CAUSE OF GOLD

This novel is for my father-in-law,

DAVID WEBBERLEY,

who told me the story first.

THE VILLAGERS

The Reverend Nathan Wohlford, *an Anglican curate*

Philippa Agnew
Carrie Agnew
Rosalind Agnew
Eleanor Agnew
Lucy Agnew

Captain Stephen Agnew, *their father*
Rebecca Agnew, *their mother*

Faithful Rowthorn, *the Agnews' housekeeper*

The Reverend Arlo Jump, *the Puritan rector of Saint Margaret's Church, Barming*

Melhuish Clare, *Saint Margaret's churchwarden*
Sarah Clare, *his wife*
Judah Copp, *Saint Margaret's sexton*
Grace Copp, *his wife*
Christopher Coates, *the local butcher*
Lion Radcliffe, *a scrivener*
Kill-Sin Magner, *the Agnews' bailiff*

Titus Waterman, *the local squire*
Verity Waterman, *his wife*
Francis Waterman
Roger Waterman   } *their sons*
Isaac Waterman

Sam Joplin, *the local blacksmith*

Dan Sloane, *landlord of The Gryphon Inn, Barming*

Jemima Wilkins
Jane Bartram   } *local girls*

Marjorie Gwyther
Anna Frost, *the local midwife*
Seth Frost, *her husband*
Polly Cater, *a maid of all work*
Amos Monkman, *a local farmer*

Jack Tannock, *a Leveller*
Master Jex, *a Leveller*

THE ROYALISTS

George Goring, 1st Earl of Norwich
Sir Gamaliel Dudley, *Military Governor of Maidstone*
Sir William Brockman, *High Sheriff of Kent*
Sir John Mayney, MP
Sir Conor Forker

Thomas Culpepper
Colonel L'Estrange   } *the Earl of Norwich's Staff*
Sir Bernard Gascoigne

Hadrian Pegler, *a County Commissioner*
Sir Ambrose Norrington Bt, *a County Commissioner*

Colonel Thomas Treanor
Captain Marchington

Parson Brabazon, *an Army Chaplain*

Tom Gomes, *a Private soldier*
Salathiel Tams, *a Private soldier*
Dick Chaloner, *a Private soldier*
Peter Jacomb, *a Private soldier*

THE NEW MODEL ARMY

Captain-General the Lord Thomas Fairfax MP, *Commander in Chief*

4

Colonel John Rushworth, *his Secretary*

Colonel Henry Ireton, MP
Colonel Thomas Hewson, *Commanding the Parliament's Regiment of Foot*

Major Carter
Captain Topping   } *Colonel Hewson's Regimental Officers*
Captain Price

Major John Callender, MP, *an Aide de Camp*

Captain Weller, *a New Model Army Dragoon*

Corporal Jesmond
Trooper Elihu Nye   } *New Model Army Dragoons*
Corporal John Probyn

1641

By the known rules of ancient liberty.

ONE

The idle spear and shield were high uphung.

Barming Place still looked the same as ever. Nathan paused, with his hand upon the gate, and studied the house. Its ragstone had gone the colour of bee-matured honey. Its tiles were being toasted to a crisp, rich orange. Its barley-sugar chimneys soared high into the blue. The hollyhocks still wobbled on their spindles. They ran the full length of the path, like a garish guard of honour.

Faithful hadn't changed, either. When she opened the door, Nathan was treated to the same old brightening of her eyes. The smell of herbs and spices from the kitchen was still a constant. Traces of flour and pastry had daubed the cracks between her fingers.

"Why, it's well to have you back, Master Nathan!"

"It is good to be back, Faithful." He ducked in to plant a kiss on her pumice cheeks.

"Along with you!" she burbled. "Pecking me on the doorstep – go save it for the Mistress!"

Nathan smiled as he stepped into the hall. He had to stoop to avoid the twisted, worm-pierced beam that had lintelled the door for decades.

Faithful examined him closely. "You have grown, Master Nathan."

He doffed his old capotain hat, revealing his nut-brown hair. "Perhaps a jot."

"They feeding you up there?"

"Not overmuch!" Nathan's new shoes sounded loud on the flagged stones. The house felt still, like it was napping in the heat. A filtering radiance, sweeping through the leaded panes of window glass, caught the silver buckles on his shoes and turned them into moons.

"Poor boy," she tutted.

Nathan's smile became indulgent. The long-haired youth of serious purpose who stood before her now, and the six-year-old mischief who would sneak into the kitchen and make off with a palmful of currants, were indivisible to Faithful.

She helped him with his cloak, folding it over her arm. "You have no bags?"

"Aye, but I dropped them at the Parsonage. Where are the family?"

"Cap'n's lame-a-bed upstairs. And don't the whole house need to know it!"

Nathan glanced at the foot of the stairs. "Where's your mistress?"

"In the garden."

"And the girls?"

"They're out there, too. Should I announce you?"

"Thank you, Faithful; I know I can find my own way," he answered, gently.

"Very well, sir. I must be about it: heaps to do. I'll be thanking you, sir."

She bobbed him a curtsey, which he found rather amusing, and left.

Sir... Hearing it from deferential, disapproving college scouts were one thing. Hearing Faithful Rowthorn assert he had truly grown up simply didn't ring true.

The sunshine blinded him as he left the shadows of the house. So it was that he only heard the clatter of wood on stone, and the tremendous squeal of, "NATHAN!" Then two little bodies collided with his, and two pairs of arms locked around his middle.

The twins had encircled him. The air was split by their chatter.

"Where have you been?"

"Could you not have got here sooner?"

"Oh, *do* say you will stay with us and dine!"

"Girls, girls!" he pleaded, but trying to struggle was futile. Rosalind and Eleanor held him fast. Their hobby horses lay discarded on the terrace. Nathan made for greater sport, and the twins were dedicated gaolers.

"We shall not let you go until you tell us how long you mean to stay!" Rosalind's eyes were sparking in her small, vivid face.

Nathan relented. His hands looked very large on the twins' shoulders. "A good while, Ros."

"How long is that?" piped Eleanor.

He humoured her elfin insistence. "Now *there* is a question!"

"Well, *where* is my answer?" she riposted.

"First, take a long time…"

"Yes, yes?"

"And then," he grinned, "tack a bit on!"

Eleanor frumped.

"Where's Pip?" he asked.

Now it was Rosalind's turn to wrinkle her nose. His question caused her to release him. "She's *reading* – the silly great book worm."

"She's in the little house," Eleanor supplied. "And been there hours!"

"Hours? Aye, probably to make her escape from you two."

"Well!" Rosalind made a great show of crossing her arms. Inspired by her sister's example, Eleanor did the same. It was an uncanny imitation of Faithful's most quintessential gesture. "Well, boo! We need him not, then!" She turned on her heel and flounced away to retrieve her hobby horse. "Come along, Elle! Nathan has forgotten how to play!"

"I'm a Clerk in Holy Orders, Ros. I'm not in the business of play very much these days." He was doing his best to sound contrite.

Eleanor tugged hold of Nathan's hand and pulled him downwards until his ear was level with her mouth. Concealing her words behind her hand, she whispered: "Go to Pip, Nathan. Go now. Go find her straight'way – she's been waiting for you all day!"

The "little house" stood halfway down the garden. In truth, it was little more than a trellis box, with a shingled roof and a pebbled floor and just enough room for a table, a bench, and a couple of chairs made from half-cut logs. Rebecca Agnew's flowerbeds enveloped it on three sides, providing quiet waves of pink and blue and yellow. Climbing plants formed a kind of nest around it and granted it shade from the bite of the heat.

He found Philippa sitting inside. A heavy tome lay opened before her. She was so absorbed in its pages that she did not even note his presence. Nathan seized the moment to sample her complexion anew. The features in the oval face were still smoothed, still fresh. He saw the faintest suggestion of her flaxen mane, curling out beneath the linen coif. He could not have denied that he found the effect alluring.

Her foot *tap-tap-tapped* upon the pebbles. She had still not detected him.

"Pip?"

She looked up. The sight of him standing before her made her sit back in her seat.

"You're back," she breathed.

Next moment, she was on her feet, and her arms were round his shoulders.

"Hullo, Pip."

They stood there, their embrace mellowing, from formality, to affection, to enjoyment. When they released each other, Philippa's hands passed over his upper body, over his chest, and around the small of his back.

"You are thinner!" she announced. "They worked you hard at Brazen Nose!"

Nathan nodded. The smell of old books and parchments had lingered in his nostrils. Before his final *viva voce* he had studied by candlelight until his eyes had jumped like fleas. "Aye, Pip. You tell the truth," he said.

"My truths were made to be told, Nathan." Philippa's voice, which had always been low in pitch, gave a shape and a weight and an edge to her arguments. "I should have met you," she said.

"Did you not hear? The twins gave me a warm welcome."

"Hoho, they would! The Bothersome Both, I call them."

He laughed, and looked over to the table. "What's the book?"

"Ovid. The Golding translation."

Her hands moved down to her side, touching the hems of her skirt as she readied herself for a compliment.

"This philly mort ... looks well upon you," he attempted.

She cocked an eyebrow at him. "Flatterer."

She plumped back down upon the bench. Her finger beckoned him.

"Come. Sit here by me, Nathan. I want to hear your news."

Before he had the chance, Philippa's tall and handsome mother had appeared in their midst, bearing a trowel and a trug of freshly excavated carrots and shallots in her hand. A hat of old straw sat casually on her head.

"Nathan! You made it at last!" She sounded gratified.

"I'll give you good day, Rebecca." He politely offered her his hand. She took it, but she also had a kiss in store for him.

"I trust that your journey did not wear you out?" she asked, solicitously.

"Oho, the college life has already done that for him, Mother!" Philippa illustrated her point by leaning forward and poking her index finger between Nathan's ribs.

"Ah, we'll soon put that back on," Rebecca declared. "Faithful is preparing roll of beef, and I have just plucked the accompaniment. I hope you will stay to taste them?"

She caught her daughter's eye. She read the meaning in that conspirator's smile, and let out a soft burst of laughter. "Well!" said the maternal diplomat, "I must be away to the kitchens. Pip will doubtless take care of you."

"Especial care, Mother."

Rebecca withdrew. They watched her stroll sedately over the lawn towards the terrace.

Nathan turned. "Where is Carrie got to?"

"She's under the ash, with Loobie." Philippa laid a hand on his arm. "But you are not going to look for them now."

He had caught the imperative in her voice. They sat down together, side by side. By way of security, Philippa's hand looped through his arm and stayed there. At last she leaned to rest upon his shoulder.

"When do you take up your curacy?" she asked.

"On Sunday."

"Very soon!"

"Aye, but at least I shall have a day or two of peace before."

He was wrong. Their peace was shattered as another familiar voice erupted: "Bolts and shackles, woman! What am I, now? An ivy-covered ruin?"

They both looked up the garden. Faithful was shepherding the hunched, complaining form of Captain Agnew. The Captain's hands were gripping the heads of two sticks as he shuffled across the lawn. Nathan thought Stephen had aged well beyond his years. His feet dragged heavily, leaving trails in the tell-tale grass. The twins were circling their father on their hobby horses, like jingling heralds. "Settle down, you little heathens!" Nathan heard him growl.

Nathan and Philippa rose. "I thought he was confined to bed?"

"He is, but you know Father." She made to move past him and go to her father, but he had already reached the little house.

"Here I am, a creaking haywain!" The Captain's face was blotched, and sweat was standing out on his greying moustache. "And here's our Nathan!" His teeth showed square and yellow. He had to grip the edge of the table for support.

"Good afternoon, sir." Nathan bowed. "I did not know you were up and doing."

The wave of the hand was dismissive. "No pardon, Nathan. Saw you'd arrived from me window. Least I could do." Her father sat down on one of the half-log chairs. The woodwork creaked beneath him. "Disturbing your frolics, am I, Pip?"

"Father!" Philippa protested.

Her father chuckled. He bent and laid his sticks on the pebbles. "My *physician*," he explained, with a curl of his lip, "advocates a complete rest. But give me me own garden to roam in. That'll be tonic enough for this tumbledown cottage of mine."

"Indeed, Father, you are a trifle out of repair!" chirped Rosalind.

"Bah! None of your brass, my girl!" Her father aimed a sportive swat at Ros' bottom, and she pranced out of reach. "Get along with you. And take that looking-glass duplicate with you!"

"Come on, Elle!" Rosalind gripped her twin's wrist with a possessive hand. The pair of them vanished with a clatter of pattens.

"Rebel Ros!" Philippa chose stinging words.

Nathan smiled. "She's sharp as a drawknife, that one."

"Aye, and she'll cut herself one day!" A sudden, hacking fit of coughing overwhelmed the Captain. His throat strained and he thumped at his chest with his fist. Nathan saw a sudden look of pain in Philippa's eyes.

Captain Agnew slumped against the bench. "Never thought I'd bring up a brood of hens, Nathan," he gasped. "'All me pretty chickens, and their dam,' what?"

It was Philippa who answered. "'Tis a poor choice of reference, Father – you'll remember Macduff's family were massacred in that play."

"Massacred? God's my life!" The Captain's temples were throbbing as he stared at his daughter. "You'll not go reminding me of massacres, girl."

"I am sorry, Father." Her head dropped, chastened. "I forgot myself."

"See what me snug old age has come to, Nathan?" the Captain went on. "Since I waded out of that heathen swamp the cartographers call *Ireland!*" His pain was evident: his eyes were livid white, and rolling everywhere. "There's dead men we left in those bogs. Good Kentish lads. To see them lying there like – like herds of rotting sheep! Why, I wept like a woman!"

His daughter strained. "Father, I beg you!"

"You beg? You *beg* me, girl? Why waste good English lives on popish swine?"

Nathan shifted awkwardly on his half of the bench. From deep pockets Captain Agnew produced first flint, steel, tinder, and then a leather tobacco bag. He puffed his thin-stemmed pipe into a glowing resurrection. It helped to disperse the midges.

One glance at Pip's tawny eyes, and Nathan changed the subject. "The – uhm – the harvest must bode well, sir."

"Aye, 'n so it should, at five shillings an acre!"

"Oh, you *must* see the peach trees, Nathan. They are groaning with fruit." Philippa was glad they were leaving Ireland alone, and winging home to Kent.

"True, true, we've had plenty of fruit," her father agreed. "My motions are as constant as the stars!"

Philippa gathered Golding's *Ovid* into her lap. Her dress flowed and tumbled to the ground as she rose. "By your leave, Father?"

"Mm," the Captain grunted back. He was preoccupied: his pipe was dying.

Nathan stared up at her. "You give place to us, Pip?"

"Aye, Headstrong. Go get to your mother," her father assented.

"So I shall." Philippa paused a moment. "Till later, then, Nathan. I am glad you are home."

Nathan looked after her as the tall girl retreated towards the house. She was holding the book close to her bosom, and her neck was strangely bowed. He wanted to spring up and go in pursuit of her. He wanted to escort her inside, see her framed again against oak beams and the burnished copper utensils in Faithful's kitchen. He wanted to learn her again.

Captain Agnew vented a deep, trumpeting sigh. "I am done with this world, Nathan. I'd fain try another."

Nathan had never expected so frank, so weary a confession. "Why, sir?"

"Why, sir?" the elder lampooned. "I'm not in the regiment now, boy!"

"Your pardon. Stephen, then?"

"Hark at his formality!" The Captain succeeded in crossing his legs. "You ask what ails me, lad?" The older man gestured with the end of his pipe. "Listen well," he rumbled. "I'm nothing but an old horse-soldier. Us Agnews always saw service with the Crown, right the way back to bluff King Henry. You follow?"

Nathan nodded.

"Mark me, Nathan. This Parliament constitutes the greatest threat this kingdom's had to face since the Dons came up the Channel! They sit there and blather on behind their walls, about how the King is answerable to the laws? He *is* the laws! Ordained, by God Almighty! You're a church man, Nathan; you should know this."

"Uhm…"

"Well? Speak your opinion, lad! Strike it home!"

Nathan panicked. His voice was losing strength. "Uhm – well, I do not believe I have one."

"Then you're blind, boy! And don't think that your Holy Orders will protect you from my talking to you like that – I've known you too long." A wry smile was crossing the leathery face.

Nathan could feel moisture draining from his mouth. The Captain was right, of course. The gossip had babbled in the streets and alehouses he had left behind in Oxford. It had gripped the highways of the Medway towns he knew so well, and spread its twisting tentacles into all four corners of the Kingdom.

The nearing shadow saved him from his labyrinth. Sixteen-year-old Caroline Agnew had carried Baby Lucy on her hip from the bottom of the garden. "Nathan!" she trilled, smiling across the top of her little sister's head. "Nathan's home! Look, Loobie! Nathan's home!"

"You're looking well, Carrie." He stood up as the girl offered him her cheek to kiss.

Carrie smiled. "Mother says I am blossoming."

"Well, that is her entitlement. And now who is *this*?" Nathan put out a finger to tickle Lucy's creamy face. "Can this be Little Loobie?"

Lucy wriggled in her sister's arms, gurgling, "Cuggle! Cuggle!"

"She wants a petting." Carrie shifted Lucy's weight. "Would you relieve me, Nathan?"

Nathan took possession, supporting the infant on his lap. Carrie sat down by her father, shaking out her hands from her wrists.

Captain Agnew smoked on. "A fine legacy of lambs for a man to bring up, eh, Nathan?"

Nathan held on to the youngest Agnew carefully. Lucy's curious, stubby fingers had found his ear lobe. She was fascinated by its pinkness.

"She has got heavier!" he observed.

"Aye, you had best to take care: she's a spirited thing!" Carrie enjoyed the sight of Nathan trying to free his ear from Loobie's grip. "But we love her."

There was a step on the pebbles, and Faithful arrived from the house. "Please, Cap'n," she bobbed. "There's two gentlemen wish to see you."

The pair she pointed out to them were waiting on the terrace, near the door. One was middle-aged and stocky, with a dark Mephisto beard. His companion was taller: a lanky, pasty youth, no older than Nathan. The cut and style of their clothes marked them both as the middling sort. The younger fellow was armed with a scroll of papers, securely tied with an official-looking ribbon of red silk.

"Oh, what's Magner had to bring the scrivener with him for?" the Captain groaned. "Don't tell me it's the Buttery again?"

"Who is this Magner, Stephen?"

"Our bailiff." The Captain dropped his pipe upon the table. "Only engaged him a month ago, and now I can't shift the blighter. Thought he was on the windy side of the law at first, but he's zealous to a fault, I'll grant him that. Pass me me sticks, Carrie?"

His daughter complied. The bench screeched as it was relieved of its load. Captain Agnew belaboured all attempts that the housekeeper made to assist him. "Halt that, Faithful! I can face 'em on me own two feet." He glanced back over his shoulder. "You're staying to dine, aren't you, lad?"

"Certainly, Stephen." Nathan was joggling Lucy on his knees, and her mouth was bubbling with delight.

"Good! I would never have heard the end of it from Pip if you hadn't." And with that, Captain Agnew straightened his back and began the slow, slow process of going to meet the waiting men.

TWO

Must now be named and printed heretics.

The sweat was running off him like rainwater. His hair, his cheeks, his nose; all were crusted with the residue of eggs, with the tang of putrid apples, and with the earthen smell of horse's grey-green dung. The pillory had been erected at the village crossroads to make it intentionally public. A platform of planks, no bigger than a small table, some four feet off the ground.

He heard the footsteps approaching first. Then came the hat, the well-appointed coat, only purchased last week from a Maidstone drapery. The spanking, blunt-toed shoes that spoke of recent acquisition. The dark-eyed face, the beard of daring cut.

"Well, well! And what employment have we here?"

It was Kill-Sin Magner, the Agnews' industrious bailiff. The clothes were convincing: the man had assumed a veneer of class. Magner no longer looked the justice's informer. He had become *respectable.*

"In the pillory, is it, Master Joplin?"

The dark eyes moved from the wretch's face, to the sign that hung about the neck.

"A Wanton Gospeller!" Magner read aloud. He nodded his head in thought. There was amusement in those deep, dark eyes. They burned with a wizard's energy. "My, but you have been well served."

The bailiff turned, and for a moment Joplin thought their encounter at an end. But his relief was short-lived. All that the bailiff was doing was to tour right around him. When next the voice came, Magner was standing behind him and Joplin had no way of seeing him.

"Contemptuous carriages, was it? Interrupting the Word of the Lord?"

Thump. Thump. Thump. Those brand-new shoes were coming up the steps.

"Breaking the respect that you owe to the Sabbath Day?"

Now the bailiff stood at Joplin's shoulder. Magner's arm came over the top of the board. Joplin flinched as the hand came to rest on the crown of his head. He shut his eyes.

"No hat? No scrap of shade for you, man?"

A pat. Then another one. Thoughtful. Considered.

Magner lowered his voice. "Does the sun boil you up like a lobster, Master Joplin?"

Joplin's head drooped. A fat drop of perspiration ran right the way down his face, and plopped to its doom from the end of his chin.

The bailiff's hands moved to rest on his in-bent knees. The voice became a whisper. "What blackness was there in your heart, Master Joplin? Mm? What moved this gross, premeditated behaviour?"

Joplin could feel the bailiff's hot breath on his earhole.

"Did they jeer you, Master Joplin? Did they pelt you for those blasphemies? Oh! My Lord, I see they did..."

The square-toed shoe was getting slicked with a film of egg white as it poked at the carpet of broken shells.

"My, but there's a few good suppers they wasted on you here." Magner tilted his head to one side. "What's the going rate these days, for blasphemy?" The bailiff's lips were now barely an inch from Joplin's ear. "Did your bowels turn to water? Does your heart smite you now, for the love of your wife? How long shall you have to slave at your forge, before you make good on your arrears? What citizen shall be seen to bring his business to you, a Wanton Gospeller?"

Joplin's nail dug hard into his palms. He was lost in a pit of shame.

"That string must fray your neck, yes? Does it? Does it itch, like the sackcloth itches?" The whisper became a hiss. "Ah, man, have a care. There's the devil's flare in your eyes, Master Joplin."

The first attempt died in the desert of Joplin's throat, but at last he forced out:

"Piss thy breeches, Magner!"

The bailiff's face lit up. "Tut. Tut. Tut." He said it slowly, lingeringly. His hand reached up and pinched the blacksmith on the cheek. "Why, that tongue of yours will wear you out, Master Joplin!" The bailiff laughed. "And so I'll leave you to your conscience."

He moved out from Joplin's ken. Magner did not jump down to the ground, but walked back down the creaking stairs with an air of grace.

"I must to the Buttery," he declared, sounding no more than casual. "The little matter of six shillings' rental that are owed to Captain Agnew. Though the levy is nothing, of course," he continued, with a significant toothy leer, "when compared to the Bench's fines!"

It was only a short stroll up the hill to the low-slung, thick-walled Buttery. The building sat on land that the Agnews owned, right enough, but the Buttery was older than anyone could remember. It had been built by enterprising ancestors, probably around the time of Bosworth Field, to make capital out of Barming's local produce. Its roof was a full foot deep in thatch. The thatch had been stained with long years of exposure to all that Kent could throw at it.

The bailiff rested his hands upon the bottom half of the stable door and leaned into the shadows. Inside, the Buttery was cool and refreshing. His ears caught the gentle sound of sloshing. His eyes, adjusting to the blackness, caught sight of Jemima's ample, rounded bottom. Jemima had her back to him, working away at the churn with the wooden dash in her hands.

While she worked, she rhymed.

> "Come, butter, come.
> Come, butter, come.
> Peter stands now at the gate -"

"Waiting for a buttered cake!" He was compelled to join in.

Jemima spun round. "Why, Master Magner!"

"Good day to you, Jemima." He he lifted the latch and came in. "Where, pray, is Master Plurenden?"

"Attendant on the Mistress. She's took'n bad again." Jemima tapped her forehead to show him what she meant.

Magner assumed a pained expression. "Poor soul. I had especial business here, d'you see?" He closed the bottom half of the door. The latch scraped back into place. "Matter of six shillings.

Well, six and eightpence-ha'penny, actually, Jemima, that's still to be accounted to the Captain."

He produced the scrivener's handiwork and showed it to her. Jemima's illiterate eyes widened. Though she could not decode the words that he held in front of her, she knew that there was no arguing with the ink on a legal writ. Her fingers went to her lip as she thought what to do. "You'd... you'd best come back later," she said.

"Aye. Perhaps I'd best."

The writ had gone back in his pocket. Then the hand left the pocket and went to the hook that fastened the door to the wall. It lifted the hook from its eye and let the top half of the door shriek home. With the door closed, the Buttery slunk into murk. The tiny windows threw what light they could upon the brass creaming dishes.

"And how fares Master Plurenden, Jemima?"

"Well, sir. He'd thank you."

The bailiff was coming closer. Jemima could smell the tobacco on his breath, and on his clothes. Her breathing changed rhythm.

"And you, Jemima?"

She hesitated. "Me, now?"

"You, now. How do you fare?"

"Well, sir. I'd thank you, too."

Jemima bit her lip with her little white teeth as his hands began to roam her body. She felt his supple fingers clutching at her buttocks. They squeezed roughly, then released. He had raised the stakes.

"And how fares Nature's Treasury, my pet?"

He had buried his confident face in her neck. It made her gasp.

Jemima put her hand on the small of his back. Now it was her turn to assume the command of the moment. "Why, only come upstairs to the loft, Kill-Sin, and you shall soon see!"

THREE

Woods and groves are of thy dressing
Hill and vale doth boast thy blessing.

The Medway was sluggish as it looped down the valley. It would not hurry to its rendezvous with the sea: the appointment could keep.

Nathan paused amid long grass. The world was sweet with honeysuckle from the hedges, and new-mown hay. Away up the hill to his right, a rank of oaks and elms guarded the bounds of the field. He was approaching the Agnews' orchard, but had yet to embark the ideas that he desperately craved. He needed points of perspicacity. Something that he could then take home and work up into something insightful, and thought-provoking...

He set himself a task. By the time he made it to the orchard, he'd have to find a way out of this tangle. Now, with less than fifty yards to go until the nearest apple tree, he was starting to despair.

A noise at his back intruded on his thoughts. It was the breathy, insistent harrumphing of a horse. He turned to find himself staring into the face of a handsome gelding, the colour of a conker. White patches formed a shooting star down most of its muzzle. He had been so engrossed in his thoughts that the fall of hooves, and the clinking of the harness had evaded his notice.

Nathan collected himself. He redirected his gaze from mount to rider. "I ask your pardon, sir," he said, retreating off the path. "I was quite distracted."

"Sir?" the rider queried back, in familiar tones.

Nathan looked again, and his eyes went the size of hen's eggs. It was Philippa, but a Philippa transformed. The philly mort girl of the day before had vanished. Her flaxen hair was buried beneath a man's wig of dark brown curls. The white-feathered hat that she had perched on the wig was also a man's. Her legs, astride the gelding's saddle, were thrust into a man's pair of breeches, encased in bucket-top boots of an oak-like leather. She wore a white cravat around her throat, a plain linen shirt with ruffles, and a broad belt buckled round her middle. Over the lot (and this was by far the most arresting feature) she had donned her father's old campaign coat.

"Pip! What – ?"

"I'll give ye good day, *Maaaahster* Parson." It was a salutation of satirical formality. She knew what she was doing.

At last Nathan managed, "What brings you out here at this hour?"

"Fulke does!" She patted the horse's neck. "And you?"

"I – I wish to compose."

"Madrigals?" She cocked an eyebrow at him.

"A sermon!" Nathan's eyes roamed Fulke's girth and reins. "You made him ready yourself?"

Fulke tossed his long head and Philippa used those self-same reins to steady him. "I am more than capable of strapping my own mount, Nathan. I thank you for your concern." Her voice had a disdainful note.

"But... what happened to Tobias?"

"Tobias? Tobias is gone. Not a sennight since."

"Gone where?"

"To the ordinance foundry; Horsmonden way."

"In heaven's name! Why does he want to work there?"

"In heaven's name, I know not!" she retorted.

"Still..." Nathan coughed. Tried again. "All this..." His hand swept through the air, from her head to her toe.

"My wearing apparel, you mean?"

"Yes."

"Parading my bravery, you mean?"

"Yes!" he said, this time with more conviction.

She flashed him a look of reproof. "Why should I prostrate myself before the Juggernaut of fashion? My father donned this coat to show his mettle and I, Nathan, am my father's daughter. And besides – " She slipped a long leg over the gelding's back and slithered to the ground " – were Fulke to take fright and I to fall, had you not better see me in my britches than naked?"

Nathan's mouth dropped open. This frankness of hers, this *vulgarity*, was new-found, and difficult to accept. "I'm surprised you did not take down that sword that's been in your family since the Wars of the League of Cambrai, and strut about the place with that on, too!"

24

"Mutton-head." She gave him a spirited thwack with a kid-gloved hand.

"Still headstrong as ever, I see!" Nathan murmured, rubbing at his sleeve.

Her fingers curled like claws about to scram, and she hissed between her teeth, the way a cat conveys its warning.

Nathan laughed. "The sun is rising high." His neck craned upwards, to look at the supernal prospects. "'Tis a jewel of a day."

She collected the gelding's bridle. "Would you object if we share it?"

"Never."

"Then go." She motioned him on with her hand. "Fulke reins well, but I fear he is quite implacable."

He led the way down the path in single file, with Fulke bringing up the rear. When they reached the orchard Philippa let the gelding roam among the trees. She watched him as he ambled off to graze. Ahead, Nathan had come to a halt. Philippa quickened her pace, bounding through the grass to catch him up. She found him pointing his chin to the skies again. She regarded him silently, giving him leave.

"You're composing again," she prompted.

Nathan looked round. "You'll have to pardon me. 'Tis a part of my vocation."

Her shoulders rose and fell as she imbibed a lungful of the morning. Insects nestled behind their shields. Squirrels were snug in their dreys. "It raises my spirits," she said. "Being closer to nature. The girls love it here."

"So did we."

"I bring Loobie here, to read with her."

Nathan said: "D'you remember playing catch as catch can?"

"And the grass stains all over my kirtle? Cost Mother a fortune in linens!" She pulled off a kidskin glove, revealing the creamy white flesh of her hand. She turned, and when she faced him again Nathan saw that she had put the index and middle fingers of one hand over the index and middle of the other, leaving a little hole. Her smile was lively. "Remember this?"

"Put your finger in Foxy's hole –" He performed the action.

"Foxy's not at home!" her singsong came back.

"Foxy's out at the back door – "

"PICKING AT A BONE!" they chorused, as she snared his poking finger. They laughed exultantly. Suddenly he was ten and she was eight again.

"I play it through with Loobie. You should hear her squeal!" Her eye fell on something round and red, lying in the grass. Then more than one. She stooped to pick them up. "Here," she said, throwing it to him. "Have a windfall. And tell me about your sermon."

"Tell you about it?" He rubbed her gift upon his sleeve to give the apple back its ruby shine.

"Mm! You clearly wrestle with it. And a struggle shared, is halved." Philippa dropped amid the cuckoo buds. She sat with her knees drawn up. The soles of her boots were flat. "Come now. What's the text?" She bit through the crisp red skin, feeling the apple flesh give beneath her teeth.

Nathan sank to the grass opposite her. "Second Book of Samuel."

Philippa frowned. "Second Book of Samuel..."

"*'The beauty of Israel is slain upon the high places,'*" he furnished.

Her tawny eyes closed. "*'I am distressed for thee, my brother Jonathan; very pleasant hast thou been unto me; thy love was wonderful, passing the love of women.'*"

"That is the text."

She pondered. "Hmm. Now, let me think."

Nathan kept expectant eyes upon her. She chewed long, and loudly. Her face had retreated to its work, sunless beneath her hat. The only noise was the crunch of grinding molars.

"Fellowship!" she said at last.

"Fellowship?" he echoed.

She gestured with her apple. "The bonds of fellowship. The fellowship of man."

"Of course!" Now a wheel had revolved in his mind. He was excited now; inspired. The words were tumbling out of him. "So must it be between – between Christ, and those who would follow Him. Between Him and His people."

Philippa looked at him keenly. "You preach extempore! Which scholar taught you that at Brazen Nose?"

"Why, nobody!" he answered back. "I inferred it myself."

She appeared to accept his rejoinder, and that made him happier. Finally, she swallowed and said, "Of course, it is also David's cry of lamentation."

"Certainly, it is."

"But a cry brought on by guilt. And foolishness."

Nathan frowned. "You lose me, Pip."

"Well, it is what I 'infer', to borrow your word." Her voice picked up in speed. "Now, what is at the root of David's weeping? His conscience. The conscience of a fool. Think about it: a young man, a hot-headed Prince, who's suddenly confronted with the cost of war that *he himself* has engineered."

Another, loud crunch.

"David knows what he has done, yet all's too late. He knows he has blood on his hands, but all is no good. So, what does he do? He sits there and he wallows in his folly. The folly of war."

Nathan stared at her. She wore her father's coat, but was this her father's voice?

Unprompted, she asked: "What really turned you theologian, Nathan? I never understood."

Nathan conceded a smile. "*You* don't understand? How about Faithful? She probably still thinks of me as a cunning little sneak-thief, for all her show of kindliness."

"You forget something."

He looked at her. "My little accomplice, you mean?"

She grinned, and a little apple juice leaked from her lips. "Well, I could not let you face it all alone! We were allies! Still are, I would hope," she added.

Nathan munched on down to the trove of pips. "If you ask me for the truth," he said, "I'd presume to say it all started once Father married Theresa."

"You'd presume?" she queried.

"That is, after he declared to me that it would make difficulties if I... after he and she had... You know."

Philippa eyed him. "It hurts you. I can see it. I am sorry I brought it up again so soon."

She extended her hand to him, palm upward. Her fingers waggled, seeking his. Nathan took hold of them and squeezed. Their solidarity was absolute, their closeness unreserved. Suddenly the whole world seemed reasonable again.

"Oof!" She tugged her digits free. "You've forgotten I bruise like a peach."

Nathan swivelled his neck to watch the careless swooping of a blackbird. Some fifty feet away, he could see Fulke tearing up great clumps of yellow grass, frisking his tail to fend off the flies. From under the brim of her hat he heard Philippa starting to whistle. It was an old, old air, filled with bucolic longing.

My Robin is to the greenwood gone...

"You taunt me, Pip," he said.

She whistled another bar before she understood him. "You mean you still can't whistle?"

He shook his head.

She laughed so hard and so suddenly it came out of her mouth like a snort. "Well, upon my living soul!"

Nathan carefully dismembered a stalk of grass and ignored her. But he found he could no longer ignore her once he'd discerned she had gone deathly quiet.

"What ails you, Pip? That head of yours might hold the cares of an empire!"

"I was – thinking." He saw unspoken questions in her eyes.

"About my sermon?"

"No. I was thinking about myself, not about you." She said it with some asperity.

"Then – what?"

Completely without expression, Philippa answered. "I was thinking of Arthur."

"Arthur?" Now Nathan was worried. "But why? You – you never mention Arthur."

"It was what you said to me up there. About this." She meant her costume. "You remember the words of Viola? *'I am all the daughters of my father's house, and all my brothers, too – and yet, I know not.'*"

"Pip?"

She took time to admit: "Father named Carrie 'Caroline' for the Caroline Court. And Mother named me for a Queen."

"Aye! And for a woman who knew her own mind."

"Did she?" she said stiffly.

"Why, yes! Do not forget that it was Philippa who interceded for the Burghers."

Now it was her turn to pluck a blade of grass, folding it over and over around her fingers. "I wonder if she was tall?"

"Tall?"

She lifted her head. "Mother told me that being tall would always allow me to look men in the eye. I – I have never forgotten that."

"Pip? I pray you, stop this talk!"

"Oh, Nathan." Her head was shaking. "Is it all too obvious for you?" Seeing that apparently it was, she said, "Phi-li-ppa." The word pulled the air to the back of her throat and sent it out again with a pop of her lips.

"I – I don't -"

"Philippa. Pip. *Philip.*"

Her meaning had a sudden, desperate clarity. "Have done, Pip!" he warned.

"One syllable away." She held up her index finger. There was granite in her voice. "Just one, that's all I am! One syllable, from Father's precious son." Her chin went down again. She was huddled up tight into a private shell. "He lived only ten months. Yet in all, he will always be older than me."

At last Nathan got himself up onto all fours and crawled across the grass. He was kneeling directly in front of her. "Pip?"

She turned away. Her face was burning.

"Pip? Face me, Pip."

She was cornered. The curly wig swished.

He took her hand and held it for a long moment. She did not resist him. "Arthur's dead."

"A swift one, you are!" she grunted.

"He's dead, I tell you – buried."

"*And cannot come out on his grave*..."

Now he was annoyed with her. "Stop this quoting Shakespeare! Shakespeare will not help! Must you be so pretentious?"

His sudden spurt of anger sent tremors through her face. "Then answer me this," she said, and this time she did not avoid his gaze. "D'you think you would have made a friend of his?"

"What?"

"If Arthur had been let to live? Would you have been friends with him, Nathan?"

He hesitated. He had to put force in his voice: he *had* to get through to her. "I do not wish to know this. I do not wish to hear it from you."

"I must discharge my thoughts; speak my mind," she hit back. "You told me I could always tell you anything!"

"Aye, and I respect that. But you have to stop this talk. It does not – cannot matter."

Philippa folded her bottom lip underneath the top one and left it there a while.

"I'm well rebuked," she sighed, and now a smile was almost piercing her cheek. "Nathan, I fear I must ask your pardon. As a nincompoop."

She tapped the end of his nose with a kid-skinned finger.

"We must get back. You must stay and break your fast with us."

The vulnerable girl had vanished. She had resumed the veneer. Mature, considerate; the eldest Agnew, hostess in the making.

"Thank you. I should like that."

"I shall retrieve Fulke," she announced, as she got to her feet. "We shall take him back on foot. I have been in the saddle since dawn. My legs need a walk."

Now it was Nathan's turn to scramble up out of the grass. Far, far above, an arrow's head of wild swans went beating across the sky. He followed their flight towards the neat veil of yew trees across the meadows. Their trunks marked the boundary wall of Saint Margaret's Church, a well-tended, isolated oblong amid the rolling fields. Tall-towered, and still.

No! Not still! Even at a quarter of a mile, he could see that the churchyard was busy with people. It could have been his folly, it could have been the softly carrying breeze, but he was convinced he could hear raised voices. Short, barking, masculine shouts.

Nathan turned in puzzlement. "Pip?"

The girl had got hold of Fulke by his reins. "I am ready."

"Philippa, look."

She followed his outstretched finger. "Oh!" she squinted. "What – ? What are they at?"

"I cannot tell." He shielded his eyes with his hand. "There's no service being held."

He felt Fulke's muzzle brushing his shoulder. Nathan turned, and opened his mouth, but stopped when he saw Philippa staring down at him from the saddle with a purposeful look.

"Come on!"

"What?" Nathan dithered in the grass.

"Stop faddling, and climb up behind me!" she commanded. "Fulke will get us there more rapidly."

"Us?" he said, stupidly.

Philippa thrust out a hand. "Come *on*, Mutton-head!"

Nathan mounted Fulke without much grace, finding an awkward perch upon the cantle of the saddle. His face was filled with her periwig and hat.

"Away?" she asked, over her shoulder.

"Away!"

Philippa steered the gelding's head towards the church, and urged him into a gallop with her father's tarnishing spurs.

FOUR

License they mean when they cry Liberty.

Saint Margaret's was in uproar. Men in blackened iron corselet were dashing about like ants around a ruined nest. They were weasel-eyed, unshaven Militia, dragged from a pre-dawn bed with no time for niceties. They could not move fast enough, nor carry enough in their gauntleted arms, for the little man who raised his tiny fists when he harangued them.

"Bestir yourselves, sirs! Would you not spring to the Lord's work?"

Philippa reined in by the wall. She and Nathan gawped at the scene from Fulke's back. A man they both knew well, a man in shabby working clothes, stood in the churchyard, facing away from them. He was watching the Militia darting in and around the church. He was elderly, and what white hair he had left clung bravely to the back and the sides of his head. His hands were pressed to his face in anguish.

Philippa cried out to him. "Melhuish! What's the upset?"

Melhuish Clare turned round. "Mistress Philippa!"

"I said, I want to know what's going on! Who are these men?"

"'Tis the Parson, Mistress." The old man ran to the wall, stretching out his arm to them as though in supplication. "His order's to strip the church!"

Now it was Nathan who goggled. "Strip the church?" Philippa shared his look of uncomprehending shock.

"Aye, sir! His business is to gut it. And he's brought this platoon down as to accomplish it!" There was agony in the voice of Saint Margaret's old verger.

"But that – that's – !"

"I'll not lift a hand to the work, so help me," Melhuish vowed. "But you'd best be quick about it, Master Wohlford, else there'll be nothing left for you to stand in, let alone to preach in!"

Nathan didn't hesitate; he dismounted at once. Pain stabbed him like a dagger as he twisted on his ankle.

"I'll tether up Fulke, and join you soon," Philippa promised from the other side of the wall.

"Hurry. Please."

She caught his eye, and nodded. Then she kicked the gelding forward.

Nathan limped towards the lych gate. He had contemplated vaulting the wall, but his nerve had gone. He could count twelve Militia men, all told. More were probably inside the church. The rest had remained in the yard, moving searchingly from grave to grave. Occasionally a drawn sword took a swipe at a memorial.

Nathan rounded the ancient building. Now he could hear the Reverend's voice. That piping, hectoring voice.

"Quick, fellow, quick! Profane no more with it – it shall be gone!"

Nathan went on a few paces, then he heard it again.

"'Tis the Lord's work we do, His name ever have the praise!"

Melhuish Clare had retreated to the cover of the chestnut tree that overhung the wall. He stood there now, with his back to its bark. Nathan went to him.

"Master Wohlford! In your conscience, have you ever even dreamed the like?" Criss-crossed veins, the colour of a rich port wine, were glowing in the old man's cheeks. "Did you see 'em at their work?"

Nathan nodded. "Round the back, among the graves."

"Aye. But they're not our fellows, though. They come over from Malling way. Lopped off the head of the Saint herself, they did." The verger looked on the point of tears. "Took a half-score of blows, but they done it. She's lying inside. I couldn't look."

"Where is the Reverend now? I heard his voice."

"He's in there with 'em – you've just missed him." Melhuish drew his lips against his teeth.

Another figure, a square man, powerfully built, came round the other corner of the church. It was Judah Copp, Saint Margaret's sexton. Younger than the verger by a decade, his eyes had seen enough this morning. He was wringing his work-roughened hands

"God's wounds, Master Wohlford, this is wanton work!"

"I see it, Judah. I see it."

"There's been no stopping 'em, Parson! No hand or word o' reason'd do it!"

Nathan listened to the cacophony coming through the Norman doors. *Should he intervene?*

There was a hurrying of boots, and Philippa arrived. Judah touched the brim of his old felt hat to her. "God keep you, Mistress."

Philippa said nothing. Her eyes were on the short, elderly figure that had just emerged into the sunshine. The Reverend Arlo Jump lacked height, but he'd more than adequately made up for it with his thick, long beard. His fists were held high above his head, Old Testament-style. His face was a picture of gleeful victory.

"Ah! Master Wohlford!" The words were expelled through that Abrahamic fur. "I had expected you earlier to superintend our purposes, but 'tis better late than never."

Philippa stepped forward. "Parson Jump!"

"Mistress." His respect was gruff and reluctant. Her choice of costume perturbed him.

The girl closed with the bearded man. "By whose warrant do you do this?"

Jump's tight smile was mirthless. "By the warrant of the Parliament at Whitehall. You may read it for yourself." He pointed to a large sheet of parchment, stamped with seals of red wax, that had been tacked to the opened door.

"They brought that with 'em, Mistress," Melhuish could affirm.

One of the soldiers appeared through the porch. Flushed and sweating, he looked older than most of his confederates. "Beggin' all pardon, Parson?"

Reverend Jump turned. "Well, Sarjeant?"

"There's prayers for the dead in Latin on the west wall, Parson – what'll we do with them?"

"Latin?" Jump squawked. "'Tis the language of the Beast! Away with it!"

"Right y'are, sir." The soldier retreated. Philippa turned a horrified face to Nathan, but Nathan was staying where he was, beneath the chestnut's branches.

Judah Copp moved closer to stand by the tall girl's shoulder. "Rough waters, Mistress."

"Aye, Judah – as rough as the Straits of Magellan!"

"By the rood, Parson Jump's one of the hold-fast breed."

Philippa could think of nothing, in all the limits of astronomy, to account for this brutality. She could *feel* herself trembling. "By the rood, Melhuish... the Parson's run mad!" she replied.

"P'raps you should go see what the warrant reads, Master Wohlford?"

"Do!" Jump stepped back, his arm extending towards the porch. "Step up, and read the ways of the right-thinking men!"

The four of them trooped over, doing their best to blot out the unsettling noises they could hear inside. Somebody was enthusiastically smashing glass. The document had been set up in type, doubtless for easy reproduction, and to give it a legalistic heft. Nathan scanned its sentences. The two older men saw a tightening in his jaw.

"Would you narrate it, sir?" Melhuish was diffident. "I – I have not got the lettering."

Nathan obliged: "*By the order of the Commissioners, given in Parliament this seventeenth day of September, in the Year of Our Lord Sixteen Hundred and Forty-One... all edifices tending to idolatry, to whit all superstitious pictures, all statues of any of the three persons of the Blessed Trinity, or of the Virgin, or upon any cross or memorials in the yards adjoining thereto, are to be demolished forthwith.*"

He looked at the verger.

"No popery, in short."

"By the Lord Harry! It'll be the Dissolution all over again!" old Melhuish breathed.

Philippa wailed, "Can nobody do anything to stop this?"

"Stop this, you say?" echoed that spine-clutching voice. They turned. Jump was walking very slowly across the grass towards them. His eyes were like jets of flame. "Would you preserve this Romish blindness, any of you? You of all, Master Wohlford?" His finger pointed heavenward. "Any there be, who would forget the memory of the life Christ led upon this earth, shall be judged guilty. Guilty, as Judas Iscariot."

"Watch your words, sir!"

All the men exchanged glances. None of them had said it.

Jump stopped in his tracks. "Eh?"

"I said, Watch. Your. Words," Philippa snapped.

"What?" Jump stared at her, then stuttered: "Do you defy me, girl?"

Philippa stood her ground. "Yes!" She augmented this waspish assertion by folding her arms across her chest.

Jump drew a long, long breath. "Mistress," he began, and his voice bubbled with a corrosive criticism, "your father may be a quality man, and you yourself be a lady of breeding, but you are still, in fact, a *lady.*"

Philippa stared him down. "My family has worshipped here for three generations, Parson Jump – does that count for nothing?"

"And does the sin of idolatry count for nothing?" the cleric fired back.

"I beg pardon?" she blinked.

Jump was cool with her now; uninterested. He had toppled her. "Search your heart well, Mistress. Archbishop Laud shall answer at the Latter Day for the perfidy he has wrecked on our Protestant Church. Remember that the heathen faith of Rome did make mockeries of worship. Would you now have those superstitions spared, for the sake of your family's 'traditions'?"

Philippa was still trying to assemble her reply when the Sarjeant of Militia brushed her elbow. He had snatched the long, brass candlesticks from the altar. "What about these, Parson?"

"Show us." Now that he'd silenced the Agnew girl, Jump had more pressing priorities. The brass caught the light in his hands as he turned the candlestick over. "Aye!" he confirmed. "It bears the image of Mary – smash it up!"

"Aye, sir!"

The Sarjeant was making for the nearest bit of masonry when Philippa's voice returned to her. "You, sirrah! What mean you with that candlestick? Put it down at once!"

The Sarjeant looked twice at the well-spoken figure wearing the braided, weather-beaten coat, before he determined the sex of the youth who was wearing it. Confusion made him pause.

Jump's control abandoned him. "What brazenness is this, girl? Has privilege made you insensible?"

Philippa ignored him. "Put. It. Down."

The Sarjeant looked to Jump for confirmation.

"Keep your tongue between your teeth, Mistress!" the cleric squawked. "You know the commandments!" He turned to the gawping soldier. "Sarjeant? Do your duties!"

The Sarjeant sloped away down the path. Best take the sticks round the corner and smash 'em up there.

Melhuish and Judah admitted defeat. There was nothing to keep them here. They made for the lych gate. When the Gryphon opened, they'd drown their sorrows like puppies.

Nathan and Philippa watched the older men's despondent retreat. They hung about on either side of the door, avoiding any eye contact. Philippa put her hands behind her back, flat to Saint Margaret's wall. She bent one knee and lifted the heel of her boot to the ragstone.

First in ones, then twos, and then in one final phalanx, the Militia withdrew into the sunshine to declare that the work was done.

Jump was jubilant. "Well done, my men! The Lord of Hosts, which is the searcher of our hearts, knows with what sense and willingness you went about this service. You will sleep well tonight."

One of the soldiers grinned, "We'll sleep better after we've struck the church at Farleigh from the list first, Parson!"

"Go with God." Jump smiled a satisfied smile, but the face withered into scorn once he turned back to Philippa. "Your conduct shall reach the ear of your father, girl. Depend upon it."

Philippa tossed her head. She would not even look at him.

In an attempt to douse the flames, Nathan said, "Perhaps we ought to repair to the house."

"Oh, I think not!" Philippa's face wore a sour sneer, and her eyes were cold. "The Lord's work has been done. It behoves that we should see it, don't you think?"

Nathan sensed danger.

"Go along, Nathan," she commanded. "I think it only proper that *you* lead the way."

Nathan obeyed her. This was the last straw for Jump. "By my life! Does the Captain's daughter intend to enter the house of God in the guise of a *caballero?*" he yelled.

Philippa paused in the door to the porch. "Strength and honour are my clothing, Parson, and I shall rejoice in the time to come."

Her riposte came from Proverbs, and Parson Jump knew it.

She stopped to survey the capsized likeness of Saint Margaret. Nathan could feel the crumbs of masonry beneath his feet. Someone had been punching ugly looking holes in the stained glass windows. Some of it still clung in crazy patterns to the framework. Pure sunlight poured through the gaps.

"The alms box is untouched, at least," he announced when she'd joined him.

Philippa crouched to pick at the curling pages of print. The pages littered the nave. They were like leaves on the floor of a forest, after a generous autumn. She stood up, and smoothed out a sheet on the thigh of her breeches. Nathan heard her sharp intake of breath.

"Pip?"

"They've... they've torn up the Bible."

She could hardly get the words out.

Nathan lowered his gaze to look at the papers by his feet. *In the beginning was the Word...* The unfolding, circuitous opening sentences of John's Gospel. Illuminated work; painstaking no doubt. But their colours had spelled their doom. Such Tudor craftsmanship meant nothing to vengeful soldiers, armed with Whitehall edicts and keenly-whetted blades.

Philippa stared at the mess in misery. "They want whipping," she hissed.

"Pip – I beg you!"

She disregarded him. Her eyes were stinging. "They're *Visigoths!*" She stamped her foot, and her boot made a harsh, cracking sound in the empty space.

Nathan found the words. "They did what they were bid," he said. "This was the very time they looked for."

Philippa looked up sharply. "You... knew?"

He shrugged. "Who could be a church man, and not know?"

Her gloved hands moved to her hips. "Explain." She asked the one word quietly.

"I – I had heard there were mutterings," he gulped.

"What mean you by that?" she pursued.

"I'd heard tell of defacements. Canterbury; the library at Rochester…"

"Barming," she completed.

Nathan used his shoe to turn over a buckled brass plaque from the time of Elizabeth. Holes in the plaster betrayed where it had been wrenched from its anchorage in the eastern wall.

'*Search your heart well, Mistress!*" she mimicked, with malevolence. "I tell you, Nathan. Those who talk with about God, and the Book, would be well served to look to themselves!"

"Philippa….!" Nathan shot a quick, nervous glance at the chancel arch.

He heard the crunching drumbeat of her boots. He readied himself for her onslaught. He even wondered if she'd walk right up and strike him. But when he looked round, she had vanished.

"Pip?"

Nathan forced his legs to move. They carried him shakily down the aisle and out through the porch. The moment he left the building, he started to run. He burst into the sunlight. The coolness of the dawn had disappeared. The morning air was now as sticky as a dog's breath. He was glad to learn that Jump had disappeared. The last thing that he wanted was another, hot-tempered interview.

He arrived at the gate in time to see her hopping, *one-two-three*, up and onto Fulke's back. She gathered the reins in her hands. Her face was the colour of alabaster.

Nathan stopped in the gateway. He dared come no closer.

"You are obviously a glutton for punishment," she said from Fulke's back. "That's absolute. May you be happy."

Fulke could detect that something was not well with his mistress. His ears were twitching, and his hooves began to dance.

Nathan ran his hands through his hair. "Pip..."

She bent low in the saddle to fling her parting words at him. Her tone was filled with ice.

"Forgive them, Father. They know not what they do!"

FIVE

Thereby to set the hearts of men on fire
To scorn the sordid world and unto Heaven aspire.

Denuded. That was the word he'd pick for it. And even after Melhuish and Judah's dutiful attempts, the wounds remained. The altar rails had been wrenched out, leaving ugly craters in the painted plaster. The chancel's protective icon of Margaret, a consort to the larger statue at the door, had been mutilated. If the scars were anything to go by, her features had been gouged away with a short-bladed knife. Probably the kind the Militiamen used when cleaning out the pans of their muskets.

The breeze gave tongue. Nathan heard it singing through the jagged remains of the stained glass. Jump had left the traces there intentionally, until plain glass could be appropriated.

"Plain glass, Master Wohlford. For good, plain services," he'd said as they were making ready for morning service. With a reduced audience, and with infinitely less to prove with Nathan, Arlo Jump could sound almost comradely at times. "Verily, 'tis all for the best. You'll allow I am for the Law, be it temporal or spiritual. The Law is not mocked."

"So let it be, Arlo. So let it be," Nathan answered in muted tones.

"Aye, that's the stuff! And when the Law compels it – "

Jump stopped. People were filing in through the porch. Nathan recognised local farming families. The peal from Saint Margaret's carried far along the valley. They would have been up at first light to walk through the lanes and across the fields.

"You are peeved. The task vexes you, Nathan?"

"No, Arlo."

Jump's face wore a fox's expression. "Hear me, now. I can smell an untruth before it is even uttered. I think you were unhappy with what I said to the Agnew girl yesterday. Am I not right?"

Nathan could confirm that, and nodded. Jump's white fingers pinched his arm. "I follow your reasoning, Nathan. Whatever loyalty you've borne to the Captain's family is to your credit."

"They were always good to me." As an excuse, it sounded pitiful.

"They are Christian souls; I know that full well. But I did not treat that girl with gentle courtesy because these matters are too pressing for diplomatic talk. We must needs be Alexandrian. A quick, clean cut."

"'Twas not a quick, clean cut that decapitated that statue," Nathan hazarded.

"Superstitious dressings, boy!" snapped Jump. "Popish decorations, which only detract from the Word of God, as you shall very quickly hear."

Nathan looked to the back of the church. The congregation was swelling with fresh arrivals. A group of faces leaped from the general throng.

"The Watermans, Arlo."

"Here? That is well!" Jump watched that family's progress, watched them collect their hymnals from the verger. "If we can win *him* over, we have the rest." He looked Nathan in the face, and laid one of his tiny hands on his curate's shoulder. "I need you by my side, Nathan, as a fellow in Christ," he confided. "County folk are not easily malleable."

They bustled up to meet the burly man who was escorting his wife, and their three adolescent sons up the aisle. The Waterman boys were turned out smartly. Doubtless their father had paraded them to check their appearance before he had let them out of Briarwell Hall. Their cloth was of decent cut, and fragranced with choice herbs. Superiority radiated like an aura from their faces. Their heads were being upholstered with Latin and Greek, courtesy of an expensive private tutor. Their father hoped for Cambridge for his boys.

"I'll give you good day, Squire," said Jump.

"And I you, Parson." Titus Waterman's voice was deep and cavernous. His soldierly frame, with no spare flesh, testified to years of service on fields of smoke and pikemen. "I trust that the House of the Lord is now fit for His habitation again?"

"It is, Squire."

"And will the newly ordained here be leading our act of worship?" the squire enquired, with a half-smile in Nathan's direction.

"Master Wohlford's turn is yet to come round," Jump explained. He shot a look of corrective venom at his junior, but Nathan never even noticed. He had noticed the tall, cloaked figure who'd appeared in the doorway. Rebecca Agnew had come to church this morning dressed head to toe in mulberry. She had hold of her hobbling husband. The Captain's sticks came tapping and rapping on the flagstones. Nathan had duped his brain into thinking that the family would not come to church this morning. Now he resigned himself to sorrow.

Rebecca detected Nathan's gaze. She smiled back, but it was a weak smile of vocational civility. Nathan's stomach clenched. He resigned himself to sorrow.

The girls were coming up behind. Philippa entered last. She had charge of the toddling Lucy. Nathan had no luck with Philippa's face. Pip was hard to read when she wanted to be.

Jump got a grip on Nathan's elbow and piloted him back towards the chancel. "Steady, Nathan. Courage, now."

It was a struggle for Nathan to retain some semblance of calm. His neat little world was crumbling, as were most of the assumptions that had framed it in the first place.

"I – I am alright, Arlo."

"Right. Stand fast, and true." The grip became a clench. "Together, we'll soon straighten their philosophies."

The congregation sat down with a shuffle and a creak on the back-breaking pews. They were quiet and attentive, but undeniably on edge. Word of what had happened had been impossible to contain along the valley. Stories had been swapped, improved, and swapped again. Saint Margaret's had been ransacked by godless traitors, probably masked, and possibly horned and tailed. Old Nick's pitchfork had likely pierced the breast of the statue by the porch. Tales of pitched battles between marauding Militia and local journeymen defending the church's property had gained great currency in the intervening hours.

"Let us stand and join together in a song of praise."

They opened their hymn books and rose for the song of assurance.

"All people that on earth do dwell
Sing to the Lord with cheerful voice,
Serve him with joy, his praises tell,
Come now before him and rejoice!"

Philippa had dashed into the house the minute she had got back. Ros and Elle had been playing in front of the morning room firedogs. They had heard Pip's boots pounding upstairs two at a time, and after a moment the twins had slipped upstairs after her. They were accomplished eavesdroppers.

"We are the flock he comes to feed,
The sheep who by his hand were made."

Peering around the door, Ros and Elle had seen the tears in their sister's eyes. Pip had bawled that the statue of Saint Margaret had had its head taken off; that the Parson was a madman; that their church was in ruins. And it wasn't bad enough that Nathan had done nothing except stand aside and watch, he had *known* that the men were coming! He had stood by and let it happen, and done nothing – nothing!

The twins hadn't worried overmuch. After all, Saint Margaret of Antioch had been dead for centuries. Chopping up her stony likeness presumably hadn't hurt her.

"O enter then his gates with joy,
Within his courts his praise proclaim."

Ros and Elle watched Mother put her arms around their sister, telling her not to be dramatic, and that all must come right in the end. Pip had buried her face in Mother's shoulder and cried with abandon. There had been no further mention of Nathan around the house that day. Nathan had likewise kept his distance. Wait as they would at the window, the twins never saw him the whole day.

"Trust that the Lord our God is good,
His mercy is forever sure."

Pip had been in a queer mood, keeping mostly to herself. She had barely touched the capon pie that Faithful had dished up at dinner. This was most unusual, for Pip always beat Carrie to seconds. Ros and Elle had spent the afternoon maintaining a vigilant watch, in case those Militiamen came back to lay siege to the house and decapitate Mother's hollyhocks. They tried to blot out the sounds of their bed-ridden Father, wheezing and spluttering in his chamber.

> "His faithfulness at all times stood
> And shall from age to age endure."

The service proceeded. Nathan mumbled the Gloria like an automaton. At long last, Jump mounted the steps to the pulpit.

"A reading, from the Book of Revelations."

He upended the hourglass that hung beside the pulpit. The Reverend Jump was no "spin-text". It had never been his custom to charge through the scriptures. His copy of the Testament was new, and crisp, and unadorned with anything extraneous.

"*Behold, he cometh with clouds; and every eye shall see him, and they also which pierced him, and all kindreds of the earth shall wail because of him.'*"

Nathan lowered his eyelids. Not in devotion, but in hearing his worst suspicions confirmed when it came to Arlo's choice of text.

"*I am he that liveth, and was dead; behold, I am alive for evermore, Amen; and have the keys of hell and of death. 'Thou sufferest that woman Jezebel, which calleth herself a prophetess, to teach and seduce my servants to commit fornication, and eat things sacrificed unto idols.'*"

Somebody coughed at the back.

"*Behold, I will cast her into a bed, and them that commit adultery with her into great tribulation, except they that repent of their deeds. And I will kill her children with death; and all the churches shall know that I am he which searcheth the veins and hearts; and I will give unto every one of you according to your worth.'*"

The cough came again. People were trying not to turn around and stare.

"*And I looked, and behold a pale horse*," Jump sang out, "*'and his name that sat on him was Death, and Hell followed with him. And power was given unto them over the fourth part of the earth, to kill with sword, and with hunger, and with death, and with the beasts of the earth.'*"

Lucy yawned, and the sound filled the building. Pip and Carrie joined forces to shush their little sibling.

Jump did not pause. "*For the great day of His wrath is come; and who shall be able to stand?'*"

He closed the book with vigorous authority. Nathan sat below the pulpit with bated breath, waiting for the plunge.

Arlo Jump took his time. He spoke with a most terrible sincerity.

"There are some men – misled, benighted men – who believe it lies within the powers of any man to preach. This be not so, and it is a grave error. It requires the mind of the ordained man to present a truthful picture of the world. Verily, I say unto you that the Lord would despair for our souls. We have fallen, as we are liable to fall, into tumult and strife, and our land is now awash in dissipated living. It is the lot of the unhappy and deluded multitude, pretending to the memory of Christ, to give way to sin-begotten dealings, and to sensual delights. And were these not the same, deluded multitude who were once offered the choice by Pilate, and chose the notorious prisoner Barrabas? In saving that mortal man, they did condemn their immortal souls. And they did know it, brethren. They. Did. Know it!"

His finger stabbed the black-bound cover of the Bible with the beat of every syllable.

"Verily, I say, we must be wary. Satan's temptations invest the soul in a manner most amenable. As a stone rolling down from the top of a hill ceases not till it rolls to the bottom, nor is it with Satan, to ruin both your conscience and to gratify his lusts."

The congregation sat a little straighter.

"I bid you to remember Revelations, Twenty-One. '*But the fearful, and the unbelieving, and the abominable, and the murderers, and whoremongers, and sorcerers, and idolaters, and all liars, shall have their part in the lake which burneth with fire: and this is the second death.*'"

Jump leaned upon the pulpit rail, gripping it tight with his tiny, gnarled hands.

"Wicked men forget their Creator. They think the Sabbath long and stultifying. They think the cleansing of the soul through fervent prayer, be long. But how long shall it feel to endure the undying smoke of the furnace, I ask you, brethren? Remember the wicked in Hell all wish they would die, but they cannot!

"Now. There is not one of you can fail to note that our Saint Margaret's has been expurgated of its trappings, and of all its popish blindness. Some of you I see sitting among us this morning have even been moved…" His eyes narrowed to embers "…have even been moved to give *voice* to your observations. I would advise them to take care. Be it remembered among you that Saint Margaret was swallowed by the Beast, from which she sprang alive when he could not stomach the faith which protected her. I bid you now: remember the story of faithful Margaret. Let us bear her forward as a shining example to us all.

"And be it remembered, my brethren, that during the dark midnight of papacy, the heathen church of Rome did sit in all its gloomy, ghostly Inquisition, and they did burn their fellow creatures. They did persecute those whose sole desire it was to bring the Word of God to their fellow men, in words their fellow men might understand. I quote again, from the Gospel according to Saint Matthew: *"For them that honour me, I will honour, and they that despise me shall be lightly esteemed."*"

Philippa felt a thick lump of dread in her throat.

"We are poised." Jump was using his hand to communicate this next point. "Poised, as over a bottomless gulf. The decree of the Lord is immutable. Through fervent prayer, and through trusting in the Path of the Servant King, we may yet be saved from falling all together. God grants a good deliverance. Christ, is all."

The Reverend Jump descended the steps with his beard held high. Nathan gathered his wits and helped him to make ready for the sacrament. The congregation formed a line and waited to be renewed by the Flesh and the Blood.

Nathan moved along the altar rail. "The body of Christ, keep you in eternal life."

It was a nasty jolt when he found himself supplying the morsel of bread into the waiting hollow of Philippa's upturned palms.

Nathan did his part. "The body of Christ... keep you in eternal life."

"Amen."

She mouthed the word that closed their private circle. His eyes had looked at hers with momentary hope, but Philippa's glance was uncommunicative as she rose from the kneeler and went back to join the other girls.

1642

Yet first, to those chained in sleep,
The wakeful trump of doom must tremble through
the deep.

SIX

Chaos, that reigns here…

Christopher Coates sat quietly in a corner of The Gryphon, drinking that hostelry's cats'-piss beer. The smell of his trade lingered on his hands. The local hops, thickly garlanded round The Gryphon's beams, could not win the contest. The smell of blood carried very far. It had ingrained in his skin.

He watched the rain, falling without restraint on the outside world. The bench was hard beneath his capacious backside. He shifted to get comfy. It had been a headlong dash to get inside the inn's soot-smeared walls, to draw grateful breath amid the musk of tobacco and ale. He was sufficiently close to the fire to feel its warming fingers. Coates chewed his pipe. He was beginning to feel contented.

He looked up with interest when Melhuish Clare ducked through the door. The barrier banged shut into its jamb. The weather was encircling The Gryphon like a python coiling on its prey.

A tankard was filled from the barrel. The verger raised a hand of greeting to the butcher. When his drink had been served, he brought it to Coates' table.

"Chris."

"Melhuish." Coates motioned with the bowl of his pipe that the verger should sit down on the form. Melhuish shed his cloak, shoving it away between their feet, where it lay like a wet animal.

"'Tis pelting down!" he said, lowering himself onto the form.

"Mm! We'll see the Ark go sailing by before you've finished that pint."

Melhuish chuckled and toasted: "Here's health."

"Returned!" Coates picked up his own tankard, and drained it almost to the suds. Wiping his mouth on his sleeve he said, "I assume you've heard the stink? The Queen has fled."

The old verger shook his head. His ox-like eyes were dulled. "I heard. And the children gone with her. This can only bode ill, Chris."

"I heard that popish brat of France took a tun of treasure with her from the Tower."

Melhuish stared down into his foaming brown ale. "Nay. The emblems of the state should not be hawked about like peddled toys."

Coates' eye fell on the doorway as the rain butted in on the room again. A small, square, oilskinned figure was revealed in the entry. "Ah! Our good sexton."

Melhuish groaned. "He took the news bad, did Judah. We'll have no need of prompting."

Judah Copp paid for his pint mug of mild at the bar and came to join them. He scattered a trail of drips across the floor. They saw his downturned mouth, wrenched in gloom.

"One need not be a sage to guess the content of you fellows' talk," he said.

"Nay, indeed." Melhuish sighed. "There's nothing this side of Jerusalem that carries the weight of this, boys."

Coates sniffed. "Well, I'm not worrying overmuch."

Judah gawped at him. "Why not, Chris? I thought you set value on your blood!"

Coates gave him an owly glare. "What's that supposed to mean?"

Judah's tankard went down with a clink. "Why, man, the meaning's obvious! The King's cause is imperilled. For all we know, they might be calling out for men already!"

"As the Lord disposes." Coates' moustaches soaked up the very last traces of beer. Wars were nothing new on their horizon. First there had been the war with the Scottish Bishops, those ranks of mulish Covenanters, with their Presbyterian dogma. And then there'd been the turbulence in Ulster... the plantations were running red with blood.

Dan Sloane, the purse-lipped landlord, arrived to collect the empties. He exchanged no word with his patrons, but there was nothing unnatural in that. Sloane was a spreading, Friar Tuck-cheeked figure of a man, but minus the charm.

Melhuish waited until Sloane had left before saying: "I thought I'd seen it all in Ireland, fighting with the Captain."

"Along with you!" muttered the butcher.

"No, no," Judah reproved, with significance, "we must defer to Corporal Clare, now."

The erstwhile Corporal Clare wanted to thank his friend, and to assure Judah that his faith was not misplaced, but he didn't get the chance. The buffeting door told him that two more men had entered The Gryphon. Melhuish nudged the sexton and said, "Oh, see! It's Proudcock Magner."

Coates surveyed the pointy beard poking out through the collar of the bailiff's oilskin cloak. "Master Stick-Up-My-Arse, I call him."

The pair of newcomers strolled over to the bar. Melhuish looked from the bailiff to Lion Radcliffe, the gangling scrivener. "Would you look – he's brought that young streak of piss with him again!"

"Cares nothing for the law, does Corp'ral Clare," nudged Judah.

Melhuish returned: "The taller a man, the more his brains be frostbit!"

Judah Copp, five-foot-five in his stockings, could afford to chortle as he drank up.

Coates kept his eyes on Magner. He watched him closely through the plumes of smoke that were snaking from his pipe. "Doesn't look too radiant today, our Kill-Sin."

"P'raps it's an itch in the carnal stump!" Judah's eyebrows wiggled.

"Now, now, my boys," said Melhuish, "we must have civil words. Many things are licensed in a hostelry, but not to impugn a bailiff."

The old verger cocked his head at the newcomers, and motioned them over. "Hi, you two!" he called.

The bailiff and the scrivener had stood irresolute before the bar, each of them cradling their pewter tumbler of cider. Now at Melhuish's call they swiftly joined the trio. Magner bowed. "I'll give you good day, gentlemen."

"Kill-Sin; Lion."

"'Tis a blasted day, sirs!" said Lion Radcliffe, in a voice sounding strained and reedy.

Magner pointed to the vacancies. "You'll let us join your company?"

"Aye; sit down, the both of you."

Magner tweaked his dark moustache. "On my soul, I'll wager I could guess the topic of your talk outright!" he said, as he sat next to Judah.

"So *you've* heard, then?"

Magner gave what might have been a laugh. "I'll doubt there's a man in Kent that hasn't!"

"Out of doubt, 'tis a bad business."

Lion Radcliffe indulged in an audibly loud gulp of his cider. His hands were shaking. The tumbler made a clinking noise against his front teeth. His tongue felt the tang of old pewter. The cloak that swathed him was new, and unseasoned, so the artful rain had sneaked into his clothes. He had a weak constitution at the best of times. The last thing he wanted was to catch cold, and be sent to bed for a week.

Melhuish said: "If God ever lay ear to the earth, He'd not know the place!"

Judah lifted his tankard and held it steady with his elbows on the table. "There'll be a fair few noddles broken over this," he prophesied.

"Aye, and hearts as well," said Melhuish.

"What mean you by that?" the butcher demanded.

"I mean a lot of girls left portionless, Chris, if the nation's bent on war."

Judah paled. "You think we are headed that way?"

It was Radcliffe who said: "Pandora's chaos could not be contained just by shutting the lid!"

They all looked at the youth. His allusion to the Classics was their first real reminder of the scrivener's presence.

Coates rubbed his eyes. "God damn me, it's enough to make any man get as tight as a tick!"

His fingers tattooed the tabletop. Judah took up the rhythm. Melhuish caught the hint, and he rose to his feet. "I'll stand my round, my boys."

The old man's shoulders were hunched as he made for the bar. Judah looked after him. "He's worried, Chris. No sooner has he kicked off his cavalry boots than the kingdom's imperilled again. It's of little wonder he's took'n it bad: his heart is sore."

"It's iniquitous," said Radcliffe.

"It might be!" said Coates, who had no idea what it meant.

Magner considered. "The King is trusted with the security of the Commonwealth. He must do what he sees fit."

"Even so, Lion, it follows that he must be held to account for it!" said the sexton.

Lion Radcliffe would not pass up an opportunity to use all those years he had spent in Articles. "Nay, sirrah. Princes are not bound to given an account of their actions, save only to God."

Judah's lip showed he was unconvinced. "I'm not for that. Things are as they are."

"The King has his pride," persisted Radcliffe.

"He can't afford pride! Just look where it's got him!" growled Coates.

"Alright, alright…" The younger man made a placating gesture with his palms. "I'll grant you gentlemen that His Majesty has been… uxorious."

"Uxorious!" Magner hooted. His face pulled into an expression of comic delight. "My, the longhead has spoken, gentle friends!"

Radcliffe shoved his cider out of the way. "Attend to me. The law of this island – *attend to me, gentlemen* – the law of this island is no yoke for His Majesty. His Majesty is set above the law, else where be his sovereign power?"

"What fecundity!" The bailiff laughed aloud.

"Aye, but even Kings must answer to the Lord. In the end," Judah pointed out.

Radcliffe turned on him. "Weigh those words of yours, sir," he warned. "As a man who has studied the law, I say again: have a care!"

Coates had had enough. He took the stem of his pipe from his lips, and used it to jab the air around him. "The King's got rights. He should put that Francoy shrew of his back in her place."

Magner's laughter met the beaker he'd just lifted to his lips. "How so?" He produced a dainty kerchief to mop the cider from his whiskers. "You suggest he use the rod on her? Put her in a cold, dank dungeon? Give her the last brisk walk with the priest to Tower Hill?"

He heard a footstep at his back and a voice said: "So these be your thoughts, lads, the minute my back's turned? For shame!"

Melhuish had come back with the drinks. His sharp tone silenced the lot of them at a stroke. They sat upon their forms like chastened schoolboys, not looking at each other.

Melhuish set the bailiff's refill down in front of him with a disapproving thud. "God save me, Kill-Sin. I never had you down for a Roundhead Dog!"

Captain Agnew beat his sticks upon the lawn. "No, *no*, Pip! Your posture's wrong! Your feet need firmer placing."

"I am sorry, Father." She let him see her correct her stance. "Is that better?"

"Marginally." He handed her the doglock pistol, holding it out to her by its blackened, foot-long barrel. He glanced at his wife; at the audience of goggling siblings he had ordered to stand well back. "You're sure I'll not persuade you, Rebecca?"

Rebecca's reluctance held firm. "I'll not touch a firearm, Stephen. It is not in my nature."

"As you wish."

Rosalind bit at her thumbnail. "Where is the sense in this, Father?"

"What, girl? With the way this nation's headed? Are your senses quite shut up?" He turned back, to his more promising, eldest daughter. "You'll want a strong grip. Support your hand at the wrist, if need be."

"Should I load it?" she asked.

He credited her keenness. "Nay, I'll do that, Pip, so's you can get the hang. Come! Swap!"

She held his sticks for him whilst he primed the pan from the mottled powder horn he wore on a string around his neck. He withdrew the rod from its hidey-hole beneath the pistol's barrel. Then he rammed the ball home, with a square of material to keep it in check.

"Bit of old hat," he explained, when he saw she was watching. "Otherwise, the ball'd roll out the end, and all you'd do is blow smoke in his face."

She nodded. The powder horn was discarded on the grass.

"There." Captain Agnew clicked back the lock with a callous-thick thumb. "Now. Swap?"

Philippa accepted the weapon.

"Oh, now think what you're doing with it, Pip!" He snatched the doglock out of her hands. "D'you want to blow my head off? Now, take it again. And keep those fingers clean off the guard till I tell you."

"Yes, Father," she complied.

"Right. Bring it up till it is level with your shoulder, and aim straight for that trunk." He jabbed with the end of his stick at the ash tree at the bottom of the garden.

Philippa shook her left hand out of its sleeve, and used it to grip her right wrist.

"Remember the feet, remember the feet!" He tapped her right ankle with his stick, watched her adjust again. "Now. Curl your finger. *Slowly.*"

She applied pressure, then a little more. She could feel the indentations on the trigger. Finally, the mechanism gave and the hammer fell. The pistol breathed fire, leaping in her hands. Loobie stuffed her fingers in her ears. Birds exited the ash's uppermost branches with a flapping of outraged wings.

"Did I hit it?" Her voice was very eager.

"Hard to say." The Captain hobbled the fifteen paces, and ran exploring fingers over the trunk. "Aha!" He turned his head. He wiggled his finger in the chip that the ball had made. "See there, Pip? See that? A hit!"

"A palpable hit..." she murmured.

Captain Agnew set his jaw. "Alright," he said. "Now, take this here horn and reload it how I showed you. Then we might let Carrie have a turn."

SEVEN

The scene now changes to a sumptuous palace, set out with all manner of deliciousness.

Nathan had always imagined a giant had planted Briarwell Hall at the end of its drive. It made a fitting image: a great model, fashioned by a giant's crafting hand, planted in a rolling landscape of his choosing. The house looked so sure of itself, with its thick chimneys, its tower, and the windows peering out of the dignified walls. Even the guttering had been given due attention, and had been carved all along with simulated arrow-slits. Excursions to visit the Squire had come few and far between in his lifetime, and Briarwell had been built to impress.

He had ridden abreast of Jump, up the yew-hedged driveway, past the boars' heads on the gate piers. The house rose to welcome them. They dismounted in the lea of its stony gables. A groom scurried forward to take the bridles.

"Chill night, Parson!" he rasped in salutation.

"Aye." Jump braced his wiry shoulders against his cloak.

"Evening, Master Wohlford." The groom "capped" the younger of the clerics.

"Evening, Zeb. Chill night, indeed."

"Still, with this moon you won't be going home in the dark. I'll give yer good evening."

Zeb led their horses away. Jump walked briskly up the steps to the double doors. His cloak was too long for him, and it spread behind his feet like a coronation robe. The knocker beat heavily, authoritatively, shattering the stillness. Nathan shivered at the anticipation that he would very shortly be toasting himself before one of the Watermans' massive hearths.

Jump stared up at the great stone lintel above the doors, where the Waterman family motto had been boldly engraved:

CONEMUR TENUES GRANDIA

Jump eyed the Latin with deep-set suspicion. Nathan, no stranger to Horace's *Odes,* translated it for him. "'Though we be but little, let us strive for great things.'"

"I have no need to construe what it says, boy," Jump shuddered.

The door was opened to them by Windigate, the squire's grizzled steward. Nathan stepped inside, coughing as the night explored his lungs. They were surrounded by dark, finely-carved furniture; the handiwork of Dutch and French craftsmen. Over there was a cave's mouth of a fireplace. The floorboards had been polished to a pleasing sheen.

Windigate took a respectful charge of their cloaks. "This way, your Reverences."

The steward led the way into a high room off the hallway. The panelled chamber was filled with people: some upon their feet, some upon the well-appointed chairs. Piled logs of seasoned elm crackled away in the enormous hearth. The draught down the chimney was voicing a moan that could have been human. The windows kept the deep, dark night at bay.

Verity Waterman came to meet them. The squire's wife was an erect woman in her late forties, and her dark blue eyes were kind. Tonight she swished along in an expensive blend of periwinkle satin and bobbin lace. "Parson Jump!" she enthused.

"Madam." Jump gave a frigid bow.

"So splendid you accepted the invitation." She turned to Nathan, a surer audience. "And Nathan! How nice."

Nathan bowed in turn.

"You'll take a drink on a night like this. Parson Jump?"

"If I might have a beaker of milk, is all, Madam?"

"Milk?" she blinked. "Why… yes, we shall arrange that straight away. And for Nathan? Milk, as well?" The Lady of the House sounded amused.

Nathan demurred. His lips felt very tender from the cold. "No, thank you, Mistress – I shall take drink with the company."

"Very good. The Agnews are here. You must mingle."

She moved away. Jump's fixed smile flattened away to nothing. "Mingle, eh?" he muttered. "What lot has been cast for us, Nathan? Are we to stand about and prattle, or to tope with the company?"

Nathan looked hard at him. The old man was in one of his curdling moods: he had been nursing his spleen all day. "What ails you, Arlo?"

"What ails me?" Jump spun Nathan around by his elbow. "Parliament brands our squire a delinquent and a rogue, and we flock round to treat him like a conquering Caesar!"

Nathan licked chapped lips. "We really ought to mingle, Arlo."

Jump let go his elbow and picked his way in the direction of their host. The squire was showing Rebecca the family portraits. The Waterman gallery had been leavened with an Oglander or two, for Titus had no qualms in showing off his wife's Norman blood.

"Yes," the squire baritoned, "it was my grandfather. The work is by Antonio Moro, which really is the only reason for its existence. I've heard it said that there's an example of his work to be found over at Penshurst Place, though I've never met the man who has actually glimpsed it." He turned at the old man's approach. "Ah! Parson Jump. You are welcome, sir."

Glad that Arlo had found a berth, Nathan stood by himself and studied the room. Only now did he see that the Waterman boys were studiously keeping their own company in a corner. Francis, Roger, and Isaac: Titus in triplicate. Francis was the centre of his father's universe, hence his permanent look of cocksure vanity. Roger and Isaac were merely misaligning planets.

Windigate materialised beside him. "Your drink, Parson Wohlford."

"Thank you." Nathan accepted a sherry. He raised it, in polite toast, in the direction of Francis Waterman. The smile he got back was thin. The brothers nudged at one another. Nathan saw them snickering. He moved to stand unobtrusively beneath the soaring chimney breast.

"Hullo, Nathan."

Nathan spun round. Philippa had risen from a settle set against the wall. The black, high-necked gown accentuated her flaxen hair, and Nathan liked how it cascaded from its oval bun.

"Oh! Pip."

She stopped when there was still a good yard of air between them. "Such a guarded tone!"

"I didn't see you."

She tilted her head to one side. "You throw a strange regard upon me, Nathan."

"I thought – you wouldn't want to speak to me," he said, in a pinched voice.

Her gaze was very piercing. "Would you strain friendship to destruction?" she asked, quietly.

"Not with you," he breathed. "Never, with you."

Her countenance thawed. She walked right up to him. "Then you are still the Nathan I grew up with."

Her hand came to rest on his arm. Nathan began to relax. "What are you doing here?"

"Why, sir!" The look of playful challenge was back. "Am I not a growing lady?"

At least she had made him laugh.

"We were invited here tonight to share in the squire's good fortune," she explained. "Same as yourself, I suppose. Or are you too ashamed to be the guest of such disreputable Royalists?"

"Pip!" he half-protested.

The squire's booming, mouth-stretching laugh made her glance across the room. Nathan used the moment for another sip of sherry to recover his composure.

"'Tis uncommon, you'll allow, to sit down and dine with a proscribed man," Philippa said.

"Titus is not proscribed: they bailed him."

"Aye, and for a petition of good conscience," she reminded him, with the glimmer of steel in her voice. "For presenting the not so impertinent notion that Parliament ought to petition for terms with the King!"

Nathan looked at the parties dotted round the room. The Waterman boys held fast and aloof. Their mother did valiant service with Arlo, trying to engage him in pleasant conversation.

"I heard that the public hangman burned the document in Whitehall," he said.

"So had I," she murmured back. "And what do you say on the matter?"

"Nothing. At present."

There was movement by the fire. Windigate the steward whispered in the squire's ear, then Titus gave a loud, commanding cough. "Ladies, and gentlemen, if you would? Dinner is served!"

With a mighty effort, Captain Agnew heaved himself out of an upholstered sofa and steadied his weight on his sticks.

Rebecca stepped in to offer assistance, but he batted her away. "Pip!" he called, motioning at her with his head. "Stop hugger-muggering with Nathan over there, and come and be sociable!"

"Oh, Father…" she sighed.

Nathan turned to her. "Is something wrong?"

Philippa's eyes hid nothing. "He's not well, Nathan."

"Is it the ague?"

"In part, it is. But he also has… such fits." She shook her head. "'Tis the news, you see. It brings it all back."

"Brings what all back?"

"The things he saw, in Ireland."

Hurried strides signalled the arrival of Francis Waterman. "Philippa?" he quacked. "I do claim my right to take you in to dine." He crooked an arm for her in readiness. That glance he gave could run the world.

Philippa studied his gesture for a few, silent seconds. "Thank you, Francis," she returned, and she kept a mild voice. "But Nathan has already volunteered for that duty. And it *really* would be churlish to refuse him, don't you think?"

She took the sherry out of Nathan's hand and parked it on a nearby credence table. She threaded his arm through his and steered him away without another word. They left Francis, open-mouthed, his arm still ludicrously crooked in that attitude of courtesy.

Nathan bit down on his tongue. "*That* was flat blasphemy."

"I do not care!"

"He'll be snubbed," he mock-rebuked her.

She shrugged, and her arm squeezed tighter. "What if he is? He's no Endymion."

They passed through the double doors, beneath a barrel ceiling painted in pastel colours, and out into Briarwell's dining hall. Nathan marvelled. Here was space indeed. Sturdy beams supported a vaulted ceiling. The table gleamed contentedly in the mellow light of the candelabra. A crusader's sword hung dormant above the fireplace, the fight for the Holy Land long over. The walls were liberally dressed with antlers, for the squire's land teemed with red deer, and all the Watermans were dead-shot hunters. That giant who'd erected the house must have also furnished the enormous dresser that showed off the Waterman family plate.

"Don't *fuss* me, Rebecca – I can still sit meself down!" the Captain harangued her.

"Philippa?" Verity Waterman patted the back of a chair. "If you would? You are here, Nathan: next to Parson Jump."

Titus assumed the head of the table, in a chair replete with ornamental scrollwork. "Parson Jump? A word of grace from you?"

Their heads bowed. The beard twitched out the familiar cadence: "For what we are about to receive, may the Lord make us truly thankful."

"Amen!"

Their meal was set before them. River pike, followed by a boiled mutton and stewed potatoes. Platters of hot rolls were fetched in. Nathan always enjoyed the sound of the freshly-broken bread, sitting on the side plate and popping in its own heat. A thoughtfully-placed pitcher of milk helped top up Parson Jump's supply. The talk was of trivial things, and the company seemed to be working hard to keep it that way. Down at their end of the table, Roger and Isaac largely kept themselves to themselves, very conscious of their juniority.

"Marchpane! Mmm!" Rebecca smacked her lips at the sight of the dessert.

Verity smiled back. "We thought a treat was in order."

Titus lifted his goblet of claret. "By your leave, friends? I would propose a toast."

The Company made ready.

"The Queen!"

"The Queen," they echoed, and drank.

The squire detected a pause from a certain quarter. "You hesitated, Parson Jump."

Jump's smile grew, then shrank again. "If you would press the matter on me, Squire, then I cannot deny that the notion of a papist Frenchwoman having the ear of an English king is one I find abhorrent."

"Yes. Well." Titus coughed. His voice had changed key. "This is a time for community, not politicking, Master Jump. Stephen? The claret is with you."

Nathan had certainly not expected the very next voice around the table to be Philippa's.

"Was Herodotus far from the mark when he wrote, 'Circumstances rule men; men do not rule circumstances'?"

The squire looked entertained. "I cannot answer you that, Mistress Philippa!"

"Oh, I do not expect you to argue *contra*, sir. Yet surely we can all agree that a rightful monarch should not aim to dominate, but rather to compassionate?" she went on.

"Pip...!" her father warned.

Titus said mildly, "Nay, nay, Stephen; let her go on."

Philippa inclined her head in a grateful gesture. "It presents itself to me that, as the Lord's Anointed, would it not follow that the King only strives to discharge his office to the utmost, as he swore in his Coronation Oath? To my mind, the King can have no wish to make slaves of his subjects, either by measures political or theological. Surely his ministers of state, likewise, only want to do the right thing for their country. His Majesty's great love for this nation is well known, after all... is it not?"

Silence fell on a period of mental gestation. That is, until Francis Waterman tried to fill it with a spout of laughter.

Captain Agnew dabbed his moustache with the linen. "My *learned* daughter," he faltered. "You'll have to excuse her, Titus."

The squire gave a little, light laugh. "Nothing to excuse, old friend!"

"Rebecca, d'ye see, vowed that no girl of ours should ever grow up unlettered," the Captain deflected.

Philippa flushed, for she had seen her mother wince. She folded her hands before her on the cloth and said, "If I may, our minds were a gift from the Lord when He made us. *Ergo*, to learn is God's gift. And for us to be learned is to please Him."

Titus rolled his tongue around his mouth. "I – I can find no fault in your logic there, Mistress Philippa," he admitted.

Francis risked another laugh, and surprisingly got away with it. "Doubtless the good clerics will have something to say on the matter, Father!" he crowed.

Nathan could feel the eyes of the company upon him, but refused to be baited. Arlo, however, had no such qualms about retaliation. "I, for one, am also keen to guard the minds of men from the influence of so-called educated females, sirrah!" he croaked at Francis. "And whilst we find ourselves on the topic of insidious influences," he added, turning to address company in general, "I maintain that too much is still being done to the Holy Institute in the name of popery. I'm for keeping our Church free of the Laudian sway. Those bishops preach a doctrine of sedition by suggesting that Man has some inherent right to choose whether he be saved or not."

The squire arrested his goblet, halfway to his mouth. "And what if those bishops should be acting at the behest of their King, Master Jump?" he asked.

"My faith is in the eternal, Squire," the cleric snapped back.

Titus set down his goblet again heavily. "Why, Parson Jump! I'll own that I'm astonished!"

"No astonishment, Squire," said Jump, and a lean smile cut across his beard. "I am merely one who believed that Christ was who he claimed to be. The man from Nazareth spoke many and many a truth. '*It is easier for a camel to pass through the eye of a needle than it is for a rich man to enter the Kingdom of Heaven.'*"

Two ridges furrowed the face of Titus Waterman. The lava was beginning to bubble. "I caution you, sir, for your own good, because you are still yet new to our community. A bellicose Parson is one thing; a dangerous sectarian is *quite* another matter."

Verity stepped in adroitly from her end of the table. "Come, come, Titus, we're all reasonable people. Parson Jump, why not another cup of – of milk, and restore amends?"

Titus sat back in his chair. "Nathan? What think you of this?"

Nathan, in the act of lifting another morsel of marchpane to his lips, tensed. "Well, Squire, I – I'm as certain as I can be that Parliament ought not to assail the Church," he stuttered.

The squire approved of his answer. "Quite right."

Nathan shifted in his seat. He had won Waterman favour! "After all, we are all of the one body: one Anglican communion," he continued, warming to his thesis. "What else unites us all around this table, if not in our Protestant faith? And, at the last, we are all subjects of the same King."

"Hear, hear!" Philippa smiled comradely at him.

Titus looked impressed. "The voice of moderation, Nathan! I really must commend you."

"By your expression, it would seem you are not in accord, Master Jump...?" Rebecca asked the older man, in tentative, temperate tones.

Jump did not turn to acknowledge her. "Christ is King, not Man, *Master* Wohlford," he said, caustically. "In Him, at least, we shall always have a monarch who serves us."

"You will retract that statement, Parson," rumbled the squire.

The old man snapped, "So will I not!"

Titus' face had darkened. "You will retract that statement, or you will remove yourself from this table forthwith."

Captain Agnew started stuffing his mouth with blocks of marchpane.

"I would remind you, sirrah," the squire went on, "that you are sitting in the presence of those loyal to the Crown. Men who have grown grey in its service."

Jump broke out into a full-blown sneer. "And would that be the self-same Crown that His Majesty now has in pawn?"

The two wives started violently, and even the Waterman boys looked shocked. The squire's glare was bull-like. His voice was like a scythe.

"Parson! Quit my house!"

Jump looked genuinely flummoxed. He switched his gaze to the dessert that still awaited him. "But – but I have not supped my fill!" he spluttered.

"You've supped enough, sirrah. Aye, and you've said enough, too!" Titus jabbed a finger at the old clergyman. "I'll not bear these defamation in my presence – by God, I will not!"

Jump's neck twitched. "It is not for the unordained to dictate to the men of God, squire."

"Damme, sir!" The squire's fist pounded the arm of his chair. His face was distorted with fury; his spittle flew high in the air. "Damme, indeed – you'll pardon me, ladies – if you will drag us into disputations of this kind! Remove yourself, sir! And take your calumnies with you!"

He seized the hand bell from the cloth and rang it violently. The door in the corner opened. The steward was revealed.

"Windigate? Parson Jump is leaving. Be so good as to locate his cloak."

Nobody moved. The silence was heavy. Jump gave himself a dignified veneer before he pushed back his chair. He walked crisply towards the double doors. Halfway there, he stopped.

"Master Wohlford?"

Jump jerked his head for him to follow. Philippa's wide-eyed gaze tried to hold him down, but Nathan jumped to his feet. It was the involuntary manner of a hound who has been alerted by the command of its master.

"So. You side with him, sirrah?" The squire could not hide his disillusion. "Well, sooth to say, you Puritans must have your *principles*." He turned his head away. "Show these persons out."

Nathan went on shuddery feet. As from an incredible distance, he heard Titus saying: "'Twas ever thus with the base-born. Pass the wine."

Laughter. The Waterman boys were laughing. He heard Francis' unmistakable, hee-haw bray. He wanted to rush back in and take his seat back; ask the squire's pardon, and redeem himself. He wanted Pip. He needed her to forgive him with her eyes...

"Your cloaks, gentlemen." The steward's tone was glacial as he handed them their things.

Jump led the way outside. The night was getting bitter. The stars were white and naked. The yew hedge was shivering in the night breeze. Someone was sent round the back to tell old Zeb to bring round their mounts. Windigate firmly shut the door upon the pair of them.

Jump fastened his cloak at his throat. His scornful eyes roamed the facade of Briarwell Hall, settling again upon the Latin motto above the door. He shook his fist at it. "God shield us, they will buy this dear! Aye, confound them, and their kickshaws! As a man soweth, so let him reap!"

The old man looked for Nathan's affirmation, but Nathan said nothing.

"What is it with you *this* time?" The old man was losing patience with him.

"I – I don't know. Mayhaps we should have – "

"You're addled, boy." Jump stepped up, and pushed a crooked finger into Nathan's chest. "Hearken, now, to what I say. You must put any thought of being impartial out of your mind. This is no time for placating the fallalery of the landowning. This is a time for choosing *sides!*"

Hooves were sounding on the gravel. Old Zeb the groom had come back with the horses. Jump quickly followed through:

"'Tis your God, or your King. For you cannot have both!"

EIGHT

But he, her fears to cease,
Sent down the meek-eyed peace.

The first week of March was hot, with a sky like brass. Christopher Coates stood, his arms akimbo, reading the printed text that now graced The Gryphon's door.

A PROCLAMATION, *hereby forbidding all His Majesty's subjects, belonging to the Trained Bands or Militia of this kingdom, to rise, march, muster, or exercise by virtue of any Order of Ordinance of one or both Houses of Parliament.*

Coates rubbed his chin. Why did these official documents take such *time* to say what they meant? He felt like he was floundering in a sea of commas.

To the King it belongs to defend wearing of Armour, and all other force against the peace, at all times when it should please him, and to punish all which do the contrary according to the laws and usages of the realm.

"Usages of the realm"... That was a good one!

We understand that, expressly contrary to the good laws of this, our gracious sovereign kingdom, under pretence of an Ordinance of Parliament without our consent, the Trained Bands and Militia of this kingdom are intended to be put in arms in a warlike manner, whereby the peace and quiet of this kingdom may be disturbed.

Coates took off his hat and used it to fan his brow. He had been looking forward to bagging his usual table, and settling down with a lazy drink or two. This notice had spoiled everything.

We are desirous to prevent that malignant persons do not seduce our subjects from their due obedience to us, and to the laws of our land, whilst subtly endeavouring to hide their mischievous designs under the pretence of putting our Trained Bands into a posture only to draw and engage our good subjects into a warlike opposition against us.

Coates heard footsteps coming his way. The square little sexton panted up.

The butcher nodded. "Judah."

"Chris."

Judah's sleeves, turned back almost to the elbow, spoke of toiling in the churchyard. His knees and pattens were caked in the Kentish loam. He reminded Coates of a burrowing mole that had come up for air.

The sexton read his mind. "Aye, I've sweated to it, right enough. Nasty job. A baby. Baby girl, it've been."

"Care to say whose?"

Judah shrugged. "It's no secret. That Jemima Wilkins, from the Buttery. Bad business."

"When's the interment?" asked Coates.

"Sunday." The sexton sniffed. "Parson weren't too happy. Wages o' sin, he says."

"And...?" Coates left the question of paternity unsaid.

Judah shook his head. "No word. And she's not saying."

"Slut." The butcher spat on the ground.

Judah nodded at the door. "What's all this, then?"

"Them sons of Belial in the Commons."

"Oh, what now?" Judah read the Proclamation with down-turned mouth. "Pshew! The old Blunderbore's stirring again."

"I'll go bail half of 'em don't even empty their own jakes-pots!" Coates muttered grimly,

"Mayhaps this is the signal?" Martial fires were flickering in the sexton's eyes.

"Aye, old friend," said Coates, with a viciously cutting smile. "The signal to march out in great companies and to bleed the nation dry!"

"'Tis well to be alive, then." The sexton slung his arm around Coates' shoulder. "What say we float our kidneys, and give health to the King?"

Coates smiled, but movement in the lane behind Judah's head made him pause. "Hold hard, hold hard," he said. His face picked its way from disbelief to staggered, staring humour. "May the Lord's saints preserve us!" he choked.

Judah looked. "What the – ?"

Who should it be but Melhuish! Old, angular, bow-legged Melhuish, decked out in the garb of a Corporal of Horse. His bald pate was hidden under a green Monmouth cap, his trunk beneath a "back-and-breast" cuirass. He was hung about with matchcords and bandoliers. He had his old snaphance musket over his shoulder, and he held it by its muzzle. He'd even buffed the buckles on his shoes.

"My eye!" the sexton chortled. "Goliath rides again!"

The Corporal walked right up to them. His face was shining. "Chris; Judah. Fine day."

"Uhm – Melhuish?" Coates hesitated. "Have you been taking drink?"

"Certainly not!" said Melhuish, hotly. He tapped the tacked-up paper with his finger. "I could read enough o' that to know the King has called for fealty. Well! This is it!"

"Aye, but I think you'll now find this get-up contravenes the letter of the law!"

"What, *that*?" Melhuish looked at the warrant with derision. The musket was brought down from his shoulder. "Clean out your eyes, man! I'm a private citizen, in me own wearing apparel. I'm oathed to no Militia."

A sudden thought struck Coates. "What does Sarah think of all this get-up?" he queried.

"She says I'm brave: she's proud of me!"

"And you are not at all worried about – ?"

"About what?"

"About people – ?" Judah's hand rotated in an interpretive fashion.

"People what?" frowned Melhuish.

Coates was not so coy. "Laughing at you, man! Making mock!"

The verger defended himself. "Let 'em split their sides! I am for the King, tooth and nail."

Judah placated him. "None meant, none meant. First pint's on me."

Melhuish patted him gratefully on the shoulder.

Coates fanned his face with his hat before he said: "Whichever way things happen, please God it will not be allayed with a shower of blood."

"A shower? Pish, man! Please God it ain't a deluge! " Melhuish scoffed. "I'm the only one of us who's ever seen a war! Soon as you know, if Parliament has its way, it's a cannonful of shot shall fly in your smiling faces. Just you remember *that*, next time you get down on your hunkers and pray! And I ain't the only one in martial get-up, believe you me." He jerked his thumb up the lane. "I seen the squire, with a morion on his head – on his own lawns, too! Thing probably hadn't been worn since Flodden."

"Trying it for size, were he?" the butcher chuckled.

Judah joined in. "Next thing he'll be taking them sons, and setting 'em all on high to captain the rest of us."

Melhuish eased the bandolier that he had slung across his left shoulder. The belt was hung about with wooden charges, commonly nicknamed "the Twelve Apostles". His gesture made the charges knock like listless wind chimes. "Aye, and if he builds up his biceps, they might even make that little Jack Pudding Isaac an ensign!"

"'Tis vain. 'Tis more than vain," Coates grieved.

Judah suggested a practicable solution by sidling towards The Gryphon's waiting door.

NINE

Himself is his own dungeon.

Nathan couldn't sleep. A lot of half-formed images were drifting about in his brain in search of colour. His mind was tightly-wound. His head was one, uninterrupted, chugging rhythm.

He lifted his head from the pillows and turned his face toward the window. Moonlight flecked the darkness of the room. He hadn't drawn the drapes across the little latticed windows. At this rate, the sun would find him hollow-eyed, his face smeared with lack of rest.

Up.

He kicked his legs free of the imprisoning blankets. Legs over the corded mattress, feet to the floorboards. Standing made him reel like a whirligig. A splash of water from the china basin chased away the very last of his drowsiness.

He dressed himself mechanically, with blind man's fingers. Then he slipped down the twisting staircase, pausing only to lift his cloak from the peg. He took the big key from the sill by the door. No need to be a clod and lock himself out. Try explaining *that* to Arlo at three in the morning!

The door creaked open softly for him, like it was trying to be helpful. Then he was outside.

He kept off the path. The crunching gravel would betray him. He went over the grass on cat's feet. When he reached the lane he glanced back towards the Parsonage. Its gables had stood there since the reign of Bloody Mary. The trees leaned over the half-timbered building, sheltering it from the world. Their branches whipped the sky. Nathan wobbled his way down the lane, over the road. The meadows were there to receive him. The moon had spread the valley with its shining. The trees were parading under its beams. The world was as quiet as a library. Heaven itself might speak. The desert night had probably been tomb-still like this when Moses heard the Voice on Horeb's slopes.

His questions still beat in his brain like a hammer. With every clap, the sparks went flying, the way he'd seen them dance on Sam Joplin's forge. The long grass, recently sodden, parted before his pattens. The Medway dragged its feet down the shallow, V-cut valley. Its surface was pricked with starlight.

A bird swooped past him, making him start. The swallows were back now, and had been for several weeks. By day, you could watch them wheel and swerve in their unerring unity.

Quite without thinking, he had wandered into the Agnews' orchard. Nathan selected a particular specimen, the one with the rock at its roots. He stopped and sat down. Everything else stopped with him. It did not take long to realise that he had not outpaced his thoughts.

How many hours must the two of them have spent in one another's company?

His mind raced ahead, and went on without him. Detail piled upon detail. While their mothers spread themselves in their companionable chairs, he and Pip would up, and be off. In those days the whole world had been their province. Sooner or later they would find themselves a snuggery. They did not care wheresoever it was, provided it was somewhere they could sit and be alone.

The image twisted. Mere playmates took the shape of closest friends. Then came the exchanging of trust and ideas. Then came the growth. He, slightly-built and mousy; she with her height and her lengthening mane of fair hair.

Now another memory was before him. That time when he was about ten. That time Captain Agnew had teased them with the threat of a ghost that lived in the ash branches at the bottom of the garden, which liked to abduct disobedient children. It still made Nathan smile to think of how he and Pip had held each other's hands as they'd crossed the garden, brave in words but not in their hearts, to hunt the spectre down. Pip had armed herself with a stick, determined to shoo away this unwanted lodger.

He heard her thirteen-year old voice again now. *"What, Nathan? Do you think I am only a weak woman? Race you to the house!"*

Then had been the accident, leaving Mother to spend her tenure of eternity in the graveyard of Saint Margaret's. Leaving his father a husk of a man, unable to reach out to the son who badly needed him.

And then, almost too fast for him to contemplate, had come the separation.

Pip had clung to him when he'd left for Bicester. *"Be here for you when you come back!"* he had heard her mumble through her tears, and had rejoiced to hear her say it at the time. He'd mumbled something back about writing whenever he could. He had had to bid farewell to all the Agnew girls, even kiss the baby twins... But Pip had been the only one he had gone back to embrace a second time. He remembered her cheeks had been wet, because she'd been crying.

In retrospect, he could understand Father's decision. After all, Father was an Oxfordshire man; his wife had been the Kentish one, and Barming was sullied with memories. But at the time, as a confused thirteen year old boy, it had been a wrench. After a while, Theresa had come into their lives. She was handsome and had money: her father owned a lucrative printing business. What the old county types liked to disparage as "Trade" behind their hands. But there was something graver than that: Theresa was a Brodnax, and the Brodnaxes had long adhered to the Church of Rome. Not good enough for an *English* God.

The tension had been palpable. Nathan had buried himself in his books, and studied for his life. At last he'd moved on, into the sponge cake stone of Oxford University.

Oxford had been another hushed world, too. One of too much candlelit thinking, on not enough to eat. Trying to meet the exacting standards of his tutor, old Melchizedek White. Finally the Chancellor had conferred his degree, and in due course he had been ordained.

Father had stared painfully at him from his chair by the fire. "Nathan, of course I know that you did not take this decision out of spite, but you must not fail to recognise the position that this puts Theresa in."

The son had held his ground. "This is my vocation, Father. I know that I am called to it. I had thought you would be cheered."

"Well, I am not. And to hear you've been appointed to the curacy in Barming I find personally injurious!"

"But, Father! Barming is my home."

His father exploded, "Bicester is your home, boy! Lord knows I made it so for you, and so has Theresa! Do not have the temerity to mention that wretched place again!"

"In that case, Father, there is nothing more to say."

Nor there had. And so, as through the landscape of a dream, Nathan had come home.

Home. To Saint Margaret's, and the care of souls in the parish, and Barming Place, and —

And the afternoon when he had found her again in the little house. And the morning when she found him, in this very field, wearing her coat and her oak-like boots.

His mind was falling back into the groove again. He'd had it all worked out. He would meet her in a secluded woodland brake, here, between the dawning and the day. Probably beneath that round-topped beech that sentried the Tunbridge Road. She would be wearing a hooded cloak of dark red. The disguise would help make their escape furtive and at the same time titillating. He would set her on a horse (it would probably be a white one, but he would not quibble) and he'd whisk her away, out of the County forever. Her cloak would billow out behind her as they rode...

He stared at the twisted wood, standing gaunt on top of the hill. Some hope. That white horse had *long* since ridden off to Camelot.

There'd have been nothing but scraps of joy for them, anyway. Their excitement would be fleeting. Pip would be fretting for all those they'd be leaving behind. It would be like a canker. Young ladies of breeding were supposed to conduct themselves impeccably, were they not? They would inevitably have had to come crawling home, and throw themselves on the mercy of the court.

Sometimes, when their eyes met, he thought that she'd mined the secret out of him. He wondered if it had made her laugh.

He flung the thought away from him. He got up, and resumed his walk. Pip was creeping more and more into his dissonant brain. Always there. A character in a drama, awaiting her entrance.

He stopped peeling the grass into shreds. Someday, he would marry Philippa Agnew.

"Which is an honourable estate, ordained of God in paradise in the time of man's innocency."

The Common Prayer embraced him in its cadences, sanctified by years of usage. It was like slipping into warm water.

Edward the Sixth had granted men of the cloth the right to get wed. He would become a – what was the word? An uxoriat!

"And is therefore not to be enterprised, nor taken in hand unadvisedly, lightly, or wantonly, to satisfy men's carnal lusts and appetites like the brute beasts that have no understanding."

His palms were sweating.

The more he thought about it, the more he thought he might succeed. The girls were very fond of him; Elle and Ros would certainly have held nothing back if they weren't. And Rebecca and Stephen's feelings towards him had held, for all that Arlo Jump had tried to drive between them. The door of Barming Place was always open. Their house, was always his.

And if he squared it properly with Stephen, their eldest would always be his.

Unless –

Unless he got it wrong.

Pip would be gentle, indulgent. She might even put her arms around him for it. But her laugh would still cut him like a dagger. It would beat him more effectively than any club.

And what about Jump? If he mentioned the matter to him, Arlo would probably advocate a Justice of the Peace to solemnise the union, rather than see it performed in a church he found distasteful. The Word of Man, being energised against the Word of God.

It was true. The Word of Man *was* being energised against the Word of God. Why, the rumours were igniting everywhere! All those desperate debates in the Commons were blowing on the fire. The Jeremiahs spoke of Parliament wresting back its power from the King's Personal Rule. The result would only be an irreparable fissure with the throne. Those who looked to the future saw it rather differently. Putting down an authoritative Scot meant breaking from the more benighted traditions of Monarchy. Breaking down an attitude that they shouted was more suited to Herod, or Caligulan Rome, than to England in her prime. An England that had shed the cocoon of the Renaissance, withstood those angry Tudor redheads, and swapped them for the orthodoxies of the heavy-lidded Stuarts. An England that had inked out new dominions, far across the oceans. An England filled with right-doing, right-thinking men.

Nathan knuckled his eyes. He was a right-doing, right-thinking Englishman, wasn't he?

Wasn't he?

The Word of God, or the Word of Man.

Pugnacious words were giving way to falling doglocks. Talk was becoming the strenuous beat of armed and marching men. The guns of civil war would split Saint Margaret's tombstones, and make the dead jerk from their graves. What place had he in that?

None.

Nathan's mind could not – would not – accommodate the image of his putting on a uniform. There would be no "breastplate of righteousness" for him. His thoughts stood like a mountain.

He had no idea how long he had stayed in the orchard. But when he looked, he saw the easternmost end of the valley had been treated with the first touches of dawn. He took care to rearrange his cloak around his shoulders. The others of this world might go marching on with many hallelujahs towards their own inferno. Let them. He was only a puny little parson. But even this puny little parson knew his mind.

TEN

Dare ye for this adjure the civil sword.

The foam from Melhuish's pint slopped down his sleeve. "'Tis a tyrannous usurpation!" he spluttered. "The man is a King, and they have laid him by the heels!"

Judah said nothing. He was stealing little sips of beer. At threepence a pint, in the oppressive heat of summer, the fruit of Maidstone's hops would have to last him.

Melhuish wasn't done. His voice bordered the hysterical. "How can the Parliament dictate to the King? Is the Crown nothing but an empty toy? A trinket, for some bauble-hoarding whore to brandish?"

"What eloquence!" Magner surveyed him sardonically through wisps of curling tobacco.

Radcliffe tried to intercede. "The Commons would make respair. Their motives are sincere."

"Pish!" The verger had had enough of the Commons' "motives". He still bore Saint Margaret's scars personally.

Judah asked: "What be *your* opinion, Chris?"

Christopher Coates licked the drips out of his beard. "It's got me beat, I'll own. You have all those squireens sitting in Westminster, all a-cooking up their brain-pans, and where has it got them?"

Melhuish said: "I always knew as writing and ciphering avail a man nothing, no matter the brains he's got in his head."

The scrivener was aghast at such a slur on his vocation.

"Nay!" Coates brought the flat of his hand down to meet the table, making the pewterware rattle. "To write naught but his own name should be sufficient for a man. 'Tis all he ever needs after all, believe you me."

"Nay, now that is brabble!" The scrivener scoffed at his elders without camouflage.

"Brabble?" blinked Coates, unhearing.

"Ha!" quacked Magner. "The brabble of the rabble!"

Coates' eyes squinted away to nothing. His index finger leaped in Radcliffe's direction. "See here, you dandied pup, you! Who you calling rabble?"

"Nay, settle down, lads, settle down…" attempted Judah.

"You call me rabble one more time, long-head, and I'll rattle your teeth!" the butcher snarled, revealing his remaining crooked teeth.

Magner reached over and pushed Coates' hand back down towards the tankards. "Put up your blades, my bucks, 'afore you get yourselves thrown out, and the rest of us with you."

The armistice took effect. "My apologies, sir, if I have given offence," Radcliffe said in an undertone.

"Aye, well," sniffed Coates. "Bygones be bygones."

Melhuish attempted to draw the warring parties onto more communal territory. "I'll tell you what 'tis. 'Tis Puritan talk."

The trick worked. His ruse elicited a lot of assenting grunts. The Puritans were the target of every printed newssheet being churned out in London. Their Low Church pieties proved irresistible fodder for ridicule. They were Pharisees in sad-coloured dress, and their posturing needed puncturing. Most of them probably indulged in the very vices they abhorred the minute the shutters were up. Shutters up, britches down…

"Aye. Puritan talk," Coates concurred at last. "Short tempers, and long prayers!"

"God blind me, but I'd give those windy tripehounds a drubbing they wouldn't forget!" declared Melhuish.

"Oho! And what next?" chaffed Magner. "I suppose you will advocate we all enter into pay, and go and fight the Roundheaded dogs?"

Nobody said anything for a long, long time. Their expressions changed around the table.

"Well… What about it, my boys?"

The afternoon was muggy, so Nathan had taken his thoughts outside. At least the churchyard yews brought a bit of shade. Sweat ran like mountain springs from their source at his temples. He was pacing through the graves wearing a suit of faintly mildewed black, with a copy of Holy Writ opened in his hands. He dabbed the perspiration from his eyebrows and tried very hard to focus on the words of Saint John.

Then the Jews took up stones again to stone him. Jesus answered them, "Many good works have I shewed you from my Father; for which of these works do ye stone me?"

The Jews answered him, saying, "For a good work we stone thee not; but for blasphemy; and because that thou, being a man, makest thyself God."

"BOO!"

Two index fingers had jabbed him in the sides of his abdomen. Nathan yelped and dropped the book. The churchyard rang with peals of girlish laughter.

Nathan whirled to face his adversary. "Carrie!"

Carrie's long hair flowed over her shoulders and over her shift. Her face was creased from laughing. "You make such a squawk when someone does that to you, you know!"

Nathan stooped to retrieve the Bible. Picking it up, he dusted it off where the moss had kissed it. "This is hardly politic behaviour, Carrie."

Carrie's answer was to stick her fingers in her ears and caper about someone's headstone, chanting, "La-la-la-la! I am deaf! I am deaf!"

Nathan hunted for the chapter in question among the hundreds of onionskin pages. Carrie stopped prancing abut at last, to come and stand beside him. "You look so serious," she said.

"It's the Word of God, Carrie. Hardly fit material for joking and jesting."

"No. I suppose." She coughed to expel the last of her jollity. "What part are you reading?"

"This." He used his thumbnail to show her.

"*Though ye believe not me, believe the works*," she read aloud, "*that ye may know, and believe, that the Father is in me and I in him*." She looked at Nathan. "What's that for?"

"The sixth will be Trinity Monday. I must prepare for Sunday's Service."

That evil smile was back on her face. "You yowled just like a scalded cat, you know."

Nathan parried her with: "Does your mother know you're roaming?"

The gaiety was fading out of her eyes. "To tell you the truth, I had to get out."

"Why?"

"All sort of reasons." She trailed the toe of her shoe through the grass. Then, quite abruptly, she asked, "Nathan, can I talk with you?"

"Well, if not with me, then with whom?"

"Walk with me. I have to tell you something."

She pushed her arm through his and began to pilot him off down the path. He counted twenty paces — almost as far as the porch — before he hesitantly began, "Is it your father?"

"No!" Carrie almost sounded unimpressed with him. She came to a halt. "At least, not truly. Not wholly."

"What does that mean?"

"It means Father is a part of the problem, not the entire. No, Nathan, it's — it's me." She drew breath. "You don't know how it is for me. I mean, it's always *Pip*. Or Loobie, just because she's still the baby. Or it's the twins, if Ros and Elle have anything to say in it. Sometimes I feel like nobody at home ever wants to make the time for me."

When Nathan made no comment, she wondered why. Then she saw the gravestone that stood closest to the path.

SACRED TO THE EVERLASTING MEMORY OF
JUDITH AGNEW
1597 – 1633
"SHE IS CLOTHED WITH STRENGTH AND DIGNITY"

Carrie blanched as she let go his arm. "Oh! I — I did not stop here intentionally, Nathan."

"I know. I know."

She licked her lips. "What… was it like? You do not speak of it."

Nathan said, "There are some things that are left better unsaid, even to you." Then he sighed. It had come out stronger than he'd hoped, more callous. "First Mother, then our moving. Everything that I had ever truly known was taken away from me."

"Oh, Nathan, I remember. Our mother was beside herself!" Her arm went round his middle. She looked at him deeply. "You must not think me insensitive… But I must ask, is the accident the reason we so seldom see you on a horse?"

He grimaced. "The memory, you see; the association."

"Aye. It makes sense."

He went on, "When I left Oxford last year and came here... you will laugh, but I took the Drovers' Road. A few carts gave me a ride. Help the poor parson!" He managed a weak smile. "But enough about me. Shall we see if we can find a way for you out of your troubles?" He comforted her with a hand on top of hers. "Adolescence can be an exceptionally difficult time," he said. "I remember how things looked black when we had to move to Bicester."

"Pip didn't want to let go of you."

He nearly admitted, "And I didn't want to let go of *her*," but instead he said, more cheerfully, "But I am back now. And back to stay. And I know that Mother and I shall meet again. Let the dead bury their own dead, eh?"

Carrie squeezed his arm. She held on to it with both hands, like he might float away. "The honest truth, is I feel so *spare*."

"You're not spare, Carrie. You are much beloved."

She turned to him properly now, so that she might stand before him. "Do *you* love me, Nathan?"

Nathan gulped. "You know how I feel about you, Carrie. How much I care for all of you."

"Especially Pip!"

"Yes. Especially Pip." He did not flinch, or blink.

Her lips curled up like petals. "Then we have something in common, we two,"

"Indeed, Pip cares for you deeply."

"I did not mean that." She studied him awhile. "You do not see?"

"N-no?"

Carrie heaved a sigh. "Pip was right: what a mutton-head you are." She leaned in to whisper: "I mean that I, too, have somebody who cares."

"You *do*?"

"There's no need to sound so shocked!" she pouted. "I've seen you and Pip go about together – all you ever do is talk!"

"We enjoy talking."

Carrie said: "Pip speaks languages, without book, you know."

"I know she does."

"Silly goose. Now I'll admit that Roger's not a talker. But he is quite the gallant."

Nathan looked at her. "Who did you say?"

Carrie put her fingers to her mouth. "Oops!" she smirked.

"Roger? Roger *Waterman?*"

"Mm-hm." She brushed very casual fingernails against the front of her bodice. "A girl could not resist!" She put her arms behind her back. "And no man could *ever* forgo us Agnew girls. We are *quite* irresistible."

Oh God, and Christ, and all His suffering saints together.

"But, Carrie! Do they know?"

She shook her head. She was biting her lip as she smiled. "Roger, is my big secret."

Nathan was completely lost. It had never occurred to him that Carrie was now of such an exploratory age. Something still made him think of her as "Little Carrie", the hoyden who'd raise the rafters in complaint Mother would say it was time for her supervised afternoon music practice, and she must try to evoke a tune from her *viola da gamba.* Now here stood the same "Little Carrie", starting to draw the attentions of others, and to seek attention in her turn.

"The squire's son," he murmured.

"Aye, and I could do very much worse!" Carrie said, with some spirit.

"He's only the second son, mind."

"It does not matter to me. In any case, he says he's due his equal share when Titus dies."

Nathan was staggered to hear the distinguished squire addressed with such casual informality. "You – " he failed, then rallied. "Have you – ? That is, has Roger – ?"

She bit her lip again, this time to nod her head. "May morning, it was, when he asked. By the riverbank."

"Oh, Carrie."

"He cares!" she stated simply.

"But – you are only seventeen."

"Oh, do not start to panic, Nathan. Roger has laid no plans to elope. Mind you," she threw in, "I might do, if he begged me!"

Nathan shut his eyes. His face tingled in shame.

"Nathan?" Her hand felt for his wrist. "You've gone away."

He inclined his head. "I – I'm speechless, Carrie."

"For once!" Her arms went round his middle. She nuzzled at his chest. "Can you not at least say that you are happy for me?"

He relented, enfolding her at last. His fingers were still thrust between the pages of his bible. "Truthfully, Carrie, I *am* happy for you."

"Good!" She stood up on her toes to plant a quick peck on his cheek. "And now you know, you have to keep it to yourself." She made a little, lip-locking gesture at him.

Nathan looked into her face. She was toeing the grass again, rejoicing in her cleverness.

"Carrie, what is that look in your eye?"

Carrie giggled. "I told you my woes as a friend. But I tell you my secret as my priest."

"Confession's for the Catholics."

"What's to confess? I am not ashamed."

"And what if I told Parson Jump?" he broached.

She visibly flinched. "You wretch! You wouldn't?"

"He'd have to know. Eventually."

"Oh yes, *eventually*." That girlish pout was back. "I love Roger, and he loves me, and someday we will wed." She had begun to sway her hips a little. "And maybe one day you will be the one to solemnise it! So there!"

Nathan could not look her in the eye. He felt like he was standing on quicksand.

"Oh, my!" Carrie's attention had wandered over the churchyard, into the fields. She followed where it led her. Finally, Nathan went after her and found her leaning on the wall. Carrie's hands were clasped before her. All her focus was on the display of martial vigour taking place in the water meadow.

"The Militia! They're at it again!"

Carrie nudged him with her right hip, intending to draw interest out of his uneasy face. "Some sight, isn't it?"

"Oh – uhm, yes." He laid the Bible down on top of the wall. A lot of wispy lichen had covered its stones like a skin. Together they watched a score or so of armoured men, practising their foot drill in uneven columns of four. After a few minutes' halt, the ranks broke and the platoon began to form the various postures of musketry. Beams of light winked off a lot of tempered steel, and locks, and barrels.

"Oh, look! There's Roger!" She waved exuberantly at the aloof-looking youth who carried the halberd.

"'Our trusty and well-beloved'," Nathan murmured.

She dragged her eyes away from the crimson sash that Roger wore knotted around his middle. "Come again?"

"That is the wording of the King's Commission," he explained. "'To our trusty and well-beloved Roger Waterman, Esquire, greeting.'"

She looked at him with interest. "How do you know that?"

"A fellow I knew at Brazen Nose had commission the Militia. He showed me the scroll. He kept it in his chambers."

"Well, Roger is certainly *my* trusty and well-beloved."

He studied the pacing ranks again. "I see even Melhuish and Judah have joined them."

"And so's our bailiff, Magner. See? There, at the back." Then she turned to him. "They have been at drill a lot recently. What is it they are doing, d'you think?"

"The King rejected Parliament's terms."

"Huh! Men!" Carrie copied her elder sister's tossing of the head. Her long hair shimmered with the gesture. From her face, Nathan watched her arrive at an inward decision. She turned slightly side-on, regarding him imperiously.

"When are you going to marry Philippa?"

It felt like she had kicked him in the midriff.

"You should wear a love knot!" She had pinned a confident smile to her face. Carrie enjoyed her mischief. "Why haven't you procured one, mm?"

Nathan was tongue-tied. "I – I can't deny that my feelings for – for your sister, run deep."

Carrie stared at him. "Is that all?"

"Will it not suffice?"

Her eyes strained in their sockets. "But you have both been so *slow*! It's like watching a flower grow!"

"Flowers need to be nurtured, Carrie."

"Well, hurry up and bloom!" she ordered, hotly. "We're all waiting for you to ask her. For her to come into the parlour, wearing your ring!"

Nathan's mouth could not stay closed at that. "ALL of you?"

Behind them a voice shouted: "Carrie! Oh, Carrie!"

Nathan turned, relief sweeping through him. The twins were bounding down the path in their direction. Rosalind was calling: Eleanor did the waving.

Carrie's shoulders slumped. "What *is* it, you little imps?"

"Headstrong has sent us out to find you!" Eleanor panted, doubled-up to get her wind back.

Rosalind flung herself into the situation. "Have you asked him, Carrie? What did he say?"

There was a big, mooning leer on Ros' face. Nathan released an exasperated breath. "Girls, this is an elaborate conspiracy!"

All Carrie's attention was on Rosalind's ten-minute junior. "What's this? Do not stand there making mouths at me, Ros! Why does Headstrong want me?"

"She doesn't: it is Mother wants you back." Eleanor stood straighter. She could speak more coherently now. "It's Father."

Carrie's whole aspect changed. She looked nervous, like a bird looking out for danger. "Oh, Nathan! I – I must …"

"Go! Go!" He urged her along with a flap of the wrist. The Bible was back in his hand.

"I –" Carrie began. Then she caught his eye, and her nerve deserted her. "Nay, never mind."

She hitched up her skirts and made off, pausing only to grab Elle by the hand and heave her along. Ros bestowed a fluttering wave of adjournment before she, too, stumbled away through the graves. Nathan leaned back against the wall and stood alone. Left to contemplate how Carrie schemed of a life as "Mistress Caroline Waterman". How the massed ranks of the Agnews were waiting for Philippa's betrothal with bated breath. And to the irony of Stephen and Rebecca picking one of Mister Shakespeare's more uninhibited heroines to name the elder of their twins.

ELEVEN

Bitter restraint and sad occasions drear
Compels me to disrupt your seasons due.

Nathan climbed the stairs of Barming Place. His tread was slow, like an old man's feet. His satchel contained the sacramental necessaries. Rebecca watched his ascent from the safety of the bottom of the stairs. Her heart was in her mouth. She had spent much of that morning on the first floor of the house, and could not face another trip.

He stopped at the head of the stair. At the end of the corridor, a closed door faced him.

Philippa swam out of the gloom. Her face was arrestingly pale. Her eyes were very wet, and she was snuffling. Her red eyes told him she had been crying for some time. She leaned against him while Nathan put his arms around his shoulders.

"I came as soon as I had word," said Nathan.

Her nose was streaming, so she fished a square of cambric out of her apron. "We found him on the floor. He's in there now." Her sentences were unnervingly simple.

"The spare? Why not the master chamber?"

"Mother – couldn't bear it." She gulped down breath. "Those sticks do him no good. Not now. He needs a line of chairs just to cross the room."

"Your mother intimated ... it must be the end."

She nodded. "Faithful is with him."

"I will do what I can," he pledged. His hand began running up and down her sleeve. "No man should die alone."

Philippa cuffed back a tear. "Make him – make him ready."

"Is he really sinking?"

Her glance grew sharp again. Her head tossed ominously, and she spoke with the force of rage. "It's my father, Nathan, not the *Mary Rose!*"

Anger flickered in Philippa's eyes for an instant, and then quickly passed. Her face was strained, and full of pain. "Go in." She was trying to choke back another sob. "You have not much time." Her manner became curt and dismissive. "I'm going downstairs. Mother needs me."

I need you. His words yearned for their freedom, but he kept them imprisoned.

Philippa left him. Nathan brushed the whitewashed wall, icing his elbow in the process. He stopped before the door. A pause. A gathering of courage. Then he mounted the short flight of steps *one – two*, and lifted the old iron latch.

The smell made him reel. It was the smell of too little ventilation, of long, slow, sweltering hours; of the exhausted slump of Captain Agnew.

"Hullo, Stephen," said Nathan from the doorway.

In his spleen, the Captain's hand fluttered a greeting. "Gimme me physic again, woman!" spluttered the voice.

Nathan walked over to the bed. Its curtains had been drawn back, all round, and made fast to the posts with their cords. Faithful was sitting on a three-legged stool beside the bed. She held a bowl of water in her lap. The light in Stephen's eyes was awful. His forehead, dabbed clean by Faithful's linen cloth, crackled with the fever that consumed him. The plump and ruddy flesh had stretched to parchment over the cheekbones. The eyes had lost their lustre. The jaw was gritted with pain.

Nathan came closer. "Faithful, would you be so good as to leave us for a short while?"

She set the bowl down on the floor by the bed and stood up with a look of relief.

"Perhaps you might – attend on your mistress?" Nathan suggested.

Faithful quit the room without another word.

"I'm pretty well pickled, Nathan!" The Captain's voice was still blunt.

"Nonsense, Stephen."

Nathan thought he had best find a place for his satchel. And he needed to put a bit of distance between himself and the dying man. He went to the opened window, hungry for air. He heard the whinny of a carthorse. Peeping out, he could see the sheeny beast, heading head-bent down the Tunbridge Road. The load in the waggon was heavy. The June haymaking was well underway.

He set down his things under the sill. A game of chess had been laid out on the occasional table. Contesting red and white ivory pieces stood stranded on their squares. Nathan picked up a red knight, threatened by white bishop.

"Pip's playing white," the Captain explained. "Give her a half-hour more, and she'll smite me hip and thigh."

"I mean to improve my own game, Stephen," Nathan said, with a feeble attempt at humour.

"Philippa'll teach you," the older man rasped.

Nathan unpacked what he'd brought. He used his body to shield the leavened Host, the phial of communion wine, and the silver chalice he was laying out upon the table. "This summer will be wealthy with harvests," he said.

The Captain opened his mouth to agree, but all that came out was a squeaky croak.

"You ought to save your strength, Stephen. Try not to speak."

"Why?" the Captain wheezed back. "Are they fearing I'll meet me Maker with a curse on me lips?" He vented a lot of hollow coughing, which might have passed for laughter.

Nathan crossed the room and sat down on the three-legged stool. The Captain eyed him sidelong. "They sent you in, didn't they? To usher me out?"

"On no account!" Nathan protested.

"Don't contradict your elders, boy!" The parchment stretched tighter as the eyelid came down in a wink. The old, commanding mien was back. "I am not afraid to go, boy. I know how to die."

Nathan was sincere. "You're a true soldier, Stephen. And a sterling fellow."

"Muzzle it!"

Nathan cleared his throat. "Now, Stephen," he began, hoping he sounded practical. "I have brought the bread and wine for you."

"No! None o' that!" The eyes stared in sudden panic. "I'll have none of your 'Take this, my son'! Not yet." The eyes closed. "Still. It could be worse. They might have sent me that mad dog Jump!"

Nathan bridled as he listened to the gurgling phlegm in the Captain's throat.

A wasp began to fuss around above their heads. It was trying to find a warm crack in the oaken beams. The Captain's glazed eyes followed it, pinning his hopes of life on a mundane insect.

"That Jump would indict a Bergomask for a nuisance!" he muttered.

Nathan attempted to smile.

The Captain's hands were stilled upon the covers. "There is one thing..."

Nathan leaned forward. "Go on?" he encouraged, prepared for every syllable.

The Captain's head rolled upon the neck. "This island, now. It's pustular with war. All those blood-witted Westminster Members; God's teeth, they're nothing but a lot of bellowing cranks!" There was bile in his voice. The dewy moustaches shook. "I'll not draw me sword for that, Nathan. Not for a thousand crowns. Be like cutting the nation's throat!"

"I — I know what you mean, Stephen," said Nathan, with perfect honesty.

Captain Agnew must have read his mind. "Chasing Irish bograts be one thing. But to set neighbour on neighbour. That's not — not —"

"Christian," Nathan finished.

"Christian, aye! I've heard 'em out there, in the meadow. Been practising two rounds a minute. They're sounding our doom, boy!"

He fell back and gasped into silence, like a swimmer who has heaved himself at last upon the shore. Nathan thought he had caught the squeak and the shuffle of feet on the landing outside. But as he turned to try to listen, the noise disappeared.

"That Waterman pup!"

The voice made Nathan jump. "Which one, Stephen?"

"Roger," the Captain said, curtly.

"What — what about Roger, Stephen?"

"Titus bought him his commission, didn't he?" the Captain sneered. "First Francis had one, so Roger got the same. Now the word is Titus has said he'll do the same for Isaac. Bought 'em all the King's Commission, like a nosegay for some bloody trull!" He was practically shouting. "Fine match that jackanapes *Roger's* going to make for any hoyden with her heart a-flutter!"

Nathan's head bent lower over his arms. He was thinking of Carrie, confiding her secrets.

"Nathan?"

He turned back to the drenched face. "I am here, Stephen."

Captain Agnew was struggling to sit up. "Nathan? Listen to me, for I mayn't get another chance." The fingers slipped from Nathan's hand, then found purchase again. "You're a good lad. Always were. There's something I want you to do. For all our sakes, now, listen to me!"

Nathan's heart beat triple-time. *Philippa! Philippa! Philippa!*

"I hear you, Stephen."

The fingers tightened. "I urge you to do something, boy. For all our sakes; for *my* sake... Get to the King's Party, Nathan. Before it be too late."

Nathan paused. "Stephen, I – "

"The Church *must* stand by the sovereign!" The eyes were wide and pleading.

Nathan swallowed. "I – I think, we ought to say a prayer now."

The Captain had expended his strength. His head touched the pillows in a show of surrender. So Nathan began. He never took his eyes off Stephen's face. He owed him that.

"The Lord is my shepherd, I shall not want."

The fingers clawed. Now Nathan saw fear in Captain Agnew's face. Real fear. Morbid faces of those Kentish lads he had left rotting in Irish swamps would be coming for him, reaching for him, dragging him down to their festering hell.

"For thou art with me; thy rod and thy staff they comfort me."

Stephen's lips squirmed in time. His head was trying to lift.

"And I shall dwell in the house of the Lord forever."

The pillows received the head in their valley again.

"Stephen, there is something that *I* have to ask you..." He sat up straighter. "Stephen?"

Too late.

Silence flooded the room. Nathan had to check, of course, but the truth was a wall. He let go Stephen's hand and patted it in gratitude. It took considerable fortitude for him to reach out and close the Captain's gelid, hazel eyes.

Nathan rose and walked the half a dozen steps to the door. He lifted the latch and drew the door open. The light from the windows behind him revealed that two figures were sitting side by side at the top of the stairs. Rebecca and Pip. Their faces turned to meet him.

Nathan stood with his hand on the edge of the door. "Stephen... has gone," he said.

Rebecca did not cry out, for she did not want her girls downstairs to learn the truth that way. She was the first to stand, then she turned and helped her eldest daughter to her feet. She put her arms around Philippa's shoulders and helped her along the passage. Nathan watched Pip walk like a stumbling puppet, all out of step.

When they stepped up into the bedroom, the daylight showed their faces properly. Pip's tears were falling fast; Rebecca remained dry-eyed. A mask covered her own, private whirlwind. She mimed the words, "Thank you," and her hand went out in Nathan's direction. At once the gesture comforted him and drove him away. She was confirming his duty done.

The widow went to the bedside. Nathan saw her throat constrict. She studied her husband's dead face. Then, quite without warning, Rebecca gave way. She fell to her knees like a collapsing tower, and buried her face in the sheets.

"Oh, Stephen! Oh, *Stephen!*"

She cupped his dead hand in hers, and pressed it to her cheek in desperation. "Dear Lord in Heaven, let not my Stephen die!"

Philippa started to tremble from head to foot. The bedclothes could not muffle Mother's wails for the husband she had loved, and lost.

Nathan moved in. "We must leave her, Pip. Pip? Let us go and tell the girls."

Philippa remained rooted to the spot. He put both arms around her shoulders, trying to drag her away.

"Pip? Pip! There is naught else we can do here. Come on, Pip. Come *on!*"

TWELVE

Their moans the vales redoubled to the hills.

Arlo Jump's voice cawed across the churchyard as they bore the Captain's coffin to the door of Saint Margaret's.

"'I know that my Redeemer liveth, and that I shall rise out of the earth on the last day, and shall be covered again with my skin, and shall see God in my flesh; yea and I surely shall behold him, not with the other but with the same eyes.'"

Nathan peeped over his shoulder. Rebecca had wanted to look strong and forward-looking. Today, this day of days, she must be brave. She owed it to the girls, to herself; to the train of black that walked behind her.

"Before the mountains were brought forth, or ever the earth and the world were made: thou art God from everlasting, and world without end."

Loobie toddled along on her chubby little legs. One of her hands enveloped by Mother's glove. She felt all out of place in this sombre raiment. She had seen her mother's bending head, and her quiet, melting tears. The proper response to this defeated her. She was trying to choke back a giggle, gagging herself with her fist.

The wind was rustling in the sleepy yew trees. A single bell tolled for the death of a man.

"In the midst of life we are in death; of whom may we seek for succour, but of thee O Lord, who for our sins are justly displeased?"

They trailed into the church. All the Waterman boys had donned their new uniforms to say their farewells to their Father's old friend. They observed the propriety of surrendering their swords at the door. Jump led the familiar prayers. The biography was brief. "Life of service... person of rigid principle... respected by all who knew him... devoted to the family of daughters that he headed."

When it came to the reading, it should have been the cadences of Paul to the Corinthians, reminding the faithful of their mortality whilst earnestly anticipating the salvation secured by the Second Coming. Instead –

"'Think not that I am come to send peace on earth: I came not to send peace, but a sword. For I am come to set a man at variance against

94

his father, and the daughter against her mother, and the daughter-in-law against her mother-in-law.'"

Across the nave, Rebecca's face betrayed nothing. The mask had been put back on.

"'And a man's foes shall be they of his own household.'"

What was Arlo doing? Was this an ominous diagnosis of the health of a sickening nation, or was it Arlo's cock-a-doodle of revenge? Stephen had never given offence to the Parson, had he? At least, surely not to his face?

"'And he that taketh not his cross, and followeth after me, is not worthy of me. He that findeth his life shall lose it; and he that loseth his life for my sake shall find it."

Nathan suddenly knew where he was. There had been just enough about the immortal soul to leaven the message behind it: impending bloodshed. The old fox had been clever!

At the graveside, birdsong trilled from the surrounding trees, and the rain, which had been spitting all morning, stopped. A watery sun peeped down upon the tableau and upon the widow's dear expense. The symbolic palmfuls of dirt thudded down upon the coffin. No common parish box in this grave. The Captain's coffin was a varnished, ten-shilling affair. Its oak had been inlaid with stamped sheet brass. The villagers were suitably impressed. Some of them even wore the gloves and deep black hatbands that the Agnew family had thoughtfully provided for their mourners, as custom dictated they should.

The condolences began. Hasty, dilatory, polite, well-meaning, heartfelt. Verity Waterman walked up and kissed Rebecca on the cheek. Titus tended her his deepest sympathies and repeated their undying amity.

Judah Copp had already prepared to oversee the filling-in, but he would not pick up his spade in the presence of the widow. He whipped off his hat and gave a mannerly tug of the forelock. "God keep you in your ordeal, Mistress. The Captain will be missed about these parts."

Now Judah's wife Grace stepped up. She was a small, fair, perpetually flustered woman. "A great loss. Great loss. So *dreadful* for you, Mistress."

Rebecca tried a twisted smile. "Thank you, Judah; Grace. That is – a true comfort."

Corporal Clare raised his hat to his commander's widow. "God bless you, mistress. And God bless your girls in their darkest hour."

"Oh, Melhuish." Rebecca's smile was fuller now. "Your visit to him meant a deal at the last."

She had sat in the hall, glad to have her embroidery hoop to distract her, while the old horsemen relived their campaigns.

"I'll draw comfort from that, Mistress." Melhuish flicked something out of his eye. "'S not a man in the Captain's command as wouldn't 've took on the Devil himself, if your husband had asked 'em."

Rebecca laid her fingers on the older man's sleeve while she whispered her thanks.

Philippa stood to one side, in her pocketful of darkness. She stared fixedly into the grave, hating herself for her own rigidity.

Nathan sidled round the margin of the hole and went to her. "Shall you be... alright?"

Philippa said nothing. But her gloved hand emerged from under the fall of her cloak, made contact with his body, and pushed him away.

The mourners began to disperse. They had been standing about for too long in this high-noon humidity. Faithful also took her slow and wet-eyed leave. The Mistress and the girls ought to be alone while they had the chance. Besides, Faithful had three pounds' worth of cakes and a hogshead of beer to serve to the mourners. The crowd were all repairing up the lane to Barming Place: they'd have an appetite by the time they made the trip. Death did not come cheaply.

Jump dipped his neck in adieu and tramped back inside the church. Rebecca and Philippa bracketed the grave. The mother at the head, the daughter at the feet. Nathan remained among the girls, helping to thwart disaster when it looked like Loobie was about to venture too near the hole.

The sexton's labourers waited at a respectful distance. They were in no hurry. There'd be beer all round when the task was finished.

Nathan said: "I'm – I *am* so sorry, Rebecca. Truly."

Rebecca sniffed. "He is at peace now, Nathan. We must swallow our tears. All of us."

Nathan cast a look around the girls. Pip, still sunk in fathoms quite unreachable. Carrie, with her arms around the shoulders of the quietly sobbing twins. Loobie, still too young to understand the situation properly, with her lips around her curving thumb. Grief was not a secret indulgence at Barming Place. The Agnew girls had cried till their insides hurt. Only the night before, Pip and Carrie had come in search of their mother. Their nightgowns showed lint-white in the shadows, and they had pattered across the boards like barefoot ghosts. Pip had kept very quiet, stretched out upon the bed; Rebecca had been unable to tell if her eldest had slept or not. Carrie had snuggled down in the crook of her mother's arm. She kept making little mewing noises in her dreams. For Rebecca, there had been no dreams, and only fitful imitations of sleep. She had held her girls tight while she stared and stared and stared at the pre-dawn dark.

"He had no desire to suffer any longer. Or for us to have to watch him as he suffered," Rebecca went on. "At least you were there to bring him comfort at the end, my dear. I shall be forever in your debt for that."

Nathan was moved, but he bit his emotions back and said: "No debt, I assure you, Rebecca."

She said: "Walk with me, Nathan."

Her arm went through his, and they moved a few paces away from the grave.

"What – will you do now?" He was almost afraid to ask.

She sniffed, and stifled her breath. "Stephen has apparently bequeathed us a small stipend." Her gaze moved back towards the yawning, earthen mouth. "Not much, but it will be enough to live on if we rearrange ourselves a bit."

"Rearrange?" he questioned.

She shrugged. "There is no possible way we can remain at Barming Place."

Nathan's heart squeezed. "Then... who will – ?"

"I hear he's a Cheapside merchant, seeking to buy somewhere rural for himself and his family."

"I see." He had heard the chagrin in her voice.

"It will only be to Maidstone," she confirmed. "A house is to let, on Week Street. Quite modest, but enough for our needs. We will not pass our days on a pension of thousands, but neither will we find ourselves sleeping under ricks and hedges, if that were your concern."

"You are – fortunate."

Stupid word.

Her pallid smile forgave him. "We have a fortunate agent," she said.

"Magner?"

She nodded. "It is providential that Stephen's funeral takes place upon a Saturday."

Her abrupt *non sequitur* sent Nathan's eyebrows shooting up his forehead.

"You noted, no doubt, that our bailiff did not number among the mourners?"

Nathan gave the confirming sign.

"There remains, I regret, the question of one or two rental arrears still outstanding to us." Rebecca blushed to speak of it. "Had Stephen been interred on the Sabbath, then of course Master Magner would not now be at liberty to discharge his office. You may think me quite indelicate to speak of such a thing here, Nathan, but I *have* to consider the girls."

"That seems very considerate of Master Magner," he said.

Rebecca agreed. "Stephen always thought him quite an overweening fellow. But say what you will, our Master Magner is a conscientious man."

Her palms were pressed flat to the wall, and she was moaning. His thrusts were strong and deep as he pounded into her. Her pelvic muscles clenched; he jerked his hips on his release. As he did so he brought his hand down, hard, upon her bottom. It made her scream. He placated her by leaning in to nibble the nape of her neck. He felt her hunch her shoulders beneath him, heard her throaty laugh of triumphant pleasure.

He untangled himself. She gasped as he slipped out. "My, you boiled over!" she remarked as she turned to face him.

"Oh, I did. I did indeed."

She used her wrist to rub her cheek. Her face was now shot through with rosy blush. "You enjoyed yourself!" she quipped.

His pointy beard accentuated the satisfaction on his face. He was breathing hard as he wriggled back into his breeches. She watched him as he shamelessly adjusted himself. She was pleased to see the perspiration in the hairs of his moustache.

She moved away from the wall, beating the powdery lime from her fingertips. "I ought to have known you were a man to combine business with pleasure, Master Magner!" She picked up the jingling, lambskin pouch from off the table.

He had not even removed his hat for their breakneck romp; now he swept it from his head and held it out before her in a gesture of exaggerated courtesy.

"To such a one as I, Mistress McParlan, pleasure *is* my business."

She laughed, and dropped the purse into the crown of his hat with a sportive expression.

THIRTEEN

Cheerily rose the slumbering morn
From the side of some hoar hill
Through the high wood echoing shrill.

An escarpment outside Nottingham called Edgehill had been the place of reckoning. Men primed their pans and gripped their pikestaffs tight. Big, square regimental standards broke against the breeze. The hosts had glared, and stood, and shot, and hacked at one another. The well-born and the base-born rode out to meet their maker waving swords and feathered hats above their heads.

Holed up amid the quads of Oxford's colleges, the King's Party rubbed their aristocratic chins and wondered how to retake the capital. Surrounded by the silver plate and dark panelling of the ancient seat of learning, they drank their sack, and schemed. The Headington stone resounded to the pacing of their bucket-top boots. They denounced a fickle populace of Puritan ingrates that had turned their backs on Monarchy and renounced the whole order of being. Meanwhile, the Horse Artillery practised their drill in the deer park of Magdalen, and were occasionally inspected by King Charles.

"'The people that walked in darkness have seen a great light: they that dwell in the land of the shadow of death, upon them hath the light shone.'"

Nathan had entered the bedchamber to find Jump sitting up in bed, wheezing. The room smelt faintly of very old, very dried-out, lavender sprigs. The darkness of the morning was only warded off by the two, tall, tapering nightlights that flanked Arlo's headboard. Their flicker fell upon the creases in Jump's antique features. Ravaged by sickness, the old man appeared even tinier. His wizened face was nearly lost amid the pillows. His beard had frayed at the ends like old rope. His eyes looked colourless and filmy in their stare.

Nathan kept a secure distance. "How do you fare, Arlo?"

The thin lips puckered. "I have not heard the bells." Jump turned his head to the verglas window panes. "Bed-headed layabout! I'll wager the devil is with him. Make sure he is prompt to his post. A quarter to eight, and not a jot longer!"

"I shall make a point of it," Nathan promised. Then, "The church will be like ice, I fear."

"It'll keep 'em attentive." Jump tugged the bedclothes higher, til they almost covered his mouth. "You'll take the service."

Nathan heard the peremptory order and nodded. "I am for all waters, Arlo," he reassured.

"Not a word too fast, now, Nathan!" Jump warned, raising a severe finger. "Assure yourself I shall learn it if you do. Now go."

"Stay as warm as you can. I shall look in on my return."

Jump was seized by a spasm of coughing. "God's lifelings! Where is that fool of a woman?"

"I have not heard her."

"Tell her to warm up some honey from the larder and bring it me. My throat feels like a toad's!"

Nathan couldn't disguise the first glow of a smile. He trooped downstairs, into the welcoming warmth of their kitchen. Hannah the Parsonage's housekeeper was absent from her haunts, though a hot kettle hung over the fire, and there was a dish of honey and a dipper all ready on the table. Arlo would get his electuary in good time.

Nathan collected his cape and unbolted the door. The light had stolen back into the sky. It was stinging cold and everything was rimed in white.

The world was a world of ghosts and gaps these days. With the advent of war, Barming had quickly been pruned of its usual faces. Now there was no Faithful, waving to him with her dust beater from an upstairs window. No Rebecca, maternal, warm, enquiring if he had had enough to eat. No rambunctious twins. No Loobie, smallest, youngest, and forever underfoot. No Carrie, running through the water meadows with her long hair streaming out behind her.

No Pip.

The ruddy sun was rising over the hills. The bells swung to sonorous life in the tower. Sam Joplin the blacksmith was warming to his Lord's Day post. Before long the path to the gate would be trodden by people's pattens and galoshes as the congregation came out to brave the unfriendly cold.

His gaze swept the graveyard, and its undulating surf of snow and frost. Thinking of the Agnews made him stare across the burial ground. Nobody could trim the grass like Judah Copp. Nobody tended the church with more love than Melhuish Clare... But now the pair of them had gone. A nation, hungry for uniformed men, had marched them off to a life of shouted orders.

The air was taut with rumours. News was scratching at the door like a homing animal that no-one wanted to admit. With London so close, and Parliament's Trained Bands straining at the leash, the Western boundaries of Kent were deeply perturbed. The Kentish Militiamen kept a beady-eyed watch on events in London Town, and the Parliament's Trained Bands stared right back. Neither side seemed willing to stomp on the hornet's nest first.

Nathan coughed into his hand and declared: *"For unto us a child is born, unto us a son is given: and the government shall be upon his shoulders, and his name shall be called Wonderful, Counsellor, Almighty God, the Everlasting Father, the Prince of Peace."*

The view from his lofty tub was tame and colourless. Saint Margaret's walls had never looked so bare. Plain glass had been installed, but the memorial tablets had not been put back. The decapitated Saint had been bundled away, and long grass now grew all around her on the other side of the wall.

"'Of the increase of his government and peace there shall be no end, upon the throne of David, and upon his kingdom, to order it, and to establish with judgment and with justice henceforth even for ever."

Isaiah's divination been intended to rouse, and make people rejoice. It had never sounded so completely uninspiring.

FOURTEEN

And those pearls of dew she wears
Prove to be the presaging tears
Which the sad morn had let fall.

Nathan left blue footprints in the snow as he walked through the graves. At first he did not see her, because she was sitting low on her haunches, and her black cloak enshrouded her body and her broad hat had buried her face. She manoeuvred herself upright but she did not turn to face him. Nathan moved alongside the brim of her hat. It masked her remarkably, extending all the way out to her shoulders.

Philippa continued to stare at the grave. Then she incanted, Scots burr and all,

"Unto the deth goes all estatis,
Princes, prelotis, and potestatis,
Baith riche and pur of al degre;
Timor mortis conturbat me."

Nathan took his cue.

"He takis the campion in the stour,
The capitane closit in the tour,
The lady in bour full of bewte,
Timor mortis conturbat me."

"It feels strange, you know," she said. By her manner, they were resuming a conversation after five seconds' pause.

"What does?" he asked.

"To walk in the lane past the house. Just to walk past it, and to see it from the road."

"You ... walked?"

She inclined her head to peer at him. Their dragon's breath smoked thick. She had placed that curly brown wig on her head, and that surprised him. "What else may I do, without Fulke?"

"But, suppose you had been waylaid?"

She did not appear to have heard him. Her face pointed towards the gable end of Barming Place. "Do you imagine houses retain some legacy of the people who inhabited them, Nathan?"

Nathan shrugged. "They might. Mayhaps they do."

She scratched at the tip of her nose. The gesture unveiled her attire to him for the first time. The cavalry coat, the belt. The leather boots. The stock as white as the snow. Her outfit was just the same: the only difference was that her kidskin gloves were black.

Nathan looked down at the oblong block near their feet. Fingers had brushed away the night's deposits to reveal the engraving beneath.

ARTHUR AGNEW

1621 — 1622

A TRIBUTE OF AFFECTION

TO A BELOVED SON

NOW WITH GOD.

"When you said we would meet by the church..." he began.

"I know. I know." There was an iron-hard ring to her voice. Her hands were digging deep into the pockets of the coat. "But I had to come. It would have been quite ill-mannered not to!" she added, with the same old flicker of her previous, privileged self. "They might have been getting lonely."

Nathan had taken note of her choice of pronoun. His eyes moved on, to the adjacent block.

HERE LYETH THE BODY OF

STEPHEN AGNEW

HE DEPARTED THIS LIFE

AUGUST 27TH 1642

IN THE 56TH YEAR OF HIS AGE

DEARLY BELOVED.

"How fare the girls?" he questioned her.

"They adjust." She pointed a toe and studied it. "They make themselves useful. All got very excitable when I told them where I was headed."

"I shall visit again, before the twenty-fifth. When my duties permit. I promise."

"Do."

"I – I'd feared you would not come, you know."

Philippa sniffed. "How fares the venerable Jump?" Her tone had become sardonic.

"Not well, I fear to tell."

"We have heard. The influenza, yes?"

"'Tis pneumonia, now. It cannot be long," he said.

She looked at his satchel. "What bring you in there? It looks heavy."

"Aye, it is, rather." He slid the strap from his shoulder, and enjoyed the relief. "It contains a gift, for you."

"For me?"

"Only a little something for the Christmas." He fiddled with the buckles, awkward with the cold. "Close your eyes."

She screwed them shut.

Nathan drew the bulky object from the satchel and held it before his chest. "Open them."

Philippa squealed when she saw what he had brought. She clapped her hands together, jumping up and down upon the spot. Her boots crunched into the snow.

"A happy Christmas to you, Pip." He broke into a big grin as he handed her the *Folio* of Shakespeare.

"But this – this – !" She ran excited fingers over its calfskin binding. "This was mine! I would swear this was mine!"

"It was. And now it has found you again."

She looked at him, unseeing. "But how?"

"I saved it. At the auction."

"Oh, Nathan..." She opened the cover. The portrait stared back with that egg-shaped forehead and that small moustache. Below were the names of the printers Jaggard and Blount, and the date 1623. Right at the bottom had been inked the words *Philippa Agnew. Her book.*

"It just needed the opportune moment to give it you back."

She showed it to the headstone by her feet. "Look, Father! Now I may be learned again!" Her face was shining with excitement. "Nathan, I fear this is a debt I can never repay."

Her chin tilted down upon the cover boards, and she hugged the book tight to her chest. She pinched her lower lip between her teeth. She lifted her head to whisper her thank yous. Nathan smiled back with great affection.

Nathan stepped closer. "Anything for you. You might have known that, Pip."

Philippa put the book into his hands again. "Here. Keep it safe for me. Just a little longer."

He stuffed the *Plays* back in the satchel. When he looked at her again, Nathan saw that her look of wide-eyed joy had disappeared. It was like the closing of a shutter. "What ails you, Pip?"

She licked very pink lips. "You rebuked me once, for dressing in these brilliants."

"I never rebuked you, Pip. You were honouring him, and proud to do it. You honour him now."

Her eyes darted back towards the grave. She betrayed a little shiver.

"You're cold," he remarked.

"I am. Bone-deep. But his boots keep my legs warm. And the coat..." She ran her leather-clad fingers up and down its forearm. "It's like feeling his embrace again."

"I understand."

"No, Nathan, I do not think you do!" Her gaze crossed his: a beam of tawny anger. "He taught me how to ride. He taught me chess; to play pall-mall. He taught me leisure angling. He even showed me, once, how to fly a hawk. He taught me things... he should have taught a son."

At first she seemed entirely calm, but as Nathan looked her mouth twisted, a crease appeared between her eyebrows, and her gloved hand covered her nose and her mouth.

Philippa turned gratefully into the open arms of his embrace. The brim of her hat curved upwards against his head. Nathan held her close in wordless comfort. He had no idea how long they had remained there like that, but his toes had begun to curl with the acidic cold.

In the end, she drew away and stepped out of his clutches. "Sorry," was all she said.

"It does not matter."

She flicked away a tear with her thumb. "I — I did not bring a handkerchief."

"Neither did I," he admitted.

"Oh, well." She dabbed at her nose with the back of her sleeve. She was self-consciously, bashfully, smiling. "I must be a sight!"

At length he said: "He was always — very proud of you."

Her head dipped. "You cannot win, Nathan."

"Would you not — talk to me, Pip?"

"Talk?" She could not meet his gaze, but her voice was very steady. "Mother and I were talking, only the other day. With things as they are, Mother said — she intimated, rather — that we could go to the New World. All of us."

He was stunned. "America?"

"New World. New life," she ruminated, studying the treetops. "An escape from all this; find better hills to journey over. 'For the former things have passed away'... *N'est pas?*"

Now he had her by her shoulders. "Philippa!"

Her eyes went wide. "Holy Mary! You sound serious!"

"Listen to me, Pip." Talking was difficult. Her words had tightened his tongue. "The thought of you, sailing away to the other side of the sunrise — it's a damp on my spirits."

She put her hands in the crook of his elbows. "Oh, Nathan. You haven't caught us in the nick of departure!" She spoke gently, even gaily. "But with Father gone, these days we are lucky to have a jakes pot to call our own!"

"I — I do not want you to leave!"

"Things have changed, Nathan," she said.

"*We* have not changed! Not so that one would notice."

Now she was looking at him as though he were a dunce. "What blindness is this? We *are* different people!"

"I — I need you, Pip."

Her head drew back. She appeared to be divining his intentions, mapping his next move. "You... you do not really need me, Nathan. Not when you have your God."

He drew a sharp breath. "I cannot believe you mean that."

"My truths were meant to be told." She laid her hands on the front of his cloak. "I knew always that you liked me. Liked me hugely. I have felt it in my heart for years."

"And more! I loved you, Pip!"

"You... loved me." Her eyes roamed every quarter of his face. Then she tenderly cradled that face between her hands. "You are a true friend, Nathan. And a good man. And I trust you always will be." She paused, letting her eyes look deeply into his. "But my position's pathetic enough. And I do not desire admiration, Nathan. I do not *expect* you to love me."

Nathan summoned his voice. "I want to care, Pip. I – I want to care, for you. If you would let me."

Philippa let go of his face, and backed away. "Nathan!" she gasped, "I do believe that the cold is affecting your brain! Was that a proposal?"

"It... it may have been," he mumbled.

"It *may* have been?" She gawked at him, her face in disarray. "You would ask me, now; here, of all places?"

His admission hobbled out. "You must know how I care for you. And I *would* care for you. Lifelong, Pip. I love you."

"You – you do not really mean this." She was trying to convince herself that he had only been joking.

"Yes, I do. And it is no laughing matter."

"No. Indeed."

She shouldered past him. She extended a single upturned finger, to indicate that he should not follow her immediately. She stood with her back to him, staring across the frosty meadows, down towards the river.

Nathan tried again. "I swear, I would not be inconstant! I would protect you, and care for you. And it says, in the Book, to love your wives just as Christ – "

"'Just as Christ loved the church'," she interrupted. "Do not cast texts at me, Nathan. I know that: I have read it."

She still resolutely refused to confront him. All he could see was the great obscuring hat, slightly tipped back over her snow-spattered cloak.

At long, long last, her hand burrowed out from the folds of the cloak and reached up to pull the hat off. The dark wig came away with it. It flopped to her feet, bounced once, then lay there in the snow like an animal brought down. When Philippa finally turned, the breeze was disturbing her flaxen hair.

"Ask me again," she commanded.

Nathan stepped forward. "Would you marry me, Philippa?"
The big hat dropped from her hand. She reached for him.

FIFTEEN

To scorn delights, and live laborious days.

They were married in Saint Margaret's, when the crocuses were blooming in the graveyard. Old Reverend Webbe officiated in the presence of the bride's family. Where Arlo Jump would have scratched like a crow, Reverend Webbe put real music into the narration of the Order of Service.

"Forasmuch as Nathan Wohlford and Philippa Agnew have consented together in holy wedlock and have witnessed the same before God and this company..."

Pip had been wearing a gown of yellow taffeta. She carried a posy of wild violets. Rebecca had made the bride a present of her grandmother's pearls. The bride had looked tall and proud, and brave, which was more than Rebecca could feel during these insane days. She had sat in the pew and wept without a sound. Carrie had felt for Mother's hand, pressing it while the older woman bowed her head and let the long tears flow.

The wild violets moved to the crook of the bride's left arm, while her right arm was through her husband's. It had been Pip's idea to lay her posy upon the grave of Judith Wohlford, the mother-in-law that she would never know.

They had been married a matter of months when Philippa learned she was pregnant. "Bring forth men-children only," he had said, reaching for a line from *Macbeth* to chaff her. She had been getting on towards her term at the time, and feeling too much like she resembled a stranded whale to appreciate his choice of reference.

The contractions felt like stomach cramps at first. Philippa worried about what she had had eaten, and whether it would harm the baby. She had started to pace the kitchen, moving from the door to the window and back again.

When her waters broke, it frightened her. It frightened her more because Nathan was out of the house on a parochial errand, and she wanted him there, to hold her. He had returned to find her in the kitchen, on the floor. She was moaning and sweating. Her head was tipped back against one of the cupboard doors, her hands clutching the curve of her distended stomach.

110

Nathan had got her on her feet by degrees. She doubled over, hissing in agony. He manhandled her upstairs. Ignoring her cries, he doubled back down the staircase three at a time, and dashed across the lane to enlist the experienced hands of Anna Frost. Anna was an unfussy, feathery hen of a woman. She'd had six children of her own, and helped deliver a score around the village in her time.

It had been a difficult birth. Searing contractions had made Philippa writhe on the soaking sheets and scream her throat out. The pain was unlike anything she had ever felt in her life: she had to be dying.

Then, it was over.

"Aha, he's a fighter, this boy!" said Anna, as she cut the umbilical cord with a pair of sharp shears, and listened to the newborn's wailing.

"I wonder where he inherited that?" Nathan mused aloud. He had been looking at Pip as he'd said it. Her hair was wet with perspiration, and her voice was rubbed raw. She tried to readjust, to prepare, but every trace of her strength had left her. The very compass of her being had changed its cardinal direction.

The boy had slept. His eyes were pinched shut as he'd snuggled in Philippa's arms. "Look at him…" she whispered, giving Nathan her free hand to hold in both of his.

"He is ours," was all he said.

"Aye. I am his and he is mine." Her arm had tightened round the little bundle.

They'd called the boy Stephen. Rebecca had emphatically approved.

Stephen had rallied. He'd cried. He grew in strength, and teethed on his new wooden rattle, lying in the very same cradle that had succoured his mother. Rebecca had saved the crib for one daughter to the next. She willingly donated it for the birth of her grandson. The twins adored their nephew on sight, and bickered over which of them should hold him first. Shortly afterwards they made him a present of their old hobby horses, which they'd carefully hidden when the inventory for the auction of Barming Place was being drawn up. One horse had been for Stephen, and its pair was for Stephen's future little sibling… But as the years had gone by, Stephen still found himself with the choice of two.

"Bring forth men children only…" Or just the one. Philippa's monthly bleeding had not been punctual. Sometimes it dried up altogether; it could take weeks at a time before it would happen again. Attempts to provide their firstborn with a sibling (and they had made numerous and effortful attempts) had not borne fruit. There had never been a fellow to ride the second hobby horse. Eventually Pip had gifted it to the children of some neighbours in East Farleigh.

Sometimes Nathan wondered if Pip was still expecting him to blame her. But he swore he never would. He had chosen to think that Stephen was a blessing. Their blessing – his, and Pip's. A gift from On High. So it was that Stephen had become the centre of their universe.

At first his hair had been his mother's shade of flaxen, but it had darkened over time. Philippa made it her mission to help him as he learned to walk. Nathan would look up from his latest impending sermon, to watch her through the window of his study. Up and down, up and down the garden they would go, till the muscles cracked in her back and she was nearly hunched from stooping. Inside, she would wash Stephen's hair in the bath before the fire. He cried lustfully as the water had gone in his eyes. He caterwauled with feeling. His parents had discovered soon enough that there was power in his lungs.

Pip looked after their lives with a sedulous care. She acquired medical tracts from a Maidstone shop. She brought them to read upstairs in bed by candlelight, with her knees drawn up under the blankets. When she fell on the word "miasma", and uncovered what this concept conveyed to men of science, she insisted on opening windows, and hooking back the doors whenever possible. She knew full well that Nathan's living was small in this rural incumbency. To that end, she had saved him the expenditure of a cook. She had learned enough from Faithful, after all. She washed her hands before handling food, and scrubbed out copper pots with vinegar solutions. Flies and lice were pursued without check. Stephen would sit at her feet while she combed his head for nits. Whichever towel she would use for the job would then get thrown onto the fire in the kitchen. When her son was full of a cold, she would dutifully sit by his bedside and spoon nourishing preparations into his mouth – chicken broth, and herbal electuaries she had sweetened with honey to soothe his throat. Philippa loved to read to Stephen. She loved to tell him stories. She had an inventive mind, and made a natural story-spinner.

Of course, for all her industry, the Parsonage could not be managed by Philippa alone. A few enquiries about the village had procured them Polly Cater. Polly was their day-woman, their fifteen year old maid of all work. The Parson's wife had sized her up at once: Polly was but one of the adolescent thousands to whom books and penmanship were alien things.

At long last, Philippa had broached the subject whilst they were working in the kitchen.

"Polly? Forgive me if my question sounds a little harsh, but do you have the gift of any alphabet?"

"I know my letters, Mistress." Polly was staring at her shoes, and her shoulders were shrugged up around her ears.

"What would you think of it if I were to help you turn those letters into text?"

Polly looked up and stared at her. "I – I could not pay you no fee, Mistress," she stuttered.

"I would not ask for one."

Philippa saw the girls' eyes narrow. "I'm not wishing to sound an ingrate, Mistress, but... why are you claiming you would do this?"

Philippa was gentle with her. "My own mother gave me lessons. Me, and my sisters. I owe my Mother much, but I may never repay her for that." She left the room briefly, only to return with a slate and a piece of chalk. She set them down on the table.

"Can you write me your name, Polly?"

Polly eyed the writing materials with the look of a prisoner in the Tower, being confronted with the instruments of their impending torture.

"Will you at least let me try?" persuaded Philippa. "Mayhaps you'll surprise yourself."

And so it was. For an hour a day, before Polly went home after finishing the chores, they would sit with their heads together at the table, while Stephen played around their feet. On the tenth momentous day, the girl had been able to write "Polly Cater" in wobbling capitals, rather than marking a simple X. The writing lacked polish to be sure, but Polly had assured the Mistress Wohlford she would practise. Their spade had broken the ground. Before a month was up, Philippa resolved that Polly would have a grasp of grammar. They would start, appropriately enough, with Chapter One of Genesis.

"A messenger arrived. Just before you did."

Nathan hung his hat upon the peg by the kitchen door. "What did he bring?"

"This letter, for you." Philippa went to retrieve it. She had left it propped against a bowl of proving dough. As she handed it over, she grinned, "Don't tell me they are handing you a bishopric already?"

Nathan did not smile. He was too preoccupied by the handwriting on the front of the folded paper. He recognised it at once. The same hand had been on the occasional missive that would be delivered to him at Brazen Nose.

"This is from Theresa."

"Mm-hmm!" said Philippa profoundly.

Nathan drew back a chair and sat at the end of the table to read it. His stepmother's writing was neat and careful, but he could tell it had been set down in some haste.

> My dear Nathan
>
> I pray you will forgive any presumption in taking up my pen to write these lines to you. I know that all is yet not well between you and your father, and I hoped that a calm communication would be welcome to your spirits.
>
> In spite of your father's emotions, we miss your company and he talks of you often. You will have to believe me when I say that it is only your father's choice not to understand your feelings to match with the maiden you knew so well in your youth. For my part I am convinced you shall enter into matrimony with the same devotion as you entered your

studies for the Church. I essay what I can in your defence, but I fear that sometimes my entreaties are not received. You may judge me presumptuous, and you may have just cause. I would only ask that your eyes consider the thing from the perspective of one who only cares deeply for you both.

The truth unvarnished, Nathan, is that your father blames you for a situation that is not of your own making. When he pleaded my consent to be his wife, our nuptials were duly ceremonised before the Church of Rome. Had we proceeded thence to an Anglican ceremony so as to bind our hands together under English Law, all would still be well. Yet this has been a contentious point between us. As time as gone by, your father's thoughts have tended more and more to an adherence of the Roman faith.

I esteem he has all the zeal of a true convert. Your father professes that this decision would be a gift for my sake, though I would have you know plain that this has never been through any influence on my part. Nor is there an irreparable schism in my mind with the observance of English law. I trust you would not believe it was in my heart to be so devious.

Forgive me if I sound unsparing when I remind you that your father spoke of your marriage as a calumny. He vowed he would not witness a ceremony setting Law upon Faith. He must perforce watch your marriage as valid before the law of the land, whilst his own remains condemned by the Puritan rabble, and averred as extra-legal by the Courts. It is because he cannot follow his own inclination that he has treated you thus.

Should you wish to make reply to my letter, the servants are primed to retain any communication that arrives at the house addressed in your hand, so that I may first read it privately. In the meantime, I pray that you may draw some consolation from the knowledge that you shall always have my blessing, and my only wish is for a life of happiness with the lady you have chosen.

I trust you will commend me to your Philippa.

I remain, your affectionate friend and confidante,

Theresa

Philippa had been watching his face. Without waiting for his assent, she took the paper from his hands and read the thing through for herself.

"The old bull! His own son!" Her eyes were blazing. She threw Theresa's letter on the table. "Speak not to me of the sins of the father, Nathan! I can hold back no longer!"

Nathan licked his lips. "I must confess," he began, "that I shall look at Theresa with a totally new complexion." He said it with humility, as though he had just walked into a cathedral.

Philippa studied the crown of his head for a minute or two, before she stooped to twine her arms around his neck from behind. "Oh, Nathan. My Nathan." She felt his head slump as the letter caught up with him. "It will all be well," she shushed him, and commenced a rocking rhythm. "I am here."

Nathan twisted his head to stare through the window. "It grows dark!"

She looked for herself. "Aye. Almost time for Evensong."

"Where are the candle and flint?"

"Under the window."

When Evensong concluded, Philippa prepared some supper and they ate it in the candle-glow. Occasionally they could hear the sea coals falling in the kitchen grate. In bed that night, when Stephen had settled upon his truckle, they had cuddled down close. Nathan made a pillow for her with his arm, and Philippa wrapped one of her long legs across both of his. She used her knuckles to trace an 8 across his chest, back and forth and back and forth until she could feel that his body had relaxed into sleep.

1645

That bawl for freedom in their senseless mood,
And still revolt when truth would set them free.

SIXTEEN

And all the spangled host kept watch in squadrons bright.

It was six o'clock in the morning of the Summer Solstice. The Militia were on parade, performing the ritual of beating the drum and displaying the ensign. Their standard was blood-red, embroidered with the rearing white horse of Invicta, and with the promising motto OUR STRENGTH AND REFUGE in golden stitching.

In command of all this was Captain Thomas Treanor. He was a stocky landowner without any previous experience of soldiering, and an incurable habit of smoking his pipe on the parade ground. He cut a strange figure when he stood beside his Adjutant, the unwearying Captain Marchington, who reared over six feet tall. Marchington would shadow the Colonel during the morning inspections. He appreciated how Treanor liked to work the men hard of a morning.

Treanor paused before a weedy-looking Private in the leading file. "Sirrah!"

The Private snapped to the attention. "Me, sir?"

"Aye, you, sirrah. Where is your baldric?"

The man glanced helplessly at the bared left shoulder of his doublet. Overriding his doubts, he replied, "I know not, sir! It must've been took!"

The Colonel looked him closely in the face. The defaulter's eyes were circled with the dark grey rings of tiredness. "I am a straightforward man, Private, and I care for deceit in none of its forms. We shall try again. Where is your baldric?"

There was a shuffle of embarrassment. "I – I forgot the thing, sir. In my haste."

"Damme. You forgot it," repeated his inquisitor. "'Twas not so hard to say, now, was it?"

"No, sir," the Private capitulated.

Treanor widened the conversation to include every man who stood in earshot. "Who is this rogue's platoon Sarjeant?"

A dark-eyed man with a pointed beard took a brisk pace forward. "Me, sir!"

"Ah, Sarjeant…?"

"Magner," supplied Captain Marchington.

"Magner, is it not?"

"Aye, sir!" The tapering beard jutted high.

"You will note this man well, Sarjeant Magner. This man is improperly dressed, the Company being paraded for my inspection. You will be so good as to give me his name."

"Answers to the name of Private John Cripps, sir."

"You will see to it he is docked a day's wage."

"So shall I do, sir!" Magner brought the flat of his hand against the shaft of his half-pike in salute.

Colonel Treanor stared at Private Cripps. "You make no complaint, sirrah, against your punishment?"

Gulping, Private Cripps did not answer. Neither Treanor nor Marchington had detected the look of dreadful menace that shot from Sarjeant Magner's black-brown eyes, but Cripps had. Sarjeant Magner would have this Private Cripps, like a worm on a hook.

More than anything, being in the Army learnt a man tricks. Take saltpetre, for instance. No chance of making powder for the charges in a man's bandolier without saltpetre. When supplies were running low, the Army even learnt a man that it was possible to harvest saltpetre from the pews of local churches. Women who had pissed in their seats during Divine Service would leave workable traces of the stuff in their urine.

When Corporal Melhuish Clare had a few reflective moments to himself during the day, he had to laugh. The air had been rich with promise when they had first mustered. Him, Judah, Radcliffe, Chris. Soldiers of the King. Corporal Clare's Irish service had been sniffed out, and his rank reinstated. Magner had been made up to Sarjeant within a month. He kept himself clean. He said all the right things to the officers.

It was a great joke about the camps that the Trained Bands were trained, alright – trained to drink the day away! It had to be said: living out on the Weald like this, with the sun beaming down and the harvest coming on, Death seemed such an alien thing.

One year, long before the war, the Trained Bands had been commanded to raise a thousand Kentish men to sail north from

Gravesend to take the fight to the pugnacious Scots. Few had ever been heard from again. And for over a decade, county squires (already beset by the financial uncertainties of the farming year), had had to dig deep in their pockets to pay for His Majesty's Ship Money. What had become of their "investments" now was any man's guess.

Corporal Clare knew that all this arsy-varsy waiting would get a good soldier down. A man would seek diversions elsewhere, such as how he might best live off the bounty of a "free country". For above all, the Army taught a man to forage. When Private Copp appeared around the campfire with a pheasant for the pot in his snapsack, all Melhuish got out of him was an enigmatic, "Them as asks no questions, Corporal…"

Pheasant stew had gone down well in the Corporal's section. Sarjeant Magner remained unaware.

Night-time would find them round the cooking fires, grinding their misaligned teeth on barley bread that they used to mop the gravy of whatever they had eaten. When they'd finished their food, they would sing. Broadsheet ballads, mostly, which were easy to pick up in chorus. Sometimes sentimental songs, and patriotic verses that reached back to the deeds of Drake and Martin Frobisher. Flagons would be passed from mouth to mouth. Then would come the boasts: the soldierly boasts. The kind that would have left even Homer feeling uninspired.

A perpetual sore point was the summer of 1643. Parliament had long been eyeing up the Wealden iron fields and foundries. Then, in the July of that year, a lot of unrest had flared up around Sevenoaks and Tunbridge. It was the match to the tinder. Sir Henry Vane's cavalry had made a sortie in force out of London and confronted the Royalist foot at Yalding Bridge. The Kentish men had lost. They had been outfought and outnumbered by the Londoners, but History was all about interpretation.

"By the lap of the Virgin!" One of the Corporal's bullish messmates smouldered furiously at the thought of it. "If we had stood there, we'd have carried the day! We'd have driven the shitheads all the way back to London Town!"

"Oh, yeah?" said a Doubting Thomas on the other side of the fire.

"An Englishman's home is his keep, mates, and I says death to any man who trespasses upon it!"

Private Radcliffe glared at him. "Even if that man who treads on your preserves be a fellow Englishman?"

"'Specially so, if the thief sells his soul to the Parliament!"

Corporal Clare shook his head, gripping his dead pipe between his teeth. "Nay, but will you listen to your prattle? By the rood, you've had it easy in this war."

The others mocked him amiably. Drummer Coates looked up from whittling a piece of wood and grinned, "Would you listen to the old Spartan?"

"Nay, man, but you've had it easy..." his Corporal repeated.

The Company was drawn up in hollow square. Parson Brabazon, the Chaplain from Kemsing, had attached himself to them and their spiritual wants. Now he stood atop an old wooden crate and breathed heavily through the sermon. He had sweaty fingers, meaning they stuck to the prayer book. His Church Parade's text was from Psalms.

"Blessed be the Lord my strength which teacheth my hands to war, and my fingers to fight..."

"Man is like to vanity: his days are as a shadow that passeth away..."

"Bow thy heavens, O Lord, and come down: touch the mountains, and they shall smoke..."

"Cast forth lightning, and scatter them: shoot out thine arrows, and destroy them."

As Chaplains went, Parson Brabazon was as contemptuous of Laudism as the best of them. He had a fondness for preaching sermons that appealed to the hardy, and the masculine.

"Mark my words, lads. Around the world the soldier will sweat, like a brute and a beast in a uniform. Sure as Death, he will descend into what is unbecoming, and will be led into temptations that deliver him unto evil. And unless he follow the path of truth, the God of Adam and of David shall curse the wayward to a life of eternal tortures!"

He paused, to see for himself what effect this promise was having upon the assembled men.

"Yet be uplifted, lads. For it is written, "*O God, thou art a strong tower of defence to all that flee unto thee: O save us from the violence of the enemy. O Lord of Hosts, fight for us, that we may glorify thee. O suffer us not to sink under the weight of our sins, or the violence of the enemy.*" You would do well to pay heed to those words 'ere the life of the world to come. Now go, with peace amongst you, to love and serve the Lord. Amen."

Colonel Treanor plumped his hat back on his head. "Carry on, Captain Marchington."

His Adjutant saluted, and then turned to the assembled men. "Sarjeants? Dismiss the parade. We parade for care of arms in twenty minutes!"

SEVENTEEN

As if to show what creatures Heaven doth breed.

The woods were being bathed in splintered sunlight. Magner hummed a favourite air as he pushed through the tangled greenery.

"Down in a vale, diddle-diddle,
Where flowers do grow,
And the trees bud, diddle-diddle,
All in a row."

He had cause enough to sing. In his hand he clutched a fat half bottle of Francoy brandy. It had been quietly sequestered from Colonel Treanor's baggage.

"My hostess maid, diddle-diddle,
Her name was Nell.
She was a love, diddle-diddle,
That I loved well."

The going was slow. Brambled bushes snared on his sleeves and his breeches. Beds of nettles were after his ankles. And Sarjeant Magner was not quite steady on his feet. The brandy was a potent brew, and he was taking it on top of an empty stomach.

"I heard a bird, diddle-diddle,
Sing in my ear.
Maids will be scarce, diddle-diddle,
In the New Year!"

Magner paused. The neck of the bottle was nearly at his lips. The brandy filled his nostrils. But he stopped. Some deep, animal instinct that had never failed him yet was lifting the hairs on the back of his neck. The woods were no longer his private palace. Somebody, not so far away, was in here with him.

He ducked behind the nearest rowan, holding himself flat to its trunk. His eyes narrowed while he weighed up his options. If it were a Roundhead, then an ambush could spell a ball or a sword through his back before he could even turn. Mayhaps it was a gamekeeper? He had no idea whose land he was walking. There might be officious questions. His name would be round all the alehouses by dinner time, spoken of as a trespasser, and a common felon. If it were one of his own Company, then how was Sarjeant Magner to march the villain back to camp without having to account for his presence in the woods also? And if it *were* one of Treanor's men, and if Sarjeant Magner *were* to march he villain back to camp, and even *if* they shot the villain for a cowardly deserter, it might still get around that Sarjeant Magner had been found in the woods with a battle of officer's brandy. You couldn't keep a titbit like *that* from running round the camp.

The brandy must go. Magner stooped and wedged it tightly between a couple of the rowan tree's roots. He made certain it wouldn't capsize. Straightening up, he looked down at his waistbelt. The pistol, or the knife? It would have to be the blade. His hand closed on the hilt of the dagger and he pulled it from his belt. The steel winked roguishly at him as it passed through a shaft of bright light.

Whoever it was, they were somewhere on the other side of these bushes. And they were humming a country air.

Holding the dagger before him, he hopped out from behind the rowan. A figure was not more than ten feet away, but down on its hands and knees amid the roots of a beech, which explained why it had escaped his detection. The linen kirtle, rounded shape, and worsted blue skirts denoted its sex.

Magner stepped forward. "Make no move!"

The girl squeaked. The head lifted to reveal a coif and a crown of fair hair.

"Turn not around!" Magner challenged. "Your name, and quickly!"

Her reply stammered out: "Jane, sir! My name is Jane Bartram. My father is the forester." The girl put up her hands, palms flat and fingers spread, where he might see them.

Magner saw her head starting to turn in his direction. "Turn not around!" he barked. And then, "What be *your* business here, then?"

"M-merely gathering mushrooms, sir." She was trying to sound placatory. "For my father to have for his supper."

Magner's eyes flicked to the old wicker trug on the ground by her knees. Several oyster mushrooms were indeed nestling at the bottom.

The girl tried again. "Please, sir! I meant no offence, and I'll do you no harm."

He waited, saying nothing to see what would happen. But this "Jane Bartram" made no further requests. More importantly, she wanted no account of *his* presence. All the better! Magner had gone years without needing to explain his actions to anyone, so long as nobody was looking.

He stepped closer. "Remove your cap. Slowly."

The hands was trembling as the girl obeyed.

"Shake out your hair."

A fraction's pause, and then waves of honey-blonde spilled out across her shoulders. From his three-quarter back view, Magner was treated to the sight of a straight nose, and high cheekbones. The face might have been fuller, but it betrayed the look of one accustomed to going hungry.

Magner wanted what he saw. His voice became a growl.

"Strip."

He heard the girl gasp beneath the intensity of the word.

"I *said*, turn not around, you wanton drab! Strip here, and strip now!" He emphasised the "now".

The girl tried to rise. Magner snatched up a hazel branch that was lying beside his shoe. Three feet long, perhaps half an inch wide. His arm outstretched, measured the distance, and took a good aim at her rump.

Whoosh – CRACK! Jane cried aloud. Tears came at once.

"When I say strip, I mean you frigging strip!"

His wrist drew back for another, heavier strike, but then a thought stayed his hand. If he whipped her until she submitted, it was only a question of time before someone would hear. He trusted his mind

"Enough! Put your hands off! I'll do it myself."

He moved behind her and knelt down. The hazel switch was laid down in her eyeline, and he chucked the dagger down with it for good measure. He turned his attention to her clothes. Jane's kirtle was heavily patched. She was not a good seamstress, and somehow this lack of domesticity impressed him even less. He hiked up her shift with one, quick movement. The linen felt cool to his touch. He cupped one of her buttocks with his fingers, letting his fingers sink in, relishing how it felt.

Jane gave a vigorous squirm that half threw him off, but those strong hands had her again by the waist soon enough.

"Oho, so the pet is in heat!"

His hands moved upwards, running over the curves of her shoulders. He leaned around her upper body, so she might feel his lips coming close to her ear. She failed to shy away.

"My lads are a wild crew, Jane. It comes in their blood. You have to ask yourself, now, will it be them… or me?"

He shook her shoulders. Watched her head as it lolled and wobbled on her neck. Heard the sound in her throat like she was fighting for breath.

"I'll be gentle," he whispered. "Just relax, and take what I give you." Then he added, 'Less you want me to slit your throat from ear to ear."

The girl simply broke down in tears.

He shushed her, petting her, stroking her hair. "Suppose how I were to take you back to camp, and tell 'em you waylaid me on the road with the promise of your sweet meats. Luring a soldier away from his duties? Tut tut! You'll be hung as high as Haman, for a whore."

"I am no strumpet!" She was beginning to moan more than to speak.

"Nay, my sweet Jane, nay… I spoke to you too harshly." He luxuriated in the effect he was producing. "Nay, for this is virgin flesh, I'll warrant me. Not ever lain with a man, have you, eh? I am honoured, m'dear, I am honoured." His lips were at her ear again. "You wish to know me well, sweet Jane?"

The sobbing girl nodded.

Magner reached underneath her and squeezed the girl's breasts. His eyes widened with the thrill. "Christ's eyes! I'll enjoy making these beauties dance the tarantella!"

Satisfied that her resistance had ceased, Magner made ready. The girl's head dropped and she gasped at the insertion. Each contact resulted in a loud slapping noise as his body rammed into her rump. Her nails dug deep among the roots. A squeal escaped her lips. Jane had heard enough about rutting with a man to know of the risks that came with it.

"Do not make me an unwed mother!" she whimpered.

Magner let out a deep grunt. He looked at the clenching bottom cheeks beneath him. He risked one, momentary glance over his shoulder, but he could see nobody moving about amid the rowans and the hornbeams. Only the sound of Jane's little squeaks that were urging him on to climax, and the cacophony of sheep in the pasture on the other side of the words. His luck would hold again. So many girls had been dishonoured in this war, all across the nation. Men had learned to enjoy their screams.

EIGHTEEN

Sometimes let gorgeous Tragedy
In sceptred pall come sweeping by.

There was fog on that Wednesday morning. They stood in close ranks two hundred and fifty strong, their elbows almost touching, awaiting the sun to break through over the rolling valley. Like all others in Lord Astley's regiment of foot, Lieutenant Roger Waterman stank. It had been a hard march to this homely little slice of Northamptonshire. He had had no taste of meat since Sunday. His uniform was flecked with small traces of powder, and it carried the whiff of last night's woodsmoke. Even his linen shirt had been soaped clean in mutton-fat. That morning he had made do with the end of a twig from a hedgerow to clean his teeth. Only the night before, Astley's Foot had made bivouac in the tiny village of Sibbertroth. Roger had slept amid the sounds of restless horses and snoring men.

He had learned to have a high regard for Lord Astley. After all, the man had been a soldier all his adult life. But Roger's best regard was reserved for his burly Major. The man who rode up and down the leading file on his roan mare, chivvying the men with an encouraging word and calling that they look to their muskets.

It was his father. Squire Waterman had heard the call of the cannon. It would have been unthinkable to miss what was soon to take place in these fields.

Roger's eased the guard of his sword a little further from its scabbard. Father had told him it would make the job easier when the time came. A few paces to Roger's rear, Ensign Isaac Waterman leaned heavily on the haft of his spontoon. His back-and-brace had been buckled too tightly. The month was June; a farmer's sun. How warm would things get by the noonday zenith?

The roan mare was coming closer. Father looked twice as large against the morning, like a statue in a London street.

Major Waterman reined in. "Roger," he nodded. "Isaac? Come hither!"

Ensign Waterman broke rank and scurried forward, ducking round the file-closing Sarjeant of the line. "Yes, Father?"

Titus looked down at his sons. "You know what it is that we do there this morning? You know the import of this place?"

"Yes, Father." Roger nodded vigorously, in a manner he hoped would please.

"Aye, surely we do, Father!"

"'Tis well. One more blow, and we'll have the New Noddle beaten!"

"Aye, Father!" Isaac had very little immunity to this contagious, martial spirit. "We'll send 'em clean away to Northampton!"

Those infantrymen close enough to hear this suffered themselves to laugh.

Titus smiled. "Aye, sons. And come what may, your father shall bear you company, and ever keep this day in his remembrance." He let his eyes wander along the regiment. In spite of the efforts of its senior commanders, little could be called "uniform" about it. "Look to your sword, Lieutenant. And make sure of your brother. May God take care of you both, now!"

His sons looked after him as he spurred his mare off down the line.

Isaac caught Roger's eye. "I wish Francis were with us."

He got a sharp, reproachful glance in return. Then Roger added, in a voice that should not carry, "Go along, pup. Get back in rank."

Isaac flashed him a grin of fraternal glee, and turned to resume his place.

One man, standing right behind Roger, had produced a small Anglican missal, and was muttering softly about the Valley of Death. A drumhead service had been held for all ranks at daybreak. Men had rushed to settle affairs with their Maker. Until then, a lot of them hadn't felt particularly faithful, but at that moment, they poured every cell in their bodies into prayer. Roger had paced up and down and tried not to dwell on two things. The first, quite naturally, was Carrie. The second was the loss of their eldest brother. The story went that a musket had laid Francis' mount low, and that he had died under a dozen Roundhead blades on the field of Newbury. The light had left their Father's eyes when he had learned the news. Major Titus Waterman still discharged his duties as a King's man, but his boys knew that something else, something far more volcanic, had charge of their father this morning.

He had been so absorbed in his thoughts that it came as a surprise to discover that battle had actually started. Prince Rupert had commenced a heady charge through the thump of cannon. Two lines of horsemen were surging down the hill like breakers on a shore. The clash of steel carried far up the slopes of the valley. At the very brow of the hill, where his brightly-coloured standard fluttered high for all to see, Prince Rupert's uncle the King kept his spyglass firmly aimed at the mêlée below.

Roger dipped his hand into the pocket of his trousers. His fingers closed about the half a dozen conkers that had come from one of the chestnuts at Briarwell. Always a lucky mascot.

The order was brought from the hilltop. "My Lord Astley? Commit your Foot!"

The old lion nodded, and turned to demand: "Colours to the rear!"

Those squares of garish cloth were escorted into the rear rank. The men prepared to descend to the killing grounds.

Astley took off his expensively feathered hat and recited aloud the prayer he had coined at Edgehill.

"O Lord, thou knowest how busy I must be this day. If I forget thee, do not forget me!"

Then he waved that hat in the direction of the enemy.

"March on, Boys!"

The advance began, to the beat of drums as big as barrels. Two hundred and fifty pairs of shoulders braced up, and two hundred and fifty pairs of feet stepped off into the valley. Major Waterman kept his mount going with shortened reins. The whole expanse of Naseby was spread before them as they crested the escarpment. The valley was a patchwork of gorse and bogs. This grassland was named on the maps as Broad Moor. It rose like an enormous ribcage out of the earth.

Roger looked back. The men were keeping step. Many of them had been recruited from the other side of the Welsh borders. Stocky men, hidden under anonymous names. Roger had heard them in the bivouacs, heard their lilting language, and their jabbering wives. Each of them wore a bean stalk in his hat or his cap. That way they at least stood a chance of recognising Friend in the fog of battle.

Astley stabbed the air with his sword. "CHARGE!"

Roger reached into his open-topped holster for his doglock. They raced into the scalding fire of the New Model cannon, and those gunners had accurate range. The horizon ignited and burned. Whole files of men were starting to fall, like discarded peddler's packs, blooding the grass.

"Charge! Charge! Meet the buggers head-on!"

Astley's Foot fired one volley at fifty yards, and then the musketeers swung their weapons round and used them like cavemen's clubs. Their faces blurred with hatred in the winnowing fire.

More volleys now. The musket balls were thick like winter snow. The New Models had held their fire wisely. The King's stately Life Guards rode upon the spur. Blocks of pikemen advanced like warring hedgehogs to receive them.

Roger kept moving. Suddenly a Private behind him went down, his head opening up a vivid bright red. The Private was trying to speak but there was too much blood frothing from his head and neck. He was beyond all human help.

The chaos engulfed them. Roger's eyes began to stream from the clouds of smoke. He could see little beside thick, wriggling curtains of cannonfire. Titus' lovely roan wheeled and plunged, her eyes rolling in terror. Then one of those cavemen's clubs smashed right into her jaw, and she went down with a kick and a crack of her legs. Major Waterman could not even rise before a New Model musketeer had put the muzzle of his firelock to the back of his neck. His Instructor had said it was a sure place to put a shot if the dastardly coward was done, and it would help if you thought of your target as no more than a rabid dog. The shot split Titus' skull with a sound like chopping wood, and blew out the curve of his forehead.

Isaac tried to make some sense of the cacophony. The powder stung his eyes. The shots were dancing in his ears. Then he suddenly felt a pain, right where his collarbone knitted his neck to his shoulders. A Parliament short sword had clawed him. It was the unfairness of it that hurt most, rather than the agony or the dribbles of red. When the blade swung down again, Isaac was ready for it. His gauntlet checked but did not stop the blow. His spontoon could no longer hold his weight. He fell to his knees. One last slice, and it was over.

"Isaac!"

Not more than fifteen yards away, Roger had watched transfixed as his brother was butchered. Another, concerted volley came quite close. A ball hit the front of his corselet at point-blank range, just above the knotted sash that denoted him as an officer, and a plumb target. The lead had flattened out and dented the steel, but it had not pierced the metalwork. His thigh was not so lucky. The slug had flattened out against the unresisting tissue, tumbling through nerve and sinew until at last it struck the bone.

Roger struggled onward. He had no idea what was in his mind, save that Isaac must not die alone. Rage had a grip of his heart. His body surrendered long before his will to keep moving. He had to bury his face in the grass to prevent crying out. The earth smelt fresh and thick with manure. It tasted of blood.

He had failed.

The fight roared on around him, heedless of one more casualty. One of those shoes kicked him on the side of his head, knocking him over and backwards. Roger blinked up into the face of a man dressed in the New Model's red. His stature was good. Hard training had put muscles on his bones. He wore a patch over one eye. Then the eye was replaced by the broad, black mouth of a wheelock pistol. There was an indifferent look about him as he stood and stared down at his helpless quarry.

Roger hadn't even the breath to plead for quarter. The redcoat sniffed and fired his pistol neatly into the space above Roger's nose. The man was a professional; this was his job of work.

Death descended on Roger's eyes. The tutor their father had hired had taught him how the souls of brave Greek warriors would race away to the Shadowlands once they had fallen in battle. Roger was having none of that. He was going home, to Briarwell, to hear the Medway chuckling through the meadows.

The King's Horse routed in panic, taking their sovereign with them. His infantry, those pocked and bearded men, began a last fighting retreat to the hilltop. They fell in heaps and clusters, many with a curse on their lips.

After the battle was over, their bodies of the dead were stripped and then abandoned wherever they had fallen. Let the elements have them. Deliver them up to those birds and beasts with a taste for human carrion. Details were told off to roam the field and gather up the clothing and footwear, and to cart it away. Whether this was a show of military ignominy, or of sheer practicality, nobody was certain, and nobody thought to ask.

NINETEEN

For Lycidas is dead, dear ere his prime,
Young Lycidas, and hath not left his peer.

The plasterwork of Number Twenty-Seven, Week Street had gradually muddied to a dirty shade of buff. Its windows were crooked and tiny. The beams in its ceilings were low and its chambers were small. The dwelling comprised two storeys, with a garret in the gable where the twins had their quarters. A clump of purple heart's ease grew outside around the door, seeded by the birds, and manured by passing horses.

The sound of the front door knocker broached the quiet of the house. Rebecca came out of the kitchen where she had been washing the luncheon dishes, wiping her hands on the cloth. "Carrie?" she called down the passageway.

Carrie stuck her head out of the parlour. "I am here!"

"No sign of the twins?"

"None, Mother. I've been watching through the windows."

Rebecca shut her eyes at the thought of her wayward daughters. "This really is too bad of them. They *knew* she was calling at two of the clock."

"Master Harrison drives a hard bargain, Mother."

Her mother pushed the Maidstone draper out of her mind by asking: "Has Loobie finished the sweeping?"

The littlest Agnew appeared around her sister, brandishing a broom that was moulting its twigs. "All finished, Mother!"

The knocking came again.

"Stay close in the parlour, and *wait*," Rebecca commanded.

"Yes, Mother." The girls ducked out of sight. Rebecca turned, threw the cloth onto the table, and went to the door. A sigh helped her collect her thoughts before she lifted the latch and pulled the door open. Verity Waterman stood on the threshold, gaunt-eyed and pallid, dressed from top to toe in black.

Rebecca bit her lip as she looked at her. "Oh... oh, my dear."

Verity turned to the coachman who sat perched on the carriage box. "Godfrey? Drive round to the mews by the brewhouse. You may return for me at three."

"Aye, Ma'am!" the coachman saluted. A flick of the reins, and he was steering the carriage and pair away up the street.

Rebecca let her old friend into the hall, and into her embrace. "I am glad you could come."

"I am glad you would see me," Verity said limply.

"Go through, go through." Rebecca shut the door and motioned her gently into the parlour. "There is the last of some sack I've been saving."

Verity Waterman's black silk rustled in the small, austerely-furnished room. Half of the parlour was occupied by the refectory table that had once stood in Faithful's old kitchen at Barming Place, and by such mismatched chairs as they'd been able to procure. The proper dining set, the mahogany one that had been in Captain Agnew's family since the Tudors, was the first piece that had gone to the auction. There remained a glass cage (nearly empty), some hangings on the wall, and a low settle before the hearth. Whatever space was left was taken up by Eleanor's spinning wheel and Rosalind's loom. Once upon a time, words like "distaff" and "bobbin" were Greek to Elle; and Ros could no more treadle a loom than stroll across the pock holes of the moon. The twins had had to come a long way, very quickly.

Carrie and Loobie rose as one from the settle to greet the visitor. At Mother's behest, both the girls had put on high-waisted, worsted gowns of holly green. This visit demanded something simple and sober, and their wardrobe was limited.

Verity gave them a tired, white smile. "Carrie; Lucy. You are quite well?"

Carrie never intended to hiccup a sheepish laugh. "I – I am, thank you."

Verity sank in a kind of curtsey so that she might kiss her little goddaughter Lucy at the girl's own level. Then she straightened, and Carrie stepped forward to brush the older woman's cheekbone with her lips. Verity smelt faintly of marigold. Beneath the silk and modest trims of lace, being scoured by grief had made the Squire's handsome widow look older than her age.

Rebecca joined them. "Sit down, dearest. I shall get us some drink." She opened the glass case and filled two small crystal sherry glasses with Malago sack from the long-necked decanter.

She filled two only. Rebecca didn't trust the effects of fortified wine on her daughters.

Verity pulled off her gloves. She sank upon one of the chairs, and Rebecca handed her her glass before she sat beside her. Verity savoured the drink, gently agitating the glass to release the ethers. "You are very kind, Rebecca."

"Take a seat, children."

Carrie and Loobie sat shoulder-to-shoulder on the settle. Loobie's young eyes seemed to be everywhere at once. For her part, Carrie folded her hands in her lap to keep herself from picking at her nails, and lapsed into a protracted silence.

Verity's voice was determined when she spoke. The wine was beginning to work. "Titus, and the boys, they did their share. We must do ours without plaint."

"You have borne yourself so bravely," said Rebecca, taking her hand.

Verity shrugged uncomfortably. "I keep thinking, did I do such wrong? I mean, had I not fixed my affections so much upon Isaac in particular..."

Her eyes looked very puffy, but this time at least there would be no more tears.

Rebecca's pressure on the other woman's hand increased. She spoke quickly, before Verity could say anything else. "Death is kinder than life. God knows there can be no more suffering, beyond the grave. And... mayhaps they are together again now, in peace."

Verity's smile was weak. "I pray they are."

Carrie watched them, feeling like a lump of wood. She was quivering with quiet anger and she couldn't smother it. She squeezed her hands together and said, "It must be hard, to determine what God wishes for his children these days."

Rebecca shot her daughter a look of reproof behind Verity's head. Even so, she *did* wish that the ordained mind were there to offer solace. She put her thoughts into tentative words. "Aye. Nathan would know what to say about that. Wouldn't he, Caroline?" she added, tartly.

Carrie avoided Verity Waterman's distressed eyes, and spoke exclusively to her mother. "No doubt that he would, Mother."

Loobie piped up at this mention of relatives. "When are Pip and Nathan coming to see us again, Mother?"

"For Sunday luncheon, sweet. As well you know." Rebecca put her glass down on the table and slipped a consoling arm around Verity's shoulders. "Dearest? Dearest, you seem tired. Are you sleeping?"

"Barely." Verity shook her head as she sipped from the glass. "The house, you see. It's too big. Too full of memory. I half expect to meet them on the staircase, or hear them all out in the rose garden. To see them, riding up the drive again." Her eyes had fixed on the sunbeams streaming through the pokey casement windows. "I can hear their voices, hear them laugh. I feel Titus' warmth in the bed with me." At long last, she turned her face to Rebecca's. A dull harshness had come into her voice. "Tell me no mother should bury her sons."

Rebecca planted a kiss on her cheek. "My dearest... 'Tis this pestilential war."

"My boys. So young. My boys. My darling boys!" A single tear was starting down her cheek. "Promise me you must cherish your girls, Rebecca. Cherish them always!"

"I shall," pledged her friend. "And I do. Don't I, Carrie?"

"Of – of *course* you do, Mother."

Rebecca detected the hesitancy in her daughter's voice. "Carrie, what is the matter?"

"If you'll excuse me, Mother."

Whether Rebecca excused her or not, Carrie got up and made a blind effort towards the door. Rebecca sat still in her seat and stared at her daughter's rudeness in flushed anger. She gritted her teeth as she heard Carrie's footsteps going upstairs. She would surely have words with her anon.

Carrie barely made it to her room before the spasms of nausea gripped her. Leaning against the door frame, she bent from the waist and vomited up her lunch. The floorboards splattered with little lumps of what had once been masticated cheese, and her half of that sausage she had shared with Loobie. She stood up, coughing and spitting, like one of those hawkers she had so often seen in the streets. She tasted acid on her teeth, and strings of slime were trailing from her mouth. She knew Mother would be angrier with her for wasting food when it was hard to get.

She dabbed her mouth dry with her sleeve. Suddenly all she wanted was to open her lungs and scream out onto the street, *"Why Roger? Why my love?"*

What callous working of the universe had sent him off to be used as human ammunition? And why had he not written to her? Chivalry was one thing, but soldiers always wrote one final letter before they went to battle, didn't they? One last chance, to say the things that truly mattered? Squire Waterman's widow would have an open invitation to go on about "her boys" for the rest of her days. What did Carrie have? Why couldn't *she* talk about hearing Roger laughing, or the touch of his hand, or his lips? Why had she been so stupid to keep him concealed?

Carrie sat upon the bed. The tears were dripping down her chin, landing down the front of her dress and on the counterpane. She shied away from her reflection in the glass. Often she had thought crying would be a relief, but it was no use. She had wept nightly for Roger. She had pictured him swallowed up by some metallic, liquid fire like a fly caught in the flame of a candle. Grief was nothing but an absurd private game of torture. She would walk into a room, any room, and half expect him to be there – and he was not. She would catch herself smiling at some small thing, and anticipate how she might tell it to her keen-humoured Roger – and she could not. The world looked vast, and lonely, and intimidating when she felt like that. She started to wonder how could she hope to wake on the morrow, and be grateful to be alive. Just one more fiancée, twisted in half by this war.

She stretched out until her feet were off the floor. All that noise from the busy streets seemed to be battering at her window.

Her bedroom door opened quietly. Looking up, she discovered Rosalind and Eleanor standing there, not the figure of a wrathful mother. Carrie's heart stood still. It could have been a trick of the light, but the twins were looking supremely self-righteous. The last thing Carrie needed was to sit there under Ros and Elle's scratch-cat sneers, thank you very much.

Rosalind looked down at that unsightly puddle on the floor. "You have been sick!"

"Don't – don't tell Mother," Carrie mumbled.

Elle approached the bed. Her arms were behind her back and she appeared to be skipping. "We just got in from the draper's.

141

Mother told us to fetch you, and send you straight downstairs again."

"Ma's very unhappy with you, Carrie, very!" added Ros, significantly. "She warned us to tell you off, for your show of discourtesy!"

Carrie caught the flickered glance of cunning between the twins. The sad droop to her eyes vanished at once. Now she was alert, and wary.

Eleanor played her hand: "This is all over Roger, isn't it?"

Carrie sat straight up. "How did you know?" So much for the indignant denial that her mind had endlessly rehearsed.

Rosalind crossed her arms in that signature gesture, appraising Carrie's show of defeat. "There is *much* that we know that you don't!"

The grin had remained on Elle's face, as if it had been painted there. "Fair's fair in all, Ros. We weren't actually sure of our facts... till this moment."

It had been a trap, and Carrie had walked naively into it. She huddled in a slight shiver, but she shook it off and replied with all the dignity she could summon. "Roger – was mine! If you two only thought about another for once in your life, you might understand me!"

Ros said nothing, prompting Elle to lower her face to within inches of Carrie's. "Mistress Caroline Waterman!" she said, in an intentionally singsong voice. "Surely you knew we could guess your clues?"

"Just when are you going to tell Ma?" asked Ros, with an unwise, superior smile.

The twins watched Carrie's expression turn from anger to sheer terror. "I – I shall tell her in my own time!"

Ros gave a passable shrug of indifference. "Oh, well. I could always go down now and tell her for you?"

"Aye, and your mother-in-law too, should it suit you!"

"You won't! You shan't!" Carrie's face was violently flushed. She had got off the bed and was staring at the twins with the whites of her eyeballs showing. She was already stretched to breaking point by the interview downstairs. Now her eyes blazed hatred. "Mother never knew, and neither did Pip, if you're so desperate to learn my secrets. You must neither of you tell!"

Ros turned. She put a hand to her mouth and, in a voice that echoed Elle's little singsong she called, "Oh, Mother! Might you come here a minute?"

Carrie shoved Elle aside and lunged at Rosalind with both fists. "God's pox, get away from me, Ros, before I kill you!"

With these words, she chased the shrieking twins out onto the landing, and slammed the door shut in their faces. She clenched her fists harder and harder till they turned the colour of marble. It occurred to her that, in spite of her rage, in spite of the round little rug she had made with her vomit, and in spite of the fact that Mother might come marching up the stairs to trace the hubbub at any moment, she had won something of a victory.

TWENTY

The end then of learning is to repair the minds of our parents.

Philippa put Stephen to bed. The boy had gone limp with fatigue and the late-July heat, and one of his arms trailed around her hip as she carried him up the stairs. She and Nathan typically ate their supper in the kitchen when they were alone. They saved the dining room for "hospitality". Tonight they were able to sit down to a gifted pigeon breast, which Philippa had stewed with plums from the garden. The air became thick and charged, but there was no sign of rain or wind. Nathan hooked the kitchen door back so that they might get the slightest bit of air.

They ate apple fritters for pudding before they took their tumblers of ale over to the chessboard. Chess was not a feature every evening, but after Stephen's bedtime they often sat up into the night, talking. Talking gave Pip the chance to show her quality.

She sat on the other side of the board, her chin resting on her hand. After an agonising interval, Nathan finally moved his rook. Philippa lifted her eyes from the pieces.

"Well, if you do that… it will be a smothered mate in no time."

"Oh! So it would." Nathan peered at the board, mentally turning its black and white squares into the moves of her victory. He sighed, then he put out a finger and tipped his King.

"You were not concentrating."

"Sorry," he shrugged. "I am – poor sport this evening."

She took her chin out of her hand. She knew Nathan's moods, and the sounds of his silence. "Something works at you. You look like you've a sore tooth at a banquet!"

He looked at her for a moment or two, his expression very sober. Then he rose from the game and went to remove a folded sheet of paper from the drawer in the walnut side table. "You are right. It was this."

When he had put it into her hand, it turned out to be a letter. She remembered the writing. "This is Theresa's hand!"

"Aye, but the words are not."

Philippa hesitated. "You wish me to read it?"

His hand waved her on. He sat back down to watch her as she read her mother-in-law's meticulous script.

> Son Nathan,
>
> Remember unto you hoping that you have good health. I know not by what road you might return to Bicester, since you cannot be easily absent from our occasions. But I entreat you, come to Sheep Street if you can. I wish that we may meet again in person as well as in affection.
>
> I speak openly, Nathan, father to son and man unto man. Theresa must write what I say, for I no longer have the strength. I am now struck in with the purple spots, and am preparing my soul for the end. You should be appraised that I am fully intending to die in the joy and comfort of the Romanish faith. A priest has been obtained to undertake the rites of reception. He will call in the afternoon of this day I write, Weds 12th. It remains my fondest wish that my choices should drive no further cleft between us, at the last. Let this not cause a diffidence of my true love for you, nor for your excellent wife. Forgive an old man stuck in olden days.

Her eyes flicked up from the paper. She straightened in her chair. "But – you never informed me of this!"

Nathan gestured helplessly.

An alarm was ringing in the back of her mind, but Philippa went on reading.

> Our Bicester is a most dismal sight. We are made a miserable spectacle, insomuch as when the Parliament's forces came into the town on the last Lord's day, many took to the streets to beg of the soldiers a crust of bread.

I do desire to hear from you and from your Philippa of when you think you shall travel. My whole hope lies in my brave son's firmness and constancy, and when I hear to the contrary I shall run mad. We thought you would never leave us this long without a few lines of news. I entreat you for a word that the two of you are safe, and in good health, and for a sight ere death of the son you have raised.

Your loving father
Matthew Wohlford
ever praying for you till for death I depart.

Philippa shook her head when she'd finished. "'Tis a most affecting letter."

"Is it not?"

"Still, Stephen's smile will surely win over his surly old grandfather yet!" She took up the letter again and reread a certain passage, about the townspeople begging from the Army. "Who can now look at this island without a mournful heart? Certainly not a woman. It would wrench at her bowels."

Nathan said: "There must be many who care not what form of government they live under, so long as they can still take their wares to the markets."

"My thanks to you, Diogenes!" she joked. After a moment's pause, she reopened the letter and read its painful valediction once again. "So close to the end. Poor man." She lifted her tumbler in a kind of toast before she drained off the last of its ale. "You don't begrudge his wanting to die with Rome, do you?" She was rolling the tumbler between the fingers of her hands.

"I – I do not believe that it is up to me to have an opinion."

Her eyebrow cocked. "And you a parson, too!"

"The choice lies with him. It has always been with him."

Philippa set down the tumbler. "I know that I spoke harshly of your father in the past, because of his treatment of you," she said. "I'll own, I'm regretting it now."

Nathan paused to scratch his nose. "I presume many must mellow in death," he said.

"Many, but not all." Then she asked, "I suppose it was hard for you to give him any surety of going to see him in your reply?"

Nathan said nothing.

"You have not had another letter, bringing word that he's died?"

"Not... that I saw." His voice was subdued.

A frown cut lines into Philippa's brow. "Wait a minute..." Her eyes raked Theresa's writing for one small, important detail. She looked at him, half-uncertainly, half-confused. "Your father was writing this on the fifth... And today's the seventeenth!"

She divined her answer in the shape of his mouth.

"You never wrote back to him. Did you?" Her voice was edged with sharpness.

Nathan bit his lip and swallowed hard. "No."

Philippa sat frozen and expressionless, watching him. He exuded apathy and despair. Then, incensed, she threw the letter onto the table with a smacking noise. "Holy Mary! What has got hold of you, Nathan? Why must you insist on being passive when it comes to the things that matter? Your father was offering you a Christian olive branch, and you *ignored* the thing? What, would you shut up your senses to the whole world if it suited you?"

He stared downward, staring as if at some distant vision.

"Answer me!"

He groaned. "I – I could not find the words."

She gave him a hard stare. "You are unreal. You are simply unreal! The learned theologian says he could not find the words! Did you never think to ask me to help you?"

He would not meet her eye. A memory was bubbling up from the yawning blackness. "Do you recollect that night we had dinner at Briarwell?"

"Do *not* go changing the subject!" she snapped.

"I am not."

She hesitated, then conceded. "Dinner? Which dinner?"

"Three years ago? Just before we lost your father?"

"When the venerable Jump did play the veritable fool?" The acid quip had been too good to resist. "I remember."

He took a steadying swallow of ale. "Well, after Titus had ordered us to be removed, Arlo had a few words with me while we were waiting for our horses."

147

"Huh! I'll warrant that he did!" Thinking of that old Puritan's fanaticism never ceased to rouse her temper.

"Aye, but you don't understand, Pip. Arlo told me, there and then, to take a stand; that I must needs choose a side. He said, 'Tis your God, or your King. For you cannot have both.'"

Philippa blurted, "Dear Lord!" Even in death, the Reverend Jump still bequeathed them his grisly inheritance.

Nathan's mind seized on a tendril of thought. "Supposing I were now an Army Chaplain, serving in the field. I should only be out there now, burying other men's boys. I hope I never have to live through anything like that." He was piling up his thoughts like a rampart. "I do take God to witness, Pip, that all I ever wanted was to settle down here, where I belonged; serve God. I wished nothing more than to take you as my wife, and as the mother of my child. I have achieved all that. I want nothing more."

"I see, I see." Her voice sounded flat and hard rather than moved. "So, we shall just sit here and spend our days wallowing in religious tranquil, shall we?"

The wall remained unbreached. "Both sides in this war believed they were performing the Lord's Work. I always thought that for me to choose sides would feel like deciding God's mind on the matter."

The blood rose in her face. "It is the minds of *men* who threaten us, Nathan! We are not talking of Jove and his thunderbolts! We are talking of man's base injury to man and womankind alike, which I would remind you has been going on every waking moment of our lives for the last three years!"

Nathan rebutted: "Both sides took up the sword convinced of their faith."

"Their faith? What stuff!" Philippa's eyes were blazing. "My oh my, you really are deaf to all the talk about the village!"

"What are you talking about?"

"Why, that only last week, the Militia demanded a whole cartload of bedding from the people of Wrotham, and razed four houses to the ground when Wrotham would not comply."

He looked at her in twisted confusion.

"Now speak to me of the faithfulness of men!" she challenged.

Nathan blinked. "What Militia?"

"*Our* Militia!" There was no anger in her face anymore, but something touching on satisfaction. "Those men who are out there now, fighting for the faith, so that one day I may say to Stephen, 'You see those men yonder? They fought in the war. We owe our lives to such as them!'"

At first, her true meaning escaped him. "Nay, but that could never be Judah, or Melhuish!"

"And I do not want to think it, either, Nathan, but – " She spread her hands.

"I refuse to believe it," he announced.

"Very well, then. Let us refuse to believe it. Now, answer me this." Her shoulders were hunched, a sure sign that her blood was up and she was not to be stopped. "What good does it do you, to sit there and say you know the mind of God?"

Nathan's eyes flew wide. "I profess no such thing!"

"Then why do you continue to climb into your pulpit every Sunday?" she asked, with a peevish coldness. "And if this be the set of your mind, explain why you did not read out Parliament's ordinance that all parishes were to offer their Army assistance?"

"Blessed are the peacemakers, Philippa," Nathan declared pontifically.

"Don't Philippa me, for God's sake!"

"It is not for God's sake!" Now it was his turn to be defiant. "It is for my conscience's sake! Your words are not... seemly." His voice had gone hoarse with emotion.

Philippa sat back in her chair. She glared at him. Without smiling, and without taking her eyes away from Nathan's, she started to speak. "*And when Pilate saw he could prevail nothing, but that rather a tumult was made, he took water and washed his hands before the multitude, saying, 'I am innocent of the blood of this just person, see ye to it...'* Do you comprehend what I am saying?"

He nodded.

She leaned forward into the light of the candles. "Just you look to the ways of Men before you sit there and tell me what is seemly. Or have you so forgotten your vocation that you need to take instruction in it from me?"

Nathan opened his mouth, but no words came. He looked huddled, and shrunken. He sagged in defeat. The strain of the past days, and all that he had been putting far from his mind, rushed in and swamped him. It seemed an eternity before he found he could speak.

"You are right. You are right." There was no longer any inflection of conceit in his tone. "My father shall go to his grave without seeing his grandson, and this country shall go on bleeding itself to death."

Another silence, deeper even than the one that went before. Philippa got up. Without speaking, she moved around the little table and sat herself down on the floor beside him.

"Nathan? Nathan, my sweet." Her hand was on his knee. "I do not say these things because I want to scold you horribly."

She had got his attention.

"What frustrates me is you have not got the blood to confront these problems yourself."

Nathan sat motionless. The final vindication of three years lay before his eyes. Or did it? His brain was a battlefield. He was surrounded by noise.

Philippa twisted around to look up into his face. "What was it you said about choice? The choice was always with you. You chose to ignore it too long."

"I shall never declare for either side," he said, his voice suddenly hard and determined. "My conscience won't permit it."

Her eyes were turning soft. "Nathan, listen to me." She got a grip on his wrist, and pressed it to her cheek. "I promise I shall love you till the world has stopped its spinning."

Nathan felt his jaw tighten.

"I married you because I loved you as a man of God, and as a man who said he knew his own convictions. The strength is in you. Think well upon it."

He started stroking her hair through her coif. "I am so tired, Pip."

"I know. I know." She was shivering despite the room being so close with midsummer heat "Let us to bed."

Philippa's arm reached over and touched nothing but the mattress. She patted about, and opened her eyes when she realised that her bedfellow had gone. Nathan slept well as a rule, even on these short summer nights. She rolled the other way and squinted down at Stephen who was snoozing on his truckle bed. She slid off the end of the bed and crossed the room. She struck flint to the nightlight and slipped downstairs. Her mind was boiling with all sorts of wicked thoughts. Not least that she had been too harsh with him, and that her words had driven the Mutton-head away. She could hardly leave Stephen alone in the house, and there was no way to search the surrounding fields, carrying him on her hip.

She was relieved when she saw a glimmer of light coming around the door to the study. Philippa peered in. She saw Nathan, forehead sunk forward on his hand, sitting at his desk. He was flanked by two candles and was busily writing away with the quill. The candles were reflected on the windows, shutting the dark without, and enclosing Nathan within.

Philippa walked into the room. "Nathan? I awoke, and you were gone!"

Nathan kept writing. "My mind would not close off."

She glanced at the filigree lantern clock before the overmantel. It was two in the morning. "From what? Whatever are you doing?"

"I am writing a letter. To Father. Or at least to Theresa."

"Oh, Nathan…" She sank upon the study's tiny day bed with a groan.

He was refusing to look at her. "I might be too late, yet I pray that I won't."

His quill came to a halt. Nathan appeared to read over the last couple of sentences, then he seized the sheet of paper and threw it to the floor. By the light, Philippa could see the area around the desk was thick with crumpled papers. Nathan took up another, blank sheet and the work continued.

Philippa got to her feet. She had heard Stephen's plaintive calls for her coming down the staircase. "I am going to Stephen," she said.

"Aye. I shan't be much longer."

Philippa headed for the door, but when she had reached it she turned her candle upon him one more time. "Just remember this, Nathan."

Her injunction made him pause mid-sentence.

"I did not bring your son into the world only for him to witness this effusion of Christian blood. Just try to keep *that* in your conscience as well."

1648

For what can war but endless war still breed?

TWENTY-ONE

A voice of weeping heard, and loud lament.

The Gryphon had scarcely altered down the years. Same, ale-stained tables and benches for its patrons. Same unflinching scowl on the face of the corpulent landlord Sloane. Same waxy, dried-out hops around the beams. Same old glance of anticipation towards the door whenever the ring pull handle turned.

Ex-Drummer Christopher Coates had found it difficult to adjust once the Militia had done with his services. He found he missed it at strange moments, too, like when he was drinking in The Gryphon with his friends, or butchering a heifer. His old cleaver made a poor companion after the men of his old platoon. He missed the eked-out luxuries: the sound of penny whistles round the fire, the breaking and the doling of a joke. By day, there had been the endless buffing of iron, wood, and leather. When night fell, faces were lost in thought beneath caps and hats and morions. Cloaked men huddled in tight against the night, lit by a wagon wheel of flames that climbed into the cold. Each man separate, closed off, yet ready to meld back into the group. With the return of the morning came the slow-march of thirty men, all to the beat of Drummer Coates, and all to the pig-eyed glare of Sarjeant Magner.

The more he thought on it, though, the butcher's trade did seem strangely akin to the soldierly life. Carcasses trussed-up, herded about like livestock; all so much dead weight in the end.

"Chris?"

Coates returned to the present, and the pub, and the faces around the table. "You'll pardon," he muttered. "I was..."

The sexton took pity. "Swords into ploughshares. Have another? My party, I think."

"Thanks, Judah."

The sometime-Private Copp gathered the tankards behind the wall of his fingers and returned them to the bar. Melhuish used his sleeve to dab foam from his upper lip. "Y'know what I figure?" he said.

"What?" said Coates.

155

"I figure them Roundheads have took'n a pasting. They're fearful up in London. They wouldn't keep the Army in the field if they thought they wouldn't need it."

"And what is it put *that* in your brain-pan?" demanded their former Sarjeant, who was busying with his clay pipe.

"Why, the County's petition, that's what! You sign near twenty thousand names on a piece of paper, it'll have its effect. Stands to reason!"

"Yes. Well. Reason never deterred a Puritan, Master Clare." Magner sipped carefully at his beaker. The price of a gill of good cider was an outrage these days.

"Aye. A wounded animal's most dangerous when he's cornered," the butcher could affirm.

"I'll warrant the Parliament won't wait long for a reply," said Melhuish.

"When they're not burning copies of the thing right across London, you mean?"

Melhuish's pate turned red. "If they do, Kill-Sin, mebbe Kent will rise up, and burn *them!*"

Judah returned with two refills from the landlord's keg, and they were thankful. They swivelled to look to the door as it was shoved open. The lingering afternoon outlined the breathless, raw-boned shape of Lion Radcliffe. Private Radcliffe was a parade's despair. Growing out the hair on his upper lip had invested him with little seniority. The drill manuals had only made him gangle clumsily. To shoulder a firelock had made him wilt, not straighten up.

"Hullo!" Judah's eyes lighted on the parchment roll that the scrivener was clutching.

Radcliffe loped over to their corner. "Gentles! Thank heaven I found you!" he gushed.

"Gentles, is it? The doings must be bad." Magner's voice was dry.

"By the rood, they are!" The scrivener's lungs were spent as he collapsed upon the form.

"Catch your breath, Lion," said the man who'd been his Corporal. "Go get him a gill, Chris."

Coates rose and made for the publican, leaving Radcliffe to recover his wind. The scrivener took low, calming breaths before he started to untie the ribbon from the scroll. The parchment was covered in fresh, calligraphed ink.

"From the County Commissioners." Radcliffe's hands were trembling. "Freshly engraved, and put into my hand not an hour ago in Maidstone. I thought you fellows should see it before I take it to Parson Webbe."

"Why've you got to –?" began Melhuish.

"The Commissioners say that it must be displayed on the door of every parish church," Radcliffe explained.

Judah had had enough of the Commissioners. "Oh, things will fall pat!" he said.

"I doubt it, Master Copp. And you shall learn why soon enough," the scrivener warned.

Their expressions adjusted accordingly.

"Waste no more time. Begin!" Magner ordered.

They put their heads together. Radcliffe selected the choicest cuts of text, and kept his voice down. "*'To the raising of seditions and tumults in this County,*" he narrated, "*we do hereby in order thereunto advise all whom it may concern to forbear all occasions of public disturbance, by any pretence whatever.'*"

"Well, that's football they've thrown to the dogs!" groaned a disbelieving Judah.

"Hush, man!" Melhuish put his finger to his lips. "Go on with it, Lion."

"*'We, having seen a copy of the said presented Petition of Right, do hereby signify our utter devastation of said practices.'*"

"I'll go bail they do!"

"What next? They hang a man in every parish for it?"

Radcliffe attacked the next paragraph. "*'And we do hereby require all the ministers of parished involved publicly to read our signification in their churches upon the next Lord's Day, immediately before they begin their morning sermon. And the churchwarden of the several parishes –'*"

"Whoop! Here it comes for you, Melhuish!"

"*'– are hereby required the next day after the time appointed, to certify what has been done therein to the Deputy Lieutenant, who is hereby directed to transmit the said certificate to the standing committee at Maidstone.'*"

Nobody said anything. The scroll was rolled up and reribboned. Judah broke the silence by pushing the tankard in the verger's direction using the tips of his fingers. Melhuish looked at the drink vaguely, with a sort of delayed reaction, before he took hold of the handle and drank his beer with grateful lips.

"Well?" Coates had returned with Radcliffe's cider. He was rewarded with wan smiles. "Spit it out, lads!"

"There's opprobrium in high places," leered Magner.

"Whassat mean?" Coates hopped back across the form.

Radcliffe's head dropped. "Look!" He began, slowly, and without momentum. "The Commissioners did rout the Puritans in Canterbury. The riots were contained; the merchants returned to their stores. You'll allow that not even a Puritan could call off Christmas overnight!"

Magner had an answer straight away: "When the Puritan lolls on the benches of Parliament, there's nothing to stop his fancies!"

The news from Canterbury had been discomforting, alright. Riots had broken out when the local dogmatists had tried to prohibit festivities, and impose an embargo on Christmas Day trading. Things had got ugly: a mob had marched on the Lord Mayor's mansion. Unless the Puritan dogs were yielded up with an apology, thundered the Royalist newssheets, then direful consequences could only ensure.

Coates sniffed, and said, "Gout-headed swine."

Melhuish suddenly said, "I went down to the church this morning. There's no flowers laid on the Parson's grave."

"Old Jump, you mean? Well, d'you wonder?" Judah blurted. "The man did the world no favours. Why, man, you wept like an infant the day the Militia came to gut that church!"

"They were under orders," said Melhuish, not without sympathy.

"Aye – *his* orders, you'll mind!"

"Nay, but… a soul should lie in peace!" the verger insisted.

"Some peace!" Coates huffed.

Melhuish drained his beer in one attempt. "Last drink of the condemned, me boys!" he said, as he set his tankard down.

Radcliffe's jaw fell away. "Dear Lord in Heaven! But you are implying … *Another war?*"

His voice had been too loud. People were losing interest in their pipes and tankards, and were turning to stare at the huddled knot of men.

"What next?" The scrivener forced his voice down and tried to speak clearly. "You are suggesting the Commissioners will march on the Commons with their petitions in one hand and their bullet-moulds in the other? Even to contemplate that we might embark on another war! 'Tis the invention of Satan!"

Magner tweaked a calculating moustache. "Nay," he drawled, "you cannot blame the Old 'Un for that one, ingenious though he may be."

"Christ have mercy!" Judah vanished behind his hand.

"But, we all of us gave of our services to assure that such a thing could not occur again!" Radcliffe protested, in a forlorn key.

Coates' face was fired with an exasperated fury. "And for what? Mm? We frittered away our service on that shitten Roundhead crew!"

The sexton blinked at him across the table. "Who pissed in your bread, Chris? There's plenty must a-been widowed in the last five years!"

"Judah's right! Just look at Briarwell," Melhuish assented. "That's too much death for a lifetime. All those Watermans ain't about to walk out of their graves."

"Yes. Well." Coates backed down somewhat. "We couldn't all buy our way onto the field of Naseby."

Magner weighed in. "To my mind, the right-doing man would sit as mute as fishes, and let events run their course. We could benefit from his good example, rather than stirring the pot."

Melhuish looked from Judah, to Chris, and then back from the one to the other.

"I'm feared, Lion," he hushed. "Would to God I could say otherwise, but Chris is right about the Roundheads. They will not be placated, and they could hit back anytime. The dickens is in the business, and that's the truth."

Radcliffe rose quickly. "I'll have none of this talk. Not now, gentles. Not any longer."

The scrivener was breathless with an urgent desire to leave. "This kingdom has already lost an ungodly number of its manhood. And yes, I will state without shame, I am afeared. I am very much afeared!"

They didn't look at him.

Radcliffe gathered up the Commissioners' scroll. "I will give you all good day, my masters. And in going, encourage you to keep your tongues behind your teeth!"

No word of valediction passed as Lion Radcliffe left The Gryphon and banged the door behind him.

TWENTY-TWO

The subject now, it walked the town awhile
Numbering good intellects.

As a vendor, he was a rather scrawny representative of manhood. The straw hat on his crinkly thatch of hair was old and tattered. He had pimples, red as grapes, all over his chin, and they made him self-conscious in the company of other folk, particularly women. But other folk (particularly women) were hard to avoid on a Market Day. He carried his wares-to-sell unwillingly through Maidstone's cobbled streets. He had to chirp his heart out under his blue linen smock. There were plenty to be beguiled by a bright song and a tray of peddled dainties. And to be fair to him, he sang only slightly off-key.

"Come, lads and lasses, what do you lack?
Here's wares of all prices,
Here's long and short!"

A tall young woman in a sugarloaf hat was coming up High Street towards him, holding the hand of a bright-faced little boy. Over the other arm she carried a fat round basket.

He has attracted the young woman's attention. He'd reel her in yet.

"Here's wide and straight!
Here's things of all sizes!"

She was crossing the street. Her intentions were clear. "Cash down, Mistress! Cash down!" he piped, by way of greeting.

She stared down into the wicker basket that he wore on a strap round his neck. Her little boy had stopped his hopscotch steps, and was now looking thoroughly bored.

"Pennyweight of ribbons for you, Mistress?"

Her brown eyes betrayed her considering mind. "A penny a yard, now, is it?"

"Prices do go up, Mistress."

"I rather care for the green," she announced, in her low-pitched voice.

He redoubled his efforts. "Green as the Weald in summer, Mistress. Best in all Maidstone!"

"I can believe it." She nodded to herself, then said: "Very well. I'll have a tuppenny worth."

"Tuppenny worth? Aye, just as you wish. Be the finest investment you'll make all morning, Mistress!" The youth began measuring out the length she wanted, using his arm as a rule. The ribbon caught the sunshine in a brilliant flash.

The young woman let go of her little boy's hand to reach for the linen cash bag she had tied to her apron. The boy, finding himself emancipated, watched the rain of sparks that flew from a knife-grinder's wheel across the street. His legs began to move towards those fireflies.

"Stephen!" The familiar voice rang out. "Do not wander — stay close to me, now."

The lad returned to her, hunching his shoulders. Mother had sworn she would buy him one of those penny paper windmills that were always sold on Market Day. Now she was spending twice that amount on some ribbons!

He watched her pay the spotty hawker in the smock and the hat. Then the hand with the gold wedding band went out to him again. "Stephen? Come along, sweeting."

Life was always taken at a run on Market Day. High Street was a riot of sights and smells and sounds. The mongers sold their pig iron and metal wares. The victuallers sold their drystuffs and their surplus produce. The husbandmen sold off their fruit by the horse-load. The maltmen unloaded their hops with their "Hail, fellow, well met" humour. The drovers bartered for their black Sussex cattle, which they'd driven in that morning off the sheep-cropped Weald. The drapers kept sly eyes on the prices of neighbouring mercers, and then they quickly undercut them. Market was always so busy, Stephen didn't know where to put his eyes. On that stall over there, the cabbages were so big they looked as though they might rise up and eat you. Everywhere Stephen looked were the sellers of penned-up hogs, of timber and faggots; of paving stones; of straw, and hay, and grass; of meal, and seeds. He and Mother passed down avenues of eggs, the butter, the cheese. The white breads, all warm and inviting. The dishes, the scullery ware. The stockfish, and the oysters, and the herrings.

Stephen went on grudging legs. They were on their way home now, and Mother had yet to stop for any windmills. The ginger lyne suit that his aunts had woven him for a birthday present was a silly thing to wear down to the Market. Stephen wasn't ungrateful for it, but it puckered too much, and there'd always be awkward questions if he got it dirty.

Philippa sensed he was flagging. "Are you alright, my fox-cub?"

"I'm hot!" he muled.

"Never mind. Home again soon."

Stephen peeped up at her. "Mooother? Are you going to buy me a windmill?"

He never got an answer. They had arrived on the fringe of a large crowd of people. Two men in working drab were standing in the midst of it, on a sort of wooden platform. Above them, a linen banner drooped between two poles. On it had been daubed the words, NO WAY TO THE OLD WAY. Both men were wearing sprigs of rosemary in the bands of their battered old hats.

Mother had stopped. Stephen tugged on her hand. "Mooother? Will you not buy me a windmill?"

"Just – just a minute, Stephen." Mother sounded distracted. She was listening to the words that were coming from the dark-haired, darkly-bearded man who stood on the right of the platform. His companion on the left was older, greying; he didn't hold Stephen's interest. The darker man, though, the one who was speaking, had a bandage swaddling his left hand. There were interesting gaps where the second and third fingers should have been. Stephen's imagination got to work.

"The fate of this nation rests in the hands of the generals, the titled nobility!" the man with missing fingers declared to the crowd. "And when those gentlemen fall out among themselves, they shall send for the poor scrubs – men like you and me, my masters! And they'll press the poor scrubs to come and kill each other for them!"

Whatever the man was saying, he was getting properly worked up about it. The man had showed his audience his fist, as if he were threatening to strike them. A *fight!* Stephen rejoiced in the thought. So long, of course, that Mother escaped unharmed. And himself, of course.

"I tell you again," cried the speaker, "all degrees of men should be levelled! And that quickly! Make the tenant as liberal as the landlord!"

A roguish voice escaped out of the audience. "What are you, Jack Tunnock? Wat Tyler's grandchild?"

The crowd laughed. Stephen didn't understand the joke, but he tried to join in.

Mother, he noticed, was not laughing. She was riveted on the man who was missing his full compliment of digits.

The man called Jack Tunnock made another charge. "We chose our Parliament as our lawful representatives, to deliver us out of bondage, and to preserve us in happiness and peace. And I say again that in that, they have failed." He turned to his companion. "I put it to you, Master Jex, let us have done with the wiles of Kings, or Parliaments. The Commons for the *common* man, say I. If we do not act fast, Parliament shall be naught but the plaything of tyrants, and the sword will rule the land!"

"Pistol him! Pistol him!" Mocking fingers jabbed in the speaker's direction.

"Aye! If it be so, my masters, I would die for this quarrel!" Tunnock's voice crackled with enthusiasm. "Know you, any of you, the prices in London these days? Just you try to get yourselves your meat and drink in Hounslow, or in Southwark! Scarce will be gotten for your money!"

He was quickly rebuffed on this point. "Then God be thanked there is plenty of corn in the County of Kent!"

"Aye, and at two shillings over the market price a bushel when there is!" Tunnock shot back in triumph.

Philippa looked round at their theatre of faces. A couple had drifted away, disillusioned, or perhaps pressed for time. Some *were* staring upon the speaker with a kind of devoted interest, but those constants were scattered very wide.

Stephen was tugging on her sleeve. "Mooother! Will you not be buying me a windmill?"

Philippa bent over him, trying to be gentle. "Hush, Stephen! Quietly, now. Let Mother listen."

Stephen frumped extravagantly.

Up on the platform, the grey-haired man named Jex had found his voice. "My masters, let us not be too hasty. Master Tunnock, you will observe that the earth is a common treasury, and yet there *is* a property, for the Law of God says, 'Thou shalt not steal'."

"Nay, nay, Master Jex, mine and thine cannot be!" Tunnock rejoined. "No man has power over my rights and liberties, nor I over any other man's. In essence, if I do, then I am only an invader of that other man's rights."

He was starting to lose his crowd. "Man wants whipping to his senses!" someone hollered, and a cackle of laughter broke from the onlookers.

Tunnock disregarded his detractor. "We *have* been under slavery, Master Jex! Our land's laws have been written by the men of riches, men of estates. Right the way back to William the Bastard himself, as soon as he had smashed the Saxon kingdoms. The commoners of England have been paying for it for six hundred years!"

Now he came forward, right to the lip of the platform.

"My masters, the issue is this. Nay, now do not turn tail just when I am arriving to the heart of the thing – stay and hear it out! Every degree of man deserves a say in choosing those who will make his laws for him. 'Tis the birthright of all free men. And I for one would willingly die a free man, rather than live a slave who is yoked to a driving tyrant!"

Philippa cleared her throat. "You – you'll – you'll pardon me, sir?"

Tunnock and Jex looked down, casting round to place the voice. Philippa obligingly put up her hand. "Master... Tunnock, was it?"

"Aye, Madam." Tunnock assessed as much of this woman as he could see. The tall-crowned hat. The ruff that encased the throat. The unwavering, light brown eyes. The sceptical mouth.

"Much of what you said has intrigued me very much." Philippa had hold of Stephen's hand, and she advanced with him nearer the platform. She stopped only when she stood right under

Tunnock's nose. She smiled as inoffensively as she could. "Sir, my husband is the rector of Saint Mary's in East Farleigh. I have heard him speak many times of our creation in the image of the Lord. Surely, as I am his wife, I have an interest in Christ that is as equal as you menfolk?"

Tunnock coughed. A frown of obliging philosophy had criss-crossed his brows. "No doubt, Mistress. But that is more *your* affair."

Voices were starting to ripple through the crowd. Philippa drew Stephen before her, showing him to the two speakers. The little boy leaned against the protective curve of her body. She began to put flesh on the bones of her thoughts.

"Now, if my son here were delivered of God by the hand of Nature, does it not follow that *his* birthright and privileges are as equal and alike to me, as I am his mother? After all, we are all God's creatures."

Jex replied, in a voice that was strained and abrupt, "It follows, Mistress, that God created you for the specific purpose of *being* a wife and mother. Just as it is written that Eve was created for Adam."

"Yes," she said. "I am a wife, and I am a mother. I have fulfilled those purposes. Does that therefore imply that any further rights of mine are terminated?"

"Uhm – "

"Am I not, as a woman, due a proportionable share in the freedoms of this nation, which you've so keenly pledged to be every man's birthright?"

"Uhm – " Jex looked to his fellow on the platform. Philippa did so too, though with less desperation.

"What, sir, are *you?*" she pursued. "What purpose has the Almighty given *you?*"

Tunnock stuttered: "I – I am a soap boiler."

"A soap boiler," she repeated.

"Yet I wore the King's coat in the field!" His chest puffed out as he held up his hand. "And I'm now two digits less for it, as you will observe!"

"I do, sir, I do. And therefore I must ask you, if God created you to be a soap-boiler, just as he created me to be a wife and mother, what right do *you* have to demand – yes, demand – any freedoms beyond that?"

Tunnock blinked. "I – I do not understand your question, Mistress."

Philippa set down her basket by her feet. "The Lord created you to do your duty to the King, just as he created you to boil your soap, correct? Very well. You have done your duty, for your wounds are clear to all of us, and you have boiled your soap. *Ergo*, what rights have you to anything beyond that?"

"Well, I – " Tunnock broke off.

"And *if* you are entitled to those rights, which were bestowed on you by God, then by your own reasoning ought I not to have a share in them as well? After all, I too have fulfilled my purposes by marrying my husband, and bringing forth my son. Have I not?"

Somebody clapped. Others cried "Shame!" and craned their necks to trace the applause.

A yeoman farmer nudged the flabby brewer standing at his elbow. "Cap'n Agnew's eldest, that is."

His neighbour's eyes widened. "You certain?"

"Aye. I knew him back in Barming, rest him." The yeoman tapped his forehead significantly. "She knows her mind, does that one."

The brewer's chins wobbled. "I don't hold with females."

Neither, it seemed, did the mellifluous Master Tunnock. "It is not for the womenfolk to so petition, Mistress," he said, witheringly. "In my view, you'd do well to take that lad away with you, stay home, and mind your business."

Philippa flinched. Observing her hesitancy, someone behind her guffawed, "Aye, Mistress! Go home, and wash your porridge pots!"

The crowd began to snicker. Soon the snickering had mushroomed into fuller, richer fits. It was the kind of laughter that can only come at someone else's embarrassment. Philippa turned to stare at the scathing crowd. Only a couple of faces looked sympathetically female. Looking back at the platform, she saw that Tunnock had crossed his arms at her in victory. His cheeks had filled out with a smile.

"Sir." She cleared her throat, for her voice had gone hoarse. "I would well inform you that we have scarce any crockery left us to wash, and those we do have we are not sure to keep." She bent to retrieve her basket, and to mask her blushes. "I can only regret I appear so despicable in your eyes."

Stephen squinted up at her. What was going on? Mother looked like she was in pain.

"Come along, Stephen."

Bodies stood aside to let them pass. Before long they were heading down the throat of swarming Week Street.

Time was running out. "Mooother?"

Philippa drew a long, long breath. "I am sorry, sweeting. But we are going home."

Rebecca met them in the hall. She opened her arms to her grandson. "Here comes my little cinnamon!" She kissed him on the crown of his head as Stephen hugged her round her ribs.

Philippa divested herself of her capotain hat. Her face was mellowed by the shadows. She felt shaky and short-of-breath. The reaction was setting in.

She watched her son go running out of his grandmother's embrace; go clattering through the door leading into the front room. They heard Elle's tender call of, "Hallo, bunny!" Next moment, Stephen had reappeared. His Aunt Loobie, barely three years his elder, had seized his hand and was spiriting him away on fresh adventures.

"Careful, lambkins!" Rebecca looked after them as they dashed upstairs, then turned and stepped forward to greet her very quiet, very static, eldest daughter.

"Your proudest achievement, Pip."

"*Nathan* was my proudest achievement, Mother."

"You found what we need?"

"Fear not, little flock." Philippa passed her mother the provisions.

Rebecca drew back the linen pall and rifled the purchases. "Ah, I see you did not forget the bottle of peas."

"Where are the twins?" asked Philippa.

"At their work." Pip's abrupt tone made her mother look up. "Something bothers you?"

Philippa shrugged. "There were men. On High Street."

"Men? What sort of men?"

Her daughter said nothing. Rebecca's concern only grew. "Pip? Tell me! What were these men doing, that so riled you?"

Philippa's reply was one of simple significance. "Giving speeches."

Rebecca raised her eyebrows. "What manner of speeches?"

"A prognosis, on the health of a sickly nation. *Sickly!*" she sneered. "They were numskulls, both of them! Why, even if I could bring forth *ten* sons, I would still be reckoned lesser to them in this world!"

"I do not understand – ?" her mother said in puzzlement.

Philippa strode forward. Her distress was welling up. "I think they must knead their bread with ale, for they were drunk, Mother, I swear!"

"Drunk?" Rebecca was staring at her. "I do not understand! On what?"

Philippa's anger rang out. "On *rhetoric*, Mother! Rhetoric! And their cleverness!"

She had grabbed her mother's bicep. The look on her face was frightening.

"Pip, you're hurting me."

Her daughter had curled back her lip and her teeth were showing. "O judgment! Thou art fled to brutish beasts, and men have lost their reason!"

She said no more, but let go her mother's arm and abandoned her to wonderment.

In the front room, she found the twins spinning and weaving. Ros threw the shuttle with an artisan's dexterity. The loom, more intricately rigged than any ship, was creaking and sighing as she treadled with her bare toes.

> "The man in the moon
> May wear out his shoon
> By running after Charles his wain,
> But all's to no end
> For the times will not mend

Till the King enjoys his own again!"

Elle joined in. They harmonised the chorus:

"Yes, this I can tell,
That all will be well
When the King enjoys his own again!"

Ros looked round at the shutting of the door. "Headstrong! You are returned!"

Philippa gave her a weary glance. "The *King*, Ros, is unlikely to be enjoying anything at the moment, since he is penned up in Carisbrooke Castle!"

She stood a while with her back against the door, watching Ros' mobile hands. She was beginning to calm down.

"The work fares well," she said, brightly.

"Gewgaw," Ros sniffed. "Might fetch a few pennies, is all."

Philippa planted a kiss on the crown of her sister's coif. "You are too modest, Ros."

"Huh! You were the first that ever found me so," Ros flashed.

Stepping into adulthood had been an ugly shock for the Agnew twins. They would rise at dawn, share a beaker of milk in the kitchen, and then work in the parlour till dinnertime.

Philippa asked, "Where is Carrie?"

"Upstairs." Ros volunteered no further information.

"What is she doing upstairs?"

Now it was Eleanor's turn. "Hiding."

Philippa rounded on her. "What mean you, 'hiding'?"

"I mean what I say: Carrie's hiding!"

"*Why* is Carrie hiding?" It was all Philippa could do not to stamp her foot.

Ros paused at the loom and swivelled on the bench to look at her. "Because Verity Waterman will be calling on Mother at noon," she replied, with a gleam in her eye.

Philippa moved away and placed her bottom on the edge of the table. Her knuckles gripped the woodwork very tight. "It is three years since Roger was killed," she said at last.

"Roger; Francis; all of them."

Elle said, "'Afore God, it cannot be much of a life for her these days."

Ros threw the shuttle before she treadled again. "I still have no idea why Carrie kept Roger all to herself, you know."

Her comment ignited Philippa's temper. "We are *not* discussing this again!"

"Oh, but you're all right, Headstrong!" said Ros, indifferently. "*You* are married off, and *you've* got Stephen. Carrie has scarcely looked at a man since Roger. And Elle and me can go hang, I suppose."

"ENOUGH!" exploded Philippa.

Eleanor shrugged in the awkward silence. "As you wish."

"As you wish!" Ros parroted, and went on with the treadle.

Philippa could not see the look of sly congratulation that the twins passed to one another. The years had made no difference; their two would always outnumber the eldest *one*.

"I suppose ... I should go up to her?" she said aloud.

"Huh! I'd not!" said Elle. "We tried. And we're lucky to have our heads left!"

TWENTY-THREE

To scorn delights and live laborious days.

The scene never altered in any particular.

He would be standing, very straight, on the rug before the fire. Feet as far apart as his shoulders. Hands crossed in the small of his back.

"Father, I am in love."

First Father would frown from irritation. Theresa would look up from her embroidery hoop. Then Father would rise from his chair, and his eyes would flash like topaz, and he would say,

"In love, sirrah? And who, I beg, is the object of these affections?"

Nathan would meet that tiger-like stare. "Philippa Agnew."

Father would go terribly, eerily quiet. "Who – whose name did you speak?"

"Philippa Agnew."

"Heart and hell!" his Father would whisper.

Nathan would shift the weight on his feet. "We are in secured in our affections, and are pledged soon to wed."

As the weight of those words sank in, Father would exchange a fleeting, glance at the Catholic Theresa. Then he would walk over and stand by the fireplace. He would bend his head and stare at the velvet tapis before he'd begin to speak. "Nathan. Heed me, now. You are not in love with Philippa Agnew. Nor are you in love with any other Agnew girl."

When Nathan did not reply to his charge, his father would lash his body round, face reddened in fury.

"I know not what damned stew this is you have got yourself into, boy, but by my life, if you go through with this falal of a marriage, you shall no longer be welcome in this house!"

Nathan would draw breath and say,

"Then that is the end of it, Father."

Then he would turn, and quit the chamber. He had not tried to justify showing his father his back.

His father would start after him. "In love with that Agnew girl? Nay, boy, for I know who you love! You love yourself, and you're too dunderheaded to own to it!"

172

As Nathan passed out languidly through the door, his father would boom his last denunciation.

"God rot you black! I don't care if you're a parson – you're a fool! And a blind fool to boot!"

Nathan would not stop to watch Theresa's attempts to placate her husband. But he would hear his father's cry, "Unhand me, woman!" He would hear Theresa's tears And he would hear the sound of a toppling chair.

Their bedroom in the Parsonage faced eastwards. Nathan awoke into the slab of orange brightness where the curtains didn't touch. He rolled onto his side, and his arm went round Philippa's midriff. His lips found her upturned cheek.

Philippa stirred from her sleep-fogged mind, feeling her skin start to tingle. A smile spread inch by inch across her face. "You and your butterfly kisses," she murmured.

Her arm was trailing over the edge of the flock mattress, suspended in space. She drew it back onboard, then put it round Nathan's neck so that he might greet her properly. At last she used a finger to push him away.

"Along with you. You have a busy day ahead."

He left her, and she heard his footsteps striking out across the room, heard him spread the curtains back. The sky had begun to lighten. Apricot swirled into the palest cerulean. He heard the birdsong rising with the morning. Nathan was moved to dip his head in silent, thankful, momentary prayer.

Philippa gave a mind-resisting roll onto her front. She lay there, stretching her limbs while she blinked into the daylight. Her hair was hidden under the hanging, rabbit ears of her nightcap.

Nathan was now at the wash-jug. "You burned the candle late last night," he said, with a glance at guttered wax. "Was something lying on your mind?"

She returned his look through unfocused eyes. "Aye; I could not sleep." She yawned, and removed her coif. Her mane of hair tumbled free across her shoulders.

"You seemed uncommonly pensive since you both came back from town."

She used her palm to scrub dust from her lashes. "I know."

"What was it? The twins?"

"Partly," she grimaced.

Nathan stopped, halfway into his breeches. "Were they beasts to you?"

Philippa was careful in her reply. "They worship Stephen, both of them. They treat him like a doll and kiss the very ground he walks on. And yet..."

And yet they would still ally themselves to chastise her, because she had found her herself a husband, and gone on to have a son, while Ros and Elle had little to enjoy but the prospect of throwing a few coins into Mother's diminishing coffers.

Nathan perched on the lid of the chest in which they kept fresh linen. "I am done at the schoolhouse at two. We could – take a walk."

Philippa giggled. "My heart's heart. My most *devoted* abecedarian!"

His eyebrows rose. "There are worse names you could cast at me."

Her shrug was very stoic. "You cannot lead the gay life on forty pound a year."

Nathan changed the subject. Talking about his beggarly clerical stipend was never an easy topic, even with Pip. "I heard there was a meeting in the Market."

Philippa drew up her knees. "Meeting?"

"Aye, those – those what d'they call 'emselves – Levellers!"

Philippa swallowed hard. "How – did you hear this?"

"I encountered Seth Frost, on his way home."

"Did Seth... tell you any more?" Her voice sounded shaky, though her face remained unmoved.

"Not really. Why? Did *you* see something happen?"

"No!" she falsified. She promised herself to make peace later for that later.

Philippa watched him, padding about the floor in his stockinged feet as he finished getting dressed. Her chin rested on her knuckles. The public meeting, and the twins, were beginning to recede. She vented a short, sharp laugh. "Ha!"

"Ha, what?" He did not confront her as he sat down on the bedclothes.

"I was just reminded of something, is all."

Nathan looked round, hearing an arch little trill come creeping in her voice. Her eyes were teasing him. Then she puckered her lips, and whistled the opening phrases of *My Robin is to the greenwood gone.*

Something like four cautious seconds elapsed before he asked, "What are you at, Pip?"

"Why, the text of your first sermon!" she answered.

Nathan deflated.

"Second Book of Samuel. 'Passing love of women'. You remember?"

"I remember," he said, as he affixed his collar.

"You never got the chance to deliver your thoughts on David and Jonathan. No thanks to Arlo poxy Jump!"

Now he did confront her. "It is not meet to speak ill of the dead in that way."

"Nathan, I am your wife," she parried. "That old man did nothing, nothing whatever, to advance your vocation, nor your happiness – you would do well to remember that as I do. I defy contradiction!" she added, raising her hands at him.

The only words he let go were: "Oh, Pip."

Philippa scratched her nose. "I heard tell his exit was petulant."

Nathan, who had been there when it happened, said, "Not more than usual." He rubbed his chin. "Do I need to shave?"

"Show me?" She cupped his jaw between forefinger and thumb, and rolled his head from side to side. "You'll keep," she said.

He got up again, this time for his coat.

"I shall tell you what it was that set me to thinking," said Philippa. "Verity Waterman paid Mother a call yesterday."

Nathan stiffened. "You did not say so."

"No; I needed to think on it first. I suppose, when I saw the two of them together, her and Mother, both having lost so much…"

"How was Carrie, when Verity called?"

"What are you expecting of her? The rending of cloth and the gnashing of teeth?"

175

He did not answer her. A look of consternation was growing in his face. "May I relate to you something?"

She spread her hands. "If not to me, then…?"

"I have got a bad conscience," he admitted, sitting down beside her again on the bed.

Philippa was amused. "Indeed? Does the archdeacon know this?"

"Please." There was the tinge of a plea in his voice. "Don't jest with me, Pip."

Her smirk only broadened. "You are in Holy Orders, Nathan. I thought your conscience was inviolate."

"*Philippa!*"

Her mirth caved in under the weight of his reprimand. She laid gentle, mollifying fingers on his arm. "I think you should tell it me, and quickly."

When Nathan's confession came, he made it to the blankets. "Carrie told me."

"Told you what?"

"About her betrothal, to Roger."

"She – ? You – ? WHAT?" The words tore out of her.

"It is true."

Now she was kneeling upright on the bed in front of him. "And just *when* was this?"

"That summer, before the war."

There was a long and knotted silence.

"Nathan! Face me!"

He obeyed. Their eyes met level.

"Speak honestly, now," she warned him.

"I do speak honestly. We were in Saint Margaret's yard. She wanted to talk. And the news, it just slipped out. She swore me to secrecy," he said, limply. "She made me take an oath."

"Merciful Heaven! What a pastoral tragedy we do make, on this beautiful earth of ours." She scratched at an itch on the back of her head. "You know, thinking upon it, I do not know what good would have come of it if you *had* told me. Save that Carrie now would be a grieving widow, instead of a grieving spinster."

She laid her ring hand on top of his, the fingers splayed out flat. She patted him.

"And, for all Father's friendship, Nathan, I think we both know that it would have been an onus to have had a Waterman as in-law."

The door popped away from its frame. A tousled Stephen pattered in in his nightshirt rumpled, towing Daddles the wooden duck on his string. "Mother! Mother! Mother!"

Philippa at once saw his look of apprehension. "Oh, my sweeting!" She stretched out her arms to him. Relinquishing Daddles, Stephen clambered on the bed, searching for rescue in her embrace. "My, what a squirmy worm you are! Whatever is the matter?"

Her son's answer fell from his lips. "I *dreamed!*"

"Did you, my darling?" His mother touched his small, uncomplicated face and kissed him tenderly. "Hist, now, hist, you wriggling little piglet... It is over." She was hugging him tight to her warmth.

Nathan asked: "What was this dream of yours about, Stephen?"

"Don't remember!" Stephen mewed. He had the same, dimpled look that Loobie used to get.

"Oh. What a shame." Philippa rolled her eyes at Nathan over their little son's head.

"Never fret, now, Stephen. It was nothing but a dream." Nathan laid a hand between his son's barely pronouncing shoulder blades. "Now, I am afraid that I must be away, Best Boy, but Mother is here to be your soothsayer if your dream should come back to you."

"Now is that not typical of your father, Stephen? Going off and leaving me to wrestle with all the bother!"

Nathan met her dancing, jester's eyes. "Peace be within our walls." He ran his finger across the soft expanse of Stephen's dimple. "Now, see here, Best Boy. You must help your mother around the place while I am at the school."

"He will. He likes to help me knead the dough," she reminded him.

Nathan kissed her on the cheek and headed out to the narrow landing. At the head of the stairs, he stopped. Stephen and Pip had commenced the old, sing-song chant.

"Put your finger in Foxy's hole-"

"Foxy's not at home!"

Nathan was smiling as he descended the stairs. Three steps down, he picked up Stephen's garishly-coloured teetotum. The last thing he wanted was to return to the Parsonage and find Pip at the bottom of the stairs with a broken neck.

The impermanence of a parson's lodgings was reassuring. Everything he *really* needed in his life was at play above his head. He welcomed the long indigo nights of the summertime, and the winter's slapping gales on those chilly afternoons, because he could share them with Stephen and Pip. Stephen was the only legacy Nathan truly knew he had. Everything else was nothingness. But Stephen was a second chance, *post mortem meam.*

"PICKING AT A BONE!" The joyful chorus came drifting down from the bedchamber.

He cast an eye upon the long shelf affixed to the wall by the stairs. Here Pip kept her most treasured possession: her "Christmas" Shakespeare, as she liked to call it. Alongside it sat *The Anatomy of Melancholy*, the Essays of Bacon; Augustine's *Confessions*, and *An Anthology Of English Wit*. There should have been more, by rights. Herodotus, Cicero, Spenser, the old copy of Ovid translated by Golding – those had all been auctioned away with the rest of the library after Captain Agnew's death. The gaps had not been filled. In many respects, their library was the most valuable thing in the Parsonage. Pip was always saying that knowledge was priceless.

Last of all, kept separate from the rest, was Foxe's *Book of Martyrs* that Stephen was on no account to touch. Those woodcuts between its boards left nothing to the imagination. Besides, Stephen "dreamed" too much.

Their kitchen was southward-facing. It was a small and sunlit room in the early mornings, filled with brassware and pewter utensils. The remains of yesterday's loaf still stood upon the table. Nathan sawed off a crust, and ate it. A mouthful would have to be sufficient for the moment. He had yet to make his rounds about Saint Mary's, and there was always a good hour's work to do in his study before he could return and sit down to his breakfast.

The light was growing stronger. He slipped his pattens over his shoes, put on his hat, and went outside. East Farleigh was stirring. He could see the same old figures, bound for the fields, or the forge, or to Maidstone on business. The same smiling, genial glances.

"God keep you, Master Parson!" boomed a thickset specimen in brown worsted.

Nathan waved back. "And you, Amos! Commend me to your wife!"

From the lane, he could see Saint Mary's Tower, staring back at him over the tree tops. Should he look the other way, the hill descended to the Medway like the broad back of some giant, reclining beast. The road dipped down through the village towards the narrow medieval bridge. From the far bank, it was only a short trip up the hill to Barming. Back to the crossroads of his life.

"I'll give you good morning, Parson!"

Nathan stopped. The voice came from behind a load of washing that had been pegged up in a nearby garden. A hand drew the curtain aside and out peeped the face of Anna Frost. Round, broad-nosed, rosy-skinned, motherly, and quick.

"I'll give you good day!" she repeated, this time with a wave. She liked their young Parson. He'd had a college education, and he'd married the Captain's daughter, and he had tidy manners.

Nathan raised his hat to her. "And I you, Anna. You'll pardon – I did not see you."

Anna moved out from cover. She held a rattan carpet beater in her hand.

"Hard at it already!" he observed.

"I am that. The days are never long enough. You see this?" She drew back a plump wrist and gave the carpet an especially heavy drubbing. "I pretend it's them County Commissioners!"

Nathan shared the joke.

"How's that little scamp of yours? Isn't he a mischief?"

"Yes, Stephen certainly can be," he had to agree.

"Bless him. How he loves the muck!"

"He does, Anna, he does."

"I'll wager he keeps his mother busy with the linens!"

"Aye! Particularly since his mother has made it her business to show him how to climb our apple tree!" he confided. "It is an ongoing battle."

His choice in metaphor had struck a chord. "War news ain't good, Parson," she said, and now there was gloom in her voice.

"I fear you may be right." He nodded a polite farewell. "Good day, Anna, and God buy you."

Anna did not heed his benediction. "I said to Seth only the other night, should we lock away our pewter and linenware, d'you think? And he said yes, we should bury the whole lot in the garden. There's thievery about, Lord knows, when a war is on!"

TWENTY-FOUR

If this fail
The pillared firmament is rottenness,
And earth's base built on stubble.

The elderly Earl of Norwich looked down at the broadsheet he held in his hands. The image depicted a castle, founded on the outline shape of the Isle of Wight. Its walls were bristling with cannon mouths. Poking through the prison bars was drawn a drowsy, bearded face. A crown surmounted the head, and a golden sceptre was in the hand. The words "BEHOLD YOUR KING" were emanating from the mouth in rather nonplussed, bleating tones.

Norwich crumpled the paper and chucked it into the hearth. The broadsheet would make good kindling. He was staring intently into the bed of ashes that lingered in the grate.

The other man in the room watched him. "I thought the likeness rather good, m' lord," he said, mildly.

"An ill augury for our persecuted monarch!" growled the Earl. The sexagenarian Norwich was a fine figure of a man. He stood over six feet tall, and he was barrel-shaped. He could traverse the room in ten strides or less. His riding boots boomed loud and deep upon the floor. He hesitated before the suit of armour which stood on a marble pedestal. His eye travelled from the suit's great helm, running the length of the reversed *zweihänder* sword. Something moved him to reach out and tap the curving breastplate with his knuckle.

"This ... Army of Sectaries?" he wondered aloud.

"Not fit to waste good spit on, m' lord," said his companion.

Norwich spun round, heels squealing on the floor. "Hell's teeth, Sir Gamaliel! We are beset by a concatenation of perils! I'd have been better off stopping in Flanders!"

Sir Gamaliel Dudley didn't blink. He sat in the chair by the open hearth and looked at the Earl of Norwich. In contrast to His Lordship, Dudley's voice did not clang with unfettered emotion. "Things do not wear a bonny aspect at present, I grant you, my lord. But they shall – they shall."

Norwich's countenance was one of strong but often cryptic emotion. In his younger days, when his hair had not been grey, the Court had re-echoed to his jovial wit. He had been esteemed a most promising officer, gifted with the carriage and the tact of a prospective Knight Marshal. A tried and trusted courtier, he had not only been invested as Knight Marshal and later an Earl, he had escorted the Queen over the Channel on her fund-raising venture for the Cause in 1642. By then the winds had been blowing irrevocably towards all-out war, and the King had looked to the Dutch for some rapid financial injections.

"I trust you will take the very greatest care of the Queen, Lord Norwich," His Majesty had said, in that rather halting, softly-spoken way of his. "It would grieve me beyond measure were she to run to any harm."

The Queen had certainly been in want careful escort. Henrietta Maria was an extremely striking woman, but with a halting grasp of English. What is more, the Queen was not well. She'd been troubled by a persistent bout of migraines for the duration of their venture, brought about by the stresses of the mission. The Dutchmen drove hard bargains.

"God blind me!" He glared dejectedly at the door. "What can have delayed him?"

"He will be here," Dudley placated.

Norwich moved to the table. He had attacked a late breakfast of beef olives, and his used plate and cutlery had yet to be cleared away. He surveyed the enormous map that had been spread across the table for him. There lay the diamond shape of Kent, divided into its facet-like Lathes. The borders of the map had been brightly decorated with the heraldry of its Earls. One corner was held down by a plate of sweet rolls, the other by a goblet. His eyes roamed the hand-painted layout of the West Kent towns like an interested deity's. He ate up the miles of brown, round-topped hills, the iron-grey roads, the azure rivers, the little red churches.

"And still no word from the Commissioners?" he asked over his shoulder.

"Nothing." Dudley shifted in his chair. "The word is that Parliament will likely meet whatever force is sent to London with everything they have."

"But 'tis a lawful petition of right, man!"

"Not, m'lord, when you recall that those same men who would butcher the petition have made themselves the lawmakers," returned Dudley.

"Hell's teeth!" Norwich cursed. Since he could not straighten out the skein of the situation he snatched up the goblet, only to find it was empty. "Just whom do we blame for all this?" he demanded.

"Blame?" Dudley got up at last. "Why, blame the Committee of Kent! Blame those God-damned Independents! Blame the exciting times in which you and I are compelled to exist!"

He stalked over to the window. From this grand, square, mullioned portal he was equipped with a most arresting view of the Barham Downs.

"We could always try prayer," he observed, dryly.

Had the mood been different, Lord Norwich might have laughed. But he would not even grace the remark with an answer.

Footsteps could be heard approaching down the passage. More than one person. A few brisk, no-nonsense knocks were unleashed upon the door.

"Come!" His Lordship called.

The door was pushed open by a tall young Major wearing a buff coat and a sash of deep maroon around his middle. His anticipating hand remained upon the door-ring, poised for swift retreat. "My lord? Sir William Brockman is here."

"Let him enter," said Norwich. "And ensure that we are left undisturbed."

"Very well, my lord!" The Major withdrew, to be replaced almost at once by a forty-five year old man. The High Sheriff of Kent was broad-framed between his beard and his boots. Dark ringlets framed his round features. A pair of large green eyes questioned the world they saw.

"Lord Norwich!" he bowed, speaking in a tenor voice.

"Sir William." Norwich sounded curt.

"You'll pardon me, my lord, but it is some way from Beachborough." Brockman had draped his cloak "artistically" across one shoulder. He thought it lent him dash.

"We have great need of your intelligence, Sir William," said Norwich. "A glass of wine?" he offered, indicating the stoppered decanter.

"I thank you, no."

"A courteous veto, Sir William. You know Sir Gamaliel Dudley?" Norwich queried, while he poured a measure for himself.

"Of course!" Brockman bowed in turn to the bearded, gnomic man over by the window. Dudley, by way of contrast to his two fellows, was shorter and slight of stature. A few puffs of grey hair enrounded his glistening dome.

"Sir William," Dudley nodded back. "'Tis well to have you on hand for our endeavours."

"Come here, Sir William." The Earl beckoned Brockman to the table, and to the map laid out in readiness. "We are relying on you, please Providence, to help us out of our despondency."

"I believe I can do so, my lord." Brockman jabbed a finger at the map, right on the estuary towns. "That Presbyterian Warwick has declared for the King. The Fleet is with us."

"Whoa-ho! That's geck and gull for Parliament!" cheered Dudley. "Dover Castle itself would be ripe for the plucking, if the Fleet could bring their guns to bear…"

Norwich's smile came and went. "And Deal? And Walmer?" he pressed.

"'Tis certain sure they'll follow us," Brockman pledged.

"How sure?" retorted Norwich.

"As certain sure as I am standing here, my lord."

Dudley joined their little conference from the window. "Then Gravesend and Rochester are also sure to swing our way."

"So will they, if not already!" Brockman pronounced, hotly. "I could levy a thousand men off the streets of Rochester and have 'em entered into pay within a week."

"Rochester…" Norwich considered the map. He thought of the ancient town which oversaw the Medway's last meanderings. He pictured its keep and its ancient cathedral. "It is a veritable arsenal."

"Aye, my lord, and fiercely loyal to His Majesty!" Brockman reiterated.

Dudley's stubby fingers drummed the table. "And what with our brethren in Wales, and over forty thousand Scots

Engagers massing to march south any day... Why, even General Cromwell, damn his hide, cannot be everywhere at once!"

Lord Norwich straightened up. Slowly, barely perceptibly, a belligerent gleam was beginning to spread in the old peer's eyes. "God's holy hair! I'll soon have fifteen thousand men in arms!" he whooped, as he clapped Brockman on the shoulder with such force that the younger man staggered. "I'll pull 'em from their beds by their hair if I must!"

"I cannot conceive of anything to stop you, my lord!" Brockman cried. There was a grin on his face, in spite of the ache that the Earl had put into his shoulder. "This force should rally to your call just as pretty as you please."

"How long?" Norwich asked, through a jubilant mouthful of sweet roll.

"Well, m'lord." Dudley, ever the pragmatist, was rubbing the side of his nose with his thumb. "I would bring to mind that we would be relying *in extremis* on a lot of untrained levies. More crudely, a rabble in everything but name."

Norwich challenged him. "But how can that mar our account, with 'For King Charles and Kent' behind us?" Inspiration was blazing in his eyes; he was in no mood for any man to pour cold water on his scheme. "By the veil of the Virgin, Sir Gamaliel! You are Maidstone's Governor, and yet you cannot vouch for the capabilities of your own men?"

Dudley flushed. Swallowing hard, he said, "I merely raised what I thought was a pertinent point, m'lord."

"*However – ?*" bated Norwich.

Sir Gamaliel hesitated. He watched Lord Norwich's expression carefully for clues. He read where His Lordship wanted the cards to fall. "*However*, where Maidstone goes, the rest pursue. That I can guarantee you, be assured."

His Lordship went quiet. A lot of very active, febrile thoughts were picking their way across the plains of his mind. Nothing showed outwardly: the face kept them well concealed.

"How long d'you need, Sir Gamaliel?" the Earl cast again.

Dudley turned his head to him. "I could not tell at present," he said, pontifically. "If the Kentish womenfolk would wish themselves safe from the clutches of Parliament, then let them persuade their sons to come forth and stand with us. We need strong, horse-owning men," the Governor reminded him.

Norwich's expression started to clear, and he nodded briskly. "Take things as they arise, eh?" he agreed at last. "Sounds sensible. Would you not say, Sir William?"

"Your Lordship has my fullest support," said Brockman. He was glad to have been allowed a conduit into the talk once more. "And I can promise you the concord of many other county gentlemen of note. Why, for one, Sir Thomas Peyton was particularly keen to be commended to your service."

"Ah, Peyton," Norwich reckoned. "A Sandwich man."

"Correct, my lord. He holds a great sway in the eastern lathes; his loyalty is above all question."

"His loyalty shall not go unrewarded." Norwich smiled a satisfied smile. "Let us trust His Majesty may yet ride out at the head of his Kentish army, Sir Gamaliel."

"Provided the Roundheads do not take him back to London in a cage, m'lord, I have no doubt he will," replied Dudley.

Norwich peered at him with mounting distemper. "No idle wagging, Sir Gamaliel. Speak plain to me, now. Mere minutes ago, you swore to me the fidelity of the Medway towns rested squarely with the King!"

"Aye, and so they do." A grim smile touched Sir Gamaliel Dudley's lips. "There's talk along the riverbank, m' lord, that even God himself's turned Cavalier."

TWENTY-FIVE

Now fresh rebellions raise their Hydra heads.

The Gryphon was full to bursting. They had had to contend for their usual spot in the corner. Now, comfortably lapped by local ales, they beat time with their pattens and struck up a song.

> "We be soldiers three,
> *Pardonnez-moi, je vous en prie!*
> Lately come forth from the Low Country
> With never a penny of money!"

They had a very willing audience. Some rocked to the rhythm, or held their tankards over their heads and sang with a Judgement Day zeal.

"Sing up, Chris!" called Private Copp. "Give us a thunderbolt, 'fore we go live on His Majesty's bounty!"

Coates, who had his feet up on his enormous corded drum, flapped his wrist disparagingly. "Down with the New Noddle Army, and its blockhead commanders!"

"Aye, man! Here's to ye, Brother Clare!"

It felt strange, yet somehow incalculably reassuring, to look at Melhuish and Judah and see them both back in their uniforms. Thick wool and buff leather encased them all again, and even the prickly Monmouth cap felt a comfort.

The singers struck up another stanza. They bounced through the lyrics the way a cutter might bounce across the waves.

> "Charge it again, boys, charge it again!
> *Pardonnez-moi, je vous en prie!*
> As long as there is any ink in the pen,
> With never a penny of money-y-y-y!"

When the call had gone out, the verger and the sexton had walked right out of the churchyard to answer it. Coates had met them on the road. They'd walked down the road into Maidstone together. They had queued and been embodied, one after the other. They had been handed their first down-payment and their uniforms, told to change into them, and to report back the next day. Their down-payment had gone to The Gryphon.

Grace Copp had been chopping up watercress when she'd seen Judah walk through the door in his uniform again. She had volubly protested. "And what are *you* a doing of, Judah?" she demanded, wringing her hands and staring at the bounty he'd brought home. "You've run mad, quite mad!"

Judah had stood there and brassed it out. "Aye, chuck, mad. Mad as any right-thinking man when his King's a-calling for him!"

Then he had had to duck, for Grace had lobbed her hairbrush at his head.

Further down the lane, Sarah Clare had been more stoic. When her man had broken the news, she had held out her arms and hugged him.

"Do not expect me to cheer for you, Melhuish," she said afterwards, as she held him by the wrists. Tired and emotionally drained, she no longer felt the pangs of parting ways when the military came knocking for its Corporal. "But duty must be done, and I'll take what comfort I can glean from that!"

She'd polished his waistbelt with a chunk of beeswax for him. Worked late on it, too; sitting up late into the night in the parlour by the glow of a candle.

"'Tis a boon the old Captain isn't still walking abroad to witness all this," she'd declared, as he'd buckled it on..

"Aye," said Melhuish, as the strap was drawn tight round his middle. "He were always loath to take up arms against his own nation. The ways of the Lord is a mystery, Sarah."

The cry went up around the inn again. "For God, King Charles, and Kent!"

The tankards clinked. "'Ooray!"

"It'll be the Tunbridge Road all over again!" someone hollered, and cheers broke out afresh. That bloody stand of 1643 had lived on in local minds.

"Where's Cromwell and his friend King Jesus now?" sneered Coates.

"Pish, man!" warned Corporal Clare. "It's Charles that will be King, for all King Jesus!"

"A king can't serve us his days from the inside of a gaol."

"Aye, that's why we're bound to spring him out!"

"I never squarely saw the Roundheads' point in keeping that Army in the field, I don't really," said Judah. "Not now the whole county's in rising."

"They were asking for it, right enough," nodded Corporal Clare. "Certain as Christmas!"

"Christmas? Certain?" Coates crossed his ankles on the drumhead, feeling the drum's skin tautening beneath the heels of his shoes. "'Tis well you ain't no prating Puritan, Judah."

Judah leered at him across the table. "Tush in thy teeth, man!"

Melhuish was unbowed. He turned round and lifted his pint pot aloft. "Another round, good Master Sloane! Our throats are dry as dust!"

Sloane, who'd been mopping the bar with a rag, scowled upon them. "You've had enough."

A salvo of jeers was launched at him from the corner table. Sloane jibbed, but held firm. "Them as drinks 'em, buys 'em. No cash upon liking with me, Melhuish Clare. Lord knows you've drunk enough in here to know that."

"The Devil take him, lousy skinflint! Run him through!" Judah bawled.

The door had been pushed open. A pair of new arrivals were persuading their way in.

Melhuish sat up straight. "Aye, aye! The bawcock's come to sniff us all out."

Six eyes fixed on the uniformed figure wearing the sash, and the luxuriantly feathered hat. Sarjeant Magner had entered The Gryphon.

"My God," said Coates. "Proudcock's put on his bravery, and no error!"

"No wonder in it – see!" Melhuish nodded his head, not towards the Sarjeant but towards the Sarjeant's companion: a shapely, raven-haired brunette of seventeen, whose dark tresses cascaded like silk to her hip-bone.

"Ohhhh, *look!*" said Judah. That third pint was taking effect. "He's brought his new button-smock whore with him!"

Coates frowned. "Ain't she Tom Gwyther's daughter, up the mill?" he pointed.

"She may not be, by sundown!"

Coates shook his head. "I dunno. The minute he hoves into view, they lift up their skirts and they fall on their backs."

"'Faith, and hope, and charity. But the greatest of these is charity'," quoted Melhuish.

"He's probl'y had all three."

Judah spluttered into his beer as he laughed at the joke. Melhuish waved. "Kill-Sin! Over here!"

Magner smothered his smile when he heard his given name. It was a fleeting look only, but one of ire and lack of trust. He cursed himself. He should have guessed that the Boys would have secured that corner table. He turned, lifting her fingers to his mouth so he could kiss them. "Be so good as to excuse me, Marjorie." His voice was respectful. A gallant *caballero* – nothing more.

He went to their table. "Men." His voice was colourless. Drummer Coates was making no attempt to sit up straight in the presence of a senior non-commissioned officer.

"Pretty dell you've got there. I'd fain discover where you find the strength for it, Kill-Sin!"

Judah, who had the security of a drink in his hand, creased up again with laughter. He punched his congratulations into Melhuish's shoulder.

Magner frowned. His beard wobbled aggressively. "Sarjeant Magner to *you*, Corporal Clare," he said in upbraiding accents.

"Alright. Civil words, then, civil words." Corporal Clare seized the handle of his tankard. "Here's health unto His Majesty, and a health to the good Sarjeant Magner."

"Amen!" said Judah, in his Sunday morning voice of gratitude.

Irritated at the way he was being treated, Magner shot a glance at Marjorie. She was still waiting for him near the bar. There was much whispering going on at the sight of her. The Gryphon had plenty of unattached men in it today, and Marjorie was the proper stuff of fantasies. Unaccompanied ones were openly staring, those with female companions glancing more or less when they could. At this rate, Sarjeant Magner could lose his relished monopoly.

Magner looked at the faces around the table. "Only three of my bucks, I see. Where's Private Radcliffe?"

"What, *him?*" Judah looked like he would spit. "He's nailed hisself shut in his chambers in Maidstone! The Last Trump'll find him holed up in that office of his. I says, let the arsworm go, and there's an end to him! "

Coates was similarly incensed. "Aye, that weak streak o' piss said he'd done more than his share o' time in the military's pay, thank you kindly, and he'd no stomach for anymore! I says we are rid of him, boys. And I would tell him so, to his head!"

"Leave it, Chris!" said the Corporal, sharply.

Judah made so bold as to nudge Magner in his buff-coated ribs. "You'd best go for a proper gesture, *Sarjeant,* or else your doll'll be losing interest!" he said, with open innuendo.

The Sarjeant flushed defensively. It wouldn't do for him to raise his hand to one of his own men... not in uniform, in a public hostelry, with more witnesses around him than you could shake a stick at. And for all his brown-ale impertinence, Private Copp had a point. A "proper gesture" would be fitting, but Magner would work on that later.

Before they knew what was happening, Magner had mounted the form, and so on upwards on to the tabletop itself. His feathered hat brushed the beams and rustled the hop garlands.

"'Ere, now!" Sloane waddled out from behind the bar, brandishing his rag.

Magner flung his arms wide, and declaimed with all the panache of a leading Thespian.

> "O! that Tom Fairfax and his rout
> Should be so banged by Kent!
> He forcèd by his pokey gout
> From life, and Parliament!"

The drinkers applauded and roared for an encore. Magner swept off his hat, dislodging a dusty shower of hop seeds. The smile he flashed at the girl across the taproom showed all his teeth. The raven-haired Marjorie watched him, her eyes growing wider and her lips a little open. Beguiled. Besotted. Ensnared.

TWENTY-SIX

Peace hath her victories, no less renowned than war.

By rights, the man should have died seven times over in the last six years. He had twice endured a horse fall out from under him. He had been shot at close range through the wrist. He still wore a deep cut in his cheek from a cavalry sabre. A hail of grapeshot had gone clean through his shoulder. A monumental explosion of gunpowder had shaken his frame to its marrow. And only two winters ago he had been doubled-up in agony by kidney stones.

His uniform wore a patina of ingrained muck. His coat was unfastened, and its small, round, ball-shaped buttons drooped dangerously on their threads. The ruff had been discarded long ago, for want of good starch. Only a linen collar poked out above the doublet. The man himself was lanky and slim, with rich brown hair. His eyes were dark and, like his mouth, tended to tinge with melancholy when in repose. His teak-like complexion had led the rank and file across the divide of the war to nickname him "Black Tom".

The night was still warm. The shadows had slid into the darkness.

He set down his glass of claret and threw a look towards the man who shared the waking hours of his life. Colonel John Rushworth was a most faithful field secretary. Before he'd assumed his current post, Rushworth had accompanied the Army on its campaigns as a journalist, attempting to convey the butchery of battle after battle. Now he sat at a linen-draped table, writing up his General's dynamic scheming. Dutifully collating this plethora of disconnected notes into a set of cohesive instructions that yet might keep the Army in the field.

Captain-General the Lord Thomas Fairfax pursed his thin, shrewd lips. "Have we had word from Rochester?"

The nib barely paused. "None, my lord."

Fairfax gasped as his big toe curled up under yet another, throbbing hammer blow. Rushworth watched his chief with sympathy, but even he must admit that His Excellency cut a bizarre appearance, with only the one boot on.

"The joint-evil troubles you much, my lord?"

"Troubles me?" Fairfax snarled, out of a pain-twisted mouth. "Am I not stabbed by the devil's own pitchfork?"

Fairfax leaned on the table to catch his breath. His right foot was wrapped in bandages. He had not dared stuffing the thing inside its matching boot.

He hobbled to the entrance of the tent. He peered into the darkness, past the totemic, halberd-wielding figures standing outside. Hounslow Heath was lit for him by the banking moon. Somebody close by struck up a tune on a plaintive and inaccurate recorder.

He looked bemused, and not a little disappointed. He had a lot to think about. His men, his living name, had all been cast into the fire. He was a slave to a higher power, leagues beyond his paltry reckoning. Something else had chosen him as Parliament's protagonist. It was a role he had been given, and he could not shrink from it now. For Fairfax, it was a question of honour. It was honour, not the name, that kept the corpse alive.

He came back, using the central pole as his support. "I don't understand these Kentish men, John."

"Riddles are not my way either, my lord."

"We offer them our indemnity, and all they do is turn round and imprison our delegation!"

Now Rushworth paused in his writing. "Rebellions grow like grass in the county of Kent. 'Tis their confounded county motto of 'Invicta'."

"True, John, true. Ah, 'tis the devil of a business."

"Aye!" said Rushworth, with a punitive veracity. "And it'll keep too many a man like myself from his hearth and home, so long as our King makes war upon his own people."

Fairfax succeeded in a smile. "That is your opinion, of course, John. I'll not upbraid a man who took up arms because his conscience dictated it."

"Nor, I you, my lord; I do assure you."

"Won't kick a man when he's down, eh?" Fairfax patted his leg: the one that ended in that excruciating foot.

"Nay, my lord. Not unless he has a chance of kicking back!"

"Huh! Not much chance of that when a man's in the gout, I declare!" Fairfax limped back to the table and sank upon a stool.

By the inadequate light of the candles, he watched Rushworth manoeuvre the quill across the pages. His secretary's features were dominated by his long, straight nose. It might have been hewn from Roman marble to furnish a likeness along the Appian Way. The chin was oval in shape, fringed with only a slight ring of flab. Like his master the General, Rushworth was a Northcountryman. He went about his work with all the diligence and quiet mockery of the Dales.

Fairfax sighed. "In truth, John, I am still fervently convinced that we may bring our King to honest terms."

This time Rushworth did not look up from his labours. "Indeed, my lord?"

"Indeed." The General sank his bearded chin upon his breast. Let other men keep their Charles Stuart, the Man of Blood, the bogeyman. Fairfax had imprisoned him: he'd guarded him; respected him. Liked him, at a pinch. He'd found the King to be small, demure, and rather stick-like. A correct little man, who loved his children dearly, and always found time to play with them.

Fairfax started enumerating on his fingers. "Consider the face of it, now. Trade is slowly reviving. The merchants go back to their wares. The people return to their shops. The artisans, to their crafts. It'll avail the King nothing to prosecute this war," he said. "By my heart, I know it."

"Then 'tis an avowed shame that such a thought has not crossed any minds in Chepstow, or in Pembroke!" was Rushworth's prim response.

Fairfax chuckled. "Indeed! General Cromwell will find himself much belaboured by the people of *that* belligerent little nation. But my eyes are elsewhere, not in Wales."

Rushworth sanded the still-wet ink. "You wish to move against the Scots, my lord?"

Fairfax adopted a fierce scowl. "Colonel Lambert's expedition shall suffice to deal with the Scottish Engagers," he countered. "To my mind, it would be not only foolish but brainless for us to hurry northwards in his train. No. My eyes are on these Kentish men. Supposing they march on London? Supposing they combine with those levies in Essex and Surrey? Nay, John these rebels must be proceeded against as traitors; I do believe that most profoundly."

Fairfax craned his neck to peer at the paper between them.

"That is the order for Skippon?"

"Aye, my lord. Framed just as you asked."

"Very well. Pass it here, and I'll sign the thing." He half-rose, and held out a hand. "Lend me your pen, if you would?"

Rushworth turned the order in the General's favour. Fairfax leaned across the table and wrote his name with a neat little flourish.

"There'll be blood on the moon, my lord, should we turn on Kent," warned the secretary.

Fairfax appeared to be grinning as he poked the quill back in its pot. "You are as shallow as a pond, John." He sat down again with an almighty groan. "Take my word for it, the half-crown is the only cause the Kentish man will fight for. Their cider is the spirit of their patriotism. And half of 'em only think venery's the reward that is due to the brave!"

This sally brought a smile to Rushworth's lips. "Aye, those levies cut cards with the devil alright."

Fairfax shrugged. "Misguided; the majority of them, I mean. They've all been swept up and borne along by a lot of ill-designing squires. Hullo! What is this?"

"This" turned out to be a figure wearing the red-and-blue cut of the General's own regiment. He stood stiffly, high-chinned, at a youthful and impeccable attention. "My lord?"

"Thunder forth, Lieutenant!" Fairfax barely concealed a yawn behind his fingers.

"There is a messenger outside."

The General groaned under his breath. "Tell him that I am glutted with messengers, Lieutenant. They are tiring my ears!"

"My lord, he brings news of the doings in Kent!"

That had the General's attention. "Does he, now?"

"The very disposition of the rebels. Or so he says," the Lieutenant added, less credulously.

Fairfax glanced at Rushworth. The secretary had already made a pre-emptive move on a fresh sheet of paper.

"There is no time to be lost, Lieutenant. Go bring the man forward."

The subaltern withdrew, only to reappear with a short, pink-cheeked, breathless individual in a uniform of green and black. Upon sighting the lanky General in the buff coat, the messenger snatched his cap from his head and began to knead the tousled wool between his fingers.

"Alright, Lieutenant. That'll be all," said Fairfax.

The officer's departure sent a starburst of panic across the messenger's face. He knew where he stood with Lieutenants, but with a General – !

Fairfax rose with an effort. "What name do they call you, sirrah?" he asked.

"It – it – it is Inskip, my lord." The voice was shaking with nerves.

"Inskip... D'you hold military rank, Inskip?"

"Aye, my good lord. Rank of Trumpeter, if it please you."

"Shilling a day man, is it?" Fairfax nodded. "What unit?"

"Skinner's Regiment; Kentish Horse. I was sent up from our forces in the south."

"And you can offer us us news of the positions of the rebels, yes?"

"Y-y-yes, my good lord!"

Rushworth was tired of being off-stage. "Zounds, man!" he said testily. "Hold yourself straighter when the General addresses you! Don't stand there like some bedazzled rabbit!"

Fairfax watched Inskip's mouth opening and closing, and was reminded of the dying, desperate spasms of a landed trout. Ignoring the irons that were burning in his joints, the General sat down again. His fingers indicated to his secretary that Rushworth should relinquish his perch.

Rushworth divined these pantomimed intentions. "But! But my lord!"

"Do unto others, Colonel Rushworth, do unto others."

Rushworth got up, not very graciously, and Inskip scuttled forward to occupy the stool. Rushworth took up a new position across the table, pen in hand, paper ready.

"There. Now, Master Inskip. Tell me what it is you have to say, and Colonel Rushworth here will write it down."

To stop himself worrying at his woollen headgear, Inskip let his cap drop to the floor. "'Tis the Earl of Norwich they've appointed to lead their forces, m'lord," he said. He spoke more confidently. He was cheered by the General's quiet affability. "Nearly a thousand of the dogs have already reached the purlieus of Dartford. Now Rochester itself is in rebellion."

"We knew *that* much already!" grunted Rushworth, but Fairfax silenced him with a hand.

"The rest are awaiting their reinforcements in the vicinity of Maidstone," Inskip finished.

Fairfax coughed his voice free. "Maidstone, you said."

"Indeed, my lord. They've made its crossroads their rallying point." Inskip formed a cross with his hands, as a visual aid. "There's men as marched up all the way from Dover and the Thanet to link up with Lord Norwich's contingents."

The noise Rushworth made could have passed for a snigger. "No doubt," he remarked, "there are many county gentlemen keen to offer up their little fiefdoms?"

Inskip blinked at him across the pool of candlelight. "N-no doubt there be many such men, sir," he assented. He turned back to the General. "I tell Your Honour no lie when I say that the Earl of Norwich commands a considerable host!"

Fairfax's eyes were were dark and penetrating. His fingers ceased their rhythms on the table. "Master Inskip, I must ask you one more time. You are certain that these rebels are congregating in the vicinity of Maidstone?"

"Yes, my lord."

"You are *absolutely* certain?"

"True as gospel, my lord!"

Fairfax turned. "Colonel Rushworth?"

"Your Excellency?"

"Let food and drink be fetched for this man. Put a guinea in his purse."

"I'll see it done, my lord." Rushworth indicated with his eyes that Inskip's interview was at an end. The Trumpeter rose with many a muttered obeisance and stumbled out of the tent with the secretary at his heels.

When Rushworth returned a few minutes later, he discovered Fairfax huddled over the table, cradling a claret.

"I want every man ready to move at first light, in battle order."

"We are marching on Kent, my lord?"

"We are. We must." Fairfax picked up a thick document from the table and read its contents quickly, several times. It was his Warrant from Parliament, and he wanted to settle a question in his mind about its wording. *"Full, discretionary powers... So it shall be."* He tossed the commission down upon the table. "Maidstone, Maidstone, Maidstone. Always Maidstone. First there was John Ball and his Peasants in revolt; Jack Cade and his crew; the Wyatt rebellion. Now this."

"Perhaps, my lord, there's something in the waters of the Medway?" Rushworth snickered.

Fairfax was silent a minute or two.

"You... you have orders, General?"

"Evil times, John. Evil times." Fairfax folded up his Warrant and tucked it away in one of his coat's deep pockets. "These days offend me very much. Yet at the back of my brain is a nag that I cannot placate." He met Rushworth's eye. *"Shall* we stand?"

His secretary shrugged. "The Army is behind you."

Fairfax sniffed, shook off his melancholy, and then continued with a more pronounced authority. "Repress all attempts at looting. Let our Provosts line the Kentish byways, if we must. Any man caught dealing in anything they have not paid for shall suffer the fullest penalty."

"You may rely on it, my lord."

"Any infractions, mind!"

Rushworth started to leave with resilient stride, till Fairfax's voice made him pause.

"John?"

Rushworth turned round. "My lord?"

"There is just one more thing. These villages will have been deserted by their menfolk. The rest will be defenceless. The women, the old, the babes. I'll not have their lives endangered by our regiments. Let 'em see we are coming only to deliver 'em from the folly of their husbands, eh?"

TWENTY-SEVEN

Ladies, whose bright eyes
Rain influence, and judge the prize.

Carrie and Loobie stared dreamily out of the ground floor window. Week Street was absolutely packed with incoming troops. So, this was an army! A host! The word evoked images of things that should descend on angel's white-spread wings.

Carrie's face broke into a smile a mile wide. She ran the flat of her hand down the front of her dress. She had on a reed-stiffened bodice beneath her shift. It lent her a flattering, conical shape, and she wanted to keep it that way.

To look at the busy street made Loobie breathless. "What a birthday present for you, Carrie!"

"And what about *you*?" her sister shot back. "Loobie, if you had a tail, this is the moment it would be wagging!"

A cannon appeared before them. It was being trundled down the street on a sturdy carriage. Then another appeared in tandem, the gun wheels turning slow. Some of the crews were scurrying around its horses to keep the halter chains in check. A few livelies even rode the guns themselves, sitting atop their brass barrels in the noonday sunshine.

The latch lifted on the door into the hallway. Their mother came in, cradling fresh linens.

"Carrie? Lend a hand. Pip and Stephen want to be on the one o'clock stage waggon, and I must air their room."

Carrie turned. "But Pip will not be coming till tomorrow!"

"Still."

Loobie pouted. "I think shameful Nathan cannot come till Thursday."

"He is taking an interment, Loobie," said Rebecca. "He'll be with us, as soon as he may."

Rebecca deposited the linen *pro tem* on the dining table and joined them. She wanted to see what had enraptured her girls this much. She was startled when she found the roadway teemed with men in arms. Going by their dress, this contingent shuffling past looked like river men, who plied their trade on the tidal Medway. Some were tramping along carrying billhooks, the fighting weapon of the rural man since time immemorial. Some had been issued with a pikestaff, tipped with iron top and bottom. Others carried nothing more lethal than a spade, and some who went by shouldered no weapon at all. Their drill was slack. Their obedience was spongy. Her husband would have had an apoplectic fit to look at them.

"Look at them! By my life, they'll rob the cradle and the grave to keep the army in the field," she sighed.

"I think they came in from Aylesford way," supplied Carrie.

"Did they? Did they, indeed?" Rebecca's interest switched to the traffic that was headed the other way. Little knots in a string of people. People carting packs and linen bundles, dragging wide-eyed, recalcitrant children by the hand.

Exodus had begun.

"Oh look! There's Reuben Igoe!" Carrie undid the catch and pushed the casement back upon its hinges. The sounds of the military instantly intensified. They could hear the drums, and the yapping of commands. Carrie waved at the figure who was shunting his handcart along. Lucy copied her sister's lead and waved as well. Two, pale palms, fluttered through the gap.

The middle-aged cordwainer saw them, and paused. His fists remained clenched round the shafts of his barrow. "Ain't you gone yet, Mistress?"

"We – uhm – we have not yet decided," Carrie replied.

"You had best be quick about it!"

Rebecca reached between the heads of her daughters. With a very long arm she clapped the window shut again. The iron catch swung down, tapping against the leadwork. "Enough of that, Caroline. Shouting our business on the street to the populace? The idea!" She was shuddering as she gathered up the linen and stalked towards the door.

Carrie watched her. "Mother?"

Rebecca spun round. "Carrie."

"Those men, out there." Carrie nodded her head at them. "There must be hundreds of them."

"Doubtless there may be – what of it?"

"Well... Might we have to accommodate them?"

"What mean you by that?"

"I mean, shall we have to put some of them up?"

She was treated to her mother's famous *look.* "We might," was the icy reply. "Now, are you coming to help me with the linens, or not?"

Rebecca left the room.

Carrie counted to twenty before she undid the catch and pushed the window open again. There was a rather dashing young officer out in the street, just level with their vantage point. He had girded on a sword, and he carried a halberd as a denotion of his rank. Carrie admired the well-toned legs that took him hither and thither. He was giving orders to his Company who were milling about in the gutter, calling them to attention while they were leaning on their weapons. He sounded well-spoken, and his voice carried far.

Carrie put her head between the window frame. "Don't anger our mother too much with your men – she's a beast!" she hollered in the officer's direction.

The Company Commander never even turned round. Maybe he hadn't heard her.

Lucy nudged her sister. "Clearly it's not your *words* that'll bewitch him!" she jibed.

Carrie squirmed in her seat. "Shut up, you."

"Serve him glad, I say!" Loobie stuck out her pointy pink tongue at her sister.

Carrie turned back to the street, but the officer had vanished. She put her chin on her knuckles, and dreamed. Without much surprise, she was dreaming of Roger. Her mind was behind a wall in a cool Medway meadow on the Waterman estate. It was late afternoon, and nobody back at the house knew where she was. Roger's back was against the wall. She was straddling his lap. Her knees were up around his ears, his face between her hands. They were newly betrothed. Her kisses were greedy.

The air was suddenly rent by three sharp raps upon the front door. Then they sounded again, louder and more insistent.

Loobie moved her hand, rapidly, up and down, before her sister's glazing eyes, but Carrie was going nowhere.

"Go answer that, Loobie. Mother must still be upstairs."

Loobie slipped down from the settle, squeezed herself around the loom, and out into the hall. When she came back, it was with no uniformed dandy, no huddle of leering men who reeked of beer and powder, but with Rosalind and Eleanor. The twins had come back from selling their surplus wool to Harrison's on Earl Street.

"Mother locked us out!" Ros was nettled.

"You, or *them?*"

"Don't remind me – it took us an age to get through them!" Ros sank upon the bench before her loom and put her arm round Loobie's slender little middle.

"How are things in town?"

"The town has run mad! They're building barricades, or something!" Eleanor sounded positively cock-a-hoop.

"What?"

"We saw them! On Gabriel's Hill!"

"And Earl Street!" Ros chipped in. "They're digging up a lot of trenches." She twanged one of the cords on the loom like it was a harp string.

"And they're dragging furniture out of the shops and the houses – we saw them!"

Their mother came back, looking peppery. The linen was still in her arms. Too late, Carrie closed up the window again.

Mother was cross. "Haven't you girls anything better to do? Caroline? Caroline! What addles you? I've asked you once already."

Carrie looked at her. 'Caroline' always spelt trouble, but to hear it twice was doom. "Yes, Mother." She hopped obligingly off the settle.

"I wish Father was here!" Loobie declared, out of nowhere.

Nobody could think of a response. In time, Rebecca's thoughts pulled themselves back to more pressing, more mercenary matters. "Well, girls?" she asked the twins.

"We sold it, Mother," said Elle. "Two-and-six." Her fingers dug for the half-crown in the calfskin pouch she had strung round her waist. "It wasn't easy, but we persuaded Master Harrison into a sale."

"Wouldn't keep us so much as in peas!" snorted Ros.

Rebecca brushed aside her flippancy. "Half a crown is not a King's ransom, I'll warrant you, girls, but it will all add up in time." She pocketed the coin that she took from her daughter. "Master Harrison has not shut up shop, then?"

"No, but I don't doubt he has by now."

Rosalind rose from the stool. She was keen to gossip. "We met the Reverend Wilson in the street. He's quit All Saints', saying the Roundheads are welcome to it, and he wanted to know why we hadn't all tied up our bundles and quitted the house altogether."

"So did Reuben Igoe!" Carrie imparted.

Ros turned to her. "Saw him, did you?"

"Aye, just out there. He's probably halfway up Blue Bell Hill by now." Carrie shot another glance at the casement.

Rebecca looked at the twins. "Master Harrison is also leaving town?"

It was Elle who replied. "This very afternoon, he said. He says he'll take what he can carry, and the Army take the rest. Or the devil."

"Language!" warned her mother.

Elle protested. "I'm only repeating his words!"

Rebecca's lips flattened. "What did you two tell him?"

"Nothing!"

"Good," her mother nodded.

"Saw Master Radcliffe in town, as well. You know, the scrivener? He'd bolted up those chambers of his. Carrying about a ton of his books on his back. Looked white as a sheet."

"Well, wouldn't *you*?" demanded Carrie.

"What about it, though, Ma?" asked Ros. "It would seem that town is emptying!"

Rebecca bridled at the word "Ma". She trained her eyes upon her girls. She stood like one of the trees by the Tunbridge Road.

"And just *where* would we go?" she said. "Would you have us all load up our bundles, if you please, and spend our nights in a ditch, or under the stooks?"

"And why not? They are!" Ros pointed to the windows.

"I want Pip," mewled Loobie.

Carrie tabled: "Loobie's right. We should leave, now, and go to East Farleigh."

"Out of the question!" her mother snapped back. Her voice had gone brittle. "We have all of us known how it feels to be driven from our home, and once was quite enough. We stay."

The Agnew girls all looked from one to the other. None of them felt like drawing the unpleasant distinction between the spacious house they had ruled over in Barming, and this pokey little warren that Mother was forced to rent.

Rosalind's eyes had gone lively and defiant. She put on her pertest expression. "What next for us, Mother? Must we sell up the loom? Must Elle and I work the streets?"

Everybody stared at her.

"You impudent child! How could you DARE?"

Pale with rage, Rebecca stepped forward and slapped her daughter's face with all her strength.

It was one, eternal moment of stupefied shock, and nobody looked more shocked than Rebecca. Carrie's hand was at her mouth. Elle flinched; Loobie simply gawped. A smarting mark had blossomed on Rosalind's cheek, already showing livid and pink. She blinked at her mother. Her eyes began to bleed with tears.

Rebecca gasped. Her loss of control had appalled her. Her arms went out. "Oh, Ros! Ros, my dearest, I – "

Ros dodged her mother's embrace and stumbled from the room. Elle heard the beat of her twin sister's pattens as they pounded up the stairs.

TWENTY-EIGHT

Then to advise how war may best, upheld,
Move by her two main nerves: iron, and gold.

Rushworth traced the words with the dried-black nib. "'*Major-General Skippon to unhitch his forces from this, our main body, and proceed post-haste to take control of the Trained Bands, whereby he must ensue the welfare of the capital,*'" he read aloud.

"Good!" Fairfax assented. "And send Barnstead to move on Southwark with all haste; secure the left flank."

"So ordered, my lord." Rushworth scribbled down the gist of the General's words. He would cast the orders into proper, military shape in due course. His mood was buoyant. The move from Hounslow had passed without mishap, and not a single Royalist had appeared to oppose their forces. If the General kept on as they had, they could be at the coast in a week.

Fairfax smoothed his moustache with a long finger. "Our strength..." he commenced.

"Colonels Whalley and Rich will form our main body, in concert with Hewson's Foot. Commissary-General Ireton's Horse will safeguard the baggage."

Now the General turned to the smooth-cheeked, small-mouthed Commissary who was sitting at his elbow. "You must have your men ready to commit at a moment, if we need them," he said.

"So be it, Your Excellency." Henry Ireton was a slightly-built Midlander, of Puritan gentry stock. Thirty-seven years of age, his manner was aloof, and often silent. He did not believe in spinning words into the air unnecessarily.

Fairfax massaged his foot. "May the Lord's saints preserve me, this joint'll do me yet!" He had passed an agonising night upon his cot. The day had found him up and doing well before dawn.

Ireton studied the agonised foot. He was undismayed by its inflamed appearance. Gout was gout, and the cost a main paid for intemperance. "Mayhaps you'll get the chance to take the waters at Tunbridge Wells, my lord!" he remarked sardonically.

Fairfax didn't answer.

Ireton reached for a crust of bread and began to munch it absently. "May I assume it's your intention to give battle to these rebels when we meet them, my lord?"

"Or else tuck tail, and scurry back to London?" Fairfax winked at Rushworth, and the secretary grinned right back.

Ireton looked rather less frivolous. "Enough of these desert wanderings, my lord. The Medway is our Jordan."

"Or our Rubicon!" said Rushworth.

An officer had appeared in the tent flap. The secretary got up, and went to him. After a brief, whispered conference he turned back to the General.

"My lord? It seems – the delegation has arrived."

Fairfax, who was still digging away at his toe with his fingertips, looked up sharply. The news had made Ireton sit up, too. "Here? Already?"

Rushworth edged helpfully backwards. "Should I - ?"

"Aye, go," said Fairfax. "I'll join you presently."

Ireton rose from his stool. "Wait a minute, Rushworth! My lord?" He sounded agitated. "Uhm, my lord...?"

"Aye, man? What say you? Speak up."

"You intend to meet on terms with these fellows?"

"Certainly!"

Something twitched in Colonel Ireton's face. "They – they *are* traitors, sir."

"Mayhaps they be," shrugged Fairfax. "What point would you be about making?"

Ireton hesitated. "Well... now they're in our compass, I would have imagined that the most politic thing to do would be to put them all under close arrest."

"Now they're in their compass, Colonel Ireton, the most politic thing to do is to hear them out." Fairfax's gaze moved on to the waiting secretary. "John? Drive on. Go meet them."

"Aye my lord!" Rushworth hurried from the tent.

"I must say that I find this all quite unseemly, General." Ireton's disapproval was written large upon his face.

Fairfax spoke craftily. "Doubtless you will shortly furnish your father-in-law with the news of my misdemeanours?"

Ireton stared at him. "My lord! I'd not presume!"

"You would not presume..." Fairfax looked at Ireton with an expression that glided along on the borders of humour. "You know that, and I know that. But does the good General Cromwell know that?"

Rushworth surveyed the small huddle of uniformed men. They certainly didn't *look* like swaggering, dissolute braggarts. All their belts and scabbards were empty. Most were even without a back-and-breast cuirass. Doubtless they had had their weapons confiscated elsewhere in the camp as a precaution. The eldest of the pack held the Petition itself. Nine others were convened around him. Now they merely looked the part of county gentles who had assembled for a stroll in the late May sunshine.

"Gentlemen." Rushworth could almost smell their timidity.

The one with the parchment stepped forward. "Have I the honour of addressing His Lordship's secretary?"

"You do, and I am."

The delegate removed his floppy hat. The sun winked off a high forehead. "My name, sir, is Pegler. Colonel Hadrian Pegler." He kept things affable across the gulf of unfamiliarity. "We represent the interests of our King's subjects in the county of Kent." He showed off the officer who was standing by his side. "This is my second-in-command, Major Norrington."

A thirty-something man with a beaver's overbite made a show of salutation.

A new voice broke in behind Rushworth's back. "And that, I presume, is your oh-so valuable Petition?"

Rushworth turned. Ireton had joined them from the tent.

"You have guessed correctly, sir," said Pegler. He gave an optimistic bow, but Ireton looked upon the Kentish men with detached dispassion.

Major Norrington spoke up. "You'll pardon, sir? When the General joins us, I would prefer to be introduced as Sir Ambrose Norrington. I hold the Barony of Kemsing, in fact."

"Do you? Do you, now?" Rushworth was unimpressed with this bag of southern wind.

All conversation ceased as General Fairfax came hobbling out of his tent, his baton in his hand. The sight of the lankilyelegant General in his buff doublet and lace-fringed sash impressed the Kentish squirearchy. "Black Tom" Fairfax had to stand two yards high in his stockings!

The General was limping. Colonel Pegler, no stranger to the joint-devil himself, sensed a fellow in affliction. He tried a look of pity.

Ireton coughed. "Gentlemen. May I present and salute the Lord Fairfax?"

"My lord!" Pegler bent low. The others followed suit.

"Gentlemen. May I take this opportunity to greet you all?" said Fairfax, careful to return the civility. "Colonel Rushworth? Introductions, if you please?"

"These two gentlemen speak on behalf of the rest, Your Excellency. Colonel Pegler; Major Norrington."

"Ha-hem!" the Baron coughed.

"Your Excellency's pardon. I should have presented Major *Sir Ambrose* Norrington." Rushworth's voice increased its dose of acid.

Fairfax smiled upon them. "Colonel Pegler. Sir Ambrose. If you would be so kind as to step into my quarters? I shall not detain you long."

Pegler nodded, and turned to the ring around him. "Wait here, my men." He shunted Norrington before him. Ireton went with Fairfax. Rushworth brought up the rear, leaving the Petitioners to their own devices. Some seven thousand, heavily-armed soldiers were penning them in. What mischief could they make?

Back inside the stately tent, Fairfax hopped back to his customary stool. "May we help either of you to some refreshment, gentlemen? Some fruit? A glass of wine?"

Ireton ground his teeth. This was no time to sit around winebibbing! For their part, the Royalists declined with muttered thanks. They all sat down. Pegler held the Petition across his knees.

Fairfax surprised the pair by asking: "How does young Ned Hales these days?"

Norrington's look was blank. "Sir Edward Hales, my lord? I – I could not rightly say."

"Your county has thrown in in their lot with him, am I right?" Ireton's voice was icy. "With him, and with the Earl of Norwich?"

Their squirms could deny nothing.

Fairfax stroked his beard. "Sir Edward is very young, for a General." He conjured the face of his fellow MP from former, smoother days. He thought of Ned Hales' prim little mouth, and his failing moustache. "I trust you will extend him my greeting, should you encounter him."

Pegler took the helm. "Your Excellency, we are keenly desirous of being allowed passage to London, so that we may present this document to Parliament."

A smirk lit up Ireton's face. "Colonel Pegler, I regret to inform you that the Parliament may not even read it."

Pegler went white. "But – !"

"Thank you, Colonel Ireton - !" Now that they had finally broken through to the real issue, Fairfax looked upon Pegler and Norrington with a kind of tolerant pity. "Gentlemen, I do not doubt your worthiness. You are clearly held in high regard by those who sent you. But I cannot let you pass to London with that piece of paper."

"Then you violate our sovereign right of remonstrance, my lord," Pegler said earnestly.

"Colonel Pegler. You violated *your* sovereign rights the minute your pretty little towns declared for the King!" Fairfax said, unblinking.

Norrington looked openly vexed. "We only take up arms to defend ourselves, and our county's lathes. We make no trespass on the rights of the Parliament!"

"The Parliament, Sir Ambrose, might say otherwise." Fairfax saw the anger flickering to life in Pegler's pudgy cheeks.

"Gentlemen, let me be frank. I am fighting to defend the capital from rebels in arms. From *you*. Now, on the other hand, were you to lay down those arms and appeal for clement treatment, I am sure that the Parliament would forgive you."

The Kentish men exchanged a rather panic-stricken look at this departure from the script.

Pegler wetted his lips. "We — we have no mandate to negotiate such a thing, my lord."

"Such powers do not rest upon our shoulders!"

Fairfax's response was simple. "Well, then, Sir Ambrose. I suggest you come back when they do."

He rose to his feet.

"Colonel Rushworth will see you out."

"Rather too much liberality, I thought, my lord, for men in their position?" queried Ireton.

The General shrugged. His face was empty as a mask. "These Kentish squires are merely ciphers in this business. They know the truth — they've seen it. They'll scurry back to their masters with the news that Lord Fairfax is rolling down upon them with an army like an avalanche." He hefted up his foot and started to give it another massage. "Every hour, they'll fear the hooves of our Dragoons. And every night they'll lay them down to rest in fear we'll give them battle in the morning."

Rushworth returned through the tent flap. He had finished playing shepherd to the tottering Royalist delegates.

Fairfax looked up. "Escorted off the premises, John?"

"Aye, my lord. I believe we can say we sent 'em packing!"

"Ah, we have not landed 'em yet," said Fairfax, "even if they are on the hook. This is, in all, a civil war. The most distasteful thing Mars has among his chattels."

He sought solace in skinning a pear with a pearl-handled knife.

"This is no foreign invader we may drive into the sea," he went on, "this is Briton fighting Briton."

"Our cause is just," rapped Ireton. "And God will give us the strength."

"Aye!" affirmed Rushworth. "Your men, my lord, will do their duty. However distasteful they reckon it."

"And you think these rebels won't act in like manner?" The General's mouth had dipped at all its corners. "It's their county, isn't it?"

Rushworth had to yield to His Excellency's point.

"And what then?" Fairfax pursued. "No matter who emerges with the victory, we shall all still be Englishmen. What ways shall we devise for ourselves, that we may coexist when this business is over?"

TWENTY-NINE

*Where throngs of knights and Barons bold
In weeds of Peace, high triumphs hold.*

To the Earl of Norwich, the sloping shoulder of Blue Bell Hill seemed to be sneering at him.

"Where, in God's arse, is Fairfax?"

Dudley had learned to withstand the Earl's saturnine wrath. The shrug he returned was deprecating. "Rebuffed the Petitioners at Blackheath was the last of our intelligence – and coming on hard."

"What have the scouts seen?" Norwich demanded.

"So far, only *his* scouts. The occasional Troop of Horse. It'll avail us nothing to pick 'em off piece-work, m'lord."

"Hell's teeth!" Norwich surveyed the tented, sprawling expanse of his army of rebellion. Its camp on Burham Heath was a one big din: hooves on hard ground, the clink of trace chains, the perfecting of drill manuals under the eyes of Sarjeants and harassed Corporals. The anvils were raging. The farriers were working apace. All across the scene, men squatted at their saucepans of molten lead, casting ounce-weight balls for hungry muskets.

Some concentrated action attracted the Earl's peripheral eye. A long, coiling, column of men marching in fours were entering the outskirts of the camp. Norwich watched them, picking their way around guy ropes, past the ranks of grazing horses on the picketing lines.

"Who are they?" he pointed.

Dudley looked. "The East Kent men. Been on the march since Monday. All the way up from Hythe, I believe."

The Earl looked them over. Grizzled, stubbled veterans were trudging along with boys whom Norwich thought had barely cut the apron strings. All of them shouldered a matchlock. Some looked like they had even taken down their grandsire's ancient arquebus.

"They seem well accoutred. Half-decent order."

"Aye, my lord, they're hardy men."

"I'll grant they *look* like they know what they're doing... 'Tis well that someone does."

Dudley looked at the older man, alerted by the shift in tone of His Lordship's voice.

Norwich brushed it off. "Ah, pay me no heed. It was just a passing thought, Sir Gamaliel."

Dudley coughed. "Perhaps, m'lord, you'd care to pass it over my way?"

Norwich sighed, then turned his back once and for all on Blue Bell Hill. He leaned upon his heavy-topped cane. "I'm an old man, Dudley, but I'm not a fool. We cannot fight this war alone. We can only sit on daily expectations of assistance from our fellows in Essex."

Dudley was practical. "Then, m'lord, I will say that I shall pray nightly for the coming of that day."

Abruptly, Norwich stomped away among the tents. Dudley waited a bit before he followed him. Neither of them said a word until the Earl had retraced his steps to his own bivouac. He needed to bury himself in the security of his maps.

"We must now consider the division of our forces," he said, as Kent was spread out upon his lap once again. "Be so good as to round up Sir William Brockman and his Lieutenants. Tend them my compliments, and prevail upon them to join me forthwith."

Dudley slipped away, returning presently with the Sheriff and his two companions in authority, Sir John Mayney and Sir Conor Forker. Mayney and Forker were middle-aged, experienced Kentish hands, and Norwich had high hopes for them in the fighting to come.

His Lordship rose to greet them. "Gentlemen! I will be brief in my orders. Sir John, you are to proceed with all dispatch towards Aylesford. You must protect the passes of the river from General Fairfax's troops. Is this in any way unclear?"

Mayney had a quick, sidelong look at Brockman and Forker. "In no way, my lord."

"Very well. You have your orders. The men under your command are to deny the enemy his axis of advance."

"They are honest fellows, my lord. They'll serve you faithfully," Mayney guaranteed.

Norwich nodded. "Go with God, then."

Mayney about-faced, his brace of Lieutenants following in his wake. It wasn't long before the Trumpets commenced to sound, and the tempo of the camp began its exponential quickening. Brockman's men would march within the hour. Norwich sank upon his camp bed and, resting his elbows on his knees, pressed his fingers into his throbbing temples. His throat had dried up. The stimulus of light had begun to stab him in the eyes. He could sense a dawning migraine. How he wished he could awaken some heart-buried energy of the professional soldier.

"A glass of sack, Sir Gamaliel." It was more a command than a request.

Dudley decanted the vintage into a goblet. "Would you care to confide your woes, my lord?" he asked, as he handed it over.

Norwich's breathing laboured with his lassitude. His coat felt very tight across his ribcage. The enterprise was weighing on his soul. He felt crushed with the stress of the thing. Military adventuring spelt careful preparation, and nimble action when the moment required. This was suddenly so much more than lines on a map, and the movement of phantom chessmen. This was blood, and bodies. This was men cut down like sickled grain.

"Damnation, I am no General, man!" he groaned in a grey voice. "To be Master of the King's Horse stood for little but a glorified groom!"

Moments passed, tedious and hard-edged. Then Dudley said, "Well, then, going by his youthfulness, m'lord, it follows our Sir Edward Hales ought never designated a General, either."

"That remark is flat mutiny, Sir Gamaliel!"

Dudley performed his characteristic gesture of rubbing the side of his nose with his thumb. He looked more than ever like a figure from a folk tale. A brownie, in a buff coat. "'Tis a curious thing, m'lord, how the avalanche of mutiny is often triggered by the grains of truth."

The Earl's broad face still concealed what the voice could not. "Ought I to annul his Generalship? By whose authority?"

"Your own, m'lord."

"Condemn a man for his inexperience and youth, while I, his elder and commander, am less experienced myself?"

"M'lord?" Dudley recommended. "The generalship…"

"Throw generalship to the dogs, Sir Gamaliel! This expedition is worth more than the name or the face of one man."

Sir Gamaliel Dudley studied the peer's fast-dissolving dignity. "The choice is with you, Your Lordship," was all he said.

"But... who else – ?" The question was not rhetorical.

Dudley stroked his beard. "Sir Henry Washington?"

"Of Worcester fame?"

"Aye, m'lord. Or Colonel Thomas Culpepper. He's a local man – from Leeds. He knows the byways, and we might well have need of them if the business turned tough."

"Our aid must come. It *must* come!" Norwich lifted his eyes to the northward horizon. He envisaged the county town, skirted by dumpy hills, and veined by high-banked lanes. He drained his crystal goblet. It helped him begin to recover. "Let us put out of our mind how things count upon the eye; come take a look at this." The Earl's index finger tapped the map, right on the Medway's course to the south-east of Maidstone. "Here. The crossing at East Farleigh."

"I observe it, m'lord."

"Know this spot, do you?"

"Aye, m'lord. The road descends the hill from Barming, from the crossroads near the Heath."

"Describe the scene."

Dudley blew out his cheeks. "Well, the bridge is fourteenth-century, and the passage there is narrow in the extreme. I consider it most unlikely that General Fairfax could make an easy thrust through it."

"A bridge is still a bridge. A useful crossing."

"Aye, but not all crossings are created equal, m'lord. That particular bridge is over three hundred years old. It is quite insubstantial for the Parliament's siege guns, or the passage of heavy transport."

"Nevertheless, we have posted detachments of our men to overwatch it?"

"Indeed. Sir William deployed his local levies, supported by a battery of guns from the Maidstone garrison. Their numbers are low, but they've stout hearts."

Norwich said: "Stout hearts? They'll need 'em."

"Let us yet be confident, m'lord."

"Confident, aye! Brockman must hold the Aylesford crossing," he declared. "By the Lord Harry, he must! Else this time next week we'll all find ourselves slaves to the Puritans' whips."

The Earl's lined forehead was beginning to burn once more. The migraine burrowed into his skull like a mole scraping deeper and deeper.

THIRTY

Owls and cuckoos, asses, apes and dogs.

Sitting on their mounts, the senior officers of the New
Model Army could see Rochester clearly through their perspective
glasses. The square stumps of the Norman cathedral were
wrapped in drifting cloud. The bridge had been destroyed. The
Earl of Norwich had brought forth his sappers to do the job
proficiently. The Medway was impassable: the current saw to that.
Rochester's priceless arsenal was still in the hands of the King's
men, and so it would remain. The New Model Army snapped
away their glasses, turned their horse's heads, and headed back the
way they had come.

Philippa knew none of that, of course.
She and Stephen were sitting in the bed of the stage
waggon. It was a fat wooden elephant on wheels, drawn along in
no great hurry by a team of bone-headed bullocks. The valley
trundled past at the pace of a snail. Stephen could not crawl about
and explore, for he and Mother had been penned in by great
baskets and crates, and a whole gallery of staging passengers.
Chief among their companions was an ageing farmer who'd kept
going on about how he had mounted the waggon at dawn from a
ditch in Sevenoaks, and who swore before the Living God that
Martha would wallop him the minute he got back to Aylesford. He
glossed his talk with a lot of growling swigs from a dark green
bottle which he declined to pass around. Its stopper had come
adrift on the road out of Tunbridge. The amber liquid trickled
down his chin and over his neck. Stephen found him very funny,
though Mother carefully looked the other way to avoid his breath.
They had parted from Father on the road outside the
Rectory. They had waved from the waggon, and waved again, and
blown him their kisses. Father had already put his vestments on,
for the interment was soon according to Saint Mary's clock.
Mother had cast a long, long look back towards the village.
Stephen hadn't worked out if she were staring at Father, or at the

big guns that were getting into position on the ridge beside the river...

Mother's hand was on his shoulder. "Stephen? Nay, do not lean so far out – supposing you fall?"

Stephen retreated into the waggon bed. He was an obedient child as a rule, but when he failed to work out the logic in what he was told, he would do as he wished with an ease that his mother found distracting.

Through his haziness, the drunken farmer gave the lad the most enormous, commiserating wink.

The waggon crunched through a particularly deep pothole. Up top, everybody lurched from side to side. Philippa caught her elbow on the planks, right on the funny bone! She tipped her capotain hat a little straighter over her brow. The aching slowness had reminded her how Stephen had never got the chance to ride Fulke. Old Fulke would have looked very well in the Parsonage's little stable. She would have dearly loved to help Stephen learn to brush and comb Fulke's conker-coloured coat, and teach him to affix the straps and girth. It would have been a proud day when Stephen could go out for a hack on his own...

Philippa looked up. Even by their dithering standards, she could tell they were slowing down. The cantankerous driver was reining in his motive power.

She got herself up into a kneeling position and peered around the driver's brawny, old-coated frame. "What is going on?"

"Soldiers." The man didn't mince his words.

They were out on the outskirts of Maidstone, at the confluence of the Len, near the old Workhouse. The ground had been scraped of its topsoil and planted with stakes. Grubbing in the earth, standing up to their waists in their trenches, was a phalanx of waiting men.

The driver was resigned. "No getting our way past that lot, Mistress!"

"Whassamarrer?" blurred their companion, shaking the final few drips from his bottle.

When he was told that he would have to dismount, and would likely be walking the rest of the way to Aylesford, he used all the impious words in his repertoire. Philippa covered her son's ears with her hands and glared daggers at the souse.

The passengers surrendered to their lot. They picked their way down from the waggon bed. They helped Philippa down to the ground with considerate caution, then passed her little son into her arms, and finally handed her that deep basket covered with a linen cloth.

Philippa walked with head high towards the huddled men. She saw the nervous tension engraved upon their faces. What a motley crew. Older men, perhaps a veteran here and there. Young farmhands, short and undernourished, and unfamiliar with military weaponry. They all had fresh matches in their locks. They were being overseen by a very fat Sarjeant, whose belt had been loosened out to its furthest little hole. He carried a spontoon in his gauntleted fist.

Stephen kept very close to Mother's skirts.

Philippa stopped. "Good day, gentlemen," she said, politely.

The Sarjeant addressed her with a gruff compassion on his well-fleshed face. "Wouldn't chance your hide around here, Mistress. Nor your lad. Things don't look too healthy."

Philippa nodded. The fact was unembroidered. When Parliament's Dragoons came sweeping down this road like the vanguard of the Apocalypse, she knew who these farmhands would look to.

The Sarjeant turned, and beckoned with his spontoon. "Let 'em pass, boys."

The phalanx peeled apart.

"Stephen? Come on."

They walked up Gabriel's Hill, past the old chapel and brewhouse, into the commercial heart of the town. Stoccados had been built across the cobbles, the way you saw the strata of ages running through a cliff. They had mostly been thrown together from a lot of domestic furniture and lumber. Behind one barricade flew the Kentish Petitioners' Standard. It was an ox-blood cross on a snowy background, with a Latin motto in silver thread.

Maidstone's narrow houses looked deserted. Even The Ship, and The George, those most reliable of hostelries, looked tired and forlorn, like they had abandoned themselves to their fate. If Philippa looked up, she could see broken windows. The holes in the panes were small and neatly punched. An accidental ball from a loaded matchlock, or a dare for a hasty bet? If she looked again, she could see muskets poking through the casements, gripped in the hands of waiting snipers.

The garrison was starting to notice the tall young woman with the basket and boy. Philippa straightened her back. She drew in breath: Stephen was no longer at her side. She stopped and turned round.

"Stephen?"

Stephen was staring at a little circle of men who were studiously busy with the game of dice they had set up on a doorstep.

One of those gambling farmboys whined: "Stand be our little piece! Will you not favour me with the tin, Corporal, and I'll pay up tomorrow?"

His Corporal loosed a snort of experienced doubt.

"Stephen? Hold my hand. That is not a request."

He scurried to join her. Once more she felt his little fingers between her own.

They were approaching a gap in the barricades, barely wide enough for a gun to squeeze through, and easy enough to shut up at the sign of trouble. What might they use to stop it up? More plundered furniture? The corpus of a raw-boned farmboy with his snaphance at the ready? Philippa shuddered at the thought.

They had reached the summit of Gabriel's Hill, only to find themselves staring down the maw of a bronze cannon. An artilleryman was exploring the back of the cannon's gullet with an enormous sponge on the end of a pole. There stood the Market Cross, where High Street smacked into King Street. The guns had been drawn up around that ancient structure, compass-rose style.

They pushed on. The twisting length of Week Street, with all its contiguous houses, felt like one of those corridors you must navigate in an unforgiving dream.

"Mooother?"

"What is it?"

"Why are the streets all filled with the soldiers?"

"They're waiting, my darling."

"What for?"

"I know not. And by the looks of them, neither do they."

Philippa quickened her stride. She would drag Stephen to the house; carry him if need be.

Clipping along beside her, Stephen attempted to puzzle Mother's words through. It made no sense to block the roads when people wanted to use them. It made no sense why anyone should borrow some lumps of tin off a Corporal. And it *certainly* made no sense to set up big bronze cannon all over the place, without anybody stopping to tell you why they were doing it.

A couple of the doors they passed were idling on their hinges, like the owners had cleared out in a hurry without bothering to make the house fast. Outside Number Twenty-Seven, though, Philippa saw nothing to indicate that anything was amiss. The house still had all its glass in its panes. Its plasterwork was still mottled and streaked by rain. The heart's ease still aimed high.

Rebecca answered their knock. She gave thanks for the return of her most resourceful ally. With uncharacteristic passion, she ha thrown her arms around her daughter before Philippa could even close the door. "I am so, *so* pleased to see you!" said Rebecca.

Stephen darted off down the passage, attracted by the sounds of someone throwing dough in the kitchen.

Philippa shook the dust of the streets from her shoes. She still stank very faintly of old wood and bullock dung. "I only half expected to find you gone, you know," she said. "I knew you would never just lock up and leave without word."

"Indeed. For where would we go?" rejoined Rebecca.

Her daughter paused in the act of removing her hat. "Well, you could have always -"

"No, Pip!" Rebecca said, talking straight over her daughter. "We have been over that before, and I will not enter into it now. That Parsonage of yours is poky enough. And I have been forced out of one house in my lifetime already. "

Philippa took the hint. "Nathan sends love." She added, with a little mock-formality, "He tenders his respect, and laments his absence from the Lady of the House."

"How very gallant of him," his mother-in-law remarked.

"Have the Turners left from Twenty-Eight?"

"Yes: this morning," Rebecca nodded. "They've sent the Army in," she added, quite unnecessarily. "Old men and boys. Since yesterday. *And* they're bringing up the guns," Rebecca warned.

"We know. Stephen and I had to walk straight through them."

"Oh, Pip!" Rebecca's hand was at her mouth.

"The troops have moved in on East Farleigh, Mother. We can see them from the Rectory They've arrayed some of their cannon at the bridge," her daughter divulged.

"Lord of mercy!" breathed Rebecca, shaking her head.

"What have we for dinner?" Philippa was being pragmatic.

"Chicken. The others are making it ready. I thought we'd roast it now and eat the rest for our supper. If anything's left, that is," she reminded herself aloud.

"We'll be strict with ourselves. I shall see to it." Philippa laid her hand on her mother's arm.

"It's a miracle to have it at all – there's barely a capon left in the whole of Maidstone!"

"Plenty of roosters, though," Philippa observed without irony.

Her mother's silence was unnerving.

"I suppose the girls have been in star-eyed reveries about the officers?" Philippa asked.

"Ros was most impertinent," Rebecca replied, with straightforward indignation. "I'm afraid I had to strike her. She actually implied that she – " She broke off.

"Implied what?" her daughter prompted.

There was quite a lot of guilty hesitation. "Nothing."

"Mother?" Philippa pressed, for she had seen Rebecca's downcast blushes.

"Nothing, I say!" Rebecca spoke her words repressively. "Come: help me lay up the table."

She led the way into the front chamber. Philippa opened a drawer in the dresser. "Where are the napkins?"

"I put them in the chest. The key is in the other drawer." The table cloth fluttered and curled as Rebecca threw it out and began to straighten it.

Philippa found the key and got down on her knees by the old oak chest that stood against the wall. Rebecca looked long and hard at the back of her daughter's head. "I know what you have been meaning to say, Pip."

Philippa twisted her head to see. "What?"

"You are wondering what your father would have done."

Her daughter said nothing, but her face confirmed enough.

"You see? I knew it exactly." Rebecca straightened the linen with the tips of her fingers.

Philippa sat back on her heels. "Well?"

Her mother smoothed out an unsightly crease in the cloth. "Oh, I'll warrant your father would have been out there, right enough. Trying to be everywhere at once."

Philippa almost smiled. It was one of their little mutual treats, to talk about her father.

"You know, the funny thing is, I could not thinking of Fulke on the ride over," she shared.

"Poor old Fulke..." Rebecca permitted herself a moment of silent remembrance before she started to place the cutlery out in acceptable patterns.

Philippa turned the key and opened up the chest. "But it is true what you say: Father would have even relegated Achilles himself if he had had the chance."

"Him, and Fulke together!" said her mother.

Loobie came bounding in, and at once flung herself on her sister.

"Alright, Loobie, alright: I am here, I am *here!*" Philippa wriggled her neck free from the arms of her clinging little sibling, and turned to give Loobie a kiss.

"Is the chicken roasting nicely, child?" asked Rebecca.

"Aye, Mother! Carrie says it surely won't be long." Loobie had picked up a fork from the table and was twirling it.

"It does smell good," said Philippa, sifting the chest's contents.

Rebecca added, "We even managed to procure some rosemary, would you believe?"

"I would! It's like gold," said Philippa.

Rebecca looked back at Loobie. "Alright, lambkin: go now and lend the others a hand."

Loobie skipped off back to the kitchen. She took the fork with her.

Philippa had nearly counted off as many napkins as they needed. Only one more was still proving elusive. Then, in clearing away a great heap of old linen, she revealed –

"Mother, look!"

Rebecca turned. Philippa had the collar of her father's old campaign coat in her hands.

"Oh!" she remarked. "So that was where I left it."

Her daughter stood up. "I suppose I had always hoped that you wouldn't be rid of it." She held the long garment up in front of her by its shoulders. It reached to just below her knees. Then she brought it up to her nose and inhaled deeply. She'd forgotten its smell, and how heavy it was.

Next moment, she was burying her hands down the sleeves. Her mother stood and watched her as the coat enfolded Philippa's frame. "Well?"

"It fits me still!" Philippa said, somewhat in wonder.

A muscle twitched in Rebecca's face. "Put it back in the box, Pip."

Philippa divested herself of the coat. She folded it over one arm and returned with it to the chest. She peered down, then stopped. A large, flat wooden box was lying at the very bottom of the chest. She knew it at once. Her father's initials were engraved on the rosewood lid. She laid the coat down on the floor, then she reached down into the chest and hauled up the box.

"Mother?"

"What is it?" Philippa showed her the box, and her eyes went wide. "Now how did that –?"

"I thought that you had sent this to the auction!"

"And I thought *you* did!"

Philippa undid the little metal hook and lifted the lid. "Empty." She showed her mother the dusty padded lining of red velvet, and the two scimitar-shaped impressions.

"But – we surely never..." Rebecca's hand was at her forehead. "Why would we have kept the box and not – ? Oh, it makes no sense."

Philippa got to her feet. "Mayhaps they are still somewhere up in the garret?"

"No, Pip!" her mother said, as a cold panic flooded her.

"It's an eventuality." Philippa's voice was bland. She edged around her mother.

"But this is madness!" Rebecca wailed. "You surely don't intend to go hunting for the things now?"

Philippa walked out into the hall. "I shan't be long."

Rebecca resisted with a grinding hopelessness. "But, we're about to have our dinner! Pip!"

She chased her daughter to the foot of the stairs, terror-struck at the idea of her daughter tearing the garret apart in search of powder horn and ball.

Philippa stopped and looked down at her. Her mother's face was a jumble of panic. "Father tutored us for a reason, Mother. And besides, with a house full of women... in a town full of men..."

Rebecca made a last appeal. "Philippa! Philippa, wait!"

Philippa simply ignored her. By the time she reached the landing, her own words were waiting to greet her.

A house full of women... in a town full of men...

THIRTY-ONE

In Vain doth Valour bleed
While Avarice and Rapine share the land.

The timber-framed cottage in Aylesford was in chaos. Over Magner's head, pattens and hobnailed shoes resounded on the floorboards. His companions darted from room to room, uncovering every cranny. An occasional curse let him know when a skull had collided with a low beam. Men dashed along the cottage's misaligning passages, up and downstairs two at a time. All was fair for their game in this house. They broke open the hanging presses, the cupboards, the wardrobes, and disembowelled their contents.

Magner stood stock still and stroked his beard. His other hand clutched an old rosary. He swung it on its beads until it looped around his fingers. Then he swung the thing the other way, till the Christ dangled from his hand like the condemned from Tyburn Tree.

In the kitchen, a low extension at the rear of the cottage, the pillagers really whiffed a profitable enterprise. Another, bigger crucifix had been tacked to the wall by the window.

"'Tis the house of a frigging Papist right enough!" one of them cried.

"Aye; explains the smell of pizzle!" his companion chortled.

A third man turned from his analysis of the larder. He had a pasty in his hand and he was munching it. He addressed the white-haired, bird-like little woman whose nest this was. "Whassis, you Romish sow?" he demanded, through a mouthful of shortcrust and venison.

The distracted little old wren looked at the tray he had meant. "They're – they're sweet meats," she cheeped. "Only a platter of sweet meats."

"Touch 'em not!" advised his fellow, who had stuffed a silver drinking cup in the pocket of his doublet. "They's probably laced with poisons."

"You're right, I reckon." Still holding the pasty, the third man used his free hand to send the tray of sweets to the floorboards with a frightful clatter. By now they had done with the kitchen, and their stampede took them back to the parlour. The Sarjeant stood before the chimney breast and watched his rollicking hounds. An elderly man, the owner of this dwelling, was huddled on a stool in front of him. His arms were crossed. His palms rested on his elbows. He was rocking very slightly, hunched in upon himself.

"Tom here says there's a store of bacon in the roof, Sarge," said the one with the pasty.

All the old man did was moan. Magner went on absently twirling the rosary.

"And Chaloner has gone to find us a fowl from the coop." The man Tom Gomes slapped his fellows' shoulders in high good humour. "We'll feast like kings tonight, my bucks!"

One of their number, a squash-nosed wheelwright by the name of Peter Jacomb, had hung back in the kitchen when the others had left. Now he entered the parlour clutching the handle of a flat-bottomed kettle. "There's more 'n a man could carry in a month of Fridays, Salathiel."

His friend Salathiel Tams grinned. "I'll warrant we'll be needing us a cart!"

Now Magner opened his mouth for the first time. "Once you have finished stuffing your face with that pie, Private Gomes, you might clear the upstairs rooms of the rest of your section."

Gomes' mouth was too full to make reply, but he nodded and went away, sucking at his fingers.

The old woman sidled round these muscly, frightening men. She kept one eye upon the soldier they called "Sarge". Not because he had a wheel-lock pistol shoved into his belt, but because he was swinging her mother's old rosary beads with an uncaring expression, and she feared for the strength of the string. A low profile seemed the better part of valour, so she went to join her husband. She crouched on her haunches beside him. She made sure that her husband could feel it when she put her hands on his arm for comfort. She felt him tremble at her touch.

The old man raised his head and stared beseechingly at Sarjeant Magner. "I do not understand!" he croaked, for perhaps the hundredth time. "Why are you doing this? What wrong have we done that we must deserve such treatment?"

"Papist bastard!" Tams muttered darkly.

Magner silenced him with an eyebrow. "Nay, the time is ripe, lads," he said plainly. "These persons have a right to see our letters of authority."

From a pocket in his breeches he produced a sheet of paper that had been folded many times. He held the warrant out, near enough for the old couple to see that it carried a couple of loopy, extravagant signatures.

The old man reached out a hand. "Let me see it."

Magner promptly snatched it back and hid it away in his pocket. "For military eyes only. Strict regulations – it is not to be read by the populace. Suffice to say it permits me, as His Majesty's non-commissioned officer at war, to requisition what I deem appropriate for the welfare of his troops."

His companions had had enough of this charade. In any case, the last of their number had returned from the small outhouse at the bottom of the garden. Dick Chaloner carried a stoppered stone jug, and had a dead chicken tucked into his waistbelt.

"Hold hard! What have you got there, Private Chaloner?" demanded Magner.

"'Tis a gallon of – *hic!* – of pear cider, Sarge."

Magner was alerted by the Private's very incoherent speech. "Did you imbibe of that stuff on an empty stomach?"

"I – I might've, Sarge."

"God strike you, Private Chaloner! You'll be as drunk as a judge!" cried the Sarjeant.

"Aw, now speak comfort to the rolling short-arse, Sarge!" leered Salathiel Tams.

The old Catholic's stool overturned as he rose to all of his five-foot-three. "In the name of heaven, are we to be left with *anything*?"

His wife hid her face in her hands.

"You'll be left with your lives, if you're lucky!" threatened Tams, with flashing eyes.

Gomes came in, mouth now free of pastry, with a couple more fellows in his train. "Finished the upper floor, Sarge."

Magner did not acknowledge this new intelligence. On the contrary, he was more concerned with Gomes and Jacomb's friend, the wayward sot. "Private Chaloner! I order you not to touch

229

another drop!" he snapped, as he saw the stopper being lifted again. "Let us conclude our business here and go!"

It was Tams who exclaimed: "'Ere! I thought as we were allowed to plunder nobody but Roundheads, Sarge?"

Magner rolled his eyes. "You are yet but young in service, Private Tams! When will you learn that we'll make every man a Roundhead that has anything to lose?" The paragon stepped down off the hearth. "Sarjeant Magner never leaves his men unfriended, boys."

"We ain't your men!" throbbed Chaloner.

"No more you are. And which of us is the better off for it, I'll wonder?" Magner's eyes locked on the newly-wrung fowl that swung by its neck from Chaloner's belt. "Mine's the chicken, thank you, Private."

"The devil it is! Turd-face!" Chaloner was swaying, and Tams took the precaution of relieving him of the precious flagon.

Magner's eyes grew darker. "Please, do not annoy me, Private Chaloner."

Chaloner merely laughed.

Magner looked at the inebriated man the way an owl looks down upon its mouse. "I'll give you one chance more, Private Chaloner, and I urge to obey me. You may be Sarjeant Beale's problem day to day, and thank the Lord, but you'd find me a dangerous man to fall foul of."

The old Catholic couple froze, not a nerve of theirs in motion. Chaloner moved first. Before anyone knew what was happening, his rage-fuelled fist had buried itself in the Sarjeant's gut. Magner sprawled on the whitewashed hearth. "You son of a whoring bitch!" spat Chaloner.

A figure appeared in the doorway. Putting a hand to its mouth, it called, "Boys! Hey, boys! There's armed men a-running up the lane. They's coming for us!"

This news proved too much for Private Tams, who about-faced and dashed for the door, dumping his ill-gotten flagon with a cry of, "Scatter, lads – before the Provosts come!"

The Section took his word, and hurried from the house. Chaloner's moment of Marathon victory was short-lived. Magner succeeded in rising and in driving his own fist into Chaloner's stomach with a snarl. The Private's knees buckled and he sank, eyes goggling, to the floor. The Monmouth cap slipped forward off his brow. Next thing Magner had drawn the wheel-lock from his belt and had cocked the hammer. His hand pulled Chaloner up by the hair, lifting his head. His eyes were full of murder. The old woman shrieked as Magner levelled the pistol at a spot just behind Chaloner's right ear.

"Drunk's a flogging. Rape's a hanging." His voice was a maleficent whisper. "You struck a superior officer, and besmirched his good name, in the presence of witnesses. You're a dead man now, Master Chaloner."

A dark shadow cut across the solid bar of sunlight. Rapid feet were crunching on the gravel. Everybody froze. A middle-aged officer, clothed, cloaked, and hatted all in black, burst into the room. A drawn cross-handed sword was in his hand. It was Sir Conor Forker, and the armed men at his back were his personal retinue. The old woman screamed again at the sight of their corselets and triple-barred helmets. She pressed herself tight to her husband.

"What the blazes is going on?" was Forker's opening.

Magner sized up his opponent. This was a hard-eyed officer, a man of weight and experience, not some green, ill-judging Ensign. His mind began to whir. Sir Conor would see right through him. He thought of it ... The shame ...

"I asked a question!" Forker was looking at the old couple, who were far too stricken by shock to give him any answers. Chaloner was still drinking gulps of air like a drowning man. Magner let go the man's scruff. It was now or never.

"This man did assault me, sir. His confederates raided this good woman's pantry, and all of this gentleman's wearing apparel they met with."

"Aye, we saw 'em running pell for leather on the road," said Forker. He sheathed his sword in its scabbard again. "Could you swear to 'em?"

Magner did not rush things. "Hard to reason, sir – it all happened so quick. But one thing's plain for sure, sir: they were Company men. And they'd have compelled this old gentleman to take 'em to where he hides his money had I not intervened. Glorying in their shame, they were, sir, when I found 'em."

Forker looked from Magner, to the man on his knees on the floor. "An assault, you say?"

"Indeed, sir! Before this couple's very eyes!"

Forker turned to the old man and wife. "Is this true?"

They nodded briskly. Their thin bodies shook with emotion. They were so terrified, they would probably have shouldered the blame for the War itself if only they'd been so charged.

"What are your names?"

The old man freed his throat. "John – John Jenkin, Your Honour. This is my wife, Mary."

Forker looked down at Private Chaloner. He curled his lip. "You two!" he instructed his men. "Get this creature on his feet."

Chaloner was suddenly aware of being in the grip of four very determined hands. Dry-throated, he tried to protest, but Forker was having none of it. "Speak me no speeches, sirrah! Keep your tongue behind your teeth!"

Chaloner lapsed into silence. Magner handed Forker his sheet of folded paper. "For you, sir, by your leave. I took the precaution."

"Precaution, sirrah? Why, what is this?"

"I found it on the floor, sir. Patently dropped by the rascals in flight. 'Tis the warrant they used to obtain entry for their plunder. A clever forgery, like as not!"

Forker read it through. "Or not so clever."

"Why, sir?" asked Magner, surprisedly.

"This warrant makes out it bears the name of His Majesty King Charles himself!"

"*Does* it, sir?" Magner peered to look.

Forker shook his head. "Why, this conduct is more infamous than Malta or Algiers!"

"I quite agree with you, sir," Magner said immediately. "And now, if you will permit me, I must return this good lady her property." He put the rosary back into the hands of the quivering little woman. "Yours, dear Madam." His smile spelt contrition. Mary Jenkin avoided his eye.

Forker folded up the sheet of paper. "We'll take this along as evidence. You are to be commended, sirrah," he said to Magner, and he sounded impressed.

Magner bowed. "Sarjeant, by your leave, sir."

"Sarjeant, is it? Then as Sarjeant you will fully appreciate the penalty for having an undisciplined Section."

Magner was nimble with his narrative. "The fault was not mine, sir!" he returned. "I was here on my lawful occasions."

"*What* lawful occasions?" Forker frowned.

"Why, an errand, sir, for Captain Marchington. A bucket of Adam's Ale."

"Adam's what? Oh! You mean water."

"Aye, sir. Doubtless you observed that discarded pail by the door?"

Forker turned to look at the thing. "Since you ask, yes. I nearly fell over the damned thing."

"I distress to have so encumbered you, sir, but so rapidly did I interpose myself on behalf of these good people, I discarded it with some haste."

Actually, it had been Private Jacomb who had discarded it with some haste, in his flight.

Forker's eyes bored into Magner. "Am I to understand, Sarjeant, that not one of these looters was under your command? This man here is not of your Section?"

"You are correct, sir. This scoundrel is not one of mine," said Magner. He dipped his neck at Forker. "I merely interceded out of concern for the good name of our Army."

Chaloner had recovered sufficiently to yelp the one word, "Ballocks!"

"Hold your tongue!" Forker whipped his words at him. "You are the rancid slags of your regiment, sirrah – you, and your swinish confederates! Who is it has the dubious honour of your Colonelcy?"

"Colonel Pegler." Chaloner mumbled.

"He shall shortly be informed of your disgrace. A fine, upstanding man, and you would shame him in this way? Well, you shall answer for it. Just as soon as we draw up the charges!"

"But!" Chaloner kicked back. "But he – "

"But me no buts, sirrah, 'less you want to be took for a goat, as well as a cur!"

Magner gave a helpful cough. "Ahem? With regard to your charge sheet, Your Honour...? Striking a superior officer;

unlawful looting of the populace? Surely the only penalty is to put a rope to his neck?"

The colour ran from Chaloner's face. His flesh had turned to chalk.

Forker was gruff. "I am quite familiar with the tenets of military law, thank you, Sarjeant."

"Sarjeant Magner, sir. Sarjeant Kill-Sin Magner, at your service."

"Kill-Sin?" Forker's tongue now planted deep inside his cheek. He was bold to say: "It makes quite the appropriate name, does it not?"

The buff-coated cavalry learned that Maidstone's Great Bridge had also been soundly destroyed. A craggy, forty foot gap had been blown in its central archway. Even so, that did not prevent the leading files from edging their mounts to the parapet and glaring at the town arrayed against them. The darkening clouds threw a queer light across the tiled roofs. About a hundred yards away across the water, scores of jeering Royalists were gesticulating at them, waving hats, and pikes, and snaphance muskets in the air. Their proprietary jeers rang loud across the river.

The Ironsides wheeled about with a slow and calculated dignity, all the while feigning to ignore those hotheaded levies. The old campaigners could sense that, in their amateurish inefficiencies, those Kentish men had left a chink somewhere. And they meant to find it.

Sarjeant Magner left the Jenkins' house with a swaggering vitality. He had collected the flagon of pear cider that Tams had so thoughtfully left behind. He had made a great show of parting with a half-crown for it, and many an oily benison upon the Jenkins. Then he'd left the couple to repair their lives, and what remained of their possessions.

A half-crown was a mere trifle, of course, compared to the stash of gold pieces he was careful to keep in his snapsack. He chose his proceeds well, and saved them wisely. You learned to judge a house; to read it like you would a face, before you fell upon it. A man's face soon showed you if he was a "cony", an easy prey. It was just like how you learned to evaluate a woman, for the warmth of her heart, and her willingness to open her legs.

> "Down in a vale, diddle-diddle,
> Where flowers do grow,
> And the trees bud, diddle-diddle,
> All in a row."

He patted the rough paling of the fence beside the road. Life was good. And life, by the face of it, was about to get a whole lot better!

That night he would sell his gains on to the men for a penny a quart. It would lend a festive air to the supping of the stew and the playing of the recorders.

> "Like lambs in May, diddle-diddle,
> Making fine sport."

Yes … the women liked their sport. A warm word, an appreciative look. Rough handling, if they wanted it, or warranted it. Take the pliant Marjorie Gwyther, now. He had been gentle with *her*. He had put his hands under her shift, feeling and exploring, and all she had done was moan. He'd wanted something to savour on that last, long, liquid evening before the march. It was why she had woken him at two, and requested an encore.

> "There lives a lass, diddle-diddle,
> Over the green;
> She sells good ale, diddle-diddle,
> Think what I mean!"

Magner paused. The flat of his hand still rested on a fence post. He felt the exposed grain of the seasoned wood. His breath was coming high against his throat. His chest was boiling rapidly. He must take especial care to cover his backside at the Court Martial. He would need to repeat his tale verbatim – verbatim! Those drumhead counsels wanted accuracy, and careful understatement. They wanted a reliable man, someone plausible. With a little rehearsal, he could cheerfully oblige. And if Tams and Jacomb and Gomes were dragged before the court like squealing piglets, it would be *their* nefarious word against the word of a man with a clean record. A man of steady, sober habits. Of courteous mien. Of…

Magner could no longer stop himself from laughing.

Sir John Mayney was justly proud of Black Rose, his strapping, anthracite mare. After all, she stood seventeen hands, and she had cost him all of thirty guineas back in Headcorn. Her colour went well with his dark uniform, and his indigo cape. A kiss of his spurs, and Black Rose trotted him down the lane to inspect the outlying pickets. He could feel her fine muscles, her puissant self-assurance. There was power in those thews of hers, only waiting to be unleashed.

It was a pleasant evening, with a promise of a late sunset. The light was shining down with single-hearted fervour. Violets were everywhere.

Three men were leaning on a fence, staring out across the fields. They looked round at the approaching hooves, and stood up straight when they saw who those hooves were carrying.

Mayney reined in and nodded to them. "Anything to report?"

"Not a thing, sir," said Corporal Clare. He wore a Montero cap, which affected a stylish peak. "'Tis as quiet as a churchyard."

Hearing the word "churchyard," Chris and Judah simultaneously started to think of the way that this sunshine would look on Saint Margaret's old tower. Its ragstone must be baked on a day like this.

Mayney nodded. "Keep a sharp watch, men," he said. "It's a likely evening. When Fairfax's dogs come roaring down the hill, it won't be a game of cherry-pits that we'll be playing with them, you can depend on it!"

"Aye, sir!"

"That we'll do, sir," Melhuish vowed.

They watched the Baronet go.

"A likely evening, is it? Make the Sexton strip to his work again, Judah!"

"I'm not a bloody grave digger no more, Chris." Judah supported this point by patting at his snapsack, the sausage of durable leather in which he now portered his world.

"Just hope that it ain't our *own* bloody graves we'll be digging soon," said Melhuish.

"Stow it, Corp'ral," said Judah.

They turned, moving their faces to follow the rays. The weather was fine, right enough. The sun might accentuate the warm, woven red of the dye, but its mugginess doubled the weight of their uniforms

"You men!"

They spun round. There, right in the middle of the road, stood a long-limbed, young, and none-too pleased Lieutenant. Nothing had awakened the three of them to his arrival, but he was flesh and blood alright. He struck an attitude, putting his hand on the hilt of his sword, which he hoped conveyed an officer's dominion.

"You make no obedience, sirs. Have you forgotten the dues that are owed to those set lawfully over you?"

Melhuish was first to recover. He knew this type. Some bold young spark whose Papa had served in the King's Foot and expected the tradition be continued. He made a show of theatrical humility, to the sovereignty of one who could have been his grandson.

"In-indeed, sir, I have not." At the Corporal's lead, they all reached for their firelocks, and stood with them shoulder to shoulder.

The haughty youth surveyed them all before his eyes fastened on Melhuish. "You look the senior. What is your current rank?"

"It is Corporal, sir. Corporal Clare." Melhuish would not have denied a slight tremor at the word "current". This pup had chosen his adjectives intentionally. "We belong to Captain Marchington's Company."

"Then I would have expected better of you, *Corp-o-ral* Clare, for you'll be letting your fellows get slack."

"Yessir. It shall not occur again, sir."

Judah piped up: "I, too, sir, beg you a separate pardon."

"Yeah, and that goes for me, too. *Sir*," put in Coates.

The Lieutenant looked squintingly at them, though that might have been due to the glare of the light. "Wake up your minds, my men!" he commanded. "Those dogs could strike upon us from any quarter."

Then he turned and left them to it.

"What proper stuff!" said Judah, when the distance was safe to do so. "He's not s'posed to haul a Corporal over the coals in front of his men!"

"Render unto Caesar, isn't it?" Melhuish agreed.

Coates turned and spat on the ground. "He's a cowson. Vague in his orders!"

They leaned their firelocks against the fence, and looked back across the fields. The one nearest to them had been carpeted with a crop of potato. Little green plumes, like the feathers you saw in the Royalist caps, were starting to push clear of the well-turned soil.

Judah inclined his head and said: "What d'we do, then, Melhuish?"

"When?"

"Well, you heard Sir John. It's a likely day. S'posing as Black Tom *were* to come riding out across this field." He pointed to the nearest natural feature, about a hundred yards away. "Say he rode out of them trees, right now, and all his hounds of hell with him… What'd we do?"

"Well, we'll… we'll tell someone," said the Corporal.

"Someone," echoed Coates.

"Aye! And, then they'll tell someone else. That's how the Army works."

Drummer Coates used his square-toed boot to demolish a powdery molehill. "'Od's lifelings, but it beats me what I 'listed for!"

THIRTY-TWO

But this is got by casting pearls on hogs.

Sir William Brockman was plucking at the collar of his doublet. The day was impossibly sticky. He braced himself for news as Mayney appeared from among the tents.

"By your face, we have no word?" asked the Sheriff.

"Not a ha'porth." Mayney gave a disdainful shrug. "By the Lord, 'tis a wasteland out there."

Brockman shook his round-faced head, and sighed. A great wing of the Parliamentary Army was marching ever nearer with long, decisive steps. That fact, at least, he knew. But they could be anywhere amid the miles of rolling country. If he looked out across the floodplain, he could see the unassuming houses of Aylesford. The old bridge flung itself across the river. A cool breeze was bouncing off the Medway, right enough, but the Sheriff stood too far away to feel its relieving touch.

"Let us repair to my Headquarters," he said. "Get out of this blasted sun."

Under canvas, Mayney removed his large hat. He was glad to sit down. He crossed his booted ankles, feeling his hamstrings strain. He had been in the saddle since daybreak: he ached in all the fleshy parts of his legs.

"Crafty man, Black Tom," he admitted. "At this rate, he could well reach Dover unopposed."

"You think so?" There was an edge to Brockman's voice.

"That is the present rumour that is running around our camp, Sir William."

"Rumours!" The Sheriff was unimpressed. "Rumours go through an Army like worms through an apple."

Mayney agreed with him there. "Indeed. The common soldiery welcomes the good Dame Rumour, for I'm certain that nobody else will tell him anything."

The Sheriff's eyes were very angry. "Well, I'll not offer first blood to Fairfax. Stuff his corpse, I wouldn't give him the satisfaction!" He allowed himself a few, deflating seconds before enquiring in milder tones: "Care for a stoup, Sir John?"

"Aye. Thank you."

"Think of it as a reviver." Brockman poured the Madeira into two stone jars with their handles missing. "How fares the Court Martial?" he asked. He put the question reluctantly: he would rather they occupy their time with the Rebellion ahead, not with matters of humdrum indiscipline.

Mayney was unblinking. "The rogue is like to die. The Sarjeant's testimony was quite overwhelming, or so said Colonel Halliday who sits as the president."

Brockman was glad to feel the wine slip down his throat. "This Sarjeant... Maggs, is it?"

"Magner."

"Magner; would you say he's a man of his word?"

Mayney considered the question. "I... wouldn't say not, Sir William."

"And the rogue, Chaloner?"

"Chaloner?" Mayney was unfazed. "Well, when he had sobered, his first action was to cite a clutch of other villains. Said they were all his accomplices. All of 'em sound like good-for-nothing picaroons. Dogs, to a man."

Brockman grimaced. "Probably scrounged their way through years of undetected crimes."

Mayney took another sip. The Madeira was tongue-loosening stuff. "Seems if Chaloner's to be strung up then he wants 'em on the bough to keep him company. He even impugned Sarjeant Magner, the Colonel said."

"How so?"

"Well, I may only go from what I have heard, but it is my understanding that things got very heated. Chaloner swore that Sarjeant Magner was a ditch-delivered bastard (his words, Sir John, not mine), and declared before the Lord he was a liar, and the greatest villain unhung. Swore *his* had been the mind that had planned the looting." He took another drink. "It was all entered in the record, of course. Halliday's being meticulous."

"Mayhaps it'll be the rope for them all, and good riddance!" said the Sheriff.

"Aye. At least the Provosts will be thankful."

Brockman asked, "Did that old couple take the stand as witnesses?"

"Flat refusal." Mayney sank the last of his Madeira and polished his lips with his handkerchief.

The Sheriff stared at him. "Refusal? But it took place on their property!"

"Forker said he met with 'em. Said that something had scared 'em into fits."

Brockman's eyebrows rose. "Try having half a dozen cut-throats plunder *your* house, Sir John, and tell me you ain't frighted!" Then he called a fact to mind. "They're papists, aren't they?"

"Mm." Mayney's reply was toneless. There was nothing to suggest an opinion.

"Papists have got a thing about taking oaths. Conflicting allegiances, see?"

A shadow fell over the pair of them and into the tent ducked an alert-looking courier. He had sprinted through the tent lines to find the Sheriff. He'd slung a leather satchel over his shoulders, and it jogged across his backside as he ran.

Brockman appraised the man. The sweat was pouring off him like the thaw in the springtime. "Get your breath back, sirrah," was all he said.

The courier wobbled a little, then began by degrees to control himself. "I have brought you Sirs a message from Blue Bell Hill. The Lord Norwich was most particular that I should put it into the hands of the Sheriff himself."

"You've found him. Give it me."

With the courier's duty done, Mayney followed through with, "Go now, sirrah, and refresh yourself as you see fit." He felt in his purse for a coin. "Here," he said, holding out the money. "Take this for your pains."

The young courier bowed, withdrawing.

"And do not wander far, sirrah, for I may need you to bear an answer in return!" Mayney called. Then, to Brockman, "Read on, Sir William."

Brockman turned his focus to the letter. Lord Norwich's coat of arms had been stamped in a blob of red wax, but the wax had softened so much under the sun that it came away easily. The writing inside was a scrawl that resembled the legs of so many spiders. Several, speedy blots had first puddled, and then dried across the folds.

"*'The Parliament's Force appear... proceeding post-haste toward the River Medway'*," Brockman narrated, decrypting the script with difficulty.

Mayney was now concerned. His knee had started jigging up and down. "God's great eyes!" he swore. "Proceeding? Proceeding when? Two hours ago? Last night? The day before?"

"There is no mention."

"By the bowels of Christ!"

Brockman finished the letter by himself, keeping Mayney waiting. At last he read aloud: "*'You will note my wording well. Take a force upon your immediate receipt of this dispatch, and make rendezvous with the Governor Dudley at Maidstone'.*"

Mayney interjected sharply: "What?"

"Upon immediate receipt of this dispatch, it says. *'Defend the town in depth, whilst our forces deny the passes to the enemy and so safeguard Rochester and Chatham. Seek not to attack... but to be attacked'.*"

When next Mayney spoke, his voice was mired in wonder. "So, His Lordship's only plan is for us to mill about like sheep in the streets of the town, and wait for Black Tom to fall upon us?"

"Do *you* read anything to the contrary in there, Sir John?" Brockman handed the other man the Earl's communication. He set about refilling his stoup of wine.

"I do not," replied Mayney, and he did not lift his head from Norwich's scratchy missive.

Brockman savoured a leisurely gulp before setting down the wine with an irritated thud. "If the New Models got into the town, why they'd break our heads across!"

Mayney made a regretful gesture with hands and head. "Sir William, let us cut our coat according to our cloth. Your men are not the diehards of Ancient Rome. They are levies, fresh from the plough and the workshops. Most of 'em have never even *seen* a battle!"

"Have *you* seen a battle, Sir John?" asked Brockman, who hadn't.

"I have. In 'Forty-four. We fought in the North." He did not feel inclined to impart any more. Marston Moor ached too deeply.

The Sheriff, on the other hand, had spent much of 1644 languishing in a stinking cell in a London gaol, until the Parliament released him back to his home in Beachborough on his own recognisances. "Then, I would assume you are familiar with the concept of disobeying a direct order?" he exhorted.

Mayney hesitated. Then he rose, and looked at Brockman calmly. "I have *never* disobeyed a direct order in my life, Sir William," he declared in a terse voice.

He looked up to see if Brockman were impressed with his words. His brows began to knit when he read the answer.

"You smile, sir?" he challenged.

"You must forgive me, Sir John," said Brockman, as he surmounted the urge to grin. "I merely wondered, there is always a first time for everything."

Mayney remained imperturbable. "Be flip if you choose to, Sir William. But if we can't hold Maidstone with four thousand men, we should be broken to the ranks!"

THIRTY-THREE

Were they of manly pride, or youthful bloom?
As smooth as Hebe's their unrazored lips.

The match touched the linstock. For a moment, nothing happened; then the barrel of the 3-pounder falconette leaped insanely on its carriage. The cannon rolled backwards, down the knoll where it had been carefully laid. A squad of ants, all of them dressed in a gunner's uniforms of blue and brown, were scurrying around it in a trice. The first had been a mere sighting shell, to do no more than tickle the Roundheads. But now East Farleigh bridge and its fat old buttresses was being forded. The Parliament was upon them.

Nathan had been in the kitchen, quietly humming "Greensleeves" while he made himself a nuncheon. Polly had left to walk home. The funeral of old Isabella Stewart had concluded less than an hour ago, and Saint Mary's sexton had filled in the grave in record time. When Nathan had finished his bite to eat, he would lock up the Rectory before strolling on round to the smithy. Here he was to collect Hayden, the matted old cob that Ben Middleton had agreed to lend him. It was a bargain of mutual convenience: Ben would lend the Parson his mount for his journey to Week Street, and in return Parson Wohlford would take Hayden round to Hesketh's, the farrier on Tyler's Lane. Hesketh's rates were passing reasonable, or so Ben claimed.

As it was, when the guns split the living air, Nathan dropped his bread and cheese and dashed out of the kitchen door. He had entered a world of noise. It sounded like the din of falling meteors.

He flew across the churchyard. The gate into the lane was thronged with armed men, all of them pushing and shoving. They were local faces, making blindly for the sanctuary of Saint Mary's lofty tower.

Nathan stopped. Away down the hill, on the other side of the river, were lots of little winking constellations. At first he was slow to process what he was seeing, and he put it down to a trick of the heat. Then he looked again. Those weren't stars that he could see. They were scores and scores of breastplates, swords, and firelock barrels. And those were hundreds of men, standing there like a treeline. Different-coloured pennants denoted the Army's regiments. Gallopers delivered their orders from Troop to Troop. Then the trumpets blared out in chorus and, with one accord, the treeline was moving.

Another swam of Militiamen went rushing past. New Model pikemen dressed in red had marched across the bridge's hump. One last puff of balling smoke, and the 3-pounders coughed no more. Nathan watched the gunners, being swamped by their foe. They didn't sell their lives. They didn't even try to. Huddled together, they were herded firmly away with their hands in the air.

Standing in his shaded watching place, Nathan treated himself to some deep, relieving breaths.

Now the cavalry were getting across. No more than two horses at a time, for that bridge was a tight, medieval corridor, but it was an irresistible trickle that nothing could stem. Once they had got over the river, the Ironsides did not linger on the floodplain. They advanced on the hill in a carefully arranged screen, nudging their horses up the slope with the regimental standard flying.

In the lane, a last fan of Militiamen were levelling their muskets and aiming them down the road. Their volley was pointless. Why, at this range, they might as well gob at the Roundheads for the good it would do!

The Parliamentarian horse trotted nearer. Their sabres were drawn and flashing. The musketeers had neither the equipment nor the nerve to confront them. Instead, they cast away their arms and made a run for it. The loss of their 3-pounder cannon had eroded their hope and put wings on their shoes. They were trying to unbuckle their belts and tear away their baldrics as they ran. Some pelted straight up the Maidstone Road. Others plunged into its bordering hop gardens, or struck out further for the woods.

A full, profundo, salvo rocked the valley. Behind the Horse had come the Parliament's own guns, and they were served by well-drilled teams.

A whistle, and a bellow, and then Hell itself landed among Saint Mary's trees. The branches writhed in their sockets. The air felt like it was being sucked from Nathan's lungs. There was a pattering of earth and tiny stones. Then an indulgent howl of pain.

Something swam out of the smoke, blinded by its own blood. When Nathan stepped out from behind the tree to accost it, it batted him away and struggled on.

Nathan ran through the gate, and into the lane. The Militia's weaponry lay where it was, as fatuous as driftwood. The New Model guns were chastened. Parliament was husbanding its shot, and leaving the job to the Ironsides. Why waste its good provisions of round shot and case on an empty prospect?

He skittered onwards, into the lane adjoining – the one that ran behind the Frosts' house.

"Halt! Who goes?"

Nathan stopped short. The words had come from a squash-nosed Trooper sitting on the saddle of a dark brown horse. He must have been one of the leading vedettes: all cross belts and boots, and back-and-breast irons. His sabre thrust in readiness.

Nathan blinked at this brawny, ugly figure in battle-array. He straightened his back. There was no thought of argument or resistance. If this was the end, so be it.

"My name is Nathan Wohlford. I am the Rector of Saint Mary's."

"Were that the church, there?" The soldier gestured with the long blade.

"It were. I mean, it is." It seemed better to play along. The lane was deserted, and help would never find him here. That cavalryman's nose could speak of quick fists.

A change swept the man's beaten-in features. He descended from his saddle. "Advance!"

Nathan crept forward. Whatever he had been expecting, it was not for the horseman to drop to his knees in the road, fold his hands over the hilt of his sword in an Arthurian manner, and to beg him for a blessing.

"What was that you said?"

"Say a prayer for me, Parson?" The look on the soldier's face was pitiable. "I were a roaring boy once, I have never denied it" he admitted, apparently with more distress than pleasure. "But

246

I try to live clean. Honest, I do! For the little woman, and my boys."

Nathan looked questioningly at him. "You serve the Grandee Fairfax?"

"Indirect, Parson. I ride in Major Husbands' regiment."

Nathan had heard enough of the man's speech to detect the accent of the Fen country. "And you would shell a house of God?" He pointed to the churchyard where smoke still hung about thickly, and his frown was stern.

"The King's men did profane it with their presence, Parson!"

The frenzied look on the soldier's face was disturbing. He had still not got up off his knees.

"You've ... children, you said?" Nathan recommenced.

"Aye, sir. Raised six sons, Susannah and me."

A family man. A soul, in need of shelter.

"Have you always been a soldier?"

"Not me, Parson! I were a tanner once, 'afore the Army found me. Naseby year, that were. I made neats-leather boots. Only a three-by-four little shop, but she paid the rental."

The words were jerking out of him, as though he could not find the proper place to start them and form them.

"There's only one thing I've got to know from 'ee, Parson, and it's this. Ain't it the Lord's Work I been a-doing in the Army? I have heard the Word, and fear it," the soldier appealed, "but tell me if it ain't it the *Lord's* Work we do here, Master Parson?"

"Do you mean the Lord in Heaven, or that Lord who leads you into battle on his horse?" Nathan parried.

The Trooper would not be placated. "Please, Parson! I obey the commandments – I swear!"

Nathan made a conscious effort to sound more gentle. He imagined this were another parishioner who had need of the clergy's mind. "You... you have been awaiting this moment a long time, I think."

"O ever so, sir! I am not a bad man! For all that I done in my youth, and there were too much of *that*, I declare, I am not a bad man!" The head dropped. "It do make a man fratchety, see, when he's got God on the brain. He gets wracked with it."

Nathan put out a hand. His fingers made contact with iron and leather. "I know... I am *sure*, you are not a bad man, sirrah," he said. "And the Lord Above knows that you would never promise one thing, only to renege and do another. Make good your conscience, now. And – please – get to your feet."

The soldier lifted his face. He looked ready to cry.

A curt, Scottish accent harangued them from behind Nathan's back. "Elihu Nye! Why d'ye not take post as ye were ordered?"

Nathan spun round. The interjection had come from a grizzled little man, sitting on a squat pony, carrying a sabre. He had a grey beard and pitch-coloured eyes, and the look on his face was that of a man who has only recently discovered something foul on the sole of his boot. Half a dozen mounted Troopers hung around him. Former drapers and woodmongers, transported by rigorous training into haughty, buff-coated warriors.

The horseman named Elihu Nye jumped to his feet. "He were only saying the grace to me, Corp'ral!" he protested.

"Well, now that he's dusted your brains, Trooper Nye, just ye get back in the saddle – quick sharp!"

Elihu Nye turned to retrieve his mount, who during their little conference had passed the time nibbling grass from the verges. The weight of authority only increased with the hasty arrival of their Troop officer, who rode up smartly from the end of the lane astride a massive charger. A brace of pistols had been shoved into their holsters on his pommel. In the one hand he held his regiment's brightly-coloured ensign. Its embroidered Latin motto was short, and sharp, and stirring.

The officer lifted the hinge on his triple-barred vizor to uncover his face. He had a cleft in his chin that a mouse could make a home in.

"No pottering, men!" he barked. "Get your men moving, Corp'ral Jesmond. Go spread yourselves out and search the village for your comestibles; if you want any dinner, that is."

"Aye, Mister Weller!" The Corporal saluted. His jabbing, gauntleted finger pointed Elihu Nye back into his saddle.

The officer named Weller looked straight at Nathan with a disapproving stare. Nathan looked straight back at him. "Dash it all – get this civilian out of the way, whoever he is!"

He dug enormous spurs in the flanks of his horse, and the beast bucked away up the lane. His mount was fresh and skittish. The smell of battle was still new in its nostrils.

Corporal Jesmond looked grimly down at the juvenile Parson. "No disrespects, Reverend, but I would scurry home and bolt the door if I were ye. This is no place for such as yourself."

"My parishioners are dying, Corporal. Where else would you have me be?" Nathan rejoined, with a dangerous note to his voice.

Corporal Jesmond made no allowances. "I would not put much mind to that, Reverend. They got what was coming."

"I am devoutly thankful we do not all esteem human life so cheaply, Corporal," said Nathan.

Jesmond sighed, and gave up. "Well, if a three-pound ball should take your head off, Parson, don't say I didn't warn ye." He turned in the saddle to address his waiting Section. "'Member, boys! Not nothing to be took as isn't paid for. Ye know the penalty for looters – the Provost'll be glad to meet you with the rope's end."

Nathan cleared his throat. "You may find a fresh water pump. Over there, by the Rectory wall. You are welcome to make free with it."

"I'm obliged to ye," returned Jesmond. He led his Section away in a road-blocking bunch. Only one glanced back at him.

"Thanks to 'ee, Parson!" Trooper Nye called back, with the sincerity of a lifetime.

For the second time, it fell to Nathan to explore what military might could do to a church. Case shot had pocked Saint Mary's ancient ragstone. Musket balls had drilled right through Sits heavy, Norman doors. The planks had more holes in them than those wheels of cheese that the landowners liked to import from the Swiss Cantons.

Nevertheless, it was what he found *outside* Saint Mary's doors that grieved him the most. Amos Monkman, the jovial yeoman farmer, lay dead before the porch. The lips were slack and purpled. Blood had trickled from his nostrils down his beard. A cloud of case shot had razored his skull. Amos still wore his regular working clothes of coarse brown worsted. His form was hunched and crumpled. A barrel, with its ribs smashed in.

Nathan said a prayer over the cadaver, trying not to gag. The Monkman farm stood outside the village. The news about Amos would take some time to reach his wife, Elizabeth. She and Amos had raised strong sons to work their farm... where would they be now? Gone back to prepare the homestead for whatever was coming next, or scattered into the woods and the hop gardens?

He stood up, and looked down at the body. He felt no anger, no personal desire for vengeance. Vengeance was the Lord's prerogative. A lot of men died in battles. Amos had simply been one of them.

Thick units of Parliament's Foot were now swinging up the hill. At the same time, the requisitioners were doing the rounds from house to house. Those Dragoons were endeavouring to whip up some grub, taking care to show their bags of money. The General's orders never left any room for ambiguity.

Nathan walked out into the lane. He looked up the road, following where the villagers had showed the cannons their heels. Up the hill, to where the Tovil Lane led on and down to Maidstone, and undulated all the way to Number Twenty-Seven, Week Street.

On the far bank of the scum-speckled river, Fairfax kept abreast of developments through his spyglass. By rights, he should have been sitting in his carriage with his gouty leg up on a travelling stool, relying on runners to paint the picture for him. But no force on earth had dissuaded him from mounting up (bandages and all) and riding forward to observe the affair for himself.

Sitting on a bay mare beside him, Ireton was restless. "The quarry's on the move, my lord! They ran at the first smell of the powder, it seems."

Fairfax did not take the spyglass from his eye. "And of our own Company?"

"Of Company men, there's not a man come to harm."

His Excellency did not look geed up by this report, so Ireton pressed: "The hill is ours, my lord. That hill – right there! Do we pursue?"

Fairfax's eye was lingering on a spot to the north-west. "What lies over there?"

His question was for Rushworth. "They call it Kit's Coty, my lord," replied the secretary. "'Tis an ancient burial ground."

"Seems awfully alive to me!" the General observed. He handed Ireton his glass. Ireton could see four thick obelisks embedded in the side of the hill, topped with a slab to leave the thing looking like a table. Another feat of primitive man at which the mind could only boggle. Then he saw what the General had meant. Confound it, there had to be hundreds – no *thousands* of men upon that hilltop. But no tents, that he could see. A migrant force. An enormous, wriggling caterpillar.

"That must be their main body!" he declared. "Moving down to invest the town, I would wager."

Fairfax had gone very quiet. His crackling mind still dwelt on the battlefield of Newburn. It had been an equally blistering Saturday in the August of 1640, when the Scots had hurled the English cavalry back over the border, and chased them all the way to Newcastle. Scores of men had been killed, and Fairfax had been there to witness it. He too had felt the grip of general panic.

And then had come the day of Marston Moor. Truly, they had unlocked the horrors then. There had been much killing on the Vale of York that afternoon. Three hundred men for Parliament, and four thousand lost on the Royalist side. Among the dead had numbered his own brother. Charles Fairfax had been abandoned to die by his own Troopers. They had run when the waves of Royal Foot had coasted too close for their liking.

"Colonel Rushworth?"

"Your Excellency?"

"Take notes for my dispatch." Fairfax waited till the secretary produced a graphite stylus and a little block of paper.

"To the Right Honourable the Earl of Manchester, Speaker of the House of Peers, *et cetera, et cetera*. This day, the First of June, we shall either force the enemy to fight or swim. Tell them we've a strong party of Dragoons and Foot across the river... You getting this down?"

"Every word."

"…Dragoons and Foot across the river, to make good the pass at Rochester," continued Fairfax. "Tell them our main thrust shall fall on the far side of the river, and that with God's mercy we'll make good Maidstone in the morning. By noon tomorrow we shall be masters of the town. Your lordship's humble servant, *et cetera, et cetera.*"

"It is written, my lord." Rushworth scribbled the last of the details.

Ireton couldn't believe his ears. "But, Your Excellency! Our guns are soon across!"

Fairfax pointed straight above their heads. "Colonel Ireton. *Look.*"

Ominous-looking black clouds had spilled over the southern horizon. An ugly shade of purple promised torrents very soon.

"A house-to-house rat war will avail us nothing with this storm in our eyes," said Fairfax. "We shall ride out the weather and then commence the assault at dawn. Send Major Husbands' fellows ahead to scout the lanes and reconnoitre, but do *not* press the attack with his Dragoons."

"But, *my lord!*" Ireton said the words as if in prayer. His control was running out on him. "Why keep our forces waiting in the vestibule? The troops are already across!"

"In the morning, Colonel Ireton."

THIRTY-FOUR

That two-handed engine at the door
Stands ready to strike once, and strike no more.

The sun had just begun to settle when Maidstone heard the first snarl of thunder.

Brockman's column braced up as they marched into the High Town behind the Colonel's horse. Sarjeants carried their spontoons just that little bit higher. It was hard to maintain the proper intervals when you marched in such a stop-start fashion. Only the county landowners who headed the troops provided a touch of class, straddling their elegant and expensive thoroughbreds. The air was as thick as cotton. The men's armpits were damp with stench and sweat, and their thighs had chafed them raw. What they wouldn't give to race down to the riverbank, and dive into the weeds of the Medway!

Many of the Maidstone garrison had given up hope of ever summoning aid to their side. They had sent out gallopers to appeal to Lord Norwich, but the Earl had proven as elusive as quicksilver. Now they took off their caps and waved them at their saviours.

Brockman divided his force at High Street, among the waiting guns. Captain Marchington's Company found themselves right-about-facing and slogging back down Week Street, the way they had just taken. Guides were appointed: men who knew the alleyways of this, their citadel.

In the lea of Week Street's timbered gables, Sarjeant Magner's section heard their orders from their pilot. "Most cleared out when they knew they had the chance. Leastways, those with sense." He nodded his head at the house behind him. "This one wouldn't budge. Silly old bitch."

"What silly old bitch?" said Private Copp.

"Woman. Living here. Her, and her ducklings – there's five of 'em. Name of... Atkins, was it? Adams?"

"Not Agnew, man?" said a dismayed Corporal Clare.

"Agnew! That was it! Agnew; Number Twenty Seven. Silly bitch." The guide hawked another dose of phlegm into the gutter. "Have fun in there, boys!"

Sarjeant Magner nestled his spontoon in the crook of his arm. The door rattled in its jamb beneath his knocking. He charged those within with the familiar call.

"Open in the King's name!"

The door was pulled back, revealing a well-remembered face. Rebecca's eyes widened at the men in their robin-red doublets.

"Mistress!" Melhuish was appalled to confirm the worst. Did she not know what would happen if a town were taken and ransacked? Had the Captain spared his wife the tales of what they had seen in Ireland?

Magner took charge. "It is not our purpose to impose upon you, Mistress, but orders are orders." He gathered his unfragrant men with the one, rapid glance. "C'm along, my lads!"

They stepped into the hall. Melhuish could cage his tongue no longer. "Why haven't you *gone*, Mistress?" he asked the stately woman. Old affinities died hard.

The smile she gave him back was very faint. "There was never any question of our leaving, Melhuish." She might have been explaining that two and three made five. "My God is in His heaven, and hath done whatever He pleaseth."

Magner had parked his half-pike by the door and had gone into the parlour. "Corp'ral? Move this loom away! Coates? Give a hand!"

"You'll pardon, Ma'am." Melhuish tugged at his forelock and went to obey.

Rebecca remained where she was. "Do try not to break anything," she said, rather lamely.

The foxy-faced Sarjeant was back in the hall. "What'll I be doing, then, Sarge?" Judah asked him.

Magner jerked his head towards the staircase. "Take post upstairs. Sing out loud if anything happens."

"Aye, Sarge!"

Magner hesitated, then trained a smile on the two beautiful girls he had just noticed staring down at him from the head of the stairs. The nearest one flapped a playful wave at him. Behind her, her twin giggled keenly.

"I'll give you good day, ladies!" he called, with a smile that showed his teeth.

The first girl was advancing down the stairs towards him. "Master Magner! What brings you under our roof?"

Rosalind, or Eleanor? They looked identical and sounded identical. He drank in her trim little figure with smouldering eyes.

The twin read his thoughts. "It's Eleanor," she toyed. "The nice half of the pair."

"You lying pig!" shrieked Ros from the landing.

Eleanor threw her head back and laughed aloud. When she turned around, Magner moved a step nearer the foot of the stairs so that he might study that pert rump of hers a little longer.

"'Scuse us, then, Sarge?" Judah Copp squeezed behind him and went upstairs, trailing his firelock. The twins vanished like giggling ghosts.

"I assume you have orders, Master Magner?" Rebecca queried.

The Sarjeant said nothing. His eyes were still fixed on the landing.

"Master Magner...?" This time Rebecca's prompt was audibly less mild in its delivery.

Magner deflected the cut. "Is this door the only way in, Mistress?"

"No. There is another portal out the back, beyond the courtyard. It would take you up the hill behind the houses."

Rebecca heard the shudder of wood-on-wood in the adjoining room. Their furniture was being dragged across the floorboards.

"I shall go and inspect," said Magner, and strode quick-legged down the kitchen passage.

After a moment's pause, Rebecca swished into the room next the street, for she wanted to see for herself what the verger and the butcher were doing. The chamber was all awry. They had picked up Ros' loom and parked it against the wainscot in the corner. That had been the easy part. The refectory table (being less portable) had been heaved to one side to make space – that was what had made the grinding noise. Elle's spinning wheel was now by the door, perched precariously atop the scattering of chairs. The dresser where the pewterware lived could remain where it was for the moment. The two men had moved the settle from its spot before the hearthstone and positioned it under the windows. They were sitting on it as she walked in. Footsore as they were, they did not rise to greet the Lady of the House.

"There's no food, is there, Mistress?" Coates tried not to sound too wheedling. "See, we've been on the march since two. No one knows quite where to put us."

"Aye, Ma'am. Our snapsacks are done," corroborated Melhuish.

Rebecca kept her voice level. "Go and take what you want from the kitchen."

Coates rose on protesting feet. He nodded his thanks as he shambled off to locate the pantry.

"We'll pay you back, Ma'am. Honest!" vowed Melhuish.

"Hmm!" Rebecca said no more.

The Corporal stood up. Before the Lady could say a word, he had swung his musket round, and attacked the window behind him with its sharp-pointed butt. Rebecca flinched at the tinkling shower of glass and the rending of wood. "What d'you think you are *doing?*" she cried.

He looked at her over his shoulder. "Making us loopholes, Mistress. Don't want all this glass to fly back in our faces." He jabbed and swung again. The woodwork cracked and flaked beneath the blows. The glass tinkled into a myriad tiny pieces. Much of it fell outwards, but a lot of it fell at his feet.

Carrie hurried in, looking disturbed. "Mother! Master Coates the butcher is in the kitchen. He's raiding our larder!"

She stopped in her tracks. The room had been rearranged. There was mess on the floor. And look at the damage that *Melhuish Clare of all people* was inflicting on their house!

"Mind your feet, girl," said Rebecca, automatically, for she had noted that Carrie had no shoes on. "I gave Private Coates leave to help himself, Carrie," she explained. "These men have been on the march all day, and they have not eaten. They are not ruffians. They have promised to imburse us for whatever they take."

Melhuish turned. The job was hardly neat, but it was done. "Mistress Carrie!" He smiled as he set down his musket. "My, but you've grown!"

Carrie ignored his compliments. "And what about us? We'll starve!"

"Oh no, we shan't." Rebecca had no time for her daughter's dramatics. She alone knew of the small bundle of provisions Pip had hidden in the garret for emergencies. "Now go fetch a broom, so you may sweep up this glass."

Carrie looked from the shiny fragments of broken glass, to the musket-clutching Melhuish, to the broken window, and back to her mother. Then she flounced into the hall. "Some damned birthday!" she muttered under her breath

Rebecca chased her to the door. "I heard that, Caroline!" she fired at her daughter's back.

Coates had come back. He had palmed the remains of a block of cheese. "That grandson of yours has pushed up, ain't he, Mistress?" he observed as he chewed.

Carrie returned. She avoided her mother's eye and started to sweep up the debris.

They heard the pounding of feet up above, and a man's voice shouting, and the sound of someone careering down the stairs.

"What the – ?"

Ros danced into the room. She was clutching a musket and laughing her head off. The weapon looked jarring and outsized in her hands.

"*Rosalind!*" Her mother was appalled.

Elle came down a moment later, breathless and cackling. She leaned against the door frame and watched while her twin worked her merry magic.

"Well, Mother! Am I not a soldier now?" Ros had dropped her voice by half an octave. She embarked on a grotesque parody of the manual of arms.

Judah arrived at last from the upper storeys. He had thoughtlessly left his musket propped by the door of the garret, where a lily-white hand had reached into the room to make off with it. He was winded from chasing the twins down two flights of extremely precipitous stairs, and he had nearly measured his length on the last few steps. He saw Magner approaching in the stairwell, holding the little Wohlford boy by the hand. "I'm sorry, Sarge!" he protested.

The Sarjeant smiled that knowing and secretive smile. "Outflanked by a pretty maid, were you, Private Copp? Shame on you!"

"Return that firearm at once to Private Copp!" Rebecca's order came in lofty tones.

"But Ma!"

"*At once*, Rosalind! Before you blow all our heads off!"

Rosalind sulked, but relented when she read the unyielding look of authority on her mother's face. "Here." She sniffed as she handed it over. "Didn't care for the thing anyway."

Satisfied, Rebecca nodded her head. "So! Now that Private Copp has got his musket back, mayhaps he will keep a sharp watch on it in future while he lodges in this house?"

It was like flexing a cane under his nose with which she intended to thrash him. "Aye, Ma'am." Judah soon made himself scarce.

"Chris?" said Melhuish. "You go with him. I'll take my post here."

Coates slunk away without a fight. Rebecca now stood toe to toe with Rosalind.

"Go," she commanded, in almost a whisper.

The twins linked their arms as they sloped off upstairs.

"She was always a spark, was that one," said Melhuish, shaking her head.

"Isn't she still? They both are!" Now that she had completed her sweeping, and had deposited the glass out into the gutter, Carrie was feeling talkative. "We call her Rebel Ros."

"Caroline…" Rebecca growled her warning at her before she, too, retired from the room.

"Alright, alright! I'm coming!" Carrie stomped after her, gripping the broom handle tight.

Melhuish gnawed on the last of the cheese while he fixed his eyes on Week Street. The heavens glowered. The light was too bright: it was the last gasp of the good weather. He watched the loopholes being smashed in the opposite gables.

A footstep approached behind him. "Hullo, Melhuish."

Melhuish turned, and saw the tall girl leaning against the doorway. "Mistress Philippa!"

Philippa went to him, and held both his hands. She looked at him with tenderness and gratitude. "It is good to see you, Melhuish. Here, of all places!"

"Aye, Mistress, the Saints preserve us!" The old man smiled an uneven, friendly smile.

After an appropriate pause, Philippa asked, "Might I have a private word?"

"Why, of course, m'dear!"

She drew him aside, away from the window and over to the table. "You would never lie to me, would you, Melhuish?"

"Never!" he replied, with enormous chivalry.

"Then speak plain." She drew breath. "What is happening?"

He hesitated. "Happening?"

"Out there. What is going on? I am not the panicking kind, as I think you know." Her voice dropped to a hush. "Please, Melhuish, we are desperate for news."

The old man blew out his cheeks. "Comp'ny runner, overheard our Captain Marchington," he said. "The word is they've met Black Tom on the Farleigh Road and so they rushed us up here."

Philippa blanched at his words. "The... Farleigh Road?"

"The word is General Fairfax cut 'cross Barming Heath, and got over the bridge."

Every hair of her body rose in protest. "My God! He's passed the river!"

"Aye, so he has, and could be on us any minute! They're putting our Horse in the High Town as a last reserve. The rest of us hold the streets."

Philippa whimpered, "Nathan...!"

Melhuish shot out a hand to steady the girl he had known from a baby. "He'll be safe, my dear girl. Don't you go a-worrying: your Nathan'll keep his head. Not even the Roundheads are going to stand him, a Man of God, against the wall and pull the trigger!"

Her head lifted with a look of fearsome admonition. "Do not *dare* to say that. Even in jest, Melhuish; do – not – dare!"

It was just as much an order as a prayer. Melhuish would try to be less lurid. The last thing he wanted was the Captain's daughter ballooning into rage. "This war is a debasement,

Mistress. Death has always wanted men, but now he wants them more 'n ever."

Philippa's ire began to dissolve as quickly as it had arisen. "I saw you marching in. I was upstairs."

"Aye. Some Army!" he agreed.

She breathed out, long and low, to control herself. She needed proximity: she needed Stephen. She needed the reassurance of having his tiny body near her.

"Where is my son?" she suddenly asked of the empty room.

"He's out in the hall, isn't he?"

Philippa went to the door. Stephen, it transpired, was sitting at the bottom of the stairs, on Sarjeant Magner's lap. Magner had put his broad-brimmed hat upon Stephen's head, and it concealed his face completely. Stephen was clucking with delight. The hat smelt musky and interesting.

"Stephen?"

He pushed the hat up off his eyes when he heard the tone in her voice.

"Come here."

Stephen hopped down off his perch and went to her. She took the headgear by force from his head and tossed it at Magner. Magner caught it deftly, smiled a fraction, and shrugged. "'Tis a fine boy you've got there, Mistress. The Parson must be proud of him!"

"If the Parson should live to see him again, Master Magner, I'll wager he *will* be proud of him!" She crouched down to Stephen's level. Her hands were on his shoulders. She was looking him right in the eye. "Sweeting? Go upstairs. Find your Aunt Elle and Aunt Ros, and make sure that they're with Loobie. Your job is to keep them all safe. You hear me, Best Boy?"

She had chosen his father's name for him intentionally.

Stephen gave a very solemn nod. "I hear you, Mother." He stuck out his chin to look brave.

Philippa kissed him quickly, on the tip of his nose. "Go along with you, then."

She watched as Stephen hopped past the Sarjeant, and up the stairs two at a time.

Magner said, "The young fry has spirit, eh, Mistress?"

Philippa stood up. She declined to make a comment as she walked into the kitchen. She discovered Carrie had filled up the bucket from the courtyard pump and was scrubbing the table. Her sleeves were rolled back. The wooden-backed brush was in her hands.

"Headstrong," she greeted her sister. "Come to watch our mother's skivvy, have you?"

Philippa came to the table. "Would you welcome some help?"

"If you would? Be quicker."

"Think of it a birthday treat."

Carrie sniffed. "Don't tease me, Pip. I am not in the mood for it. Here." She handed her the other brush. Philippa dipped its bristles in the water. The pair of them dug deep into the surface of the table with the bristles.

Carrie paused in her labours. "You know, I envy you and Nathan," she said.

"It never did to envy, Carrie." Philippa spoke in her best, censorious, "eldest sister" voice.

Carrie looked nastily at her. "Why should I not? There is never a cloud in *your* skies, is there?"

Philippa cracked a laugh. "Ha! For all you know, he and I fight like cats. We only call a truce to put Stephen to bed."

Her sister shook her head at her, assured of a deeper truth. "Not you, Pip. Not the way that you and Nathan always were."

"And what is *that* supposed to mean?" Philippa challenged.

"Your memory is indifferent good, Pip. It means you fit. The two of you – you fit!"

With appalling abruptness, the sky above turned a pitch dark. As at the touch of a wand, the rain came down. First drops, and then a patter, then another, and another. The storm was right overhead: it was drenching the world. The rain gurgled and rumbled on the tiles and in the guttering. Philippa and Carrie could hear the high voices of the children, cheering in excitement through the ceiling.

Philippa listened to the vortex. "This cold night will turn us all to fools and madmen," she whispered to herself.

Carrie screwed up her eyes at her. "What?"

"'Tis a line from *King Lear*," said her sister. "Now scrub."

THIRTY-FIVE

Heard to howl
Like stabled wolves, or tigers at their prey.

When the first blow came, the New Model Army struck without bothering to wait for its General's say-so.

"Colonel Hewson has gone for the rebels!"

"Stick 'em, lads! Or may we never see the dawn!"

"Set spurs!"

Major Husbands' regiment of Dragoons started forward. So synchronised were their mounts, they sounded like the footfall of marching giants. The Troop began the charge down the Tovil Lane. In the leading file, Elihu Nye rode knee-to-knee with Corporal Jesmond. The mane of his mount was clotted with the raindrops. He felt the flanks between his legs, felt the beast rolling side to side. The world was whipping wet beyond his triple-barred helmet.

"Make – READY!" rose from the Royalist lines.

At the margin, between those thrusting stakes, men gripped their musket stocks with blenching fingers. Their senses were as taut as violin cords. Their whole front was filled with horse and straps and steel.

Trooper Nye took a moment to choose his target carefully. Even a wheel-lock carbine could deliver a steady shot under the fifth rib at a hundred paces. That blob of grease there, the one at the stakes who was giving the orders, that wine-skin... he was a quarry, alright. Fat enough to have made quarry enough for two men. By the water of Babylon, Elihu Nye would do for him yet!

"Pre-SENT!"

The muskets went into their rest irons. Cupped hands tried to protect their matches from the rain.

"GIVE – FIRE!"

The hedgehog exploded in flame and smoke. The Maidstone men were aiming for the horses, and their aim was brisk. The blood began to fountain, and horses felt the power snap out of their muscles. Then a lance of pain shot straight through Elihu Nye's left leg. The pain burnt more than it stung. His body thumped in agony. His thigh was bathed in dark red. He could feel the world slanting. He lost his grip and tumbled to the road. Sprawling among the hooves, he lay encased in his corselet like a lobster in a kettle. The rain was trying to find his face. His comrades thundered over him. One, stray swipe from a hoof and he would be finished: oblivion at a strike.

He knew he should try to sit up. You always sat up if you were wounded, lest you risked being dragged along by passing boots or horseshoes. The lead ball must have clipped him. A direct hit could shred the bone, or yank the limb clean off. Another fellow would have to flatten that portly rebel Sarjeant. It was the thought of that, and not the pain, that brought tears to the eyes of Trooper Elihu Nye.

A second volley rolled out. Much more ragged this time. The rain had got into the firelocks, and wetted the lengths of fuse.

"Out, men! Out, and at 'em!" Brockman roared.

The defenders, wet with rain and sweat, launched themselves out of the trenches and ran straight at their enemy. More men vaulted from their places of concealment behind the quickset hedgerows. They set about the horses, snatching Troopers from their saddles. Royalist and Parliament lashed and clubbed at one another in the lane. They washed their blades and they bloodied their knuckles. Their hearts were hot with murder. Flesh crunched bone and swung again at solid flesh. Heavy musket butts joined the swinging fists, breaking in noses and cracking open jaws with a blow that sent men spinning in a square-mouthed wail.

"We are wavering, my lord! Our ranks are like to break in minutes!"

A torrent was pouring off the rim of Rushworth's hat. Through the open door of the General's carriage, his skin showed pale in the lantern-light. "My lord, I do beseech you – we cannot advance much further! The pikemen can take no ground!"

Fairfax frowned at him. "You mean our attack has stalled?"

"Aye, General! Our men are hampered by the horses, and by these ferocious rebels."

"Enough of that. No more o' that." A bandaged foot descended to the step, and squelched into the mud as Fairfax got out of the carriage. He threw off his oilskin coat with one quick, deciding gesture. "Fetch me my horse!"

Ireton, who was holding the door for him, was astonishment incarnate. "My lord! Surely you do not conceive to ride into the teeth of that infernal mêlée?"

"I've rode into a hundred fights, Colonel Ireton," said Fairfax, adjusting his hat.

Rushworth waded in. He had to stall, if nothing else. "My lord! I do beseech you!"

Ireton went one better. He stepped forward and placed himself bodily between the General and his mare. "Your Excellency should not expose your person to such dangers," he said. "I say your asset is too great for the Parliament to lose!"

"And I say, Colonel Ireton, let a man be judged by what he does, rather than what his thoughts may be," Fairfax returned. "What, would you have me call upon Joshua, to sound his trumpet? The town is unwalled! Let us take it!"

The General limped toward his mount. Ireton wondered whether he would have to belabour Fairfax with his fists if need be, and chance the consequent enquiry.

Fairfax succeeded in getting his good foot into a stirrup. Then swung his long leg over the saddle and straddled the mare. He stared down at the confusion that filled their faces. "Are you a physician, Colonel Ireton?"

"No."

"Are *you* one, John?"

"Nay."

"Do you order me to abstain from this action as medical men?"

"No," they duetted defeatedly.

"Then I'll not lie here like a palsied monk while the game is playing!" That look of frenzied ecstasy was back, scorching from his eyes. He drew his sword with the noise of protesting metal. "And which is more, you are coming with me, the pair o' you!"

"So shall I, my lord!" Rushworth was already doubling back to his horse. He had been with the Chief long enough to recognise his own particular touch of choler.

Ireton took a moment to reflect on the folly of Generals who struck out for the thick of flying battle, in spite of gout and thunderstorms. His reflections took life as he muttered, "By Grace, I am in the hands of lunatics!"

Small hinges swung mighty doors. The Captain-General Fairfax could be seen by everyone, standing high in his stirrups. His hat had been lost and forgotten; his black hair hung loose upon his shoulders. Amid the rain and bullets, it was like he was riding the storm itself.

"Come on, my brave boys! I shall run the same fortunes and hazards as you, so I shall!"

The New Models hallooed their wild-eyed General. They hurled themselves forward and clawed at the rebels. Fairfax went with them. His urbanity was gone – in its place was a possessed Hercules.

"Let us pray for it, lads!" he cheered. "The harder we pray, the harder we fight!"

The fighting ha been hard where the River Len filtered down to join the Medway. Sir William Brockman stumbled to the rear. His sword was streaked with blood and his sleeve had been torn open at the shoulder. A shot from the ranks had nearly cracked his eardrum, but he was otherwise unharmed. His eyes were streaming. He was fighting the rain to make himself heard.

"Fall back! Fall back!" he waved. "We'll make our stand on Mill Street, by the bridge!"

Brockman gathered his remnants around him, sheathing his sword as he ran. The scabbard trailed awkwardly between his legs like a monkey's tail. He had not been prepared for the blood. The tang of death had got into the back of his throat. And out of his spasming mind, there writhed the one, unabating question:

Where, in the name of all that was holy, was the Earl of Norwich?

"Ho, ho! The lambs are running!" Ireton crowed, and punched the air.

Rushworth was much more logical. "They are mauled. They fly, but they merely retreat."

The hatless Fairfax watched the limping multitude, slogging up the lane. He could still hear the occasional flash of matchlock defiance. "That's all one, now. What is the hour, Colonel Rushworth?"

Rushworth delved into a pocket. He rubbed the raindrops from the face of his timepiece. "'Tis – tis a quarter of nine, my lord."

Fairfax dabbed at the end of his nose with the back of his bridle-hand gauntlet. "We'll storm the town at nine o'clock."

That had Rushworth's attention. "What did you say?"

The fire in the General's eyes was incandescent. "We must assault them! Beard to beard! It's now or never!"

Rushworth stared at the General's intensity. Every word was going against the chief's own, explicit instructions! Besides which, any notion of sending waves of men to storm entrenched positions turned his very blood to ice. What had His Lordship called it? *A house-to-house rat war.*

"But – !" he succeeded in saying. "To pitch headlong into the town can only invite – "

"The enemy is in flight, Colonel Rushworth. By book and bell, I'll tear those houses down piecemeal if I have to!" Fairfax reached forward from his saddle and gave his secretary a cuff upon the elbow. "Order Colonel Hewson's Foot to the assault, John. Order it!"

A good two miles of suffocating silence lay between the Earl of Norwich's contingent and the Parliament's guns. At first, it had been impossible to tell these thunderclaps from the deeper, muffled shake of cannon. Then the troops in their bivouac had glimpsed the distant pearls of winking fire, staining the darkness. Intermittent cannon-flash had shimmered through the rain, tracing the shapes of the hills before it evaporated back into the dark. Then that rolling rain bank found them. Everyone scattered for cover. Cloaked fortunates buttoned sturdy defences tighter. The luckless huddled, waiting. An old Monmouth cap gave little protection from this downpour.

Then the fugitives arrived. Swept on by the storms, they had ridden full-stretch for the Rochester passes. Their hooves slithered on the greasy roads. Lime-white faces brought the news with incoherent cries.

"Maidstone is alarmed! The town is imperilled!"

The rumours thudded on from man to man. Finally the news reached the ears of His Lordship himself.

"Lord Fairfax has arrayed his force before the town, my lord – Sir Gamaliel sends for help!"

"For help?" Norwich repeated, in a voice of incredulity. The scribbled note that had been thrust into his hands had perplexed him. "But he has three thousand men to guard that town!"

"My lord, the town *must* be taken unless it is helped!"

"Out of doubt, Maidstone will fall!"

Once again, Lord Norwich felt his inexperience settle about him like a millstone. He summoned his Staff to an immediate Council of War. Men arrived belted and spurred, covered in pistols and rapiers.

"Gentlemen, our forces are close invested in the town," the peer opened. "We cannot abandon them in conscience."

A battle of looks ensued. Expressions hardened. Nobody dared to go first.

In the end, another glut of messengers (each one sent out by different routes) converged on the Staff. They dropped their sketchy dispatches into the General's lap. Each one had their own, breathless versions of events. Their corselets turned to waterfalls in the rain.

"The Parliament has all the avenues!"

"Fairfax is over the river – the town is doomed!"

"My lord, it's all up with us! Black Tom is coming!"

One man, though, refused to panic. Colonel Thomas Culpepper had been born and bred not half a dozen miles from the county town. His plan, like his talk, was plain.

"My lord, I propound we draw out every horse and man at our disposal and let us go and have a fight with these Roundhead barbarians."

Norwich could not look at him. "I... I don't know."

"But this is our county, gentlemen! The world of our birthright!" Culpepper pursued. "If we are not all of us in arms for its lathes, then what are we waiting upon?"

Colonel L'Estrange, a gangling man who buried his chin in a magnificent beard, protested. "The men are weary, Culpepper. They must rest up."

The Earl looked at the other faces, each one stained into an orange murk by the brave little lanterns. "Sir Bernard? You advise?"

He had hazarded the question of the cherub-faced Florentine soldier of fortune, who sat beside him loudly taking snuff. His little box of Amsterdam blend was a powder that Sir Bernard Gascoigne particularly wanted kept dry.

Gascoigne treated them all an enormous, eye-watering sneeze. "I fear it is too late, milord." His manner was dismissive rather than defeatist. "These fugitives, they speak louder than any writing from your Governor."

The Earl took heed of that. Gascoigne was steeped in the wars: as an *uomo d'arme* in the Duchy of Florence, he had seen action across three different nations by the time he'd reached thirty.

Culpepper much preferred to chuck the Italian cuckoo out of His Lordship's nest. "May I repeat Sir Gamaliel's own words to you all?" He snatched up the most recent dispatch from the town. "'*Colonel Brockman's levies have done strengthened our forces, still I fear we cannot hold our own without immediate aid. Help us.*' There, my lord! "Help us"! There's evidence – incontrovertible!" He spun the parchment round and held it before his chest. The rain found the ink again, diluting and misting the words. "See, my lord, see! How can the Governor's message be misconstrued?"

The Earl squinted at it. Dudley's scrawling fist testified to his frantic haste. Culpepper's wet, gloved finger had blotted the anguished '*Help us*'."

"What d'you counsel, Sir Bernard?" he asked.

The Florentine gave an extremely Continental shrug. Speech was unnecessary.

"We are lying too thin on the ground as it is," mooted L'Estrange. "We would be marching to our deaths if we turned for Maidstone now."

Another thunderclap went tearing by.

"Aye, my lord! Where are the fifteen thousands which you said we were supposed to rally? Where are they?" Culpepper stood there, unappeased, with his fists balled tight. "Those be our men, our brothers, in the town! I'll warrant most of 'em declared for the King before we did! God's teeth, are we merely to sit here and *dawdle?*"

Nobody answered. Nobody could. The only sound was the hiss of the rain, and the braying of protest from a nearby horse.

"I – I thank you, one and all, for your counsel, gentlemen," Norwich mumbled.

Through tears of frustration, Culpepper played his ace. "After Naseby," he said in cracking tones, "the New Models slashed the cheeks and noses of our force's wives to the bone when they caught up with the luggage. Good God, my lord, what if Black Tom's cut-throats do the same to the women of Maidstone?"

Norwich was visibly shocked, but not so Colonel L'Estrange. "I was not aware our county town was filled with leaguer-bitches for the Roundhead dogs to mutilate!" he remarked, curtly.

As for the Earl, he had the look of one who has walked into a wall. He could almost hear Dudley and Brockman's death rattles, drop by drop by drop. He could almost see the Roundhead Troopers, scowling in triumph over the bodies of those gentlemen. The world had become a vast plain of gloom and strident jeopardy. He felt old and doddering. His brain had been invaded by thick mists. In hope, he looked to the sky in a kind of trance-like rapture. The rain had petered out for the moment, and there were only grey clouds, scudding across the moon. He buried his face behind his fingers.

Culpepper leaned over the elderly man. It took a monumental effort not to thrust out a hand and shake the Earl by the shoulder. "My lord! Your orders! What are we to *do?*"

Slowly, excruciatingly, Norwich took his face out of his hands. "We will do... what we can," he lamented at last.

Nathan floundered through the rain, feeling lumpen and breathless. He had entered the outer reaches of the hamlet of Tovil, with its cottage walls of lime and hair. A stitch was clamping his side. He forced himself to slow the pace. His hands were slick and wet. His heart was bellowing. The sight of the dead repulsed him. Corpses lay scattered like seeds in the mud and the puddles. He grabbed at a hawthorn branch and bent forwards from the waist. To vomit would be a relief, but when he attempted it, all that croaked out was a pitiful cough of sputum.

Everywhere he looked, bodies lay thick on the rutted track. Many of their eyes were still open, seeing nothing. The way they lay was untidy and unnatural. Their skins were sheared by powder blasts. One lacerated specimen had had his face torn open by the splinters of his pikestaff.

The rain was still beating down. Its drops went *pat-pat-patter* upon the cuirasses. The lightning gave him cheerless glimpses of the night. The Tovil Lane was strewn with reaching limbs, and with horses that hung on noisily to life. Their long legs kicked and quivered the dead men that surrounded them. More bodies, now. Raw ones. Dead man's bowels. The fetid smell of organs, guts and bones.

"A surgeon! For the love of God, a surgeon!"

Nathan wanted to go to that voice. He ought to venture forth and dig for that soul, to find it in the morass of other bodies. He should play the cleric, offering companionship and the verses of reassurance at the last. But the rain outwitted him. Those who had come up to the edge of the precipice looked no different from the ones who'd already tumbled in.

He slipped from cottage to cottage, darting down the hedgerow with animal quickness. The houses looked dead in their turn. No lights to see; not even a curling wisp of smoke in any of the chimney stacks. Nobody stirred on the road. No calls, no challenges to stop and show himself. No hurricane of musket fire. There was only the rain, and the corpses.

And another anxiety, right at the back of his mind. The one, sly thought past bearing. The thought of the two of them, dead, in the gutter. Pip, and Stephen. Dragged over the cobbles and killed in the street. His wife; his life. His son; all that Stephen stood for. Bundles of rags, crushed beneath the boots of a desperate battle.

His mouth was prickling. His tongue tasted tin. Blending as best he could into the hedgerow, he tucked his chin down tight upon his chest, and hurried on towards the town.

THIRTY-SIX

With such a horrid clang
As on Mount Sinai rang,
While the red fire and smouldering clouds outbrake.

The Agnew girls huddled together under the eaves. Judah was standing at the window, with his firelock ported. He had primed the pan and all was ready. The match was idly smouldering. He had to blow on it every other minute to keep its wispy flame alive.

Judah's breathing was steady as he listened to the rain. It spattered on the roof and spilled, chuckling, into the guttering, just level with his cap. The sounds of fighting carried on the sullen black night. The girls no longer flinched at it. Week Street had yet to see battle, and the rain and the rooftops hid whatever was going on. It fell to the imagination to stoke up the senses.

The minutes dragged. Judah leaned his elbow upon the sill. He rested the butt of his matchlock on the floor and stared back into the room. The garret was illumined by three lanterns. One stood on the floor, another on a shelf. The third had been placed atop the lid of an old trunk near the door. It helped to illuminate the first few steps leading down to the landing below.

The girls all sat on the floor, with their backs to the walls. The twins sat apart, by themselves. They were holding hands with knitted fingers. Carrie sat between Stephen and Loobie, and her arms were cuddling the young'uns. The little boy's mother sat nearest the door. It seemed strange for the sexton to think that these young ladies were the same mischievous imps who play hide and seek behind the graves in Saint Margaret's yard.

Philippa looked down at her hands. She was swivelling her ring around her finger. Round, and round again. Her father's brace of doglock pistols lay by her side.

She would not cry. She had promised herself that, no matter the course, she would not cry. Not even when she was alone and unwatched.

Carrie's chin was tilted down so Stephen and Loobie might nestle against her head. Her lips were scarcely moving as she sang them the song.

"Then will I wait
Till the waters abate
Which now disturb my troubled brain.
Then for ever rejoice
When I've heard the voice
That the King enjoys his own again!"

This was no mere lullaby. The ballad was sung so softly it was practically a psalm.

Judah scratched at an itch in his chin with his knuckles. What "waters"? The flood of Noah? The Babylonian rivers? This deluge over Maidstone? It was a timeless, human metaphor.

Then there came a beating on the front door. The girls all looked up from their thoughts. A muffled shout accompanied the knocking:

"Open up! In the King's name!"

Judah leaned out and peered down from his vantage point. The voice belonged to Captain Marchington, though he was screened from Judah's view by Number Twenty Seven's prognathic gable. Sir John Mayney had instructed the Captain to amass the levies in readiness. He was rounding up these bumpkins, sots and Bedlamites he needs must call his men.

The Captain beat again, impatiently. "You, within there! Open in the King's name!"

Philippa jumped to her feet, snatching up the nightlight from the trunk and shoving a pistol in the pocket of her apron. She sped to the door with a cry of, "Stay here, all of you!" Judah was hot on her heels, trying not to scratch the walls with the butt of his firelock.

Carrie's grip increased on Stephen's ropey shoulder as first his mother, then the friendly man with the gun, left the garret. "Sssh…" His Aunt Carrie compelled him back down to the floor gently. She planted a kiss on the bridge of Stephen's nose. "Think not about it, sweetheart. You stay with me and Loobie."

Coates wrenched the door open. Captain Marchington jumped into the hall. Raindrops fell from his hat brim, and smacked to their deaths on the floorboards. "God's chest, it is dark here! Bring a lantern, someone!"

Coates picked up the lantern from the table by the door, and held it before him.

"That you, Drummer? Where's Sarjeant Magner?"

Coates turned his head to give a call, but the fox-face had already loomed out of the shadows. "Here, Captain. Yours to command."

"They have broken through on the flank, into the Lower Town. Get every man you have and march them to the crossroads. You'll be given instruction there."

"Is it really so serious, Captain?" asked the elderly figure who'd emerged from the parlour.

Marchington answered with devastating simplicity. "It'll be every man on the wall, Corporal. Tooth and nail, if need be." He looked at Magner. "Act lively now, Sarjeant! Get your men moving!"

The Captain hurried on to drum up the next quota of men.

"Jesus wept!" said Coates.

"You heard the officer." Magner had retrieved his spontoon from where he'd left it propped up in the hall. "Double up, my lads! Double up!"

"Go. Go." Rebecca urged them quietly on from the door to the parlour. She had remained in that room all the while with Melhuish, sitting watchfully below the smashed-in windows. "God be with you all."

The Corporal nodded his farewell. "Save you, Mistress!"

They dribbled into the street. The rain came dead-cold against their skin. As they pelted down Week Street, they lost cohesion among the other men who were tumbling from the houses. It was impossible to keep together, but they knew where the crossroads were, and that they had to get there. Fast.

Philippa descended the stair. Down in its pocket, the pistol thumped against her legs with the motion. "Mother?" She swung the candle's glow upon Rebecca's face.

Her mother stepped into the light. "Go to the others, Pip."

"You're coming up, too?" Her daughter started backing up, showing Mother the way.

"No. I am going to rub up something to eat, for all of us."

Philippa stared. "Something – to eat?"

"I'm hungry; I know not about you." Rebecca's voice was mild. "And there may be some scraps in the kitchen... assuming the good Master Coates has left us anything, that is."

She vanished into the kitchen. It was some moments before Philippa followed her mother's bidding and climbed to the landing. Lantern held before her, she went to the foot of the upper staircase. "Carrie?"

Carrie appeared. She had had the foresight to pick up the matching doglock. "Headstrong? Is that you?"

"They have gone. You can bring everybody down."

She heard the scrape of shoes on floorboards, and the sounds of the girls stretching like cats. Carrie copied Pip's example and stowed the pistol in her apron. Its rounded outline bulged through the linen. "What is Mother's plan? D'you know?"

"Aye," said Philippa. "To eat."

Carrie leaned against the door, hiding her eyes on her arm. "The Army's closing in on us, and Mother wants to sit around and eat toasted cheese!"

"TOASTED CHEESE!" yelled Stephen. He couldn't believe his luck.

"I am merely the messenger," said Philippa. "Bring everybody down."

Carrie stood aside. Stephen led the charge, with Loobie at his back.

It was like striding into a screen of Latter Day liquid fire. Every window on Gabriel's Hill hid a nest of snipers. And always, beating out the rhythm like the drums on a Roman galley, came that chant from the rebels' lines.

"King-and-Kent! King-and-Kent! King-and-Kent!"

The levies loaded and fired to those tripling notes. Volleys of small-shot discharged through the pelting rain. The stoccados were buried in smoke.

Colonel Hewson's Regiment of Foot pushed forward. Steady, snaphance-bearing infantry were advancing up the street.

"Fall on! Fall on! Let none of the dogs escape!"

Thomas Hewson had been in one of the first dozen, defining regiments which had answered Cromwell's call. Men like him had brought the New Model into being and given it life. Now he had been knocked down by the butt end of a Kentish firelock. He was helped to his feet by his subordinate, Major Carter. The blood was slithering down Hewson's face, liquefied by the rain. No sooner was the Colonel upright again than Major Carter's wrist was smashed by a musket ball. His broad sword dropped to the roadway with a shrill metallic ring.

Hewson's regimental ensign still flew, even as its two commanders were helped to the rear. The flag was of rich blue cloth, with the cross of Saint George in the centre. It was riddled with bullet holes and scrammed to tatters about its fringe.

"On, lads, on!" yelled an authoritative voice. "Show the slaves that they may not stand in the way of the law!"

The two sides collided. Musket butts were brought to bear as clubs. Blood and chips of teeth flew wide with flecks of spittle.

Captain Topping, another of Hewson's officers, was advancing on the rebels' barricade with his comrade Captain Price. Swords in hand, they had advanced into every fight together since Marston Moor. Then Price took a bullet. He doubled up, his hands plucking at his clothes, trying to feel for the sixpence-shaped hole where the ball had punched its way in.

Topping crouched beside his friend, hunting faces that he knew "Sarjeant Betts! Lend a hand, and aid me here!"

The brawny Sarjeant dutifully dived to the Captain's side. He helped Topping to recover Price the veteran's body.

The New Model Army peeled away down Gabriel's Hill. Now they knew that the defenders – the rebel scum they had derided round their camp fires – would not be defeated cheaply.

The puddles deepened, broadened. The hill became a river. Limbs and clawing fingers started to freeze in the rain. Dead men, eyes open and frozen in disbelief, lay where they fell. The wounded prayed through twitching lips.

Then, action. Men coming *down* Gabriel's Hill, from behind their barricade. The Royalists turned to meet this new onslaught, fearing a cunning encircling movement. But no! These were no Roundheads – their lines were being reinforced! Fresh men were being fetched from the High Town. This time the rain nourished their spirits, not put them out. The cries of "King-and-Kent!" were replaced with a chorus of warm-blooded cheers, and a lot of derision for Black Tom's retreating curs. The rebels allowed themselves to forget, if only for a moment, that the professionals would soon be back.

Before the fight began, Sir Gamaliel Dudley had changed out of his sweaty doublet and into clean linens, as one who goes to chair a meeting of the Council. A Roundhead sword had cut him about at the left elbow; now he carried his arm in a makeshift sling. All Saints' bell had just chimed the half when Sir William Brockman, dirtied and sweating, joined him in the doorway of the now-abandoned Ship Inn.

"We have brought up more men! All that could be found!"

"Do not fill your heart with any false hope, Sir William." Dudley had always been a realist, and he could feel the sands shifting.

Brockman did not care for the grey, grim look on the Governor's face. "But the longer we hold here," he tried to reason, "the more time we'll secure for His Lordship to rally his own forces."

Dudley's gaze moved from the cheering barricade, to Brockman's troubled countenance. "You think that feasible, Sir William?" The question came with a lift of those bushy eyebrows. "I tell you again: Lord Norwich will not come."

The Sheriff exploded, "POX HIM!" and stamped his foot.

Dudley sighed. He wore the expression Latimer and Ridley must have worn when they walked to the stake. "If we are bound for Glory, why not meet it in the face?"

They contemplated one another before they shook hands. Then they were both on the barricade, behind the swollen ranks. They paced from one side of the street to the other, reaching out to pat an occasional shoulder, arm, or elbow.

"Have faith, men!" Dudley called. "Have faith in God's protection!"

Something was uncoiling through the smoke. Brockman saw the nervous glances. "Stand!" he hollered. "Stand until they are within ten paces of your reach, and the day may yet be ours!"

A soldier turned to look at him. He was another raw levy. He looked young, and much afraid. "We are to take the buggers on again, sir?"

"We'll take 'em on with bread knives if we have to." Brockman drew his pistol from his waistbelt. The powder was wet through. The thing was useless!

The Governor took command. "Captain Marchington! Collect every man in three. Take them head on at any point that breaks through – you must not let them turn us!"

"I'll see it done, sir!"

He did, too. Which meant that Corporal Clare no longer had Private Copp at his side, but a stalk of seventeen who until three days ago had plied an unassuming trade along the Medway.

"Easy, son. Easy." There was a hint of a smile on the old Corporal's lips. "Shut your eyes if you want to. I'll nudge you when the time comes."

The New Models were on the move. Accompanying the scores of sturdy shoes, there arose a low, guttural noise, nearing and nearing.

"Truth! Truth! Truth! Truth!"

The monster was emerging from its depths. It bore its fifteen-foot pikes before it, each one tipped with eighteen inches of pointed steel.

"Stand, you whorsons, stand!" roared Marchington.

"Truth! Truth! Truth! Truth!"

"Hold your positions! Steady, boys! *Steady-y-y-y!*"

Melhuish looked at the young lad by his side. The boy could not wrench his eyes away from the advancing pikemen. He wore no cuirass, and had only a Monmouth cap on to protect his head. Melhuish had seen for himself what a lead ball could do, when it hit a skull in the right place.

Out of nowhere, he felt a tap on his right shoulder. It was Coates, who had reached behind the gulping young river man to pat his Corporal's bicep.

"Proudcock!"

Chris had sounded urgent, but Melhuish hadn't caught the one-word message. "You what?"

"Proudcock! Magner! Where is he?"

THIRTY-SEVEN

A thousand fantasies
Reign to throng my memory
Of calling shapes, and beckoning shadows dire.

Beyond the Tovil boundary, Nathan's luck ran out. There had been a sudden, "HEY, YOU!" and then a flash. Several shots had spat at him, slicing and bruising the air.

The aim had been untrue. Slightly to his surprise, he had not been hit. He turned off the road before anyone could reload for another try. First he crackled through the hedge, clueless to who or what lay on the other side. There was soft, wet grass underfoot again. The rain lashed him as he scuttled down the slope toward the waiting hop gardens. The weather-beaten poles were thickly wrapped in shivering seeds. Their fronds arched into the night like the vault of a church. They would hide him well enough.

When he'd got a good deal deeper into the hops, he stopped and took stock. He should have kept a look out for their armour; their helmets and back-and-brace would have shone through the dark. Trapped inside the confines of his own, deluded brain, he had nearly got himself killed by the Parliament's sentry posts!

He could almost hear her chiding voice: *Mutton-head!*

Nathan waited in those rustling corridors for some time. He barely dared to move while he wondered what had gone wrong with the world. He knew he could not turn back, for heaven knew how many New Model men must be streaming across the river by now. Besides, the Rectory would bound to be in the military's hands by now. Following their own particular views on "hospitality", they'd have gone over every inch of the unlocked house, taking the sheets from the beds and the linen from the chest. They'd have taken the cheese from the pantry; the ale that had been fetched from the little brewhouse... They'd have carried off the drinking cups and the pewterware pots from the kitchen... They'd have ripped up Pip's books, they'd have smashed Stephen's toys.

Nathan's over-stimulated mind was happy to supply him with a stealthy party of Parliament troops, hunting him down through the hop poles. He could almost see them, coming for him now, with their short swords drawn.

He moved. But he did not run until he had put a decent distance between himself, and those carbines that covered the lane. The riverbank was dark, and damp, overhung with willows and a lot of drooping alders. Nathan doubted even the most fanatical of Fairfax's men would chase a fleet-of-foot shadow to earth into this murk.

He fell over twice. Rolled once. A good roll, too, over head and heels.

Something snagged at his cloak behind him, yanking him up short and nearly throttling him. It turned out to be not one of Cromwell's Ironsides, but a gorse bush. Nathan fumbled with the cord at his neck. He freed himself to breathe. He massaged his aching Adam's apple before he picked up the pace again. The cloak remained behind, snared upon the gorse. The wind was trying to play with it.

He had made it to the very shoulder of the river. His confidence grew. The ground felt firmer, tightly packed by the tread of countless wayfarers. Somewhere he thought he'd heard the lowing of a cow. The beast had best look to itself: it would be a plumb target for the Army to steal.

And then he tripped. Or rather, something *made* him trip.

In putting out his hands to break his fall, he plunged them straight into an ambush of waiting nettles. The blistering was instantaneous. It made him grit his teeth while he tried to fight the pain. He still did not dare to cry out. Instead, he knuckled his fists and clamped his hands under his armpits. He screwed his eyes down shut so tightly that they hurt.

From a sitting position, while his palms burned, Nathan attempted to work out what had tripped him. At first he guessed it to be a particularly thick-grown root. Then, as he felt about, he realised that the trunk was soft and yielding. This tree was flesh and bone. And its roots had trousers on.

It was a man.

Nathan felt about a bit more. The man was wet through, lying on his back, daubed with fresh and sucking mud. One leg stuck straight out towards the river. Nathan bent over him, putting his head close so that the man might hear his low tones.

"Who are you?" he asked. Then, "Are you hurt?"

He shook the man's shoulder. The man only stirred, and moaned. Coherent speech was beyond him. Yet who could he be? New Model idealist, or local conscript who had declared for King Charles? The man's hair trailed. It flapped against his head as Nathan tried to move his head. A patch of moonlight nearer to the river looked promising, but moving the body was agony for Nathan's hands.

The moonlight did the trick. Deep punctures had riddled the man's body. Nathan twisted his lips. The gashes were deep and ugly. Ball, or blade? Who knew? The man could not last long: that was undeniable.

Nathan had heard plenty of tales about solitary animals who would crawl away to die. This fellow must have heard them, too. Assuming this fellow had been wounded in the lane, he would have staggered all of four hundred yards before his legs had given way. The moonlight showed Nathan that the wounded man's fingernails were filthy. They were almost gloved with muck. That detail made him rewrite the scenario. This fellow must have *clawed* his way of escape along the path. How could he have possibly lasted so long?

The man had gone limp. Only the shallow breath and straining muscles around the lower jaw communicated pain. Nathan remembered Captain Agnew, expiring with the company of God beside the his own bed, in his own house, knowing that his kith and kin were close at hand.

Nathan cleared his throat. "I am a Man of God, sirrah. I shall not abandon you now. You hear me?"

The dying man could neither affirm or deny it. Flecks of blood bubbled and popped on his lips. Nathan held on to his hand. He tried to ignore the sting, and the clammy cold that was soaking his knees. He needed a decent intercession for this moment. The man was a soldier. Or at the very least, he was ending his time upon this planet as a soldier. Nathan chose his text carefully: something with a military palate.

"O Lord, hedge up my way with thorns, that I may find no path for following vanity. Hold me with bit and bridle, lest I fall away from you."

He thought he felt a squeezing on his fingers.

"O Lord, compel me now to come to you: to bruise the serpent's head, to remember my life's end, to —"

He stopped. The man had gone. His words had merely been heard by the beyond. Nathan granted the man the decency of closing his eyes, before granting himself a moment of head-lowered prayer.

Then he was up, and off.

The river path curled round the foot of the hill. Up ahead, Maidstone's landmarks were starting to make themselves known under the moon, and he could hear the firefight. That explosive chaos seemed to be climbing up Gabriel's Hill, so far as he could judge. Soon he stood underneath the sheer, mullioned cliff of the Archbishop's Palace. He crept along crabwise at the foot of the wall. Now he knew how a rat must feel when it scurried along in a cellar. Every footfall could bring a harsh shout, and the cocking of a carbine, twenty feet above his head.

There was a flight of steps coming down to the river, but no sentry appeared to be using them. He passed beneath All Saints' churchyard without a hitch. No musket balls peppered the Medway; no stream of army crudities at having missed him. Fortuna's wheel was revolving in his favour! He pursued the path until he reached the blown-up ruins of the town's Great Bridge. He scaled the precipitous bank. He nearly overbalanced, but by a lot of scrambling he made it to the top on his hands and knees.

Instantly, half a dozen lanterns trained on him. A well-drilled voice barked, "Halt! Who comes?"

Nathan saw the buff coats, and the triple-barred helmets. He heard the unmistakable, bone-chilling sound of a sword being freed from its scabbard. His throbbing, muck-streaked palms spread out across his knees as he bent forward to gather his wind. There must be two or three carbines pointing right at his head. He was too spent to defend himself, either with words or fists. He was finished.

"Carry you a weapon?"

Nathan managed to shake his head. "I — I am unarmed!" he gasped out.

"Deserter, are you, sirrah?" The voice was not impressed.

Nathan's muscles protested as he straightened up. "I — I am no rebel. I'm a Parson!"

A pause. Someone brought a lantern bobbing nearer.

"You say... you are a what?"

What had he to lose? "My name is the Reverend Nathan Wohlford. I am the Rector of the parish of East Farleigh."

Slowly, unaggressively, the Trooper walked closer. His sword was lowered level with his hip. He inspected the unkempt broadcloth that Nathan was wearing.

"By the Powers! I believe he *is* a Parson!"

Another soldier stepped up. "Aye, that be a Parson, alright, Corporal Probyn! He's a bit out of repair, but look at those roast-beef clothes!"

"Of course I am!" Nathan poured what faculties he had left into an act of effrontery. "And you none of you ought to hinder me in my lawful occasions."

"You'll pardon us, Vicar." The first man's tone had changed. It sounded somewhat meeker, less intractable. The sword was promptly sheathed.

Now that the light had been fetched, and held there, Nathan got a good look at his captors. Their chevron-patterned sleeves denoted them as Parliamentarian cavalry, but these "brothers of the blade" certainly didn't *look* like blood-drunk mercenaries. These weren't the pinch-faced demons of Kentish nightmares. They only hunched their shoulders and moaned about the weather in low tones.

Their leader spoke again. "Taking a risk being out on a night like this, aren't you, Vicar? There's warm work over there." He pointed toward the sounds of the racketing battle.

"You ... play no role in that?"

"Not yet," said the Trooper with the light. "Not till we get the word. Then it's all in."

Nathan sensed a champing impatience among them, a barefaced resentment at being guards to the *real* fight that they could all hear blasting away across the rooftops.

"Have care, Isaac!" Probyn rumbled his warning at the Trooper's interruption. Turning back to Nathan he remarked: "You came across country I perceive, Parson."

"What? Oh! So I did." Nathan looked down. By their lamplight, he could see he was wearing greaves of mud. "I had to, mind. The roads are clogged with troops. And, in any case," he embellished, "my horse is lame."

He had broken the Ninth Commandment, but it had sold its life dearly.

Isaac-with-the-lantern now turned out to be quite garrulous. "Ah, it'll be these jumble-gut lanes of yours, Reverend!" he winked at Nathan. "My eye, we had a struggle on the march!"

Corporal Probyn would not be satisfied so easily. "You have chosen a da – I mean, a *very* odd time for to go a-parish visiting, Parson." He was glad he'd corrected himself: he could lose a day's pay for impious language, and there were witnesses aplenty.

"A cleric's work is never done, sirrah," Nathan returned promptly.

"Nay, nor a woman's day, neither!" chortled Isaac-with-the-lantern. "Just you go asking my Esther!"

The others all snickered. Corporal Probyn appeared to arrive at a resolution. He stepped aside. "On your way, Master Parson. God buy you."

Nathan's heart leapt, but he tried not to show it. He must keep things benign between them. "God go with you, men."

Isaac-with-the-lantern nodded at him. "Save you, Parson. Safe home to you, now."

They rather lost interest in them after that. Nathan controlled his urge to sprint until he had walked fifty paces from the bridge. As he strode on, he tried to think of Maidstone's street map. He wasn't far from Week Street, yet he knew he could not take the High Street. He would have to hug the river for a bit, at least until he reached the bulk of Maidstone's Corpus Christi Hall. That way, if he turned right, he could still hope to reach Week Street via Bullocke Lane.

He was skirting the trim, green, riverside oblong that was the King's Meadow. It was Maidstone's own bowling green, where her well-heeled denizens liked to be seen on an afternoon stroll. As Nathan passed the Meadow, it triggered off a memory. When he was about ten, he'd once thrashed Pip and Rebecca's forces combined at a game of pall-mall on the long lawn at Barming Place. Rebecca had been pregnant with the twins. The Captain had watched them from the little house, smoking his pipe and cheering and jeering as the state of play required. When Nathan had won the game, he'd gone haring round and round the lawn, flailing his arms like a windmill. Pip had chased him. Little Carrie, too, as she had been then… Rebecca had stood there, heavily pregnant and wheezing with laughter, supporting the small of her back… Faithful had brought out a seed cake on a platter. Funny, the mundanities you remembered when you were running for your life.

He made it to Bullocke Lane without challenge. He leaned against a bannister of iron railings, legs burning from the run, and got his breath back.

The noise of Hell was closer. Pip, being Pip, would probably have likened it to King Harry roaring his fist-shaking menaces before the gates of Harfleur in the play.

About a third of the way up the Lane, he had to stop. The street had been barricaded. Nathan saw crates and packing cases; furniture, dragged from the houses and out of the inns. A carter's waggon. A carved oak headboard.

Somebody behind that headboard took a shot at him. Nathan threw himself flat on his face. A cry from the barricade made him guess that the sniper had fired without permission. The sniper was cursed for a half-baked fool. The aim had been sloppy, and wasteful.

"Halt! Who comes?"

Nathan groaned through his teeth. *Were the fools never trained to say anything else?*

He heaved himself back to his feet. This time his desperate exhaustion rang clear. "Nathan Wohlford. Please – my wife and family!"

Silence.

"Advance, friend."

Nathan ran to the wall. Strong hands helped him over the barricade. He jumped down, and nearly fell, but his helper kept hold of his wrist. A bearded, hook-nosed face was on the end of that hand. One man among forty, waiting on the wall with readied weapons. Recognition showed in the man's eyes. "So you made it through their lines, then, did you, Parson?"

Nathan gawped. "Master Joplin? Is that you?"

Sam Joplin tried to smile. "'Tis well to see you alive, sir."

"They – they are on the Great Bridge," Nathan succeeded in pointing. "Down there."

"Aye. They must've wheeled about the town, and they'll be rolling us up soon right enough. But we'll be ready for the bastards. No offence." Joplin's rough hand patted him away. "Go find your dearest, then. God speed."

The blacksmith turned back to the river and picked up his matchlock again.

"Farewell, Sam. Farewell."

Nathan left them. At the junction with Week Street, he ducked into a dark, recessed doorway. There were soldiers everywhere – everywhere! Most of them running like sheep.

Nathan heard the screams.

"The town is gone!"

"Get out, lads! For your lives!"

"We're betrayed! We are all undone!"

That din was getting closer, working its way to the surface of the earth. Nathan stood, frozen where he was, breathing so hard that it made his throat sore. The blood was pounding in his ears. These houses, they had taken on the quality of tombstones. Alleys and courts became charnel-houses where life was expended, with nothing to witness it but timber, and tile, and lime.

Pip, and Stephen had wandered into his mind again. Their fates grew sharp. Would they have clubbed them to death? Shot them? Cut their throats to the neck bone? Spitted his son on a twenty foot pike?

The rain and the sweat and the tears all joined together, but Nathan didn't care.

He ran.

THIRTY-EIGHT

Comes the blind Fury with the abhorred shears
And slits the thin-spun life.

Sarjeant Magner sidled through the rain from door to door. His down-at-heel, bucket boots were slipping on the cobbles. Away from the hurricane on Gabriel's Hill, the town was extraordinarily lifeless. Not even the scurrying of a rat, or a cat, or a dog fox, or any other thing that liked to explore the streets at night.

Of course, he had had to make a good show of urging his squad to meet the hated foeman. But it had been the easiest dodge in the book, to slip into a doorway and wait for the crowd to move on. Then the quiet had settled. He had cast his spontoon away, into the gutter. It had left him a clear run back for his urgent business.

Aladdin's Cave was beckoning, and he knew just where to find it. Sarjeant Kill-Sin Magner could well fall in battle that night, unless he kept his wits about him. Just another levy, martyred for a Cause. If he was doomed, then it only befell he plunder Nature's Treasury one last time, and ransack all he found there.

The house was very near. He could feel how his breath was quickening. His palms had greased with the sweat of anticipation. There was nothing unnatural in that. They always did.

The last thing he had expected was for another man's hand to alight upon his shoulder, and to draw him up short.

"A word with you, sirrah!"

Magner spun upon his heels, only to find himself looking into the searching face of the garrison's Provost. Should thoughts of self-preservation take hold, and any man-at-arms desert his post and try to run, then the Provost would funnel the fugitive back to the wall, and make him fight on.

"What mean you by abandoning your post?" demanded the immovable officer.

Magner analysed the other man's hatchet face. Excuses would cut no ice with the angry Provost. This was an old soldier, unbending as wood. It would not matter if Magner's protestations were half-baked, wheedling, or forceful. And the Provost could not be alone: his rank required the presence of shut-faced attendants… But, for that moment, he *was* alone. Where was his officious entourage?

The hand shook Magner's shoulder. "An answer, sirrah! This is the very last chance, now!"

There was nothing else for it. Sarjeant Magner played things very coolly.

"Begging your pardon, sir?"

Before the Provost could react, before he could even flinch, his detainee had whipped the officer's very own pistol out of his belt and had fired it right in his face. The Provost reeled, and collapsed. His legs spelt perfect V where he fell on the cobbles. Shot at such close range by a heavy ball, his face was now a bloodied mess of bone and pulp.

Magner chucked the weapon away. His thrill became elation when he watched the pistol tumble between the bars of a grating, falling to rest in someone's cellar.

Number Twenty-One… Twenty-Three… Twenty-Five…

They were picking at the last of the scraps in the kitchen. Extra lanterns had been procured from the cupboard in the parlour. They kept a good supply of them in there: the twins had often worked late. Carrie had stood on a chair to hang one from a meat-hook over the table. Their meal had been played out mostly in shadow.

Mother had served them the remains of the chicken which they had partly demolished earlier. She had concealed the carcass in a low cupboard, behind a stack of ancient tankards: a device that had foiled even Drummer Coates' scrounging. Ros and Elle had squabbled over the last remaining leg, till Pip had snatched it firmly from their hands and presented it to Stephen. That had settled the matter all round. They ate the last of the caraway biscuits, and a little bread and butter. There was an eked-out quart of cider, to wash it all down. Carrie had stomached the least of all, and even Mother had only made do with the hardening crust off the end of the loaf. She had nibbled it slowly, watching the rest of the family eat.

Stephen yawned. All this up-past-bedtime excitement was wearing off.

"Are you tired, little bunny?" his Aunt Ros cooed at him across the table.

"Am not!" he shot back, rubbing his eyes. He glugged down the last of his beaker of buttermilk to prove it.

"Do not slurp your drink, Stephen," his mother reproached.

His face reappeared, dripping pearly white.

Philippa stood up and took charge of things again. "Right, children! Back upstairs with you. Return to the garret, mind, not to your rooms."

Stephen and Loobie got down from the table. Philippa handed the nearest lantern to Loobie. The children scampered off. Stephen still wondered why Mother had kept that old pistol on the table all through the meal. After all, you couldn't eat it.

Philippa waited till she was sure they had reached the landing. "Carrie? You go next."

Carrie left the kitchen without a backward glance, taking the second lantern with her. Ros and Elle rose from their chairs.

Rebecca blew out a couple more of the lanterns. She wanted to save the wicks. Now they were reduced to the light from only two. "You go up next, girls. I wish to tidy up."

"What?" The look that the twins gave her clearly implied that Mother had run mad. Philippa, though, understood perfectly. Mother needed something – anything – "normal", which might distract her troubled mind. Tidying away some old pots and pewterware was as good a task as any.

Rebecca repeated the order. "Girls? Go."

Rosalind crossed her arms. "Shan't!"

Her mother sighed. "*You* go up, then, Pip. Go and look after the children."

For a moment, Philippa thought she should help Mother pitch her lines against the twins for the coming skirmish, but Stephen and Loobie won out. She took the other lantern down from the meat hook and slipped upstairs.

The darkness thickened in the kitchen.

"Now, listen, you two – " Rebecca brandished the cloth, but Ros was ready for her.

"No, *you* listen, Mother! Elle and I are sick to the teeth of that garret!"

"We've been up there for hours and hours!" Elle reinforced. She had been waiting to speak her mind, and would not pass up this chance. "It's bad enough up there when it just be the two of us; with all of us in it, we've no room to swing a cat!"

Rebecca checked herself with a mighty effort. "The garret is the safest place to be, girls."

Ros counterattacked: "You call it a garret, Mother; I call it a tomb!"

Her mother threw down the cloth. "You will go forthwith. The pair of you!"

Ros responded by drawing back a chair and sitting down. "Make us!" she challenged.

Rebecca glared at her. "Why, you little hoyden – !"

"Go on, Ma! Make us!" She had chosen "Ma" on purpose, knowing how her parent hated it. "Elle? Sit!"

Elle dithered. By the glow of the lantern, she could see the fury brewing in Mother's eyes.

The three staccato knocks, and the muffled call of "Open in the King's name!" were a salvation.

"I'll go!" Elle grabbed the lantern from the table and bounded out the door. Now deprived of their light, Ros and Rebecca had no recourse but to declare a truce and follow her bobbing lantern, out of the kitchen and into the gloom.

"Elle! Wait!"

The knocking sounded again. Rebecca thought it unusually insistent. There was a force to its blows that startled her. For all of her dizzied fatigue, she could feel her hackles rise.

"Eleanor! Don't open that door!" she shouted.

They heard the latch give, and the hinges creak. Then they both heard Elle's cry of alarm.

It was only the one man who barged in through the gap. He shut the door smartly behind him, cutting off the outside world. Eleanor stumbled backwards, trying to hold the light higher and see the face. All she could see was a pair of jet-black eyes, and a highly pointed beard.

"Sarjeant Magner!"

Magner snatched off his hat. The light made his ringlets gleam. "The same! You will excuse the lateness of the hour, my ladies."

Rebecca took hold of Eleanor's lantern. "Girls? Get behind me."

Magner looked them over before he advanced on the group. "A buck could be dead by dawn, Mistress. The soldier learns to take his comforts where he finds them."

"What mean you by that remark, Sarjeant Magner?" Rebecca's voice sounded suspiciously high and sharp.

The man leered at them into the light. "A man needs to spread it about, d'ye see? Just as God meant it in the scriptures. Your ordinary pox-vendor won't do, when a man's at the last. A man needs a doll who is fresh to the game."

He was looking at Elle as he said it. A tremor seized Rebecca's frame and made her gasp.

"No…" the twins heard her whisper. Their anxiety turned to panic.

"MOTHER!"

Eleanor's cry came just as the Sarjeant whipped a six-inch dagger from his belt. Magner stepped forward. His dark eyes were gleaming with pleasure. Their fear was growing his pleasure. Instinctively, the others started moving backwards, into the parlour.

"Stand aside, Mistress!"

The dagger flashed. He continued straight for Eleanor.

Rebecca side-stepped into his path. Now she was shouting. "No! You shall not have her!"

Magner only smiled. "The fawn, and then the doe! Panting for it, are you, Mistress?"

His arm shot forward. The knife pierced her bodice and explored her abdomen. Rebecca arched her neck back.

"Is that what you want, now? IS IT?"

He drove the blade in harder. He could feel its point scrape against her ribs. The smile became a snarl. Rebecca's eyes were staring into his. He felt her breath upon his face. There was blood in her mouth. Then she lost her grip on the lantern, and the ghastly apparition vanished from his eyes.

The twins clung together, frozen with horror, not daring to believe what they were seeing.

Rebecca sagged, wincing, clenching, her eyes no longer blinking. Then she collapsed to the floor and sprawled across the Sarjeant's boots. She lay in the pool of light, and did not move.

Magner stooped to pick up the lantern again. The candle had toppled over against the glass, but the light had not gone out. His knife was still in his hand. The girls could see the red upon the steel.

"Now…" he said, and they saw his teeth in the light of the lamp. "Is the soldier to have his doxy without any further interruptions?"

Nobody moved. Then, with a banshee's shriek, Rosalind sprang at him, claws out for her twin's defence and her mother's vengeance. Magner saw her coming, tensed, and punched her off with the hand that held the lantern. The light swung on its loop, whacking Ros hard on her chin. The flame sent awful shapes and shadows up the walls. Then he caught her with his forearm and shoved her away.

"Back, you bitch! Get off me!" The mask fell away now. The voice was hard and cruel.

Ros went flying, straight into the dining chairs that Melhuish and Coates had piled up in the corner. Her head collided with a sharp oak edge. She felt a sudden jolt of pain, then nothing at all. The chair rocked. The spinning wheel toppled with a crash and buried her under its frame.

Magner made for Eleanor. She could see his face split by a grin. It was the grin of a demon with fresh souls to garner.

"There comes a first time for everything, girl." It was the same soft, cajoling whisper from the Garden of Eden. He raked the tip of his tongue back and forth over his teeth. Eleanor started to back away.

"Oh! So we're shy, are we, child?"

Frantic, mute, Elle glanced towards Mother, willing her to rise, and protect her. She had backed all the way to the limewashed wall. Now she was up against the dresser. She bumped into it, and something behind her rattled. It was the large, pewter plate. Usually they a pyramid of apples upon it for the twins to munch.

Eleanor watched Magner as he set the lantern down on the table. His distraction was momentary, but it was all that she needed. She grabbed the plate, held it side on, and slung it at his head. The missile flew from her hand, accompanied by her grunt of desperate fear. With a tremendous velocity, its thin end caught him square on the temple. It bounced off his skull; she heard the platter clanging on the floor.

Magner blinked at her, stunned. He put his hand to his head. He could feel there was blood on the tips of his fingers.

"You SLUT!"

He got hold of her wrist, and he clamped her.

"So! The slattern wants it rough, does she? You ingrate TRULL!" His free hand lashed down through the air, and Elle felt a sharp sting to her cheek. Now he was shouting into her face. He no longer had any intention of being gentle. He was dragging her forward, away from the wall. "Please!" she heard herself cry.

Magner's teeth were bared as he barked his next order:

"Get your arse over – I want you from behind!"

He pinioned her arms and spun her round, over the end of the table. Her skirts were yanked up round her middle. She could hear a lot of fumbling and frantic tugging behind her. He had imprisoned her against the table edge. Eleanor struggled and tried to rise. At once, his hand reached around her and he showed her the knife again.

"Do that again, and you'll get *this.*"

He used the pressure from his shoes to part her ankles. Too terrified to plead, too confused to wriggle and strain, she surrendered. She felt like she was hovering at ceiling-height, looking down at what was happening to her body. She was watching herself be ruined. She smelled his sweat, his unwashed clothes, and heard his rasping breath.

Then she felt the pain.

The screaming had carried easily through the storeys of the house. It had smashed the stillness of the garret, sent the four of them staring in dread at the door. Then they had heard that crash of falling metal, and a man howling.

Carrie started to cry and could not stop.

Philippa crawled up onto her knees. "Carrie!"

Carrie went on blubbing. Her sister took hold of her shoulders, and shook her. "Carrie!" she snapped. "Carrie, stop that!"

"I can't! I can't!" her sister wailed.

SMACK! Stephen and Loobie jumped as Philippa gave her the most tremendous slap across her face. Stunned, Carrie stopped wailing. Instead she explored her smarting cheek with trembling fingers.

Philippa cradled her face between her hands. "Carrie, I did not mean to do that. Only, I had to make you *listen*."

Carrie continued to look at her out of waterlogged eyes.

"Stay here. With them. And this." She fumbled in Carrie's apron and pulled out the second pistol. She put it into her hand by force, closing Carrie's fingers round it. Carrie felt the cold, hard brass that plated the end of the butt.

"Pip…!" Carrie moaned.

Philippa collected the lantern from the chest. She ducked towards Carrie, and kissed her on her forehead. "Stay close. Shoot anything that comes up those stairs that isn't one of us."

A last smile of reassurance at Stephen and Loobie, and she was gone. She slipped down towards the hall on catlike feet, keeping close to the wall. A lamp was burning somewhere in the parlour. As she approached the doorway, she could hear little gasps and squeaks.

Philippa rounded the door frame and saw the unthinkable. The lantern was on the table. Her mother lay, unmoving, on the floor. There to the right was the insensible Ros, submerged beneath the capsized spinning wheel. And at the end of the table, directly confronting her –

For a moment suspended in time, she and Magner stared at one another. Magner's strong hands gripped Eleanor by the waist as he went on pounding into her. Philippa gazed at her sister in horror. Elle was trying to keep her face down on her arms. Her hair had fallen free and Magner had a clump of it gripped in his fist. Elle's hair was thick: she was proud of it.

Magner stopped his thrusting. His eyebrows raised at her in mocking query. "The Parson's wife! Or is it the Parson's widow?"

"Let her go," Philippa demanded in a low voice.

His hand moved from Eleanor's waist to her shoulder. Elle looked up, pleading at Pip with her eyes.

Philippa produced the doglock from behind her back. She held her lantern level with her face and aimed the pistol at him. Her hand did not tremble and her eyes never blinked. "Let. Her. Go."

He ignored her, pushing deeper into Elle with ceaseless vigour. He was pulling her harder against him. Holding her tighter around him.

Philippa cocked the pistol the way Father had showed her. She took a long, cool aim at Magner's forehead. Her voice was a hiss of venom.

"Hump my sister, would you? *Vermin!*"

The hammer fell. She shot him.

The room was suffused at once with noise and smoke. A big blue hole appeared above Magner's left eye. His head was thrown backwards under the force of the shot. Gobbets of brain spattered over the limewashed wall. Eleanor suddenly felt a rush of warm blood in her tumbling hair. Magner crashed to the floor. His member still wormed out of his breeches. Eleanor went down with him, falling sideways like a tree.

Philippa dropped the pistol, and heard it thud upon the boards. She deposited her lantern on the table and staggered back, failing to comprehend the enormity of what she had witnessed; what she was standing in; what she had done.

Eleanor managed to rise. Her senses were slowly returning and her stomach felt sick to its pit. Philippa managed to catch her as she stumbled forward. The tears spilled out of Elle's eyes.

"He killed our mother! Oh, Pip, he killed our mother!"

Philippa wrapped her little sister in her arms. Their knees buckled; they sank to the floorboards together. Elle lay limp in Philippa's arms and began to wail with abandon. Her mind was a wreck and her body was burning.

Philippa never discovered how long they had lain there like that before the shout startled her back to reality.

"Look, look! There's a light in there! See!"

It was the cry of a man. Philippa's heart plummeted.

The voices had come from the street. Then they came right into the hallway. "Hullo?"

Philippa shut her eyes. She could not even hope to reload the pistol. Magner's knife was lying where he'd dropped it – only six feet away, but it might have been six miles. In any case, to retrieve it, she would have had to let go of Elle. And Philippa was quite determined to die there, on the floor, riddled with bullets or pierced with a thousand cuts, before she let go of her sister.

Footsteps sounded behind her. She bent low, twisting in on herself.

"What the – ?"

"Mistress Philippa?"

Philippa whipped her head around to see. There, pale-faced, cut about, and cradling their matchlocks, stood a trio of very familiar figures.

It was Judah who crouched and examined the bodies. The light in the room was so bad that he could see little but huddled shapes. One figure, its feet bizarrely poking out from beneath that overbalanced spinning wheel, was beginning to stir and groan. But the other two showed nothing but the finality of death.

Coates caught his breath. "Corporal! It's the Sarge!"

Melhuish saw the spatter of gore on the walls. The smell of powder was not to be mistaken. He asked, more quietly this time, "What happened here, Mistress?"

Philippa licked her lips. "He is dead," she whispered. "He is dead."

Then she turned her back upon them and bent lower over Eleanor.

Coates moved away from the window. Men were running up the street like a tidal bore. There were voices, too, calling out above the shots and death screams.

"*The town is gone!*"

"*Get out, lads! For your lives!*"

"*We're betrayed! We are all undone!*"

Judah had heard enough. He tugged at the old Corporal's sleeve. "Melhuish? Melhuish! Come on, we can do nothing here!"

Melhuish did not move.

"Come *on*, man! Or else we'll never make it!" Judah bolted out into the street. Coates went with him. Melhuish stayed only long enough to bestow one final, painful look upon the scene.

"God be with you, Mistress." Then he was out the door, musket-first.

Elle had begun to thrash like a dying animal. As she gulped down fresh lungfuls of air she began to vomit violently. Supper spewed across the floorboards.

Philippa pressed herself close to her, tighter and tighter. "It's alright, Elle," she soothed. "Calm down, calm down. It will be alright."

She had never distrusted herself more.

A flash of lightning suddenly illuminated a scarecrow, standing in the hall. Then she looked at it again. Beneath the murk, through all the layers of mud, she could see who it was. Fat drops of rain were hanging off his ear lobes, and clutching his unshaven chin. He was coated all over in slime and muck.

Philippa's face contorted. "Nathan?"

The release of tension made her feel weak. It was feat of strength to release her hold on the retching Elle and to struggle to her feet.

"NATHAN!"

Philippa flung herself into his arms. His clothes were absolutely saturated. His frame beneath felt cold and sodden through. She wrapped her limp, long body around his. Her fingers dug into his back. She buried her face in his neck, and she cried like a child.

THIRTY-NINE

Or like the sons of Vulcan vomit fire.

Parliament tried again. Its redcoats advanced into the shouting guns. Flames stabbed the night as case shot sprayed down Gabriel's Hill. A score of men exploded in clouds of blood and muscle, lost in a final shriek. Their pikes disintegrated with the impact. One three-inch fragment of an ash staff buried itself in Captain Marchington's forearm, but he was untroubled by that.

"Stand firm, my boys! We'll hold these bastards yet!"

The driving rain damp-squibbed the falling doglocks. Men were crying out at wells of blood that had appeared in their flesh. Others simply wailed to find themselves suddenly confronted with mortality.

The New Model pikemen drew their two-foot swords from their baldrics and charged for the summit of Gabriel's Hill again. They overtook their lighter-heeled confederates. Many of them had bitterly resented this renewal of hostilities in the first place, so they went for the rebels without pity or regret. These Kentish dogs were the vainglory fools who had kept them in arms, quartered away from their families and wives. If the rumours were true, the rebels had even been firing poisoned bullets at them, for which crime alone they had forfeited their right to live.

"Truth! Truth! Truth! Truth!"

Vaulting over the hay bales that surrounded the cannon, the New Models set about the Royalists they found there. The gunners fought to the end for their precious charges, with clubbed muskets and short, stabbing swords. Then they fought with their fists before they gargled out their last, despairing breaths, and they slumped beside the trunnions.

"Truth! Truth! Truth! Truth!"

A windstorm of stink had engulfed the High Town. It was a cauldron of chaos. Figures folded into it and were lost.

"Truth! Truth! Truth! Truth!"

Men were floundering about, drenched and dripping. The rain was thinning the blood that explored the cobbles. Red rilled little by little down the slope of the streets.

It was a wild scene along Week Street. Sir Gamaliel Dudley could only look on and watch the debacle unfold. His mind raced as he stood there. The town was now stormed. His men were shocked, and bruised, and hollow-eyed. They had repulsed two desperate, bloodsucking charges and fought the New Models with every ounce of their strength, but their numbers were sapping, and so was their capability. Now they were turning back up the hill to take their chances in flight. First in little huddles, then in one chaotic flow. A few determined diehards fought on till they were cut down.

The discipline was caving in. Tom Fairfax would have his victory by morning.

Dudley held his sword low, so its point was touching the cobbles. It hurt to hold the grip with his bandaged fingers. Amidst the crowd, he spotted Sir William Brockman. Last time he had seen the Sheriff, he had been choked by the thick white smoke as the redcoats closed in.

Brockman spied the Governor in his turn. He twisted through the stream of scattering men to reach him. "The town is entered at all points. We are cut off."

"I know. I know."

"Then think, man! It falls to you!"

The Governor took in Brockman's look of unrefined terror. "Not so, Sir William. It *falls* to General Fairfax."

A wild-eyed specimen pushed his way across the street, hunting for senior officers. Brockman recognised him, in spite of the chaos. It was the same dispatch rider who had brought Norwich's instructions to defend the town in-depth to Mayney's tent in Aylesford only that afternoon.

"Sir! Your Honour?"

Dudley waited a moment, before he sniffed and ordered, "Speak, man?"

"They – they have taken the guns on High Street! We could not hold them!"

Dudley glanced at Brockman, who returned a cadaverous gaze. "We are now o'er shoes in blood, Sir William."

"I saw him. I actually saw him!" said Brockman.

"Saw who?" the old Governor queried.

"Black Tom. On his horse. Through the smoke." The Sheriff sounded spell-bound. "Close enough to have danced the Cornish fling with him. Oh, that I had *only* had that pistol!" he raged, threatening the heavens with a fist.

Dudley scratched his whiskering chin. "I'll avouch, we have drawn a bad hand."

The young courier stared at the old Governor, bug-eyed. "But– ! Your Honour? The *guns?*"

Ten seconds elapsed. Then Dudley seemed to click back into life. He nodded his thanks to the runner. "I'm obliged to you, sirrah. Now go get a weapon and make yourself ready."

The courier scampered off. Brockman stepped closer. "What do we do?"

"Find any officers you can," instructed Dudley. "Horse, Foot; it matters not. Tell 'em to post snipers into these houses; line the streets. Defend every door, every roof. Pepper them."

"To the – the finish, Governor?" gulped Brockman.

"Inch by inch, if need be. They *must* buy us time."

Brockman's eyes widened. *What Canute-like folly was this?*

Dudley looked at him. "You shake your head, Sir William."

"Shake my head? I am shaking all over! Governor, if the redcoats envelope us through the side streets, our forces are not worth a maravedi! We are all dead men!"

"And are we not all dead men already, Colonel Brockman?"

Dudley picked up his sword and advanced on a party of about thirty musketeers who were retreating up the street, all trying to pace backwards in unison. Their faces pointed in the direction that the Roundheads would come. Their matchlocks looked like quality Dutch imports. He hailed those sharpshooters. "Fall back, you men! Break off and fall back!"

A voice from the ranks almost laughed. "God blind me, but I never thought he'd ask!"

Brockman trotted forward. "Your intentions remain the same?"

"You have your orders, Colonel Brockman. Get your snipers up those stairs at pistol-point if you have to. I shall rally the remainder and retire on the wall."

"Which wall?"

"The churchyard wall." Dudley used his sword to show him where he meant: the expanse of ground behind Chillington Manor's Tudor grandeur. "The old Huguenot chapel. We shall take up firing positions along its boundary. Pass the word to Sir John, should you see him."

Dudley held his sword high aloft and began to keep pace with the fugitives. Their crisis had revitalised his limbs. "You Kentish men! To me! To me! You Kentish men, to me!"

Drummer Coates had had the personal satisfaction of smashing a Parliament jaw with the butt of his musket. He had seen the teeth get bludgeoned out of their roots, heard the pikeman's yelp of helpless pain. Life had been good in that moment. From where he stood in Saint Faith's churchyard, he could look down the funnel of Week Street and await the rogue wave. This four foot high wall could still prove a resilient breakwater.

"Watch your front, lads!" warned Sir John Mayney. "Keep your eyes peeled for 'em, now!"

A few forlorn hopes were still coming in, and fellows had gone out to their aid. Some of those walking wrecks had lost their pattens or their boots, and had limped up Week Street in their stockinged feet. Some derelicts went as barefoot as little children. Their eyes were red and watery. Once they had reached Saint Faith's yard they were sifted quickly. Those who could wield a firelock or a broadsword dripped back to the line on the wall. The hopeless were herded away to the rear. The "too far gone" had been helped into the church itself, to await their final journey in an appropriate setting.

Judah cleared his throat. "Chris?"

"What?"

"If you get out of this, and live… say a prayer for us, eh?"

The butcher looked back at him. His skin was like tallow. "Be glad to."

"Tell Grace I behaved – decently?"

"I will that, old friend." Coates laid his hand on top of Judah's, and patted it on the knuckles.

Melhuish cocked an eye at the pair of them. "By the rood, you two lay it on thick!"

No time to say anything more. The sound of heavy firing from Week Street announced that the game was in play again.

Judah knew he might not get another chance to ask: "I say, Corp'ral?"

"What is it, man?"

"What d'you want us to tell Sarah?"

Corporal Clare's face clouded. "Nothing that I haven't said to her already, Private Copp."

"HERE THEY COME AGAIN!"

The lobsters were on the move. Gleaming wet morions topped off the faces of combat-ready veterans.

"Hold this position! Courage, now!" sang out the bloodstained Captain Marchington.

Away down the line, some demented bastard was kicking up a fuss. "Where are your fastings and prayers?" he babbled on. "I tell you, we're consigned to the fires – every man-jack of us!"

They heard a biff, then a cry, then a hush. Someone had known just how to with this kind of corrosive hysteria.

The Roundheads were closing in. They'd been dealing with the snipers. They had set about the task with great method. Melhuish could imagine the train of events. New Model lobsters, breaking down the door. Boots pounding up the narrow, creaking stairways. Doors kicked open on the rooms that commanded the street. Not even the time to drop to your knees and beg.

The New Models tramped on at push-of-pike, pressing closer and closer like figures from some exhilarating dream. They were sinewed, expressionless creatures. This time they would not break into a wild, bellowing charge. They were taking their own, sweet time. With the numbers they had at their backs, where was the need to rush into the thick of it like madmen?

"God save us!" The wealthy and the poor were joined by the common bond of fear.

"Make – READY!" the old cry sounded.

Corporal Melhuish Clare returned his scouring stick to its slit beneath the forestock. Then he gobbed a quantity of spit down the barrel after the wadding and ball.

Judah had noticed him. "'Choo doing that for?"

"Luck!" returned his Corporal.

"Pre-SENT!"

Coates bent right over, resting his firelock on the top of the wall for better aim. He had long since lost its musket rest. It had jabbed out a Roundhead's eyes very nicely.

Hell's kin had advanced to fifty paces.

"Pitch 'em back, now, boys! Give – FIRE!"

The rainy night split with crazy flashes as the matches breathed life in the pans.

They shall run to and fro in the city; they shall run upon the wall, they shall climb up upon the houses; they shall enter in at the windows like a thief.

The earth shall quake before them; the heavens shall tremble: the sun and the moon shall be dark, and the stars shall withdraw their shining...

The final test. Men on both sides bellowed as they met it.

FORTY

Met in the milder shades of Purgatory.

Corporal Clare was one of the first who fell in the final charge. A blade of white hot fire cut him about the chest and torso, and waves of pain went shooting through his face. The grunt came from the depths of his body. Private Coates and Private Copp quickly lost him beneath the rushing feet. The last they could see of Melhuish's gleaming pate between the legs and the bucket-top boots, he was trying to sit upright.

Captain Marchington, whose luck had held ou on Gabriel's Hill and then the retreat along Week Street, fell to the grass in a welter of blood. One of Fairfax's redcoats had put a bullet through his throat.

"The lobsters are over the wall!"

They had retreated step by step. Ten yards, then ten yards more. Buff coats were mingling with Fairfax's red and blues. The General's own pack of hounds had to be in for the death. To go by the thinning ranks, Dudley knew this last stand would be a short one.

The Governor made eye contact with Mayney, and with Brockman. They looked at him with eyes like shattered mirrors. The Sheriff simply nodded. His ringlets glowed with sweat. His cheeks were damp, but not from the pelting rain. He threw his sword down on the grass and left it there.

Dudley spoke not a word, but he began to tear the white lace kerchief he had wrapped about his throat. Mayney supplied him with a thick stick he plucked up from the root of a churchyard elms. It was the work of a second to tie the linen handkerchief to it, and hold the stake aloft.

"Stop your firing! Stop your firing!" Mayney yelled.

"Cease FIRE!" the Sheriff joined in.

The shots began to dwindle. Only the groans and the squelching of feet could be heard. The rain was starting to slacken off, replaced by a slight, endeavouring breeze. People slipped on the wet and the blood, and began to realise how chilled they really were. Their sweat had left their skin with a pasty shine. Their nostrils reeked of rotten eggs, and their tonsils were red raw.

Their eyes stared out from underneath the grime and powder burns. The Parliamentarians stalked them, encircling them warily. Even a solitary spark could revive a conflagration.

"Surrender to mercy, you rebels! On pain of needless deaths!"

Dudley saw a senior-looking officer approaching them, dividing the Parliament's ranks. This burly, good-looking man stopped before the Governor. First Dudley wiped both sides of the blade on his tattered sleeve, then he proffered the hilt of his sword.

"We surrender ourselves to you, sir."

Colonel Rushworth did not smile. "Not to me, gentlemen. To *him*."

Without word or ceremony, a very tall, swarthy figure hobbled forward into the torchlight. Fairfax had followed a thick trail of bodies all the way down the hill. Beneath his broad hat brim, his dark eyes roved the Kentishmen. So. This huddle of wrecks were the long-hunted rebels. They glared straight back at him from under their hats and their Montero caps. Muskets, blades, and short swords still drawn. Like stags when they stood at bay. Expecting death, and prepared to kill.

"My lord?" Dudley stretched out his sword to the General.

Fairfax looked at it a while. "Nay, but you may keep that weapon, sir." He looked at the smaller, older man that stood before him. "I would know whom I am addressing?"

"Sir Gamaliel Dudley, Governor of the town. This is Colonel Sir William Brockman; Sir John Mayney; Sir Conor Forker."

They stood there in silence for a few moments. Each tried to grasp a sense of warmth or trust. Another bout of considered looking, then Fairfax took off his hat and bowed from the neck. "You fought superlatively, sirs, whereby you have shown us your quality. You have put up a most gallant resistance."

Dudley's response was cool. "We have fought with a commission from those who were our lawful superiors, and from that I justify my actions."

Hearing a footstep, Fairfax turned his head to find that Ireton had joined them. Ireton was keen to be on the scene when the Royalists had to face hard facts. He looked glassy, and grim.

"We can none of us recall the like, Sir Gamaliel," Fairfax said, turning back to the Governor, "though we have all been in the wars from the start."

Ireton struck an officerly pose. "Where is the rest of your command, sir?" he asked the Sheriff.

Brockman looked wan. The damp had got into his wound. "This is it." He fluttered his hand in the direction of the survivors. "Your men shot down the rest, or else they've run and hid in the environs."

Borne by the faintest of winds, they could hear All Saints' chime midnight.

Ireton studied those rebels who were left on their feet. Their eyes looked white and fixed. They slouched. They had been shorn of all fighting. Most of them seemed to be holding up another sagging, bloodshot comrade.

Fairfax said: "I do not want to go on killing your levies, Colonel – Brockman, was it? But if you do not surrender your forces now, that is what you are asking me to do."

Mayney's head was throbbing with the aftershocks of battle. It was like a wood chopper through the skull. "Our *levies*, General, were defending their lives, and their homes from your men," he replied.

Fairfax's was resolved to stay equable, so he stilled his sudden reflex of temper. "Gradely spoken!" he accepted. "And I give you my personal assurance that your wounded shall be retrieved, and tended by our own surgeons."

Dudley turned. "Tell them, Sir William; Sir Conor. Tell them – it's the end."

Mayney looked at Brockman. "Do it."

At Brockman's word, the weapons were chucked on the ground with a thud. Firelocks and musket rests now became the survivors' walking sticks. The New Model Army clanked in and began to usher the men away, coaxing some and booting others. Dudley watched them go. Brockman stood shoulder to shoulder with the wounded old gnome. He did not pause for thought.

"We might have been too few for this enterprise, Your Excellency, but our men fought on till we told them to. 'Tis important you know that."

"I know it only too plainly, Sir William," nodded Fairfax.

"They only wished to see the King, their Master, on his throne again."

Ireton put his arms behind his back. "You did your best. It wasn't enough."

Fairfax tapped him smartly on the shoulder with his baton. "Colonel Ireton! You are addressing a knight of the realm, sir! Have you no etiquette?"

Ireton looked more dazed than anything. "I – I make my apologies, my lord."

"Then pray have the goodness to vex me no further!" Fairfax turned back to the two defeated, wilting leaders. "Perhaps I may invite you to repair somewhere more comfortable?"

Dudley spoke for the lot. "Thank you kindly, my lord, but we shall prefer to remain with our men. They are fatigued, and have had no provisions."

"Consider it done. I'll have bread brought up within the hour. Of course, I shall have to ensure you gentlemen are escorted into custody. You may retain your blades, on your parole."

He was about to give the word when a tall, muddied figure in officer's get-up appeared on the scene. He had come down the hill from the other side of the churchyard.

"M' lord?" His voice was gruff. "I have brought you the tally of our casualty returns."

"Thank you, Major Callender."

Brockman's eyes started. He matched the remembered voice to the pudgy face beneath the morion. "John Callender, as I live and breathe! You? Here?"

For a moment, military enmity gave way to a connection of social and political acquaintance. The Sheriff had spent many long hours in the company of Sir John Callender, the county MP. Then Callender's surprise relapsed into a scowl. "Of course I am here, Sir William! I am ever for the Parliament, as well you might recall."

"Your casualty returns, Major?" cut in Rushworth.

Callender tallied his figures, and handed them to the secretary. "We have taken eight pieces of rebel ordnance this night, my lord," Rushworth relayed. "Six of iron, two of brass. And any number of arms taken generally."

"Anything else?" asked Fairfax.

"So far we've counted less than a hundred of our dead," Callender answered. "Colonel Hewson's Regiment of Foot had the hardest task, of course. Of gentlemen of note, only Major Carter has been hurt, and only the Captain Price is enumerated killed. Most of 'em fell on Galahad's Hill."

"Gabriel's Hill," the Governor corrected automatically.

Callender ignored this amendment. "The Royalists, however, are proving far too numerous and widespread to book. But I forecast not less than two, maybe three hundred dead."

Fairfax flicked a look at the Royalist officers, and rather wished he hadn't. "Does that conclude the business?"

"I daresay we'll know more, m'lord, by daybreak. But there *is* just one more thing. A report has come in from an outlying squadron of our Horse…"

"Go on?"

"They've reported contact with Norwich's forces, not more than two miles away."

This time it was Rushworth who looked at the rebels. The significance of this report filtered from face to face. The one named Forker looked ready to faint.

Ireton greeted the word with a mordant smile. "My, my! Less than two miles, was it?"

Fairfax breathed hard. He doubted that even *his* hard-eyed veterans could turn about so rapidly and take on the Earl of Norwich's advance. Not after four and a half hours of such solid, crushing fighting. First he would have to find tall buildings, from which to hang the white flag of capitulation.

"I'll own that I think little of a General who abandons his own men to fight for their lives and honour," he murmured. Then he turned back to the job, suddenly alive and flashing orders. "Muster the living. Colonel Rushworth? If these worthy gentlemen wish to stay with their men, it behoves we get a move on."

The defeated party, hemmed in by cold steel and buff serge, trudged away into the shadow of what awaited them.

Fairfax stood aside to let them through. "O ye mountains of Gilboa, how are the mighty fallen," he acknowledged.

They were swifter than eagles, they were stronger than lions, he inwardly quoted. There was much that he could genuinely admire about these Kentish men. He had a sadness about the eyes as he looked at them.

"Major Callender? I have a task for you."

"I would hear it, my lord?"

"Tell Colonel Whalley to break off, and pursue the Lord Goring. Keep his sword in his back, if need be. On no account must Norwich be allowed to link back with the rebels in Essex, or attract any of the malcontents from London. I'll on to Canterbury in the morning."

Callender bustled off, pleased to be busy.

Fairfax had not finished. "Colonel Ireton? Form legions to clear away the bodies." He made the order curt. "Let's give them something like a decent burial."

"Decent? This charnel-house, decent?" Ireton was agog. "Surely Your Excellency must have discerned that these fellows died for nothing?"

Fairfax fixed him with a stare. "They died for a *cause*, Colonel Ireton. A cause they believed to be right. Let us grant them the respect they deserve – for that, if nothing else. We are standing in a churchyard: I would suggest that you use it. Bury them decently," he commanded.

"But, my lord – "

"About your business, sir!" Now the General was brusque.

A bob of the head, but no more words. Ireton melted away. The General's demeanour astounded him. Fairfax would be inviting the gravediggers for claret in his tent next!

Rushworth looked after him. "He would argue with a chair, my lord."

"Mm."

Fairfax's eye was drawn by a lot of movement on the crest of the hill. The doors of the church had been thrown open and –

"What the plague is this?!"

Out of the doors of the church had poured a thick and struggling column of men. Their hands were in the air, and they were weaponless. They stumbled into the night with a curious, surging blend of expressions. Cold. Fatigue. Resignation. Hunger. Hope. New Model men were advancing, spreading out to receive them.

Fairfax pointed to the church. "What consecration is that?"

"They call it Saint Faith's, my lord. It was put up by the Huguenots."

"Safe harbour, for a lot of refugees. Most appropriate, really." Fairfax studied the structure, erected by those grateful runaways, sound and snug on the hill. The moon sat high behind it.

"I'll not have 'em gutting this church, John." The granite was back in Fairfax's cheekbones. "Maximum penalty, imposed *without exception*, on any attempts. Our men will respect the house of the Lord. You hear?"

Rushworth heard, but he was anything but assured. Soldiers did as soldiers did. You couldn't drill, flog, or discipline that out of a man. Spoon the Scriptures into them as best you may, but they would always find the plate, the bag of moneys. They would always find the whore who would lift up her skirts and charge a day's pay. For all that those handbills would have the Army believe, the Cavaliers did not have a monopoly on harlotry and impure conduct. Once the fire of a fight had died down, men's urges would return.

As for Colonel Rushworth, he now felt the overwhelming urge to find a jakes.

"You hear me, John?" Fairfax repeated.

"I heard you perfectly, my lord."

"Then let us have done with this place." Fairfax wiped the mud from his hands on his breeches. "Come find me in an hour. I noticed some hostelry or other, just down the lane a way. The Albion, I think? We can draft our dispatch to the Speaker there. With any luck, the House can have it by next sitting."

Rushworth paused. "Will you – will you make it plain to them how hard our men fought here this night?"

Fairfax smiled. "Our men, and theirs. Aye, and their fight is worth the acknowledging. And if words carry any weight, John, we can prescribe a day of Thanksgiving in every church in Westminster tomorrow."

The wind was gathering strength. It made the General draw his old cloak about his frame. Then he turned, and began to limp back up the hill.

FORTY-ONE

In thy book, record the groans of those who were thy sheep.

The candles burned with spear-shaped flames in their brackets. Their scanty rays cast the interior of All Saints' Church into a labyrinth of huddling shapes. The pews became the surgeon's lines. Even the church's old medieval misericords harboured wounded prisoners. Some had even been lowered to sit with their backs to the altar itself. Their faces were smutted with powder. Their cheeks had burned blue. Their knuckles were scabbed to a livid purple. Voices droned on in the agony of living. Stammered prayers were punctuated by awful, exploding, full-mouthed screams.

The standard of Lord Fairfax's own regiment now flew from the tower's flagpole. It was hoped that such an act would dissuade any hopeful relief column; it had been aped across the town. The New Model Army had surrounded All Saints', and had sent a detachment of its reserves to guard the prisoners penned inside it. Being reserves, they had largely missed the storming of the town. They were glad to stand guard over traitorous rogues.

Shortly after midnight, Nathan had quit the house of lamentation and had gone into the street. He decided he'd prefer the hostile glare of a thousand men to the sounds of the wailing girls, and the sight of those bodies in the parlour. He remembered the nightmare that lay on the Tovil Lane. From where he stood now, it was only three miles to the bridge at East Farleigh, yet every yard must be paved with dead men's faces.

Two phantoms in buff coats and lobster-tailed helmets suddenly surrounded him. They spoke without preamble. "By the cut of your cloth, sir, we would say you was a Parson?"

Nathan was guarded. "And what if I were?"

"We've heard tell from one of the wounded that there's a Parson in the town, a Parson Wohlford. Would you be he?"

Nathan drew breath, trying to guess who his informant might be. "I am Nathan Wohlford. Rector of Saint Mary's, East Farleigh."

310

"Come with us. We have want of you." The Troopers were in a hurry. They made the command crisp. Nathan had not protested.

Philippa had not protested, either. She was preoccupied with trying to get all the others upstairs. Stephen had been too tired, too young, to comprehend the massive events of the previous hours. He had been carried upstairs in the arms of his Aunt Carrie, and had gone straight off to sleep without fuss. Ros and Elle had retreated quietly to the garret. Ros, her face bruised a livid purple, had cuddled and kissed her precious twin. Philippa had crawled into bed beside Loobie, and had held her very tight while the little girl cried for their mother.

Philippa stayed with her until her littlest sister snuffled at last into sleep. Then she tiptoed downstairs and into the street. She shut the door behind her, checking twice that it was locked, putting the key in her apron pocket. It wasn't long before she caught the eye of a sentry.

"Sirrah? Might I speak with you awhile?"

The man in the redcoat straightened his back. The old, instinctive deference to the voice of a lady of breeding was still there. "Aye, ma'am? Now what be you a-doing, out by yourself on a night like this?"

"Sirrah, tell me quickly, what have they done with my husband?"

The man paused. "Your... husband, Ma'am?"

Philippa understood the hesitation in his answer. "He's a Parson. Two of your fellows came for him about a half-hour ago, saying they had need of his services. Where would they have taken him?"

The sentry considered. "Most like where they've been taking all the wounded."

"And where is that?"

"To that church. On that cliff, by the river," he added, waving his hand in the direction he meant. "There was nowhere else bigger, you see."

She had let herself back into the house. After being in the night air, her skin was feeling chilly. She needed something warm. She needed her father's coat. She had retrieved it from the chest, and put it on. She had slipped her iron-soled country pattens on over her shoes and walked out into the night to find Nathan. Carrie, dead-eyed and too enervated to argue, had been left in charge.

Philippa entered the church through the north porch. None of the guards on the door tried to stop her, nor raised any questions about where she'd obtained what she was wearing. One had even touched his morion to her. She stopped and looked about her. The smell of the church was a potent, sordid mixture. The flies would have their fill. Bundles of men littered the stone floor. She looked into their eyes as she moved past them. They watched her back, clouded with the pain.

To wile away the time, the New Model reserves had made their own amusements, and raucously set about destroying the church's monuments. All Saints' enormous eastern reredos now looked like it had been scrammed by a monstrous beast. And the Wootton Memorial had come under especial attack. Its fifteenth-century paintwork had been heartily slashed and chipped. They had left the Angel Gabriel looking like he'd contracted a severe case of leprosy.

Philippa looked down. The man by her feet had his hands locked together in frenzied prayer. His breathing was coming in short, teeth-chattering gasps. Philippa's face grew tight with compassion. She made her way slowly through the church. She passed one youthful casualty who was rocking with pain. She could not have known that he had flouted his mother and run away to be a hero. It was this which was torturing him, not the collop of flesh that one of Major Husbands' Dragoons had sliced out of his leg.

Finally, she spotted a familiar figure in broadcloth black, plastered with grass and mud.

Nathan rose to meet her. "I – uhm… They told me Reverend Wilson could not be found. They needed me."

Philippa looked at the floor. "It is plain to see why."

His eyes lingered over her coat, but he chose to say nothing about her choice of costume. "You play their Rachel, Pip?"

She shrugged her shoulders. "Somebody must weep for them," she said.

Nathan moved aside. "You had best have a good stock of tears," he said.

Philippa looked down. Melhuish Clare lay propped up by the base of the ancient font. His head had slumped to one side. His breathing was liquid and difficult. Judah and Coates were kneeling on either side. Philippa dropped to her haunches in front of him. She laid a pale hand on the Corporal's age-spotted forehead. The skin felt hot to her touch.

"Melhuish? Is it that you can hear me?"

His old eyes did not open. She glanced quickly at Judah for instruction.

"We carried him down from Saint Faith's," he told her. "It was no easy task."

Philippa stared. "You – carried him? All that way?"

"Aye, Mistress. Them Roundheads have been bringing 'em down by the cartload. Only, we reckoned as if we put him on a cart, we might never get him back again."

Philippa looked into Melhuish's face. Her expression was hard and wilful. To think of old Melhuish Clare dying was one thing. But to think of him dying here, amid these whimpering crowds, was a special flavour of agony. Even the life-like effigies adorning the Astley Memorial seemed to be looking down on them, disconsolate.

"He's like to go soon," said Coates.

The old eyes did not open, but the mouth did. "Stow that guff, Chris. I'll come when I'm called!" the Corporal wheezed. Then his eyes fluttered open.

"Hullo, Melhuish."

"Mistress Philippa!" He managed a brave smile.

"How do you fare, old friend?" she asked, moving her hand to his cheek.

"I'm – I'm burning in my guts, I'm afraid. They've done for me at last."

"Here. Give him this." Nathan dipped a tin beaker in a wooden bucket that was standing nearby on the floor. He handed it to Coates with dripping fingers.

"Just enough to wet his lips," Philippa warned.

Melhuish coughed as the water hit the back of his throat. A lot of it ended up all down his sternum. It stained the front of his tunic to a darker red. His eyes readjusted. They settled on the girl who crouched before him. Gradually he realised that this was no mere overcoat that she had put on. His hand lifted and weakly touched one of the sleeves.

"Your father wore this coat."

"He did, Melhuish, he did." Her voice was almost a whisper. "And I wear it, for a memorable honour." Philippa's poise was beginning to break. "Surely they must have surgeons with them?"

"They have a man – Turpin. I spoke with him." Nathan craned his head to locate that overworked surgeon. He caught a glimpse of him, probing and stitching amid the shadows of the chancel.

"Aye; one of him, and a hundred of us, and more!" Coates glared back up the aisle. "There's our Sam Joplin up there, somewhere. Around about the pulpit. I saw him brought in."

Philippa remembered the name. "Joplin? The blacksmith?"

"Took a ball to the skull," Coates pitied. "Be a lunatic, if he lives."

Melhuish's hand had spidered out in search of Philippa's. "You ha' suffered no hurt, m'dear?" he asked eagerly.

"I am – untouched." She squeezed his paw.

Melhuish looked from her eyes to Nathan's. Moving his head was difficult. "'Tis well this girl got you back again, Parson. Sick with worry, she were. Sick."

Nathan touched her on the shoulder. Philippa took no heed of him, or his muddy knuckles.

"You – you fair put up a struggle," he said to the trio.

They seemed awkward at first. The truth of what they had suffered had not sunk in.

Coates snarled, "Cowsons thought we'd do nothing but line the streets and wave at 'em!"

"Duty don't always lie in pleasant places, Chris."

Melhuish coughed again, hackingly.

"Give him some more water," Philippa instructed the men. Coates held the rim once again to the dying man's lips. This second draught was more of a struggle.

They were near enough to the porch to catch the *clump-clump-clump* of approaching jack-boots. A senior-looking officer,

314

and a Sarjeant-Major with a very square jaw mounted the steps and walked in. The NCO flourished a torch as they entered. For a moment the newcomers stood in their pond of light. The stench in the nave was oppressive.

Colonel Hewson had recovered enough from his ordeal on Gabriel's Hill to be sent in to talk to the prisoners. He took the light from the NCO, and held it aloft. He wanted to be seen as well as heard.

"Well, boys! You're all paroled; those of you that'll see the morning." His voice had the level quality of a bell, tolling on a clear day.

"Whose order?" The question came with a sour grimace of suspicion.

"By the order of the Captain-General, the Lord Fairfax," Hewson answered smoothly. He was rather disappointed when nothing but a lot of blank shock met his words. "You'll all be given passes at first light. Go home to your hops, to your orchards. Prepare for your harvests... It is over."

Colonel Hewson turned, and strode out through the door. The granite-jawed subordinate followed. He was glad to get out.

Judah looked bucked. "You hear that, Melhuish? Sarah will have you back by dinner-time!" He hesitated. Looked again. "Melhuish?"

No pulse beat in Melhuish's straining throat. His eyes had gone dull.

Coates stretched out a hand to close the Corporal's eyes.

Judah pushed a bunched fist up to his lips. With Melhuish gone, the last drop of hope had drained with it. "What was we doing here, Parson?" he snuffed, lifting his eyes to the young man.

Nathan shook his head for a moment or two. What had this all been for? Legally? Morally? Spiritually? His absolution failed him. "I – I don't know, Judah. I do not know."

Philippa pushed herself to her feet. "Judah; Christopher. You will be excusing us if we do not linger any further. Nathan? I would welcome a word with you – outside."

"Uhm – yes. Alright."

Nathan stood nearest the porch, so he went first. They had almost reached the door when one of those buff-coated phantoms intercepted him. The Trooper carried his wheel-lock carbine in the crook of his arm. "You done here, Parson?" he brogued in his Norfolk accent.

"Erm, no. I'll – I'll return directly."

"Bless Him that giveth the victory!"

Nathan's eyes alighted on one of those bodies that covered the floor. The Trooper looked, too. "This one's at death's door," he explained. "You read the signs. Handsome business, weren't it?"

He prodded that shivering bundle with the side of his boot. A virulent perfume arose from the parcel of clothes.

"That... smell?"

The Trooper's snort was on the testy side. "His bowels have gone. He's stewing in it."

Nathan resisted the impulse to jump a good six inches to his left. Philippa joined him. "So many boys." She invested the word "boys" with a wealth of meaning.

"They fought like lions, Mistress," said the Trooper. He scratched at an itch on the tip of his nose. "I can't recall the like, and me been in the service since Cropredy Bridge!"

Nathan heard Pip's mocking laugh, and didn't care for it. "You know, sometimes I wonder why the Christ never sanctified old age by living to his seventies. Do you not, Nathan?" she queried. Her tone was drily ironic. She made for the door.

The Trooper had an appreciative look at the tall girl wearing the braided coat. "That be your wife, Parson?"

"She is." His mind was still wrestling with Pip's uncanny perspicacity.

"Blessed saints!" the older man said, in a warm and open voice. "As dainty a doll as I've seen in a long while. My oath, but you're a lucky man!"

He found Philippa waiting ten yards from the door, on the rim of the light from the porch. She had taken up a position beside a scattering of very small tombstones. They were the graves of children and infants. Little lives, who had never stood a chance.

"Well! The rain has cleared away at least," he said.

Philippa pounced on him. She took his head between her hands and kissed him fiercely, right on the mouth. Nathan could not return such a hungry intensity.

316

At last she let him go. "Oh, Nathan! You know that I love you, Nathan. There is nothing will change that. Ever!"

"Pip… Pip, what is this?"

She lowered her eyes. Her hands had gone down by her sides. First her right index finger curled, then the other fingers followed and they clawed into a ball. Tears had started chasing one another down her cheeks. "Nathan, I killed a man tonight."

Nathan had her by her shoulders. "A murderer? A fornicating rapist? What manner of man is that?"

"You asked me: I told you."

Now he was feeling her hair, trying to warm her with his hands.

"He became… as one that has a fiend," Philippa said, and her head shook to think again of that ringleted fox-face. It ogled her from beyond the grave. Its teeth were bared in a rictus of pleasurable triumph. "He took us in, so neatly, so completely."

"The devil often does," he answered.

"Father; Mother; all of us. I feel like such a dunce!"

"I protest you overrate yourselves," he said.

"God forgive me, but I hope he's burning in hell for it now!" Philippa whispered.

"Very probably he is." In his heart, Nathan knew it would not do to dwell on the diabolism of men, so instead he satisfied his own curiosity by asking, "Their bodies. Him, and your Mother. What of them?"

"Carrie is minding the children. I left Stephen with her." Her fists had clenched again. "Mayhaps… mayhaps all I did was to save the Assizes the trouble. Of all the deaths in this town today, his was the best."

"I – I cannot disagree with you there," he said.

Philippa looked at him, renewed with an involuntary respect. "This leads me to recast you."

"What?"

"You told me once, that every life is of consequence…"

"I know I did," said Nathan.

She was blinking her way out of her daze. "What was that about bodies?"

"Magner, and your mother. What did you do with them?"

"We – we carried Mother upstairs. The other… Carrie and I, we slung him out into the street. Into the *cess!*" she hissed. "Where he belongs."

"We shall give your mother a proper burial. In a grave. That people can come and see."

Philippa got hold of his wrist. "Nathan, I HAD to do it!"

Nathan spoke to her with energy. "Of course you did, of *course* you did. Pip! You were protecting the girls; yourself. Our son."

Our son.

She was staring straight at him. "Nathan? Are you there?" she asked abruptly.

"I am here." The way she looked, she would not have surprised him if she had lifted his sleeve to her nose and had sniffed it like a dog.

"I still cannot believe it. I thought – well, you know what I thought."

He nodded.

"When Melhuish and Judah burst in," she said, "I knew not what they were. And, if truth were known, I remember – "

"Pip?"

She hesitated, loath to hurt him. Then the words spilled from her tongue, all at once, with a sincerity that made them terrifying. "I remember thinking, do what you like to me. Use me. Break every bone in my body. Gut me. Roger me to death… Only let my son live. I meant it, too. I swear it."

His hand was on her bicep, but she winced away. She pulled the old coat tight around her body. At last Nathan pushed the most important question to the front of his mind.

"Why, when you had all the chance, did you not run?"

Philippa shrugged. The gesture was one of almost childish apathy. It was hard to recall the decisions. Yesterday seemed years past. "Mother wouldn't hear of it," was all she would say in reply.

Over the wall of the churchyard, the New Model Army's burial parties were rattling down Lower Stone Street. They were marching in to help secure the conquered town.

"It is almost break of day. You can smell it on the wind." Nathan shivered at the thought of what the return of light would bring. He couldn't help himself.

Philippa noticed him do it. "What is it?" she asked him.

"The bodies. All those bodies I saw..."

"The dead, are dead," said Philippa. "We should be decent to the living." Her eyes had charred out. Tears had started lapping at her lips.

"Take me away, Nathan."

Nathan looked back at her."Home?" he quizzed. He did not mention what they might hope to find there.

"No. Away." She choked. "Away, away."

Time began to spin. "I – I think you concern yourself needlessly, Pip."

He reached for her hand, but she cried expostulation and tugged herself free. "Needlessly? After tonight? When our hearts are sick with sorrow? Nathan, are you *crazed?*"

He placated her with the palms of his hands. They were still covered in those little white bumps that the nettles had made. Nathan's face puckered with thought. He tried to contemplate the full dimensions of this sudden picture. Away. An uprooting. An upheaval. "It – This is – The course will not be easy," he amended at last.

Philippa's eyes were expressionless. The corners of her mouth had quirked downwards. "That does not matter."

Nathan protested. "After all, remember that there is my parish – my superiors! The life we lead here! You cannot mean I simply – "

She laid a single finger on his lips. It silenced him at once. "Tell them: you cannot stay here," she insisted, trying to break through her tears. "It matters not where. And it is not just for me. Nathan, I appeal to you. I beg you."

"You *beg* me?" he asked, appalled.

Philippa gripped his hand, as if it alone was preventing her from tumbling to the ground. "Nathan – our mother has been murdered. And Elle is like to go mad with the grief and the shame of what that demon has done. Think of us! Think of our son! Tell them whatever you must. Only take us away from this place."

He looked away from her, over towards the treetops. The night was being turned to pastel pink. The dawn was growing up. Before long it would set the town alight again. And Maidstone would awaken, to the mathematics of defeat.

1649

That kings for such a tomb would wish to die.

FORTY-TWO

And kings sat still with awful eye
As they surely knew their sovran lord was by.

Carrie sat at the head of the table. Her voice was quiet. It strained to form the words.

"And the soldiers led him away into a hall, called Praetorium, and they called together the whole band.

"And they clothed him with purple, and plaited a crown of thorns, and put it about his head.

"And they began to salute him, Hail, king of the Jews!

"And they smote him on the head with a reed, and did spit upon him, and bowing their knees they worshipped him. And when they had mocked him, they took off the purple from him, and put his own clothes on him, and led him out to crucify him."

Elle listened with her hands folded on the table in front of her. Ros sat in the adjacent chair and gnawed on a cinnamon jumble.

It had not snowed in the night. The sun was drilling its way through the clouds. A chilly wind explored London's twisting streets. A heap of seasoned wood was burning in the grate. The flame was powerful as it stretched for the chimney.

It was a world without shadows. An uneasy, post-war world. This winter had been harsh and sickly. The nation had been left to count its butcher's bill. Plague stalked the county towns. From shire to shire, children were gaunt and starving.

Nathan had been right, of course. It had not been easy to fashion a possible future. Leaving west Kent for London meant a wrench, and a lot of long-term planning. Securing the incumbency of Saint Mildred's off Constitution Hill had been a proper, Galilean miracle. Had Saint Mildred's not suddenly lost its incumbent to diphtheria, Nathan's chance might never have come at all. They had moved in at Michaelmas quarter-day. The Rectory that came with Saint Mildred's was small. Smaller even than Week Street. And this new dwelling must needs be shared by seven. The ceilings were low, the walls thin, and the floorboards sloped like the deck of a ship in a gale. You soon learned one another's secrets, right enough.

Nathan stood in the doorway to the dining room, toggling up his cloak. "You still wish to stay here?" he asked the girls.

They would not even dignify him with a response.

He heard Philippa's feet on the stairs. "You are ready?"

"We are ready," she said huskily, coming down with Stephen in tow. She had put on her cloak and gloves. Her father's broad, black hat was on her head. "Sweeting? Hold on to Mother's hand."

Nathan paused. Pip's tread on the stairs had been too heavy for ordinary galoshes, or the clack of wooden pattens. He lowered his voice and asked, "What have you got on your feet, Pip?"

She looked squarely at him. Then she drew up the heavy skirt and showed him. Nathan looked down. Poking out was the familiar shape of a bucket-top boot of an oak-like leather.

"Oh, Pip, really!"

Her look was challenging. "Pray tell me, then, if you have any better suggestions for this weather?"

Loobie rose abruptly from the dining table. "I want to come, too!" she announced.

Philippa tried to demur, but Nathan went under the stairs and found Loobie a cloak, a heavy muffler, and some woollen mittens.

They said their goodbyes. Nathan shut the door, locked it, and put the key in his deepest pocket. He took Loobie by the hand, and off they went. They walked with the slush of the streets on their galoshes. Across the thronging border of Westminster and into Whitehall. They passed a dead dog, lying matted in the snow. It was amazing that it was still there, that it hadn't been taken away for somebody's Sunday dinner.

Eventually, there it was. The scaffold. The stage of death, draped in rippling black velvet. Its timbers had been hammered together outside the splendid windows of the Banqueting House.

The square was packed with faces. Stephen didn't like it. He would rather be at home, toasting his toes before the black grate, while Mother sat in her chair and got out her workbox. Mother spent a lot of time like that these days, busily sewing, or knitting. The light would come in through the windows and make Stephen feel cosy and content. He would sit on the floor at her feet, wrapping his arms around Mother's long leg, and she would swing it back and forth, making him laugh as he clung to her. But he couldn't be *too* rough with her; Father had told him he needs must be gentle.

Stephen still had his dreams, of course. Dreams about the man in the black hat and the pointy beard, coming in the dead of night. The man had been Satan himself. Stephen would wake up, gasping and sweating. His dreams disturbed Loobie, whose bed he now had to share for want of space.

He was tingling with a nervous anticipation. He could feel his luncheon, rolling and rippling in his stomach. Aunt Carrie had roasted haunch of mutton. The twins had prepared the gravy and the vegetables. They had baked apples for pudding, finished in the oven and basted with cheaply-procurable spices. Father had not enjoyed his luncheon. He'd been grumbling something about "the nation's shame".

"This way."

It was hard to get nearer the scaffold. Their way was barred by a forest of halberds, and a line of men with firelocks at the slope. The cavalry prowled the perimeter. The Army was taking no chances. Ropes had been prepared upon the scaffold, in case the prisoner struggled.

Philippa came to a halt. "Nathan? This is wrong. It'll give Stephen night visions!"

Nathan found her elbow, and gently drew her on.

Stephen pulled on her hand. "Mooother?"

"What, darling?"

"I'm cold!"

"In this crush?" She stopped to make some passing adjustments to the old blanket she had wrapped about his shoulders. "There. Now stay close."

People jostled one another for a better look. The executioner and his assistant were already at their posts, crudely disguised behind masks and wigs. It was a rash man indeed who boasted of such public work. Today, of all days.

The pedlars were out, dripping through the crowd. Muffin boys carried steaming wares on oval platters. Even harlots from the local trugging-house had braved the cold to try their luck.

Philippa turned her head. A voice was singing drunken snatches in a grating tenor.

> "King Arthur had three sons,
> And a good old King was he!
> But the three sons of whores,
> He kicked them out of doors,
> Because THEY! COULD! NOT! SING!"

His audience was hostile. "Heave-to, you tosspot!"

"Been out on the piss again, eh?"

The tenor would not be cowed: he tried a second verse. Then suddenly he grunted, and fell silent. A fist had been applied to his solar plexus.

"Mooother?"

"What is it, Stephen?"

"Why was that man singing?"

"Because he has drunk."

"Oh."

"And I cannot say I blame him." She looked at Nathan as she said it.

The crowd was shoving again. Loobie stumbled. Nathan repelled boarders with both hands. "Attend there, man! Take care of this child!"

"I have got him! He is close!" Philippa's hand lodged, and then stayed, upon Stephen's little shoulder.

Stephen was tugging her sleeve again. "Mooother?"

"What now?"

"Can Father not hoist me up?"

"There isn't the room, sweeting," she murmured.

Behind them, the Clock House tower scaled into the pearly sky. Without a moment's warning it boomed the hour of two.

At its strokes, the tumultuous crowd had gone quiet. A figure had emerged through one of the Banqueting House windows. A diminutive figure, his clothes were as black as the boards that he was walking on. He was closely followed by a cleric in white robes. The cleric was old William Juxon, the Bishop of London. The venerable Bishop held a Bible in his hands: a big one.

Nobody in the crowd could hear him, but he was intoning from it. Preparing the servant's soul with words of Christian comfort.

The figure in black stood there a while. Then he opened his delicate lips and started to speak. Gradually it became plain he was discoursing at length. Everyone strained forward to listen, making the crowd ripple in little waves.

"Whass he saying?"

"I dunno, do I? Too far away, 'in'e?"

A woman's voice spoke up. "Oh! Hold me, Harry, or else I shall faint when they do it!"

Philippa looked at her husband. "What... did he say just then? Did you catch it?"

Nathan held a hand to his ear and tried to ignore the mutterings. His head was thrust forward to fish for a word or two from the figure in black. "Something about an incorruptible crown, I think."

There was a tug on her sleeve. "Mooother?"

This time she tugged herself free. "Hist, Stephen! This is not the time!"

Loobie asked: "Why are we waiting, Nathan?"

"Because nothing has happened yet," came the reply.

"Waiting's awful hard!" his son announced.

Philippa bit her lip. Her legs felt very weak. She was gripped by a vision of falling down in the crowd and being unable to rise again. Her knees began to tremble.

The condemned man removed his long, dark cloak. Then he took off the pale blue sash of the Order of the Garter. He unclipped the silver star from his breast. He gave both of these things to the Bishop with a few words of thanks. Juxon balanced his takings upon the opened Holy Writ. Then a nightcap was produced. The man in black began to tuck up his long hair. Those closest to the scaffold could just see that his dark locks were touched with streaks of grey.

A quiet conference was taking place. The headsman made sure for himself of an unobstructed neck.

The prisoner lay down before the block. The wood had been set far too low for him to kneel: he had to lie prostrate. It was an engineered act of submission in his final moments.

Nathan felt, as he had often done before in times of great distress, like he was watching some queer, suspended reality.

Seconds passed in perfect silence. The sunshine flashed off the blade of the axe. Harry held on to his woman, lest she should fall in that faint to the ground. Philippa gulped. Nathan quickly crossed himself.

The axe sailed down in the death arc. It was finished with one, neat blow. Everyone flinched instinctively. The executioner picked up the head, clutching the grisly thing by its hair as he walked to the railing. His footsteps showed red on the boards. He showed the thing off to the crowd, but the much-awaited, customary declaration about the "head of a traitor" never came. The eyelids were closed in the decapitated face. They looked almost serene.

He tossed the head down to the crowd. It fell all of twelve feet, and then bounced. Nathan imagined it rolling about like a ghastly football.

Some braves darted forward with handkerchiefs, bent on bloody souvenirs. Others broke rank with their pocket knives opened. They were hopeful of a clipping or two from the Lord's Anointed hair.

The crowd, so still and quiet only a few seconds before, now loosed a mighty groan. The noise started from the back and rolled towards the Banqueting House. Growing, growing in its strength. Higher, female voices pitched in in a frightful descant. Some guards turned around to confront the angry swarm. A couple even took a pre-emptive firelock down from their shoulders, till they caught their Sarjeant's eye.

Stephen looked bewildered by the noise of this solid protesting. "Mooother? What have they just done?"

Philippa drew her son tighter against her hip. "They know not *what* they do, my darling."

The little boy looked up at her face. Her big hat held much of it in shadow. He could see Mother was blinking very quickly, over and over. "Are you crying?" he asked, too loudly to keep the query private.

His mother caught her breath. "No!" she lied, and she gave his shoulder a reassuring shake. "I am only grateful that your grandfather was not here to witness this."

Loobie turned to look at her. Despite the pain, they both smiled.

The body was laid in its waiting coffin. The cavalry cleared the space around the scaffold. Now that the main event had been concluded, the Dragoons had to ride back to barracks and prepare for mid-afternoon stables. The memento hunters started to disperse like sullen children. A freebooting few were even attempting to tear some strips of velvet from the scaffold. They swiftly abandoned this quest when they found themselves looking into the faces of heavily-armed, hard-boiled Dragoons.

Nathan stepped in. His features were calm. "Come, Pip. It is cold. We must look to the living."

Philippa nodded, head-bent. Her tawny eyes closed and she shuddered. Beneath the soft black leather of her gloves, she had felt the baby's kick.

THE END

A Sort of Essay

The English Civil Wars (wars *plural* – there were three in total). Also known as the Great Rebellion, or the War of the Three Kingdoms. Whatever you've learned to call them, they ripped the British nation in two. They destroyed the old order with firepower and death. By the time they had ended, the British nation was left permanently altered and thoroughly exhausted. As with any such war, the reasons for the English Civil Wars are prolonged, and very involved, but it is undeniable that Charles Stuart's refusal to compromise his Divine Right in any way with Parliament was boneheaded in the extreme. The King died with courage on the scaffold that chilly day in January, 1649: nobody can take that away from him. But sticking to his autocratic principles had cost him his throne, his life, and the blood of his beloved kingdom

Now, to me.

I was born and bred in Monmouthshire. Far away from the Garden of England, but still a part of the world that had felt the whetted steel of the Civil Wars. Raglan Castle (located only a few miles from Abergavenny where I was born) had been "slighted" – that is, destroyed to prevent its future usefulness – by Parliament's troops. It remains one of the greatest ruins that Cromwell "knocked about a bit". Both my parents fostered in me a deep and abiding love of History. Stuart times in particular became a source of fascination for me. By the age of twelve, I knew the basics: "the Cavaliers (Wrong, but Wromantic), and the Roundheads (Right, but Repulsive)." School had introduced me to Richard Harris' husky barnstorming in the 1970 film *Cromwell*. I had discovered that a great-uncle on my father's side had been a card-carrying member of the Sealed Knot. Plenty of other periods of military history continued to attract my interest, but there was always *something* about the English Civil Wars. To my overactive imagination, it seemed to be a world of of eloquent politicians and the swirling smoke of battle.

Eventually there were exams to pass, and university to attend. And it was here (as they say) that the story really begins.

You see, I met and fell in love with a beautiful redhead named Jess. She was a Kentish girl, from a town called Maidstone. Eventually, Jess and I became engaged. I left Abergavenny for good and moved to Kent's county town, where for a year I became a fixture in my future in-laws' home. I was fortunate to find that Jess' father and I had a mutual interest: History. It was David who first mentioned "The Battle of Maidstone". The outline of what took place that day began to emerge under my questioning. Names, too. Gabriel's Hill. Week Street. All Saints' Church. The last, desperate stand of the King's men in Saint Faith's yard.

Fast forward five or six years, if you would. I am looking for a new subject for a work of historical fiction. I found that I had had it all along: the story that David had told me. I did some more, preliminary fieldwork. The Kentish Rebellion and the events that surrounded it, such as the protracted Siege of Colchester (origin story of "Humpty Dumpty", incidentally) seemed to be well-chronicled. Maidstone, though, got barely a passing reference in many accounts of the War. Gradually, the facts emerged. The brutal street fighting, the towering storms that fell while battle was raging, the intensity of the politics that stoked it ... it was all there. All the pieces were in place for historical drama. I plunged into the writing, and after four months of work I had three hundred pages of scribbled foolscap. It was my first, full draft of CAUSE OF GOLD. But it was David who'd begun it, and this novel is dedicated to him as a result.

So, to the characters.

Many of this novel's "ensemble cast" are genuine enough, including all the senior commanders of the two opposing armies. On the other hand Nathan, the Agnew family, the Waterman squires, and all the drinking companions from The Gryphon are my own invention. They represent those civilians from across the social spectrum who found themselves on the receiving end of social flux, religious division, and military brutality.

As for that objectionable Puritan, the Reverend Arlo Jump. I must readily admit he is a kind of Dickensian caricature. In Jump, I wanted to strike a balance between "God's awkward squad", and those learned theologians who made for sincere, suspenseful preachers and rigorous Biblical scholars. Considerable license has been taken in this book when showing the damage inflicted on the (very real) church of Saint Margaret's in Barming. Saint Margaret's appears to have escaped the War undamaged, even though plenty of churches all around Maidstone still bear the zealous scars of the 1640s. All Saints' is a particular example. The details of what happened once the Roundheads set about it after the battle are real enough

The 17th century gave birth (amongst much else) to the modern "middle class". Popular politics was starting to gain real weight with the public meetings of the Levellers and Ranters. Many families who came from the minor gentry would finish up in reduced circumstances during the Civil War. Many had to turn their hand at becoming artisans to try to keep afloat, like Rosalind and Eleanor. And speaking of the Agnew family, it was the eldest daughter who emerged first in my mind. It began with an image: a girl, a tall, fair-headed girl called Philippa, sitting astride a horse in a Medway meadow, wearing her father's old campaign coat. I had no idea who she was, or why she was wearing that coat, but I built up the rest from that solitary image.

Let us turn now to the characters who *did* exist. If you have read CAUSE OF GOLD (and I am assuming you have) you'll have noticed that Cromwell is conspicuous by his absence. He is absent from this novel just as Churchill was absent from Christopher Nolan's *Dunkirk*. The reason? Cromwell wasn't there. So, there seemed little point in trying to shoehorn in a scene with him when he was on the other side of the country at the time that the Kentish landowners rose in rebellion.

Which brings me to Thomas Fairfax.

Fairfax was a mass of contradictions. Essentially a man of magnanimity, from all accounts he was capable of the most frightening passions in battle. He was also capable of the most ruthless dealings after it. His decision to execute prisoners after the siege of Colchester still invites controversy. He was a "fighting General". He did not merely direct operations "from the gods". Instead he took his men (at a time when a General needed to be *seen* to take his men) and did the job himself. In that respect, "Black Tom" Fairfax is the direct ancestor of the likes of Marlborough, and Wolfe. Of Lee, and Sherman. Even of Patton, and Rommel.

Now, I must spare a brief word about the historical sources I plundered to write this novel. The multi-volume, gentlemanly tomes by Gardiner and Clarendon covering "the Great Rebellion" do have their uses. However, if you should be looking for something more modern, then I have some suggestions. Osprey Publishing's reference books are wonderful: they are packed with information, and illustrated lavishly. For my money, Christopher Hibbert's *Cavaliers and Roundheads* remains the best single-volume narrative available on the subject. I would also emphatically recommend Tristram Hunt's The Civil War At First Hand. As the title suggests, this is a treasure trove of contemporary primary sources. It is superb and moving witness testimony from a country that was tearing itself apart.

The English Civil War was unquestionably a national tragedy. Its cost in human lives is still debated, but even the most conservative estimates tally in the region of 200,000 lives – including some 40,000 civilians. Britain would not see a bloodletting like it until the mechanised carnage of the First World War. *Per capita*, it still remains the costliest conflict that this island ever fought.

When you look at the Battle of Maidstone, there are many elements of a Greek Tragedy. The garrison who tried to hold that "unwalled" town were abandoned to their fate through a fatal combination of skilful outmanoeuvring, and doddering indecision. Inexperience, hubris, and over-reaching confidence, abounded at high levels, and it was the common soldiers like Melhuish Clare who paid for it. Maidstone was not so much a humiliating defeat for the Royalists; on the contrary, it was a supreme Parliamentary victory. The fall of their county town knocked the fight out of the Royalist rebels, though isolated pockets of resistance would continue to hold out across East Kent for few more weeks. To many who were there, it remained the toughest combat of the entire war.

I wrote CAUSE OF GOLD because it occurred to me that while Edgehill, Naseby, and Marston Moor have entered the public consciousness, Maidstone has not. Chronologically it occupies a kind of misty no-man's-land between the King's defeats in 1645, and Charles' appointment with the block in 1649. If you go there today, you will find Naseby is presented and memorialised as hallowed ground. If you visit the precipitous slope of Gabriel's Hill in Maidstone today, all you will find is a bustling pedestrianised shopping centre. It is almost impossible to picture the sheer ferocity of what took place there, on that rainy night in 1648. The world have moved on. But I thought it was a story worth the telling. CAUSE OF GOLD is the result.

James Powell
August, 2023

ACKNOWLEDGEMENTS

I am grateful for the wisdom of my friends Hannah Brown, Ka
Merrifield, Rachel King and Amy Cornish, for reading chunks o
this novel in typescript, and helping me to work out where thes
characters would go.

I am grateful to Jess, who has always believed in this novel, and
who willed me to write a character like Philippa Agnew.

Lastly, I am particularly grateful to Eleanor Smith, whose
feedback and guidance finally made me realise that I had written
story that others should read.